LEUNGA

The Loser Trilogy

-BOOK ONE-

The Languorous Loser Legend

-BOOK TWO-

The Mayhem of Monstrous Minds

-BOOK THREE-

The Nighty Knights of Nightmares

LEUNGA
The Languorous Loser Legend

August D. Hunsaker

Prologue: Press Start

I saw what you just did, and I feel obligated to inform you that it was
disgusting. Fortunately enough, it reminds me of a tale that you may find
interesting—one filled with courageous knights, homicidal sorcery, fearsome
dragons, terrible cell phone reception, cursed monsters, mystical weapons,
magical marijuana, and other stuff—if you're into that sort of thing. And even if
you're not, that's okay too, because it's mostly about the other stuff anyway.
This is a story spanning centuries upon centuries and generations upon
generations, only to wind up in a place far from where it began, and I mean
that in a couple of ways. Still interested? Really? Wow. How? I definitely
would've left by now. And I still might. Especially if the rhyming returns.

Anyway, as I was saying...wait, what was I saying? Oh, right! This is a
story not many have heard. A legend long lost. Distorted by the frailty of
memories and dismantled by the steady tide of time. It all starts long ago, at
the bright dawn of an age of expressive emotion and beauty throughout
Europe when most folks still clung to their old ways. Out of sight in the
farthest reaches of the mighty kingdoms, many small communities dwelt in
insignificance, free from persecution and the threat of change brought by
dignitary trespassers in their land. It is because of its obscurity that so few
remain who can recall the fable of a powerful evil that once terrorized a small
farming village in the northern regions of what is now the United Kingdom—in
the land once known only as Alba, where they say that, once upon a time, a
plague of unnatural origin befell the community.

For months, horrible, demonic beasts would slaughter the livestock
of the village night after night, terrifying the inhabitants before vanishing into
the shadows from which the creatures appeared. Shocked and hopelessly left

without explanation for their torment, the people of the village came to realize that a force beyond comprehension was at fault. During the daylight of the hellish bombardment, the villagers recalled a den that reached toward the sky, surrounded by a shroud of magic. Inside lived an old recluse, once shunned by the very people he wished to aid, who thus had become a malevolent power resentful of all life. Soon after this discovery, the people began calling this evil presence *the Summoner* due to the unusual powers he wielded without mercy. None who lived in the village knew why they were victimized, but all knew it had to be stopped, and yet no one possessed the courage to face the fiend head-on—save for two.

In the township there lived a single blacksmith, along with his young apprentice, who were each eager to assist in the expulsion of the evilness. Confronted by indomitable odds, the master spent insurmountable hours struggling to craft an immutable weapon capable of quelling the brooding beast in the Tower with skills he had no need of before, but his attempts seemed insufficient and amateurish at best. All hope was waning until he heard word of a wise man proficient in a form of ancient magic that might hold the key to their salvation. The Blacksmith and the Apprentice set out to find the Hermit sage without delay.

The road ahead of them was perilous and fraught with fiends. During their quest, many foes fell before the whetted blades made by the Blacksmith—which were adequately handled by himself and his smithing student after weeks of training—but the journey was arduous nonetheless, and the monstrosities were found to be endless, for when one would be sent back to the void that spawned it, another would simply take its place. After countless battles in the wilds surrounding the village, a curious thing occurred. The demons mysteriously dispersed when the Blacksmith and his young companion finally arrived at the sage's dwelling, far from the ceremony that they deserved. Wise enough not to question their good fortune, they approached the door with hesitancy and hope.

Upon gathering the courage to knock after several silent minutes, they asked for an audience with the Hermit in the hut, only to be turned away time and time again, until the way was suddenly opened to them when they spoke of a sinister man summoning demons to do his bidding, and the repellent recluse within the cottage had a change of heart and was ready to hear their request. As they slowly entered the sacred quarters, the man before them appeared young, but the Blacksmith and the Apprentice could sense that his façade concealed his years. After pleading with the Hermit, he revealed to them that what they desired could only be accomplished with an artifact that was forged by a spirit filled with purity and peace. The master's works of warfare were created by the darkness that scarred his heart and stained his soul. The divine weapon of light would need to be crafted by the Apprentice alone.

For many weeks, the young Apprentice poured blood and sweat into the creation of a blade while the village continued to be terrorized. The monsters of merciless malice who had once been content killing animals had turned their murderous attention to the villagers, slaughtering anyone who dared to travel into the wilds alone. The townspeople quickly cloistered themselves in their houses during the night for fear of death, unwilling to venture from the safety of their community. The seclusion of the village was palpable, isolated from the rest of the kingdom by the evil Summoner's creations without hope—at least until the day came when faith was restored as the Apprentice had completed the masterwork and the Blacksmith and his pupil once again set off for the sage's hut. To their amazement, the path was free of obstructions, and they arrived in less than a day.

The Hermit felt the purity of intention with which the Apprentice had created the blade and quickly began a rite to bestow a great power to the weapon. After the ceremony was completed, the sage bade the Apprentice to take sword in hand and claim the weapon as his own. As the Apprentice gripped the hilt of the sword, the blade shook violently and symbols scarred their way into the backs of the wielder's hands. The Hermit had placed a seal on the sword so that only those of the Apprentice's lineage and benevolence could handle the weapon without fear of being destroyed by it. The battle for the safety of the innocent was imminent.

The Blacksmith and the young Apprentice said their farewells and headed off to the gruesome Tower of the Summoner. Many fallen heroes from neighboring villages paved their path as they fought through impassable hordes of evil minions. The trail was long, but they managed to make it to the gates of the Tower within a week. As they stood before the immense structure, the drawbridge opened for them, inviting them in. Slowly, the Blacksmith and the Apprentice entered the dark hall and proceeded forward steadily, and the door sealed shut behind them.

All activities in the farming town had ceased since the two left on their expedition. Villagers paced and fretted over the fate of the brave warriors, but days passed with no sign of their return. It is sometimes suggested that it was on the dawn of the thirteenth day that an old farmer was staring in the direction of the Summoner's Tower when he noticed a small flicker of light. As he stood from his chair to alert the other villagers, the small flicker became a towering beam reaching high into the clouds. The dark red light pierced the sky for over a half hour, and everyone in the community was fixed on the beacon until it dissolved, and in turn, a plume of dust filled the sky above the evil sorcerer's lair.

The villagers awaited the return of their heroes. Days passed without any homecoming, then months. The attacks against the village had completely stopped—everyone was delighted and distressed at the same time. Not one of the brave warriors ever returned. On the anniversary of the Summoner's defeat, the farmers prepared a victory feast to honor the Blacksmith and the young Apprentice's great sacrifice—a tradition that would last for only a lifetime, for as decades turned to centuries, truth turned into legend. The land changed and many customs vanished—people lived united in larger settlements while the memory of the Summoner and his slayers faded away.

Now, most people would say that's where the legend ends, but most people don't know squat like I do. Only I know that the real tale remains to be told—the stuff that happened after that—if I can remember any of it. I'm sure I do, but there is so much to keep straight. Well, maybe I misspoke. I should say I *think* I know what happened. I might have forgotten one or two very important things, but I do remember enough to piece it together, and if you're ready to sit there and behave yourself, I might just tell you the whole story, assuming I don't lose my place before we get bored and find something better to do together. Spin the bottle? We'll see.

Level One

"Leunga?"

A simple request requiring only a basic reply, the muffled shout from an invisible teenage girl's voice far beyond sight calling out resonated through the small, confining walls surrounding the brunet man in his early twenties—the owner of an inconceivable moniker and an anomalous outlook on life. A curiosity of a young man to say the least, he was complex in his simplicity, an integral part of the social minority, an underdog by his own right, carefree in almost every aspect of his life, and an oddity by all accounts—living down to the rigorous standards of his well-deserved title of *Loser* and lazily drifting through the world at his own pace, taking the shortest path and performing only the bare minimum of efforts. A pale pothead hopelessly drawn to taking great interest in activities deemed geeky by his modern society, he typically found himself indulging in fantasy and was happily uncoordinated at all times. And by no small coincidence, his name was Leunga.

Far beyond the misty moors of Alba, there is a realm over the ocean—across the sacred mountains, hallowed forests, and cosmic crop fields in a place of freedom during an era of wireless worlds and streaming socializing, where there lies a golden land in which ancient trees trounce skyscrapers and mice maintain kingdoms. Lost in suburbia, somewhere secluded along the asphalt veins between the beaches of the bays and the valley of death, a man stood at the brink of darkness, faced with a dilemma he was all too familiar with. He waited several minutes, staring blankly into his shadow, before he raised his voice only slightly in response to his caller. "Shut up! I'm in my closet." And in no time at all, he quickly shook his head and quietly decided that it would not be worth his invaluable time to seek out his sister and discover why she dared to speak his name in such an inquisitive way. "Meh. She already knows how to shut up."

Eventually jumping up to snag the stringed switch hanging high above his hair after many more minutes of absolutely nothing, Leunga had the good sense to turn on the light. With his bleak world illuminated by a revoltingly dim glow, his adjusting eyes stared up at the top shelf of his closet and observed the gray box far beyond his reach. Without changing his gaze, he reached down for his step stool, only to grab at empty air. Later that very same instant, he glanced down and, to his horror, saw that the stool was almost entirely missing. All that remained were the well-defined dimples left in the grotesque shag. "Hell..."

An average-looking young man with a long, crooked, mischievous smile, Leunga wandered aimlessly down the halls of the moderately sized suburban abode, through rooms and drawers he had no business searching in, but couldn't find his step stool. Unfortunately, he needed it in order to get his grand gray box down from its perch; after all, he was only an inch or so over five feet tall. The ideal height for a full-grown man—frankly, anything taller than that is simply obscene. Quickly forgetting what he was searching for in the first place, he found himself mysteriously in the kitchen. The saccharine summer air drifting through the sliding screen doorway to the backyard kissed his skin with a gentle peck; needless to say, it was a horrible reminder of why he was excavating his closet in the first place, but it seemed fortune was violently groping him at that moment, for he noticed the dining table seats and remembered his original endeavor.

As he was grabbing one of the more reliable chairs, he heard a rumbling on the roof above him, followed closely by a showering crash and what could've been a minor explosion. And as if by magical means, the teenage voice above was no longer muffled and traveled easily through the screen door as it asked, "Leunga, are you holding the ladder?"

The young man with the confounding query in his ear hopped onto the kitchen counter and pressed his cheek against the mesh screen of the open window above the sink. "You say something?" he said dismissively, hearing her perfectly the first time.

"Are you holding the ladder?"

"Gotcha."

"Does that mean you are?"

"Gotcha." His tone was unchanged.

"...I'm gonna come down now. Hold it steady."

By the time he heard the hobbling of the ladder, Leunga was already lugging the kitchen chair down the first of two short staircases leading to the basement of the basement of their split-level house, passing his mother's home office and the television den on his way to his room below. Once he was in his closet again, he climbed up his substitute and grabbed the box with excessive ease. He tossed it onto the bed behind him just as he heard a thud against the house come from outside; of course, he ignored it. Holding the stringy thingy for deactivating the glow overhead, the slight slacker turned off the light just as he noticed something he didn't recognize. He tugged the light on again and saw a black object hidden masterfully at the back of the top shelf, which he never noticed before—likely due to his customary point of view.

With the mysterious item in hand, he hopped off the chair and made a face while he muttered, "The hell is this," and began inspecting it closely. At first glance, it was no more than an unusual leather sheath slightly more than a foot and a half long with an adjustable harness attached and a strange design imprinted all over. His intrigue was increasing at an incredible rate when his examination of the rarity guided his green eyes to the open end of the casing, where he happened to notice the handle of a completely average sword—or at least, a half of a sword and an empty slot next to it. He grabbed the hilt with one hand and unsheathed it with the other. It just may have been the most awesome thing he accidentally found that day. At least top twenty. The light pouring forth from the energy-efficient bulb in the laundry room across the hall glinted off the untarnished portion of the blade and shone like the sun.

Mighty weapon in hand, Leunga tilted it back and forth in awe, only allowing a select few words to escape his gaping mouth. "Kick my ass."

If you ask me, it was a completely average medieval sword, unremarkable in its design, but unexpectedly intriguing nonetheless. Tempered metal in dire need of sharpening, the blade was completely straight and seemingly wider than most short swords of the same length, but far more slender in the depth of its sharp edge—somewhat like a broad version of the weapon of choice among ninja assassins in feudal Japan, but it was identifiably European. Made of a dense alloy with great heft, it was extremely difficult to wield comfortably with one hand despite its seemingly small size. Leunga turned the sharp edge away and studied the blunt side closer, pondering the abridged nature of its construction. The shaft of the handle—or, more accurately, the hilt—was a giveaway to the fact that the broad weapon was incomplete, missing an entire half of its total form, split down the lateral axis into two symmetrical parts lengthwise so that it had only one sharp edge in its present state. The hilt of his fantastic treasure consisted only of a slightly rounded, metallic, rectangular cube covered in studded leather around the outer portion where the blade's sharp edge faced. On further inspection, he found what looked like a puzzle-piece cross guard—a partial metal protector designed to shield the wielder's hands from any attack that might slide down the blade—which ended abruptly as it met the flat surface of the curtailed half of the hilt, confirming that his fortuitous discovery was far from over.

Leunga's land lacked answers, and the shortage shook his world. Quandaries like visibly absent jigsaw pieces came popping out at him and started swarming his curiosity until his brain was filled to the brim, bursting his skull at the seams. Of the two or three questions he came up with, locating the sword's missing twin was by far the most critical, and a grand investigation was afoot. This enigma needed a solution and quick.

Stumbling his way up the stairs while wildly flailing the weapon in his hand, he rounded the corner to the living room with no delay. As his socks slid an extreme distance across the recently waxed faux hardwood floors of the sitting area, the daring dork screamed in horror before calling over to his father as he calmly came to a stop. "Hey, Pop?"

"What is it, Lou?" the man nearing fifty said from behind a newspaper held unreasonably close to his face.

Suddenly standing before the middle-aged man, Leunga brandished the blade at his father and demanded answers for questions he had yet to ask. His face curled to one side. "D'ya know where this is from?"

His father set the newspaper down on his lap and put on his reading glasses. He studied the sword for a moment. "Can't say that I do."

"I found it way hidden in my closet—"

"Oh, I never would've guessed that," Leunga's father interrupted.

"No, I mean where did I get it from?"

The older of the two thought about the question for another moment. "...You mean the closet?"

"Is Mom home?" his son asked quickly.

Thinking about this new question for two more moments, the seated patriarch shrugged. "I don't think so." But the response wasn't received, because his impatient audience was already on the search for her, and so he took off his reading glasses and went back to reading.

•   •   •

Almost two minutes later, Leunga had freshly given up on his search for something that he couldn't quite remember just as his mother pulled up to the curb not so near the already-occupied driveway—and in a car, no less. Upon recalling the weapon he had in his hand, his mind snapped back into place, and he ran out the front door in his socks to meet her with a frenzy of inquiries.

"Lou! You came to help me carry in the bags? That is so sweet!"

"Nah, you can handle it. I was wanting to ask you about this," he shared, showing her the bare sword. "Like...is this mine? I mean, I can have it if it isn't. Jesus. Never mind. Where did it come from?"

The woman sighed at the thought of carrying twelve full bags of groceries into the house by herself and then glanced at the sword. "Where did you get that?"

"What are you? *Me*?! It was in my closet, behind the box where I hide my bon—" Leunga caught himself. "Box of gold coins." He averted his gaze, hoping his mother hadn't noticed his unintentional referral to his distinctive paraphernalia. Close one.

"It's yours. You got it as a very misguided birthday gift when you were five or six," she grunted as she picked up one of the bags and ignored her desire to force her family member into helping her out. Also, just so you don't get the same inept impression of this lady with wondrous respect for her children's privacy as I did at first, I assure you it was her solemn decision not to question her adult son about his bon—um, I mean, *water pipe*. Closer one.

"Cools. From who?"

"My mother," his mother strained to answer while they walked into the house. "Maybe she thought you would be satisfied just playing with its carrying case until you were older, or she wanted you to just put it on your desk or something." She grunted again as she heaved the bag on the counter with a defiant thunder.

"It's called a sheath," the boy clarified as he watched his parent set down a massive amount of provisions in some sort of paper apparatus. "So where's the other one? Half of the carrying case was empty, and this sword looks like it's not totally total, know what I'm sayin'?" Leunga stated as he followed her back out to the car. "I mean sheath."

"I don't remember," said someone who sounded slightly irritated. "Go call your grandmother."

Leunga nodded and promised, "I'll do you one better," and he headed back inside. "I'll go right into her house and ask her about it...in her house."

The crumpling of grocery bags made his statement indistinct, and even more confusing than it already was. "I couldn't hear you, what did you say?" his mother asked in vain, because by then Leunga was inside preparing for his journey. To grandmother's house he goes.

Double Play

A summer breeze wafted over the rooftop as a willowy young woman high above the earth utilized her freshly learned on-the-job experience and skillfully juiced the damaged area with a highly pressurized can of toxic-flavored sealing spray held at arm's length. A college-bound girl with an aptitude for softball, contrasted by an edgy sense of style that read otherwise—an outsider, far from the mainstream like her older brother, but with drastically different areas of interest—she was a late-teen girl covering herself in jagged metal accessories to show her disdain for the norms of traditional society on a daily basis. Pestering, unparted blond bangs, customarily draped diagonally across her forehead to the left side of her face, dropped out of place to harass each of her eyes equally as she shielded herself from an uncommonly strong, and disrespectful, gust. The thought of tying the rest of her hair back into a nostalgic wadded mess from days past had occurred to her, but the gentle tickling of her long blond hair brushing against the skin of her cheek was too pleasurable to pass up—as annoying as it was otherwise.

As she jerked her head leftward to remove the visual obscurity of her thick bangs, the warming light of the suddenly unclouded sun poured over her back as if to congratulate her on a roofing job well done. With a solar endorsement, she decided she was finished and set the hammer she thought she would need—but never did—down by her foot. Through fortified eyes coated in deep rings of black eyeliner accompanied by mascara, she watched as the tool quickly slid down the slide and right off the edge of the roof where the ladder was, smacking something beneath with a loud thud. "Son of a damn it!" She crawled down the slope a few feet and shouted a concerned call to her possibly unconscious older brother below. "Leunga?"

In swift reply, the constant wind whipped with intense ferocity once again before it promptly died off in an act of greatly delayed charity for any of the novice thatchers on rooftops ready to start their handiwork free from harassment, leaving the neighborhood in a state of fragile tranquility. Too little too late, I'd say. "*Now* it stops..." she mumbled quietly to herself no more than a moment later with a crease of contempt pasted across her face before going about her business as usual. "Leunga, are you okay?" the teenage woman wondered as she attempted to peek over the edge to view the crime scene with her own eyes, but at the last second, she decided it was too hard to see from her angle. Stifling moments passed by uninterrupted. All she could hear in the late-June air was the jubilant sound of children screaming in the distance as they basked in the sovereignty of summer. "If you can hear me, stay there. I'm gonna come down... Don't be dead."

Slowly crawling back up to where she had been working in order to collect the cap to her aerosol utensil and make her escape from the roost for good, it was then that she noticed one of the roof tiles had come undone in a sticky, sickening-looking mess. The kind of mess that might even need a nail— or at least something she could use to touch the gooey garbage without fouling up her fingers. Obviously a very generous parting gift from the windstorm. How thoughtful. She glanced back at where the hammer had run off to and decided to leave it as it was. No one would ever notice it anyway; besides, she already got paid for the job. No reason to complete it completely, and no reason to make it look nice either.

Carefully creeping around the missing puzzle piece, she slithered up the slant to the plastic cap of her spray can and a small bucket of roofing tacks waiting patiently on the apex of the roof. She grabbed at the handle of the pail just as it chose to slide off the other side of the house along with the topper to that thing in her hand. In a hasty effort to catch her runaway objects before they got too far, she lunged at them cautiously but only managed to also lose the canister from her surprisingly slippery fingers. "Shit!" The items went clattering down the roof raucously before exploding against the ground below, where the girl could already tell that the sealing spray clearly popped because she could hear the rubbery contents shooting freely from some kind of crack in its hull. Cringing at the additional cleanup in her immediate future, she crawled back down toward the exit disheartened.

Forgetting her helper's health in favor of focusing on the massive mess she just made, the weary young woman aimed her voice down at the ground and shouted, "Leunga, are you holding the ladder?"

A dismissive voice yelled back. "You say something?"

Abruptly plagued by a mixture of weak emotions once she was able to grasp the significance of her sibling's reply, she was somewhat relieved to hear the sound of her unconscious brother's voice—at least now she wouldn't have to explain anything to the police; however, a growing aggravation took priority as she noticed that he wasn't paying any attention to her situation. "Are you holding the ladder?" she asked, irritated.

"Gotcha."

"Does that mean you are?" she asked, slightly more irritated.

"Gotcha."

She rolled her eyes. "...I'm gonna come down now. Hold it steady." Slowly, she put one leg over the top rung, resting her thin, gray, high-top sneaker on the second step. She scooted slightly closer to the lip of the gutter and jiggled the ladder to see if anyone was actually holding it. The ladder jostled as if it were uninhibited by human hands. Once more she called down to her older brother. "Are you really holding the ladder?"

There was never a response.

Clawing her way up the roof for the hundredth time that day, she hopped over to the other side and shimmied down to where her parents' room was located. "Mom?" she asked loudly, her voice showing signs of a growing fear, but once again, there was never a response.

To her sudden shock, across the street she saw a boy—the very familiar face of a boy who went to the same high school that she did—wheeling out a lawnmower. Rapidly gaining her composure to the best of her abilities at the time, she stopped all unflattering activities of a panicky sort and sat on the roof as if she was just relaxing on her precarious, low-angled, fifteen-foot perch. The boy looked over and waved to her. She pretended to just barely notice him and gave a deceitfully unenthused, casual wave his way and continued sitting nonchalantly while her sights averted his gaze altogether without any permission at all. And then the boy went back to work.

Far, far away, down at the furthest end of the block, the young woman trapped between the unmanned ladder and the young man's eyes on the other side of the avenue was not in the least bit pleased to notice her mother's car turning onto their street. Not wanting her mother to make a scene in front of the boy next door—asking superfluous questions like *Why the hell are you on the roof?! Are you trying to break your neck?!*—she slowly moved back to the other side of the house. "Damn you, Leunga... Stupid little bitch."

As she was cursing her brother, another surprise gust of wind returned for an encore and assaulted her, blowing large flecks of dust into her eyes while also causing the ladder to slide. "No, no, no!" she exclaimed and skidded toward the runaway rungs, rubbing her eyes with one hand, but the slim structure was moving too fast for her and fell into the side of the garage with a teeth-cracking crash. Frustrated by the situation, she surrendered and decided to check on the boy across the street.

As covertly as she could manage, the slender spy peered over the top of the roof, using the angle for cover. She watched as the boy tried unsuccessfully to start the mower over and over to his great dismay, but she wasn't interested in his problem. Lying entirely on the surface itself, she rested her chin on the back of her forearm, avoiding facial contact with her numerous studded wristbands and the roof's uncomfortable tiles. She didn't notice her mother and older brother's conversation happening just on the other side of the house, nor would she have cared to listen in.

The boy across the street pretended to repair the lawnmower out of embarrassment at not being able to start it. She watched as he turned the machine on its side, still oblivious to the fact that her mother was already home. Not knowing if his former classmate was still observing or not, the boy glanced up at his neighbor's roof, where he noticed that she was gone; however, the young woman was startled by his momentary gaze and immediately assumed he had seen her. She hid her head in her arm and stayed there for a few minutes with her thoughts. Finally, when she was reasonably sure he wasn't looking, she gradually lifted her head back up. He was gone. Sitting up slowly, she brushed off hundreds of the small rubber pellets her clothes collected from the roof and took one more glance at her neighbor's house. Troubled by darkness, she made a mildly dejected face as memories began to flood back—little events that should have only chipped the marble, but created large, disfiguring cracks instead.

"*Sydney?* What are you doing up there?" a very familiar, fully developed, deep voice called up from the sidewalk.

Sydney's attention left the house across the street and redirected to her younger teenage brother, responding as quickly as she could recall. "Dad paid me and Leunga twenty dollars each to put a patch over that leak in the roof above my room... I mean, he paid *me* forty dollars."

Her brother mumbled something under his breath before shouting out a question to the girl on the top of the house. "Do you need any help?"

Sydney looked back toward her only possible exit with a mental nod. "Uh-huh, you can help me get down. The ladder fell, and Leunga is a jackass."

"Yeah, okay. Just let me help Mom take in these bags, and I'll hold the ladder."

"Hurry," his sister pleaded. Out of the corner of her eye, she saw some new movement across the street, easily drawing her attention while she placed her elevational predicament safely on the back burner. As her little brother went to grab some grocery bags, she looked again at their neighbor's carbon copy house. A man in his early fifties was speaking to the boy with words unrecognizable at Sydney's distance. The man pulled at the mower cord while the lad gave a defeated glance at her rooftop. Both teens peering through one another felt humiliated but for entirely different reasons. Although she couldn't see the finer details of his face, they were clear to her as if he had been sitting on the roof beside her. Accompanying him was the ache of his image, and her fractured heart began to leak into the pit of her stomach all over again.

Behind her the sound of metal scraping against metal signaled the return of the ladder, and it jarred her back to reality. The rooftop repairwoman reluctantly unlocked her stare and crawled down to her escape. "You holding it?" she asked, knowing the answer.

"Yeah, ready when you are."

Sydney descended with haste, happy to be done with the roof. When she was at ground level, she surveyed the land in search of her former construction partner. Only her older sibling's wake remained; scattered tools of nonessential function and empty beer bottles lined the grass like stars spattered across the cosmos. With both feet firmly on the patio, she stood tall and sighed with relief before looking up at her little brother's face. "Where's Leunga?"

Third Time's the Charm

A vehicular horn blared as it passed him. "Get a car!" the driver shouted.

"Nice *costume*, douche," the passenger added.

Let's just say it was a very unusual day for the tall, blond, midteen boy on his way home—that was stupid; I meant to say it was a very ordinary day. Aside from his height and boyish good looks, he was a very average high school boy on his way to becoming a junior when the summer was through. A boy who rested uncomfortably on the other end of the social spectrum so distant from his outcast elder brother and sister, and who normally wore unassuming teenage clothes not unlike those of his friends, always walking with the slightest of slouches even without his backpack or duffel bag weighing him down.

He had just left his typical Saturday-afternoon Muay Thai kickboxing lesson at the studio right by the pricey supermarket in that mini-mall just down the way and was walking the five blocks home, as he had always done. And he was accosted by an arbitrary high school student or two, as *they* had always done. All things considered, he still enjoyed walking more than driving— feeling the pavement rolling away beneath his feet had an irresistibly therapeutic quality to it worthy of an excess of unwanted eyes gawking at his outlandish outfit, along with all of that additional time it took to escape the streets on a quick trip to the sightless safety of his bedroom, because the journey would be far too abnormal in a vehicle...and far too comfortable too. Okay, that was just a lie. He totally failed driver's ed class his sophomore year, effectively disallowing him the use of any motor-powered transport, no matter how much he secretly would have preferred it. There was a small problem with the written test. Multiple choice. Too many enticing answers. Also, he failed the driving test, in case you were wondering. As a result of his indecisiveness, he was forced to retake the course sometime during the middle of summer. Not a big deal. And as far as being made fun of over his karate *gi*—a heavy-duty combat robe of some kind—he was used to that too.

During his numerous years of taking various martial arts classes from that particular dojo, his route home hadn't altered one bit, and on that day he had the urge to change it up, but the urge subsided swiftly and he went his standard course. As he watched his feet glide in front of one another, he made sure never to let his foot touch any crack—a tradition he kept alive for almost eight years of trekking that familiar path. As you might have guessed, he passed the time by counting the number of sidewalk squares it took to go from the disciplined combat studio to his house. For some reason, the number never changed, but it became ritual, so he did it anyway.

Forty-two sidewalk squares. He clicked the button on the traffic light pole, indicating he wished to cross the typically quiet street. His eyes lifted from his feet and focused on the bright red hand thirty feet away. He sighed. A car filled with girls from his old homeroom and a couple of other classes flew by him and sounded the horn, screaming something indistinct. After they passed him, he quickly and carefully slid his palms over the sides of the upper stratosphere of his intricate hairdo, checking the consistency of his carefully crafted coiffure and feeling to see if what they saw was what he wanted them to see. Reasonably satisfied with what he could only hope was golden perfection, he kept his eyes on the bright red hand before him. A short wait later, the hand was replaced with a featureless man in midstride, and the tall teenage boy quickly ceased his primping before looking both ways down the street for oncoming traffic and jogging over the crosswalk.

One hundred and eight sidewalk squares. The strap on his dark blue duffel bag began digging into his neck. He tugged at it, hoping it would relieve his anguish, but the pain was much too stubborn and continued the instant he released it. Ducking his head down, he pulled the strap over to his left side.

When his shoulder was no longer required to support the duffel, he spun the bag around and placed it on the other side, putting his head and right arm through the opening after trying a few other combinations that didn't make any sense. Miraculously, much of the pain went away.

One hundred and fifty-one sidewalk squares. While walking with his gaze magnetically locked to his toes, he sensed someone nearby. He looked over and saw an elderly man staring at him with his mouth open. It wasn't open out of astonishment: the old man left it that way usually. The boy slowed his stroll and waved to the elderly man. The man darted his tongue through the opening his mouth made and hobbled inside without acknowledging the greeting.

One hundred and ninety-nine sidewalk squares. An overgrown bush that was usually obstructing the path was once again obstructing the path. Around the obstacle he walked, along the grass next to the sidewalk, while maintaining visual contact with his feet, already knowing full well how many squares he would be bypassing. He was focused on the blades he bent so much so that when he accidently stepped in dog feces, he was aware of it immediately. He sighed as he attempted to wipe his size thirteen sneaker clean using the bush, which continued to obstruct the path.

Two hundred and forty-seven sidewalk squares. He was home.

"Hello, sweetie! How was class today?" his exhausted mother asked from the curb, out of breath for an unknown reason.

Sweetie shrugged. "It was okay, I guess."

"Would you mind carrying in some of these bags?" she requested with apparent ignorance to his response as she grunted and hauled a single bag of groceries up the walkway to the front door, which was fine by him.

"Sure," he answered from the sidewalk. Looking across the lawn to the house, he wondered if any one of the someones he sometimes spent his time with were waiting within to jump him, when he suddenly saw the face of his older sister on the roof. Taken aback by the extremely unusual sight, the teen's expression twisted with severe confusion. "Syd?" he asked her.

She didn't answer.

"Hey, Syd?"

She still didn't answer.

"*Sydney?*" he called up loudly. "What are you doing up there?"

Sydney seemed to snap back to reality. "Dad paid me and Leunga twenty dollars each to put a patch over that leak in the roof above my room... I mean, he paid *me* forty dollars."

The teenage boy on the front lawn was sore to hear he missed the festivities. "I want forty dollars... Do you need any help?" he asked in a big booming voice, knowing that if his brother was involved, the job would need twice the required amount of workers.

"Uh-huh, you can help me get down. The ladder fell and Leunga is a jackass."

"Yeah, okay. Just let me help Mom take in these bags, and I'll hold the ladder," he responded, walking toward the open car trunk and grabbing three bags.

"Hurry."

The very handsome young man balanced his load as he headed for the sliding glass door at the back of the abode where he normally left his duffel bag of martial arts equipment and shoes. He walked slowly to the east side of the house, making sure not to spill any of the groceries, where he was abruptly greeted by a small empty bucket. Recognizing it from the many times he had seen it in the garage, he remembered it being full of tacks and nails, or barring that, some other form of junk. As he got closer, he spotted the contents scattered all over the grass and pavement, along with a shimmering wash of greasy black rubber coating a great deal of the same area, as well as a decent portion of the house. "I bet Lou did this," he speculated to himself. With a twist of his tightening shoulder carting the majority of the weight in his toned arms, he adjusted his course to account for the newfound obstacles and headed back to the front door.

Overburdened by baggage but glad to be home, the tall boy awkwardly walked through the front door just as a downright quixotic Leunga was leaving. "Ricky!" the eldest welcomed his baby brother with unacceptably piercing volume. "How was football practice," he asked—more statement than question, really.

Already proficient in a few styles of martial artistry, Ricky had spent many years attending training and discussing some of the more appealing techniques in great detail with his older brother, sometimes using him for practice—as a willing volunteer of course...except for the instance when Leunga was thrown through the kitchen's screen door, but that's a story for another time. In any case, Ricky's sibling should have known better than to dishonor the belt with talk of footballs, but he happily let it go with one minor correction to the stoner's statement: "*Kickboxing* was all right. And, uh, you don't have to go back out to the van. I got the rest of the bags right here, dude. You can take one if you want."

"No time for any of that yet, my pointy little friend," the shorter of the two declined as he walked out the door. "Going to Grammy's house. Important business there. See ya tomorrow."

Certain that he heard his brother wrong, an encumbered young man noticed something black strapped to the older boy's back as Leunga swaggered down the driveway onto the street, completely ignoring his car. Observant as ever, the teen was confused. "Tomorrow?" he asked the man on the couch hiding behind a newspaper.

A fatherly figure set the news source down. "Did you say something, Ricky?"

"Why is Lou going to Grammy's house?"

"Lou is leaving?" his father asked.

The martial artist flashed his eyes wide and discretely swayed them away from the man in self-serving reply, taking the groceries to the kitchen, because when Dad was reading his books and such, it meant his mind was understandably elsewhere, and therefore, of use to no one. Just like everyone else I know. Ricky then considered putting his equipment away but generously chose to help his sister first. The first thing the teenage lad took notice of after he opened the screen door was a toppled ladder blocking his path, like an overgrown bush. He grabbed it with both hands and lifted it toward the roof, nudging his duffel bag out of the way with his elbow. While he was busy moving his bag, the ladder scraped against the rain gutter, causing a calamity he was sure there would be dire consequences for. Ricky cringed. "Oops...crap."

"You holding it?"

He looked up at the roof, both hands gripping means of descent, and answered, "Yeah, ready when you are."

The apparatus shook violently in his tight grasp as Sydney moved down the structure as quickly as she could. When she was about four feet from the ground she hopped off and sighed with relief. Ricky let go of the ladder and glanced down into the dark brown eyes of his sister who, despite being a late-teen girl of much greater than average height, stood a bit less than half of a foot shorter than him. "Where's Leunga?" she asked.

"Uh..." Ricky scratched the back of his spiky blond mane as he thought for a moment. "Oh. He said he was going to, like, Grammy's house or something."

Sydney walked into the kitchen and knelt down, untying her retro canvas sneakers next to the door. "That dumbshit was supposed to help me..." She paused and looked up at her younger brother with confusion when his statement finally hit her. "He went to Grandma's house? Why?"

Ricky shrugged. "He told me he would be back tomorrow."

His older sister stared at him blankly. "She lives ten minutes away."

"Well...yeah, but I think he's walking there."

Sydney scoffed. "*He's* going to walk *four* miles?" She retied her own shoes and subsequently picked up a very different pair of footwear she just noticed from close by. "He's gonna get so lost. He can't even find her house with directions. This I gotta see. Come on. Let's go bother him. I need to tell him something *very* important anyway." She left out the sliding screen door, bumping her little brother by accident. "Oh. Pardon me, damn it!"

"Okay, um, just let me put my stuff away first."

"Duh. Bring it. It'll only take a sec," she suggested as she slid the extra footwear onto each of her fists. Hand shoes. Those aren't even hers. That's gross. "He's probably still at the end of the driveway trying to figure out if it's left or right."

Ricky looked into the comfort of the indoors he had yet to reenter and then back at his sister who was rounding the side of the house by that point. "But like, why do I have to go?" he shouted over to her.

Sydney stopped and glanced around the corner. She scowled lovingly as she motioned for her younger brother to tag along with a wave of a boot. "What the hell are you waiting for? Come on already!"

Wanting to avoid starting his afternoon by setting his spookier sibling off in some way, a very reluctant Ricky whimpered and followed his sister, hanging his dejected head high over his feet. Little did he realize it would be one of the biggest mistakes of his young life. And little did *I* realize that I just gave away a huge part of the plot.

EPIC

Through the River and Over the Woods

The midafternoon sun trickled through a bramble of hair to reach the back of Leunga's neck like a shower of flame as he sat with his legs folded compactly on the coarse gray concrete. Propping up his weary head with his hands carefully placed beneath his hearty brunet shag, he rested his elbows against his knees. "Too damn hot out here damn hell...so windy earlier..." he remarked and squinted up at the sky. Not a cloud to be seen. Tested by the trial he himself initiated, he sank his head down and shut his eyes again.

To put it as bluntly as I possibly can, Leunga wasn't accustomed to walking long distances—especially those at a very minor incline—but he was determined to get to his destination by the end of the day nonetheless. All he needed to do was gather his strength; after all, he had already been walking for hours—or at least, what he perceived to be hours. Checking his watch was futile because he wasn't wearing it, nor did he own one. Using only the sun to establish his progress like the knights of olden days, he was mighty proud of all that he accomplished in the time it took the blazing ball of Helios to soar so far across the sky; however, he was in no way adapted to the outside, so he was unable to look toward the sun directly to know if what he assumed he saw was what he actually saw. According to him, the trek so far was a success.

Leunga was holding his face in his hands when he felt a sudden temperature change. Upon opening his eyes as much as he could, he noticed that he was surrounded by shadow, so, squinting over his left shoulder, he sought to discover the cause and found his younger brother standing over him. "What do you want?" he asked the teen, not wondering how his sibling managed to catch up with him.

"Hello, Leunga. Forget something?" Sydney squatted down next to her older brother, flanking him from the right. He turned his head, still squinting, and looked her in the eyes. She smiled politely and then punched him in the arm almost as hard as she could. "You left me on the *roof,* idiot! I could have died!"

Confounded by the sudden onset of adolescents, Leunga rubbed his arm and stared at his sister, making a quick judgment of her current status. "And yet, despite all of that, you didn't." His head whipped around, looking up at his younger brother to pose a question to their side of the group. "So that's a good thing, right?"

Ricky thoughtfully considered his sibling's inquiry. "Hmmm. Yeah. Yeah, I can see an advantage to that."

"Gross." Sydney grimaced and exhaled in annoyance. "You guys love me so much it's disgusting... Also, I'm keeping your half of the money Dad gave us."

Leunga's attention swiftly snapped back to the girl. "Money for what?"

"Oh my god! You better be kidding..." his sister suggested as she stood up and looked down the street to where Leunga was headed. She swiveled her head back the way they came and shaded her eyes with one hand cutting under her lengthy bangs, witnessing for herself the great many yards her brother managed to traverse all on his own. "So why are you going to Grandma's?"

Returning to the place he was at before he was so rudely interrupted, Leunga rested his face in his hands and handed out a response. "Gotta ask her some stuff."

"Like what?" Ricky wondered, adjusting his duffel bag.

The eldest pointed to his back with his thumb as if to reveal some unkept secret. "She gave me this, but one of them is missing." When it was clear that no one else was instantly amazed by his treasured uncovery through mere dramaticized gestures alone, he gradually staggered to his feet to further fascinate everyone around. "I'm gonna find out why she kept it. And demand that she give it back. Threats will be involved."

With decaying disinterest, Ricky looked at the black leather sheath on his brother's back. "Is that a *sword*? And you put it on why?"

"What the shit? That's *it*? Why didn't you just drive there? Or smarter yet, call her on the damn phone?" Sydney quickly questioned.

"Because you don't start an *epic quest* by driving a *car*, or a *phone*, duh." Leunga scowled at her in disbelief. "It has to be a heroic trek across windswept meadows and snow-covered mountains, ditz."

She stared him in the eyes. "Quest? Crap-for-brains, you're only going to Grandma's house—"

"Whoa!" her older brother yelled and rapidly turned to the youngest member with shock. "Can you believe?! She just doesn't get us at all!"

Ricky looked away to say, "Me either, I guess."

Abruptly bearing the burden of bewilderment brought about by the discovery that his siblings were not who he thought they would grow up to be, Leunga secured the sword sheath strapped across his back diagonally up and to the right with a cinching of the buckles around his sternum and waist. He laughed. "So you two dummies followed me all the way here to ask a bunch of dumb questions. That's really...dumb. So dumb that I'm not even going to tell you how dumb it is."

"No it's not. I also brought you a present." Sydney cocked her head. "Close your eyes."

A surprise gift. Leunga was intrigued. Sooner than humanly possible, he held out his demanding hand and closed one eye. Sydney aggressively tossed a pair of heavy-duty tan work boots at his chest. He fumbled the shoes in his open arm for a bit before ultimately dropping them. He would have caught them if he had had both eyes open. No he wouldn't.

Not so surprisingly, in his haste to begin an epic-style quest, Leunga neglected one key ingredient to his journey: footwear. Looking down, he stared at his once-clean pair of white ankle-high socks and knelt, eventually understanding his error. He glanced up at the girl lording over him and tilted his head back, staring down his nose at his gifting sister. "Thanks heaps."

"Do you know what *shoes* are? They're these things you wear on your feet and use to walk to places when you go to the *outside* of the house."

"Uh! Yes, Syggy, I know who shoes are," Leunga replied with some delightfully subtle, sarcastic undertones as he jammed his foot into a boot.

"You know," Sydney said, "I was planning on holding those hostage, but then I realized all of your stuff sucks and you have nothing that I want, so I bequeath them unto you for free out of my deep sense of pity for your sucky stuff."

"Dude," Ricky interrupted humbly, "you just put your left shoe on the wrong foot."

"You stupid kids. No one here wants you! Go home," the eldest suggested sternly without the aid of patience. It was a good idea from his youngest sibling's perspective.

However, Sydney declined the offer on behalf of herself and her other brother. "No, we wanted to bug you."

As her petite older sibling rearranged some clunky footwear without tying the laces, as per his usual routine, the young man chortled her way when he stood and exclaimed wildly in response, "You have succeeded. Bye-bye."

Without listening to a word he said, Sydney pointed with her eyes down the street and made a recommendation, choosing a tone of voice saturated with reasoning—delicious reasoning. "You can still see our house. Go get your crappy car and just drive there."

Leunga thrust his open palm forward, so very dangerously close to his taller little sister's face. Less than six inches away. "Nay," he said definitively as she swatted his hand. "I need to do this."

"What the hell is wrong with you? I've seen you drive around the block for hours, pretending you're at work! Your car is right over there!"

"Why do you care so much? Bringing me footwear and news of lost wages as you have. This is highly suspicious, and I'm starting to suspect something suspicious."

"Tch," she scoffed. "Uh, duh. It's summer. What else would we be doing? It's not like either of us has anything better to do."

"Um, *I* do."

"That may be, but facts is facts. I've already made it this far already." Leunga shook his head very slowly and began walking in the opposite direction of their house. "I can't just give up on my epic quest. Already!"

Confused by the premise, Ricky adjusted his bag again. "So, uh, why did Grammy give you a sword?"

Sydney folded her arms and began following her elder sibling as they walked the quiet and clean suburb. "You know what? I don't even care. You're probably gonna get a tenth of the way there and pass out from the heat. I mean, you're wearing a long-sleeve shirt! I bet its ninety-five degrees out here, and *climbing.*" She continued following Leunga, awaiting his inevitable defensive response. As the two created an increasing amount of distance between their current position and their shrinking house, it quickly became apparent to her that the brunet boy was unlikely to respond. "Don't be stupid, Leu-zer." She added, "Walking is not exactly something you're good at... You're too indoorsy for that. I'm surprised you got this far." He's notoriously stationary. "Just get your car and pretend it's a horse or a dragon, or something equally idiotic." The young lady looked back at the other blond teenager, who had yet to move from his place where their older brother had been sitting. "Ricky and I can go with you."

Leunga paused, causing Sydney to stop short in order to avoid colliding with him. "You want to come with?"

"Maybe, if you drive there, goddamn it," she offered.

Hearing something vaguely resembling his own name emanating from his older sister, Ricky became concerned at the aspect of actually going to their grandmother's house. He had accidently broken a valuable glass vase the previous winter during a family get-together and was hoping to avoid any contact with her. He quickly placed his free hand against his lips as a megaphone and hollered, "What?"

"Come on, doofus, it'll be fun."

Leunga shook his head some more and began walking again. "Hows about you just walk with me." He smiled as he strolled away from his sister, knowing what she couldn't resist. "It'll be funner."

The young woman was rapidly losing her patience. As much as she liked the thought of her older brother lying facedown in a gutter somewhere, she wasn't too thrilled by the possibility that she could get in a lot of trouble because of it—after all, of the two technical adults at hand, she's supposed to be the responsible one. After glancing at Ricky, who looked anxious, startled, and highly confused as he gripped his duffel bag strap with one hand, she turned back to Leunga and pictured him giving up within minutes, and she realized she wanted to be there when it happened. Sydney grinned and accepted. "Okay, we'll go with you."

"But, wait..." Ricky shouted to himself, "Why me too?"

Leunga nodded in approval. "That's better. Hurry up, Rick! We got a long way to go, I think."

As her eldest brother started swaggering his way onward, Sydney caught up to him and walked by his side, steadfast in keeping her arms tightly entwined in front of her for reasons that must make sense to her and her alone.

Ricky created a more complete megaphone using both of his hands and yelled, "Can I at least go *change*?" He waited for a response but was disappointed when neither of his older siblings answered. He looked down at his clothes and sighed. A white karate uniform is not typically considered regulation walking attire in modern society. Had he not been mildly afraid of his older sister, or mildly concerned for his older brother, he would have turned around and gone home, but reluctantly he followed behind them, hoping he could stop sticking out and blend seamlessly in with the rest of the weirdos. Luckily, his long legs glided along the sidewalk, catching up with his brother and sister swiftly, thus giving him the concealing cover he craved.

Meanwhile, obviously overjoyed and showing it by hiding his whole bottom lip behind his front teeth and swinging his sights abaft to take stock of the teenage minions he was happy to enlist in such a wonderful accident, Leunga noticed his youngest sibling walking close behind with his eyes aimed at his feet, gripping some kind of luggage tightly. He turned his hurried gaze to his sister, who was staring at the houses on the other side of the street with her hands gradually moving into her pockets all the way up to her dangerous bracelets. Leunga nodded contentedly. "This is gonna be awesome. And thereby, the fellowship of the quest is created! I'm gonna whistle."

"Don't," someone sincerely beseeched, but the other boy went ahead and whistled a heavily protected, unlawfully reproduced tune anyway.

When the journey was steadily afoot, Sydney allowed herself a look at the sword on her big brother's back. The handle on the weapon was absolutely unremarkable—a bit on the boxy side and tightly wrapped with a strap of worn-out light brown leather, but nothing special. Half of an ordinary medieval sword, she thought. What piqued her attention was the black sheath. It was a piece of equipment that, when worn correctly—just as her brother was currently doing for unknown reasons—was wrapped around the wearer's torso diagonally in a fashion parallel to the blade holster over the right shoulder, in one large cincture from the neck down over the chest to the hip, where it was connected by a secondary belt to be worn around the wielder's waist. It was held securely to his body by the cinched straps tightened through two gigantic buckles. The entirety of it was elegantly imprinted with depictions of trees, leaves, and a number of woodland animals. And even though it was unmistakably made of dead animal skin, it was pretty.

The whir of a bicycle tire soaring over pavement approached from the street behind them. As the cyclist drew closer they heard, "Halloween is in October, dumbass!"

Leunga watched the vehicle and its driver roll past in immediate contempt. He glanced at Ricky's sparkling white karate gi before looking back at the attacker. He raised his right hand and extended his middle finger as much as he could while shouting, "Fuck you!" The cyclist, however, was referring to the sword draped over his back. A fact Leunga would never realize.

The man on the bicycle quickly looked back and began peddling faster. Leunga was satisfied with his actions. Sydney was less impressed. She turned to her older brother and hissed, "*Leunga!*" as she pointed at the small children a mere thirty feet away, staring horrified at the cussing idiot.

"Egad! Dudes, sorry!" he shouted in apology a bit too late, because by then the children had already run into their house, calling for their mother.

"You didn't see them?" his sister asked, quickening her pace to avoid any confrontation that might approach.

The eldest matched her speed. "Hey! Hell! Not my fault some asshole made fun of my Rickley." Again, the cyclist was making fun of Leunga.

"Thanks anyway," Ricky stated as he caught up with the other two.

"Oh, shit yeah," Leunga assured while they jogged past the house with the traumatized children. His mind leapt at that particular domicile in order to add, "I just wish there weren't any innocent victims of my awesomeness."

"Be more careful with the swearing...assface," a swift Sydney suggested.

"Actually, I was thinking I'll just keep using the top-tier swears in front of little kidagers because I'm so stupid, thanks." Leunga slowed down as soon as they were a safe distance from the house. Let's say like fifty to sixty feet.

"Yeah, whatever." Wondering about the consequences of her companion's actions, the sister glanced back past Ricky and their shorter older brother at the house the children scurried into, where she suddenly saw a woman run out the front door, looking angrily down the street toward them. The girl's eyes went wide as instinct took hold of her, and she ripped her hands from her pockets to sprint. "Shit! Run."

Without a second to spare, the three of them began running at their top speeds. Sydney was easily ahead of the pack as Ricky trailed slightly behind her with baggage aplenty. Leunga clutched his ribs and panted as he moved his miniature muscles as fast as he could possibly manage. They rounded a corner some ways away and paused for the geek to catch his breath.

"Why were we running?" Ricky furrowed his brow, scanning the area for threats.

Leunga wheezed, "It's not like...I swore...at those kids."

Spying around the side of the fence by their backs, a teen gave her full estimation of the situation, saying, "I think we might actually have to go the whole way now."

"What?! You didn't...think we...would get there before?"

Sydney avoided her older brother's explosive question and attempted to guide the boys onward toward the end of their farce. "Come on, we still have a long way to go."

Straining himself, Leunga started strolling again—after an absurd amount of time. "Yeah. I know. So why...did you get us...out of so much breath?"

•   •   •

Half an hour passed, and Leunga was beginning to look exhausted— as if he didn't before. His feet clapped against the sidewalk as he slammed them down with each step he took. "How much more...is it to there?"

"We're almost halfway," Sydney stated without losing her breath.

"Are you okay?" Ricky asked, concerned about his brother's constant panting.

Leunga looked back at him. "Yeah. Epic quest. Going... Shut your face up."

"At this rate it's gonna take another hour," his sister said smugly as she noticed her smaller sibling's souring disposition. "We can turn back now if you want," she suggested, until she considered the confrontation. "We just have to go the long way around."

"I...not...we can't..." Leunga sighed heavily. "Silence, mortal. Keep going."

And Sydney shrugged. "Okay."

•   •   •

Almost exactly one hour later, Leunga was literally dragging each foot forward, sliding his construction-grade work boots across the cement of the sidewalk. Ricky was showing slight signs of fatigue, breathing mainly through his mouth. Sydney, however, was still at her normal condition. As they passed another street sign, the middle sister recognized the house on the corner and looked at the name of the boulevard, redirecting her vision back over her shoulder at her older brother in amazement. "Holy bitch! Almost there!"

Leunga lifted his sweat-stained eyes up from the sidewalk. "Effin' finally."

"Two more minutes," she added.

"Goddamn it!" he huffed loudly in anger.

An elderly couple on their porch acted like they didn't hear any of it.

Ricky was rummaging through his bag for the better part of ten minutes, searching for his water bottle, when he ultimately found it. He whipped it out of the smallest compartment of his bag, only to realize it was empty. "Ugh. Why?!" he groaned.

"Come on, guys. When we get there, you can rest," a sibling reassured her brothers. "We're only five houses away."

"I should've...got my...car."

Shaking her head, Sydney let out a sigh. "No shit," she said sneakily to herself and turned onto the unpaved driveway of their grandmother's house while her brothers slowly followed like an obedient pair of zombies. The smell of pine trees and pollen filled her lungs as she looked around at the surrounding forest in oddly nostalgic awe. Hastening her pace, she jogged up to the front door and pressed the doorbell. An unforgettable tune entered her ears as the melody echoed through the house. Moments later, the front door opened, and a familiar face peered through the opening. "Hi, Grandma," said Sydney with a smile.

"Oh! What a wonderful surprise," their grandmother greeted with that curiously enchanting accent of hers as she unlocked the screen door. "Come in!"

Try Not to Break Anything

Leunga flopped onto the living room couch with enough pent-up laziness to power his slothy slouch for days to come in the cool atmosphere of his mother's mother's house as he pushed his boots off with his feet. His left boot fell to the floor while his right landed squarely on the coffee table, knocking over a glass of ice-cold beverage, but he clearly didn't care because on top of his lethargy, the unequipped sword hilt behind his back was digging its way uncomfortably deep into his shoulder—and yet he was too occupied with the task of breathing to care about that either. Surely it was an epic quest indeed.

Trundling into the living room after setting the duffel bag by his grandmother's kitchen archway, Ricky guzzled the cup of water at his lips and noticed that Sydney was already lounging comfortably in his favorite armchair, staring vacantly at the TV. "So. This was fun. Anybody else wanna go home yet?" he asked, and after a few minutes of having no one reply, he caved in, turning to his brother on the sofa to make a casual request. "Dude, move your feet. I wanna sit."

Leunga peeked through half-open eyes at his standing sibling. "Hell no. Sit in the other chair."

Ricky glanced at their sister. She continued to gawk at the game show on the television, completely unaware of her surroundings. "I can't. Syd is sitting there."

"Then sit on the effin' floor."

"Can't you just move your feet?"

Leunga went silent and tried to ignore his brother's pleading. Ricky waited for a response for the duration of an entire commercial before he abruptly chose to take Leunga's advice and sat on the effin' floor. Easing down beside the coffee table, he set his empty cup next to his brother's fumbled footwear without a second thought. As he rested on the ground, the strangest squishing sound came from the carpet beneath him in a muted manner, and soon enough, he felt his leg grow more and more damp. Ricky jumped up, noticing the overturned glass that had rolled under the table, and he pulled at the soggy fabric to see the damage he knew was sure to be there. The back of his left pant leg and half of his butt were soaked. "Ah!"

"I just got off the phone with your parents," their grandmother announced while walking into the room and setting the cordless phone back in its cradle after ending a wireless conversation mere moments before— despite being told numerous times that her grandchildren really weren't required to check in with the folks back home. "Your father didn't seem to know you had left, but everything is settled now... He also said something about warning you that your mother is very angry about a huge mess in the yard, but I don't know what that means..." She stopped when she noticed her youngest grandson's pants. "Oh, hermoso, what happened?"

"I think Lou had a spill..." he said as he glared at his brother, but Leunga still wasn't paying attention.

"Oh dear," his grandmother sympathized. "Well, let me have them. I can throw them in with the rest of the laundry right now. I was about to start some anyway."

The teen winced. "Um! That's okay. We probably won't be here for that long... I'm okay with just, like, wearing them."

"Sígueme. Let's get you some different pants from your grandfather's drawer so that I can clean those for you before stain sets," she suggested while walking off in the direction of her bedroom.

Looking to his brother and sister for rescue, Ricky panicked at the thought of being alone with his grandmother after the incident with the vase so many months ago. "Uh...that's really okay. It's not that bad, Grammy. It's just water."

"Not all of it." Leunga, suddenly paying close attention to his brother's words, held up a pewter cask he kept in his pocket. "Some of it was this." And then he jiggled the flask at no one in particular.

Ricky stared down at his pants in the late afternoon sunlight seeping through the window, witnessing for himself that the wet patch was slightly brown. With a bit of sugar, some bitters, a citrus wedge, and a maraschino cherry, he could have had an Old Fashioned in his pants. Reluctantly, Ricky obeyed his grandmother, walking slowly with his customary teenage slouch, another in a long list of physical traits he shared with his sister—hopefully it wouldn't be permanent—and followed along, diligently asking himself an invaluable question in an almost inaudible mutter. "Wonder what *sígueme* means..."

Leunga strained his neck to look for his brother, but Ricky was already gone. "Hells in a half shells. Rickinny spilled my drink," he informed the rest of the room. "I'm gonna get a new one. B-R-B." Rolling out of the sofa onto the floor and ignoring someone's downturned glass, he staggered up and disappeared from the living room without a trace. The closest entrance to the kitchen was separated from the area he was just in by a small sitting room some might call a nook—unless they're me—and the entire trip should have taken less than ten seconds; however, he went the wrong way when he saw his grandmother's new display of family photos and set sail for a senseless detour instead. The curious enthusiast eased up to them, looking only at the pictures he was in, or clearly should have been in, when he shouted, "Hey! Sydiddy, come look at this."

Waiting until she had watched the entirety of the scrolling credits for the high-stakes rerun she initially had absolutely no interest in viewing before she even considered seeing what her badgering brother wanted, Sydney slid out from the single-cushion couch silently and strolled to the TV to turn it off with the push of a button on the remote control handily set on top of the set. The screen before her went motionless, and she saw her own image in the darkness. She leaned closer, viewing her hair in the hazy black mirror as she fluffed her heaping bangs to keep them in perfect form for whatever reason; following that, she then tugged at the bottom of her faded, black, form-fitting T-shirt, adjusting its length underneath one of the colored spaghetti-strap tank tops she always wore as an overshirt. That morning she chose her lavender camisole for heavy-duty roofing work. Taking her time in no time at all, her fingers slid around the edge of her worn-out undershirt until she was comfortable. An action she had done hundreds of times before, maybe thousands. Millions? Don't be ridiculous.

Sydney strode through the house toward her brother's call as he reinsisted, "Freakin' Sydney, c'mere!" Stoically situated at the assortment of family photos adorning the top of a somewhat standard, worn, widely unused, upright piano acting as a makeshift mantle, Leunga glanced back as his sylph sibling approached, and instructed, "Look at this one." He pointed to a picture of their parents on their wedding day. "Check out Pop's stupid haircut. Greasy much? Hah!"

Sydney followed his directions and studied the sepia. "Looks like your hair."

"What?!" Leunga grabbed the picture frame and held it close to his face to see his own reflection. "No it doesn't..."

His sister snickered at his reaction and turned to him. "Hmmm, you're right. He's blond." Unwittingly joining in her older sibling's illogical appreciation of the arts, she glanced down at the photos and one of them stuck out immediately. "Hey, look!" Sydney carefully picked up a baby picture of herself in a miniature chair next to an outspoken preschooler. A Halloween picture by the look of it. She was dressed as an orange kitten sitting next to her loudmouth older brother dressed as a greenish dragon—or some kind of dinosaur. "Aw...how sweet. The last time you were taller than me."

"Ha. Ha. Ha." By far, Leunga's worst impression of a laugh to date.

"That's one of my favorites," their elderly ambusher remarked as she walked up behind them with a hint of longing drifting in her smiling voice. "You two look so happy together."

"Must've been before she could talk."

Sydney glared at Leunga. "Rude."

Taking the picture from her granddaughter's hands, the noticeably older woman set it down with the others and noted, "The cookies should be done soon. Bonita, come help me. Louie, go check on your brother. Make sure he finds everything he needs."

The siblings said, "Okay." In unison.

Leunga turned to Sydney and shouted, "Jinx! You owe me some stuff."

"Yeah, um, uh, 'kay," the sister mocked her brother in the deepest voice she could manage as she followed her maternal forbearer obediently.

Satisfied with the bounty of soda pops surely headed his way by way of his foolish sister's mishandling of their final wordplay together, Leunga watched the embodiment of his family's female generational divide disappear into the kitchen before checking his hair again in the picture frame he was still holding. "It does not..."

•   •   . •

Ricky dug through another entire drawer full of his grandfather's slacks only to turn up empty-handed once more. He groaned, glancing at the wet spot on his martial arts pants from their convenient placement in front of him fairly far away from the long legs they had been covering. Reaching into the unusually deep bottom drawer one final time, he cursed, "Stupid Lou..."

"What about me?" Leunga asked calmly as he too dug through the same drawer.

The youngest jumped and yelped, "Yoowugh!" or something close to that. His heart pounded as he regained his self-control with a sigh. "Dude! Don't sneak up on me like that..."

Leunga pulled some jeans out of the drawer, inspected them, and tossed them on the floor. He looked over at his brother and noticed something strange. "Um. Okay. So here's a extremelishly excellent question—and do not you dare be insulted by me—but why the butt crack are you naked?"

More than a little annoyed with his eldest sibling, the teen scowled. "I'm not." He glimpsed down at his underwear, which he was still wearing—his damp pants happened to be draped over the dresser right in front of them with stain in plain sight. "Hey!" Ricky abruptly burst into a frenzy of incidental panic at the realization of not being alone in the proposed privacy of the bedroom his grandmother had promised. "What are you doing in here?! I'm like, not wearing pants!"

Leunga pulled more of his grandfather's trousers out of the drawer and threw them to the ground without inspecting them. "Yeah, I know. So why aren't you wearing pants?"

"Mine got wet somehow," one said, glaring at his big brother accusingly.

The shorter chuckled. "What'd you do? Piss 'em?"

Ricky, growing increasingly irritated with his sibling's lack of self-awareness, picked up some of the pants his unwanted assistant had misplaced on the floor and put them back. "Can you just leave for a second, please?"

"If you need new pants, there's some in here," said someone extremely familiar on the brawling boy's left. Leunga had moved to a recently opened closet instantaneously. Ninjutsu. As if he mysteriously materialized—or much more likely, Ricky hadn't noticed it happen.

Surprised by the slacker's stealth, Ricky joined him, not realizing it was his grandmother's personal closet. "I probably can't find anything that'll fit... Grampy is...um"—he paused to assess his statement and looked down at his older brother—"not as tall as me." He chose to avoid the more painful words in order to spare Leunga's feelings, even though that little guy was the direct cause of Ricky's predicament.

"Oh! These!" Apparently, Leunga had ignored his brother entirely once again as he held up a pair of sweatpants of a vibrant turquoise—a color trapped in the shadow realm between blue and green. "These are huge. Maybe they'll work like shorts."

The six-foot-something skyscraper clearly didn't appreciate being referred to as *huge*, but he quickly realized that Leunga's definition of the word meant huge vertically—at least from a relative perspective when compared to the other options present on the rack. The chosen sweats were indeed huge, to borrow a phrase, in contrast to every other in the oddly broad selection of jogging pants—an unusual assortment of sportswear for a woman who clearly no longer jogged—so he took them from Leunga and turned around, requiring a minor amount of privacy to slip them on. To his amazement and dismay, the pants fit, serving admirably as a greenish blue pair of extra-long shorts; they were a bit on the slightly tight and revealing side, but they performed the desired function marvelously. For the time being, Ricky approved.

"Dude." He smoothed out the wrinkles and wondered something aloud. "Why would Grampy have these?"

Leunga walked to his brother's side, wearing an absurdly large grin on his face. "Perfect! Let's go show some people." He rushed to the doorway before stopping hastily in exclamation. "Oh, wait," he stalled, pulling the framed photograph of their parents' wedding out of the pocket of his beige cargo shorts. "Does Pop's hair really look like mine?"

Feeling a bit apprehensive about his brother's unusually jubilant attitude toward the pants he was now wearing, Ricky edged closer to Leunga and glanced at the picture, and after turning his attention to the stoner at his side's hair, he agreed. "Yeah, sort of. Except he's blond."

Leunga's mouth went agape. He was stunned by this revelation from whom he professed was one of his most trustworthy siblings. Dashing over to the bedroom's vanity mirror, he studied his shaggy, unkempt, and untamed brunet mane with a dry, coarse, straw-like texture akin to hay, perpetually uncut for months at a time. Truly a man with a deep sense of style—if *messy* or *unadulterated* can be considered hairstyles and not divine tributes to laziness—Leunga often described his hair as having *extra-large curls*, although it's much more accurate to illustrate it as hairs curled outward at the ends, or *mildly curly*, if there's even any difference between the two. I actually don't know how to describe it without making myself queasy. His hair is so hard to look at directly for more than a few seconds at once that I need to wait for a bit each time I look away. It's really quite a problem for me, but I suppose the last time I studied it, his hair was long and loopy like hundreds of ludicrously gigantic, gritty fishing hooks dangling from a messy mop. An arrangement that leaves the average viewer beseeching the use of a common comb.

He violently shook his head in an attempt to change his vintage coiffure, but it did little to alleviate his situation. A driving hat perched on the edge of the mirror caught his eye and he snatched it, flinging it over as much of his hair as he could manage. "I need a haircut." Making his way to the door, it was then that he noticed the greatest polo shirt he had ever seen. It was dark red with thin yellow-and-black stripes evenly spaced horizontally—three of his seven favorite colors. "And I need this, too."

Ricky waited in the dim hall, not wanting to be seen by any more people in his condition, and was growing increasingly concerned with the issue of decreased mobility caused by excessive embarrassment due to the skintight quality of his borrowed attire in the light, hoping to use his brother as a shield. His only consolation was the fact that he would only need to wear them temporarily—a couple hours, tops. Ricky abandoned his distress as he looked up, seeing Leunga emerge from the darkness. Transformed. Into something hideous.

Proudly displaying his latest stolen hat—featuring numerous brown hairs sticking down over his thick eyebrows, impairing his vision considerably—the stupefying sibling flaunted an unclean short-sleeved polo shirt worn expertly over his long-sleeved, white T-shirt covered in permanent stains from wrist to wrist. His shorts, though belonging to him, were two sizes too big and beltless, resulting in the effect of his plaid underpants being visible at most times. And his tiny ankle-high socks, when worn with his tan boots, would all but disappear completely. Truly, it was a sight to behold. A paragon of fashion excellence.

Leunga adjusted his new hat and pulled the hair out of his right eye. "Let's go show off our new shtuff."

Ricky quickly tripped on that suggestion. "Uh... I wouldn't really say it's new...or ours."

That Special Nobody

Sydney complied with the request. "Okay." And as she said the word, she heard her brother say the same.

Leunga whirled toward her. "Jinx! You owe me some stuff."

Immediately, she noticed that her brother failed to accomplish a true Jinx, not completing the entire ritual while still expecting the traditional outcome, so she lowered her voice to match his absurdity. "Yeah, um, uh, 'kay." As her grandmother wandered into the kitchen, she followed. Into the diminishing light of the natural world outside the broad, open window, the young lady walked around the large island counter and leaned against the opposite side, away from the oven where the old woman was preparing something sweet to eat—as she usually would whenever her grandchildren were around. The view from the window in front of the teen was a perfect picture of the backyard, where all the useless junk her grandparents collected over the years resided, always aging and never changing.

Her grandmother opened the oven door, prodding one of the many cookies with her calloused fingers. "These still need more time."

Inattentively fiddling with the constricting half-inch black choker wrapped tightly around her neck, Sydney stared out the window at the all-too-familiar objects outside as she stood by, anticipating the inevitable, predictable questioning from her grandmother in the set-up scenario she just then realized would invite any, and every, thing a solitary grandmother could discuss with her only granddaughter, whether the younger wanted it or not. *Not* being the operative word. And as the air was sucked from the room in an instant, at least one of them was not pleased with what she saw heading her way.

"So, bonita, are you excited about going to college?"

Bingo. Sydney sighed as silently as she could while she thought of the response her elder would want to hear. "Yeah, it's gonna be fun." Nervous. Very very nervous. Actually, add one more *very* to that.

"Have you decided what you want to study?"

The blonde shrugged to herself. "Um...something to do with animals, I guess... It'd be kind of cool if I could maybe try to become a veterinarian." And a hell of a lot of work too. Jeez Louise. "But I dunno."

"That sounds wonderful! I can't wait to hear all about your classes when you come home for Thanksgiving. I'm sure you're going to learn lots of new, exciting things."

The girl forced a smile and nodded. "Yeah." Duh. That's what school is for.

Her grandmother washed her hands, signaling the beginning of a mounting silence that grew increasingly awkward as each additional minute passed—we'll call it four or five. Suddenly, the senior spoke. "When I was about your age, I was working at a diner to help your grandfather pay for his schooling. I never got to go to college. We were too poor for me to go with him, but I was just happy that I could help him with his dreams. You're lucky to be going to school now, and with your scholarship." She smiled quietly to herself as she dried off her hands. "I'm really happy for you, bonita."

Sydney was abruptly amazed. She never knew her grandmother had made such a grand sacrifice like that for the man she obviously loved. It made the teen contemplate her own situation more carefully—whatever that may be. Mere words would disgrace the sympathy she felt, so she simply said, "Thanks," and wondered if, in a similar situation, she herself would, or could, have done the same.

"So..." Suddenly, with that single, withered word, the mood in the room took another drastic change. "Do you have a boyfriend now? I bet he's handsome."

She stood completely motionless, stunned by the question. Sydney felt the unwelcome blood rushing to her face as she blushed. "Um..." Her mind was blank, searching for the right answer, but she couldn't think. No one had ever asked her that so bluntly; it seemed so esoteric for the direction the conversation was going. Then she heard a beep, and the question was apparently lost to the ages with the completion of the first batch.

"Oh. The cookies. Would you mind grabbing the tray? My hands are feeling a bit sore today."

Slowly regaining her poise, the young lady complied. "Sure." Her grandmother's previous superfluous question still echoed in her mind. Boyfriend. She could feel her cheeks lit up like a heat lamp, giving her reason enough to avoid eye contact with the old woman. Sydney edged around the counter and slipped on the oven mitts her ancient relation handed to her, moving on with a mind ready to crumble as she pinched the corner of the tray and tried to pull it out. Her arm briefly rubbed against the scorching metal of the oven walls and she shouted, "Ow! Shi—" before interrupting herself to choose a more appropriate ending for the exclamation of agony to suit her surroundings as she gripped her seared skin in pain. "Shoot." Boyfriend.

"¡Aý! Here, run it under cold water!"

"I'm okay, it just shocked me," Sydney stated as she grabbed the tray again without incident and quickly moved it over to the countertop where she set it down. Still filled with concern for the girl's well-being, her grandmother carefully slid the cookies off the nonstick surface of the scorching stainless steel and placed them on a nearby cooling plate that was a child-safe distance away to deny her heated treats the ability to burn anymore young hands—as any cautious, conscientious mother would naturally do. Rubbing her hurting muscle and heavy in the head, Sydney solemnly stared out the window at the growing darkness, plagued by her lonely little secrets and the disease they made while a certain senior citizen carried on the conversation and prepared more lumps of dough from the heap of batter—not that anyone present would have noticed in her state, anyway. Boyfriend.

"Okay, these are ready. I'll start the timer when you put them in. Please be very careful, bonita. I don't want you to burn yourself again..."

Brought to the forefront of her concerns by the woman's words, Sydney's conventional hopes burned brighter in her brain than ever before, keeping her unresponsive and preoccupied—traditional desires that seem to have only tied her heartstrings in a tangled knot as opportunities failed—while she tried to shake her nagging thoughts by focusing on something else, but there weren't many distractions to be had. "Okay," she said, snapping back to tentative attention. The cooking sheet ground against the oven rack as she slid it back in and closed the door slowly. "They're in." Boyfriend.

To the sound of beeping buttons, she was still struggling at coming up with a new focal point when her grandmother inadvertently helped her.

"I'm going to take you shopping before you start school."

Sydney turned at yet another odd topic from the old lady and noticed her grandmother was examining her clothes.

"Your pants are full of holes...and your shirt is fading. Wouldn't you prefer more colorful things?"

Colorful, meaning normal or average. Boring. Something Ricky would wear. Feeling increasingly defensive, especially about her choice of style, the girl looked down. Her skintight denim capri pants—color: black—were frayed to oblivion a few inches below her knees, which were also worn out completely, just like she intended. "I really like these pants," she expressed meekly in the presence of her elder, even though she should have worn them loud and proud, seeing as how she meticulously destroyed a perfectly good pair of pants in order to make them—using the family's belt sander, of course. And as far as her shirt was concerned, she had her reasons for hanging on to that old thing too. "They're kinda nice..."

"I see. Well, if you change your mind..." Her grandmother's statement, though incomplete, like most of my sentences, seemed to end there.

Sydney suddenly felt the urge to leave the room before her relative said something else self-esteem shattering without a care. Find out what Ricky is doing. "I'm gonna—"

"Do you remember when you were little," her grandmother interrupted—apparently filled with conversation topics—and went on to say, "and you and your brothers would play hide and seek right over there?" She pointed out the window at the expanse of pines close to her yard. The house was basically built in a part of the woods with few trees; only half a dozen houses were considered part of her neighborhood. "I would always worry about you kids, out there in that big open forest..."

Sydney peered out the window with her grandmother. She strained to recall anything related to her younger days at grandma's house until something jumped off the tip of her tongue. "I remember you would braid my hair so it wouldn't get messy." Realizing the mistake she just made, the teenage tomboy immediately wished she could rescind her statement. Frantically, she searched for an out to the unavoidable, but it was too late.

"Oh, I remember how cute you looked! *Muy* preciosa." Her grandmother smiled with plastic teeth. "Would you like me to braid your hair? Just like how I used to?"

Sydney resisted. "Well..." But she knew she couldn't evade it. Her desire to be left alone was overridden by the admiration she felt for her grandmother. "Okay..." Following the steps she remembered well, she sat down at the kitchen table in front of her elderly stylist and waited for the pain to begin. In no time at all, her carefully arranged, airy hair was mutilated, pulled back into one long bundle with the obvious exception of her edgy bangs—a sweeping cover of fluffy, forehead-hiding hair trimmed too short to be tied back while simultaneously too long not to fall in front of her eyes at an inappropriate time, regularly imitated poorly by her older brother's carelessly crafted monstrous brunet bangs, though his were comparably more wild. No one knows why she keeps her hair so long in the front; some say it's typical for her chosen idiosyncrasy; a few say it's a way for her to hide from peers; the rest don't seem to care. It was a hairstyle largely designed to give the appearance of an uncaring attitude despite being meticulously managed in such a way that would suggest otherwise—again, unlike Leunga's, which naturally gave that impression without outside influence. You already knew that, so quit bringing it up.

Her grandmother separated the previously alternative-styled mane into three equal parts and began humming as Sydney felt a few hairs become caught in the woman's wedding ring. She cringed as the blond hairs snapped away from her scalp in plucking pings that could be heard from miles away. Her grandmother probably could have soaped up and taken off the ring first, but it's unclear at this point.

Sydney's head jerked back repeatedly. Uncontrollably. Her mother's mother moved swiftly for a woman in her golden years, and with sore hands, no less. Aged fingers weaved with an expertise that only comes with years of training. She stopped humming momentarily. "Almost finished." Her matured movements were controlled and flawless. She was forcefully gentle with the task. "And..." With a flick of her wrist, she double looped two small elastics from the drawer nearby and strategically placed them along her towering granddaughter's new braid. "There you go. All done."

The girl tugged at her midsized stalk of hair tangled snugly against the back of her head. Tight as it ever was. "Thanks," she mumbled graciously and knew her hair would have to stay stiff for the remainder of their visit, but that shouldn't take too long.

The girl's grandmother moved around to Sydney's front, brushing her lengthy bangs in twain, creating an unfamiliar part in their concealing quality; a *very* provisional division revealing her sweetly subjugated brow. "Muy bonita. There's my beautiful nieta."

Sydney smiled patiently as she waited for *that* word to cause her head to collide with her heart all over again, while she simultaneously anticipated the ridicule her brothers would no doubt bestow upon her new 'do. What a day. Boyfriend.

Compliments of the House

"Dude, I can't go outside looking like this." Ricky stretched the sides of his sweatpants outward, displaying the vibrant shade of bluish green to his brother. "It's like I'm wearing tights. It looks stupid," he reiterated and stared down at the fate that was handed to him.

Leunga assured him, "Don't worry...no one's gonna see you. All eyes will be on me and my me-ness." He shifted his hat back and forth, looking for the right look in the bathroom mirror, and was amazed by the man he saw.

Ricky looked out of the bathroom window. "At least it's getting dark now. Kinda."

"Hey, if you need to be a butt about your rad pants, then maybe you can get Grammy to drive you back all secret-like."

"Think she'll take us home?"

"Us? Meaning *many* and including *me*?" The leading brother moved into the hallway with the other in tow. "Not a damn chance. I'm walkin' back, man. I need to be seen."

"I don't wanna go back with Grammy alone... I'll just walk with you, I guess."

"Yeah, boi! And if anyone gives you shit, I'll throw them a couple of these... *Boom*!" Leunga exploded and raised both of his hands in fists with middle fingers protruding proudly and knuckles aimed down the hallway—just as his grandmother rounded the corner with a plate of cookies. "Oh!" he screeched, retracting his birds and fleeing into the bathroom quickly, slamming the door behind him. "Don't come in! I'm pooping!"

His grandmother shook her head in disapproval at the display. "Boys, I don't want any of that in my house! When you're ready to apologize, you can have some cookies."

"We're sorry," insisted Ricky, full of guilt for his brother's actions.

"Ultra sorry, Grammy!" Leunga shouted from his hiding spot. "Still pooping!"

"Hmmm." Their grandmother nodded her head at the platter. "Well, these will be in the kitchen when you want them." And then she turned and disappeared.

"She's gone."

Leunga flushed the unused toilet and pretended to wash his hands. The bathroom door opened slowly and he peeked down the hallway. "Do you think she saw me flip her off?"

Ricky nodded. "Pretty sure."

•   •   •

Sydney leaned against the wall next to her younger brother's duffel bag, fondling her black-tipped, new, blond braid in front of her shoulder as she chewed her lip and stared blankly at the floor, unwittingly letting her thoughts hurt her in any way they wanted. The sound of her brothers' voices growing louder broke her trance. She looked up just as her older sibling and his altered digs entered the kitchen. "What the hell?!" she blurted, laughing.

Leunga turned to Ricky—who had yet to show himself—just having caught a glimpse of their sister. "Whoa. I thought *my* hair looked stupid." Surveying the room, searching for his grandmother, his eyes stopped on Sydney's braided bunch for the briefest of moments as he asked her, "Where did Grammy go?" And then, without warning and utterly unable to do anything else, his eyes were permanently fixed on her plait.

Noticing her sibling's glare, the agitated anarchist was instantly annoyed, hiding his obsession by throwing her hair back over her shoulder and folding her arms to reply, "Why the fuck do you care?"

"Lou flipped her off," Ricky whispered loudly, sneaking his spiky head around the corner of the archway, when suddenly he noticed the plate of cookies on the counter and pushed past his brother, throwing Leunga into the wall. He ate two or three at a time, proving to himself that he was hungrier than he thought—or at the very least, that he was still a teenage boy.

"She was more a casualty than a target. I wasn't aiming at her," Leunga said very convincingly and was partially convinced that he was telling the truth. Immediately, he shifted his focus to Ricky and scolded him as he corrected his hat. "Damn, man. What the butt? Leave some for the rest of the wonderful world."

"Grandma is cleaning up your spill," Sydney explained while pushing off the wall using her back. "And there's more in the oven." Picking up one of the cookies for studious purposes, she handled the warm flesh of the sugary masterpiece carefully to avoid damaging it. The taste was a memory she hadn't forgotten, so she didn't feel the need to eat any of them. She set it back down just as Leunga grabbed it from her hand.

"Well," he said, shoving the cookie into his mouth, "nuff fum mum uff non tum." Crumbs and spit flew everywhere.

"Even dogs don't bark when they eat," the young woman repeated her mother's often-used adage, instantly regretting her instinctive need to sound like the authoritative figure in the room. "Never mind. Just ask Grandma about your damn reason for dragging us here so we can go home already."

"Well, thank you for interrupting me with your nonsense." Leunga went on to chew his snack food in one side of his mouth. "And exactly what reason would I need for why? Oh sick." He pulled a long hair off of his tongue. "Ugh, it's blond...or gray. God, Sydwidge, are you *shedding*?"

Sydney's eyes widened. "You know what I'm talking about, assnut. The reason you almost died walking here? The reason Ricky is wearing women's sweatpants? The reason my hair makes me feel like I'm twelve? Don't pretend you don't know."

Ricky was horrified at the news. Staring at his newly acquired pants yet again, he muttered, "Maybe I should go change..."

Leunga swallowed. "Reason..." He looked around the room, searching for anything that might be his reason for trekking to their grandmother's house. "Give me a big hint."

His younger sibling edged closer to her older brother irritably, just as their grandmother walked in. "How are those cookies, kids?" the old woman said, smiling. She had decidedly forgotten about the incident in the hallway.

"Awesome. Hairy." Leunga nodded, grabbing another.

Another young man took his traumatized gaze off of his pants. "Really good."

Sydney stared at her littler brother and lied, "They're great." Although not tasting any from that batch, she knew there was a high probability that they were fine.

"Well, I'm glad you like them... What is that you're wearing?"

Instinctively, Ricky responded, "I'm sorry, Grammy, Lou made me wear them. I didn't know they were yours."

"Hmm?" Their grandmother turned her attention away from Leunga. "Oh those. You can keep them. One of my friends thought it would be a funny birthday gift...I never really liked her."

Her grandson was greatly relieved and embarrassed at the same time. Relieved that the woman wasn't mad. Embarrassed to realize that she wasn't asking him the question.

"Louie, where did you get that T-shirt?"

Leunga tugged at the bottom of his new polo shirt. "You mean this? I came with it. Wearing it. Is your brain okay, Grammy? How do you do feel?!"

His grandmother didn't accept his response. "That's your abuelo's shirt. It's the one he uses when he wants to pretend he can golf. I can buy you one when Sydney and I go shopping for school clothes. Why don't you put it back in the hamper?"

Sydney shook her head and looked away. As she did so, she noticed Ricky admiring, or possibly abhorring, his excruciatingly turquoise pants. When that became boring in a heartbeat, she went back to staring daggers in another brother's direction.

"Yeah, okay," a dagger-ridden dimwit stated some seconds later. "I'll do it soon." The eldest of the younglings had no intention of returning the shirt at all.

"In the meantime," his sister interjected, "you can ask Grandma about the thing."

Leunga bit down on his upper lip. Taking one last look around the room, he pursed, "Um, yes..." and still had no idea what she wanted from him. He took a bite from the cookie in his hand and shrugged at his sister.

Sydney silently mouthed the words, "The swords."

"The sores?"

She shook her head and pointed toward the living room with her dark brown eyes.

"The scores?"

She furrowed her brow directly at him and scowled.

"The stores. Wait, what about them?"

"No!" she whispered. "You suck."

"You suck!" Leunga retaliated. Not exactly clever, but effective.

"What's wrong, bonita?" asked her grandmother as she placed an empty cup in the sink and turned to her. "Is there something you need to tell me?"

And Sydney swiftly surrendered. "Leunga brought something he wants to ask you about, but he's being too stupid to know what it is." She glanced at Ricky, who was standing closest to the living room. "Would you go get it?"

The taller teen nodded with cheeks full of baked goods, and as he swiveled away from her, Sydney chortled. Her mood lightened and she turned to Leunga, who was already grinning. He laughed, before pulling out another hair from his mouth.

Ricky whipped around. "Huh?" He was positive his siblings were mocking him, but he didn't understand how or why, so he cautiously continued to the couch his brother was so adamant about not sharing, discovering a perplexing sight. The sword was gone.

He searched the floor and under the couch. Nothing there. He checked the door they entered from. Still nothing. He lifted the couch cushions. Crumbs, paperclips, candies, insignificant amounts of money, but no sword. "Where did you put it?" he hollered after swallowing and waited for a reply.

"Oh yeah! Duh." Leunga suddenly realized what his sister kept referring to. "It's on the couch."

Ricky restored the cushions. "No it's..." And there the sword rested, unmoved, exactly where the loser left it. "What?" The retriever warily grabbed it with nothing more than the quandary on his lips and scurried toward the kitchen where he held it out without question or comment.

"Took you long enough," his older brother said with a mouthful of food, and gulped it down hastily. "I'm gonna ask you about this soon." Leunga pointed to the sword his sibling displayed and made an exaggerated point to use our valuable time to stuff his face instead of furthering the plot.

Their grandmother slowly took out her reading glasses and placed them on her face, precariously close to the end of her nose. She studied the object in her grandson's grip and gave a heavy sigh. "I told your mother to hide it."

"Does that mean you know where the rest of it is?" the man it now belonged to asked. "I'm pretty sure it was supposed to come with two of them. Did the guy that sold them to you rip you off? Should we go *sword* him out?"

"I knew who had the other one, but he never knew you had this one." She shuffled toward the living room and stated, "I need to sit. Come in here and I'll tell you what I know."

Leunga stroked his chin in deep contemplation—and even deeper crunching of his cookies. This epic quest was far more epic than he imagined. He nodded in approval of the situation and spat, "Sweetcakes."

The Lost Frontier

The portly old woman eased into the recliner, her arthritic joints already aching. With one hand she steadied her descent. With the other, she clutched the ornamented sheath, drawing a long, deep breath as she settled into the chair. Her aged eyes glided along the imprinted designs enveloping the dyed leather she once thought she wouldn't have to look upon ever again. Turns out, she was wrong.

"What can you tell us about it, Grammy?" asked Leunga, leaning close to her and propping himself up with the back of her chair.

"I never wanted you three to find it and bring it here. I can tell you that," she replied and continued to study the object she wished had been forgotten, placing one hand to the side of her face and supporting her head with her arm. "Your mother didn't tell you anything?"

"Nopes." Her eldest grandson shook his head, rocking her chair in the process. "She said it was a birthday present for me from you. And something about me not being able to play pretend with it, which as we all know is some bullsqueeze if you ask me." He was somewhat accurate, as you obviously recall.

His grandmother too shook her head. "No, I told her to keep it away from you..." And for no apparent reason, she paused for several minutes before adding, "You and your grandfather."

Leunga perked up. "What about Grampy-jams?"

She stroked the sheath and glanced over her shoulder at the monkey on her back. "Leunga—I mean, your abuelo—once owned both swords." After she stopped momentarily to let the painful memories come flooding back, she softly said, "He...it was before your mother was born. One day he took them with him out into those woods and disappeared without saying a thing. Every night I sat by that window there and watched the empty trees, waiting for him until I fell asleep." She pulled the sword halfway out of its holster. "Then a few days later he returned, covered in blood. His hands were cut apart with horrible scars"—she motioned to the weapon—"and he only had this. He was trembling and he kept saying 'I can't do it' over and over, but I didn't ask him what that meant. I was just happy that he was home." Carefully, she put the blade back into the safety of its container and set it aside before continuing her account. "He slept for an entire day and a half. While he was sleeping, I took this...barrabasada...and buried it behind all of the junk in the back of the garage. I never saw him so scared before."

Sydney and Ricky sat on the couch, mesmerized by the tale. Leunga rocked back and forth on the back of his grandmother's current seat and asked, "Why'd you hide it? It's awesome as beans."

"Because it caused him so much grief that night." She shuddered at the thought. "I don't know what it was he couldn't do, and I didn't need to know. I just knew that I needed him to forget about the whole thing."

"Why not just huck it in the trash then?"

"It's an heirloom of your heritage, bonita. I would never throw away anything from our familia's history. And I knew one of you three would want it one day as a memento of your roots."

Sydney shrugged. "Yeah, I guess..."

Pondering the possibility that the thing in his grandparent's grasp was some ancient heirloom with a worth greater than garbage, one boy wondered, "So, like, why was it in Lou's closet?"

The elderly woman turned to her youngest grandson and replied, "Well, one day some time after little Sydney was born, your grandfather was finally cleaning out the garage for once to get to the box of your mother's old baby clothes, and I realized that this thing was still there. When he took a break, I went in and grabbed it, and I gave it to Aurora. She must have put it in the basement closet for safe keeping."

Listening halfheartedly, Leunga nodded. "Uh-huh. Uh-huh. So, uh...you are absolutamente positiva he just had the one then."

"Sí. That's right. He told me he got rid of the other one—actually, he said he got rid of both...When he first showed them to me weeks earlier, there were two, side-by-side, but he wouldn't let me touch either of them."

"Why didn't he just get rid of both of them?" Ricky asked, timidly.

"That I don't know. If he were still around, maybe we could ask him..." She set the sheath on the table near her and leaned back quickly, inadvertently flinging Leunga to the floor. "But he's on one of his ridículo hunting trips."

Sydney looked disgusted. "Why?"

"No lo se...He goes out to hunt for rabbit once in a while, but the only time he ever caught one was on his very first trip. Actually, it was about a week after the incident with that sword." She glanced at the table. "I just assume it's his way of relaxing."

"Murder shouldn't be relaxing."

The oldest young man in the room got up off of the carpet. "When is he gonna be back already? Just hearing about this mess—I'm super sick of waiting by now like you would not believe."

"Well, he just left yesterday. And he's usually gone for the weekend, but the last few times he's been gone for five or six days at a time."

"Man, he seems to leave a lot. Don't you, like, miss him or anything?" Ricky asked long before his brain could warn him that it would be a weird thing to say.

"Pffft! Gone a lot is right," Leunga scoffed, already misquoting his brother's statement. He looked to his sister and reminded, "He was absent at both of our graduations. Guy owes us all like...a hundred dollars is what."

Sydney leaned toward her dumber brother. "The money Grandma brought was from both of them, so-stupid."

"A probable excuse. One which I will never believe."

Their grandmother turned again to Ricky. "Hermoso, I do miss him, but I've also been married to him for fifty-three years. Any time I get to be alone is a blessing."

Abruptly uncomfortable and unsure how to respond, he smiled with only half of his face and nodded while darting his eyes to the floor.

Leunga returned to leaning on the back of his grandmother's recliner. "So you don't know when he'll be back. How absolutely inconvenient that is..." Thinking of the next phase in his epic journey left the loser stumped. Coming back to this house when his grandfather returned was out of the question—it was hard enough trekking to their address the one time—and waiting around in that place for some old man to make it back was even less alluring. The main drawback—the aspect of having to talk to his grandmother for indeterminate amounts of time—easily dissuaded him. Also, there was the smell. A loud buzzing suddenly emanated from the basement and scared him half to death.

"That's the washer. Why don't you go enjoy more of the cookies while I check on the sheets?"

Ricky was the first to get up and move off toward the kitchen, trailed closely by his oldest sibling. Leunga, now lost in thought, followed his brother blindly after releasing his grip from his grandmother's easy chair with Sydney stalling back a bit to chat with their elderly storyteller. Leunga was about to release a gaseous blast storm from somewhere in his body when he abruptly remembered whose house he was in and kept it silent.

•   •   •

"So that was a weird-ass story," stated a sibling as soon as she was reasonably sure her elder was out of earshot. "I always thought it'd be Grandpa going senile first. Oh well. At least now we can go home." Several hundred seconds after her grandmother finished, Sydney smiled, relieved that the most annoying and farcical day ever was nearly over. She glanced at the kitchen microwave's digital display and scowled. "Holy crap. It's almost ten. Why's it so bright outside?"

"Duh, dude, it's summer."

"Oh!" The girl gave a big fake gasp to match the boy's odd lack of urgency and blatant overlook of the homeward meaning of her wishes to find their way back to their usual comforts posthaste. "*Duh*, dude. Is it? I'm so duh!"

"Just saying. I don't think you need to worry about the time," he clarified as he wolfed down another chocolate-chip masterpiece. "Duh."

"Good point, Ricky." Sydney switched her speaking patterns to resemble something like that of a sarcastic whisper. "And since we're in no rush, how about we stay *here* all night! We can leave at two in the morning. That way Grandma can guilt trip us into sleeping here for some stupid-ass reason. We'll have a big awkward breakfast too. Good call."

Something said sparked a not-so-strange reaction in one of the siblings. Ricky formed a quick reversal of his lazy-bones-summer attitude when he remembered how much he really wanted to leave. "Whoa! It's ten?! That's late! We should, uh, probably, you know, go right now. That seems best."

Leunga nodded. "Yeah. I know what ya mean. We gotta go find him."

"Uh-huh. Oh. Also, Grandma just told me we can dr—what?" she interrupted herself at the sound of the stupidness. "Find who? You mean *Grandpa*? What the hell for?!"

The eldest continued, nodding nonstop, "It's the only reasonable thing to do."

Sydney shook her head, her braid remaining stationary. "We can't. Aside from being one of the dumbest things you've ever wanted to do, you have work tomorrow. And I told Addy she could come over."

"Your *girlfriend* isn't going anywhere, lassie. And besides, I practically run that place. They don't get anything done without me."

"Whoa, really?" Ricky was genuinely impressed.

Leunga shook his head and sucked on his teeth. "I don't think so."

Sydney sighed. "Seems like a reason *not* to miss work." She placed essential emphasis on the *not.* "How about you just wait for Grandpa to get back from killing innocent animals and then *drive* up here?" She placed derogatory emphasis on the *drive.*

"Hell's shells. What part of *epic quest* do you not get?"

"All of it. This isn't a video game or a movie where you have to act like an idiot and take the complicated route."

"That sounded so rehearsed."

"Well, it wasn't." Actually, it was. During the walk to their grandparents' home, Sydney decided to consider any possible situation that might inhibit her from sleeping in her own room. This happened to be one of them.

"Dude. You're gonna go into the woods and look for Grampy?"

"That's right, and it's gonna be awesome."

Burying her face in her hands, Sydney groaned, "Whatever. You're gonna get eaten by a bear."

"Fool, there's no bears in the woods. Bears only live in zoos and my nightmares." Leunga jabbed an eyebrow at his brother and added, "Besides, I got a kung fu bodyguard going with me. We'll be fine."

This was news to Ricky. "Um...what?"

"Okey-dokey. You two can go play epic mountain men. I'm going home. I'll be back tomorrow with Dad when you guys realize how dumb this is."

"I'm not really—why *Dad?*"

"Come on, Sydzy. You said you wanted to spend your 'last real summer' having fun. Just think of this as a relaxing camping trip. Even if we don't find Grampy, it'll be a chance for us to bond as brother and sister one last time before you move away." Leunga had just expressed the deepest sentiment of his life. His siblings were stunned. "Also, you really need the exercise." No, she really doesn't.

Sydney was at a loss for words. She hadn't considered the fact that in a couple of months she wouldn't have the chance to just be a sister whenever she felt like it and have carefree fun in the company of family. A three-minute silence followed as both blond teens contemplated the momentary departure of their relationship. Even Leunga was only now realizing that his sister would very soon become distant and detached from the family norm. Sydney sniffled and decided she needed to say something. "Yo—sh—s—has..." Something coherent. "Okay." Choosing to do what anyone would in an uncomfortable situation, she changed the subject, discreetly. "So...how is karate going, Ricky?"

Ricky snapped to attention. "Well, yeah, um...it's, you know, good. Actually I'm in kickboxing now, so it's not called—but it's okay. It's good. Yeah, what you said."

"Smooth..." Neither Ricky nor Sydney knew who Leunga was talking to—both of them felt a little embarrassed by their comments and the fact that they felt any emotion at all—until the eldest pushed past them to the jar of creamy peanut butter he was in fact referring to on the counter. Carefully, he unscrewed the container and plunged his filthy fingers knuckle-deep into the velvety abyss.

Sydney dug her hand into her left pocket in search of something and said, "Guess I'll call Addy and cancel." Whipping out her cell phone soon after that, she pressed a combination of buttons before placing it against her ear.

"You gotta be kidding me!" Leunga exclaimed, causing his siblings to jump. He lobbed the open, and mostly full, jar of peanut butter into the garbage can, barely making it in. "Organic..."

Big Enough for Both of Us

Ricky was lost. Unsure of his own judgment, he remained uneasy in the unexplored territory he found himself in. His mind wandered through all possible outcomes of taking each possible passage, yet all choices held a potentially unwelcome result he had no intention of discovering. An ever-present nervous tick, one that he had been predominantly oblivious to, resurfaced as he surveyed the area; out of force of habit, he began to bite little bits of skin off of his lower lip—a worried situational response he and his sister picked up from their mother. A rustling sound came from what he assumed to be the north. He froze and listened for it again.

He heard the voice of Leunga through the door. "What the hell is taking him so long?"

His sister could also be heard. "Damn it, I knew I should've gone first."

His brother continued, "Ha! Yeah, right. You'd be done in what, like, four hours?" He heard a loud thud followed by that exact same someone saying, "Hey! You don't know. This shirt could be expensive as everhell." It very much was. Once.

Needless to say, after Leunga invited them to spend the night at their grandparents' house free of charge, it only seemed reasonable when he insisted that they be allowed to use the bathroom as well. Unluckily, Ricky was chosen to go first when it was finally time to get ready for bed, which proved to be catastrophic. The youngest man desperately wanted to finish up his nightly routine in the privacy of a locked room, but in such a strange environment—coupled with the urgency his siblings made him aware of—he found it to be very difficult. He took a deep breath and grabbed the handle of a random top drawer. Steadily, he pulled it out an inch at a time. It appeared to be mostly empty, apart from a few tubes of goo with apparent purposes of medicinal sorts. Without touching any of them, he began reading their names. He read through the first three letters on the brand of the first tube before slamming the drawer shut, in shock. "Definitely wish I didn't see that..."

Slowly he moved his attention to the drawer directly below the first. The second drawer. He slid it open, expecting to find some medications or pain suppressors, but found only more feminine hygiene items—things he tried to avoid looking at in the bathroom he shared with his sister—but he couldn't understand why his elderly grandmother would need things designed for a woman of menstrual age. That's when he realized he had been staring into the second drawer for far too long and slammed it shut.

Mildly traumatized by the entire ordeal, he propped himself up over the sink using his long arms as support. He stared down at the faucet, listening to the dripping water he was unable to see from his angle. It was the perfectly horrible ending to a perfectly horrible day. His sister had dragged him here. His brother had interrupted a relaxing rest. And he could tell his grandmother knew it was him who destroyed the vase. And now he was basically being bullied into going hiking for an indefinite amount of time with the only two people in his life he never wanted to go camping with again.

Ricky looked up at the somewhat familiar face staring at him. A very handsome young man, as his grandmother would relentlessly say—and in an objective sense she was certainly correct—but the boy would never actually believe her; after all, she was heavily biased. *Muy guapo.* Sounds nutritious. The discouraged person he saw before him was also in a perplexing situation—lost in a strange world, unwilling to seek help, yet in desperate need of some, and trapped in an unavoidable plight. He considered helping this outsider but knew it would be no use; neither of them knew what to do. Instead, he turned his attention toward vanity. Noticing the deflated look of his doubtful doppelganger, he set about to renovate each of their appearances as a means of distraction from their more serious dilemmas.

The cool water rushed over his open fingers as it gradually grew warmer. When the temperature was satisfactory, he cupped his hands and tossed containers of rinsing rain on his face and over his dry, brittle, gel-encrusted hair until it returned to its natural state: lustrously thick and blond, kept short in the back for neatness, but left medium length on top—two to three inches long—to form his desired style with the proper equipment. He grabbed the closest hand towel he could locate with eyes shut tight and vigorously dried his head, realizing too late that the towel smelled awful. Carefully, he replaced the soaked cloth into a folded position over the rack, as he had always done, and gave the guy in the mirror a disgusted grimace. Forgetting momentarily that he was in his grandmother's guest bathroom, he searched the ample counter for one of his vials of hair gel, only to rediscover that he was in the wrong house. Within his duffel bag existed an emergency backup cache, which he considered making a run for, but retrieval of the object would require the forfeit of his turn in the bathroom, and he couldn't let that happen. Without using any gel for support, he went through his daily ritual of pressing the sides of his hair upward to a peak, as much as he could without his usual tools.

Upon completion, he gently ran his fingers over his freshly reconstructed fauxhawk, which—when done correctly—added a few additional inches to his already above-average height. A ferocious little lion's mane, less the stately chin strap, strictly kept for outward appearances. Staring into the face looking back at him, he edged closer to examine every inch. Although he had never actually seen himself, he trusted the figure before him to be a nearly accurate representation in the glass world beyond, where he saw a teenage boy with neutrally straight lines of natural golden hair—the color of sun-kissed sands on a beach someplace with sand—and eyes of a brown so dark they stood at the edge of black. That's what they had always told him he was—just like his sister, and just like their father. Leunga, on the other hand, was the spitting image of their mother—untamed sickles of brunet hair the color of heavily sugared coffee with just a smidgeon of auburn to it, wildly pointed tips curled every which way, and vibrant green eyes of emerald brilliance. The only common trait that everyone in the family seemed to share was their profusely large, oddly onyx eyebrows as dark as scorched wood. Blond hair with black eyebrows...impossible.

There was a gentle knock on the door. "Is everything okay, hermoso?" It was the reassuring voice of his grandmother. As if you couldn't tell.

"He's been in there for almost seven hundred minutes."

Ricky felt obligated to make his overnight stay at the odd house uneventful for the elderly woman, so he simply replied, "I'm okay. I still need to brush my teeth...but I don't really need to."

"There should be some new toothbrushes in the bottom right drawer. They were on sale." The alarmingly unlocked door opened a crack. "Also, I forgot to mention, the left side of the counter belongs to my niece when she visits from México. I don't know what she keeps in there, so please don't go into those drawers."

The young man in his crowded solitude was struck by a wave of embarrassment as he briefly relived delving into the left side drawers. He shook away the feeling and opened the very drawer his grandmother instructed him to investigate. A treasure trove was waiting within, filled with dozens of poorly crafted dental sanitation products. "I found them, I think," he assured and grabbed the first appealing color he noticed. Breaking through its cardboard housing, he added a very polite, and very meek, "Thank you."

"And toothpaste is on the counter. Take as much as you want." And with that the door closed.

"And make it quicker."

Though the boy in the bathroom was thankful that neither of the nuisances on the other side of the rampart took the obvious opportunity to thug their way into the washroom after undoubtedly seeing that the entrance was not barred by locks, Ricky's grandmother continued to converse with his siblings on the other side of the flimsy barrier at a volume that was not ignorable—and at the same time, not loud enough to conceal the sound that would certainly spring forth from the privacy-granting button on the doorknob he was suddenly, and silently, trying to secure—so he was forced to listen in. Apparently, that means we are too.

"Louie," the señora said, "did you remember to put your grandfather's hat back on his dresser like I asked?"

"I *did* do that. Yes, I did. Right where Ricky found it the first time and gave it to me. Yes. It is definitely not shoved into my cargo pocket right now at all. You can check for yourself if you want to—this one, not that one."

"Okay. Bueno. Thank you. Because your abuelo would have a fit if he ever lost it again. And I don't want him digging through more dumpsters just to find it either. It's embarrassing."

Wishing that the disturbance of his peace could end there, we—I mean, *Ricky*—was hoping his family would take their discussion elsewhere and leave him to the task of unraveling his nerves after another traumatic day as a teenager—especially since his brother just decided to add to his anxiety by implicating him as an accomplice in some sort of elaborate criminal conspiracy—but they appeared to be unmoved by his internal pleas, which was obvious when his grandmother immediately said, "Oh! That reminds me. I meant to ask you about your hair."

"Whoa! What about it?!"

"It's getting so long and messy... Wouldn't you prefer to be more trimmed and neat like your brother?"

Straining to hear exactly what potentially derisive comment his older brother was going to say about his typically flawless gold fauxhawk, the blond froze. Leunga's voice elevated in pitch. "Say *what*?! I got the best hair of anybody. Just ask Sydkins."

"I think you meant to say the grossest hair of anybody," her voice seemed to say, but was a bit unclear as she responded to her sibling through Ricky's protective, hollow shield. "Look at this. See?"

"Ow! Don't pull hair!"

"Ow! *You* don't pull hair!"

An elderly woman with a slightly off accent interrupted the childish behavior on the other side of the door. "Kids, don't start fighting. You two are so nice together when you get along."

"Well, maybe *I* am."

"If you would like, I could give you a quick little haircut tonight before it's time for bed, Louie. Wouldn't that be nice?"

"Ha! You're a cool old lady, Grammy, but I like my hair this way. It's *me*, ya know? Yeah. You know."

"Oh, you're right, lo siento. Of course you do! Your style is your own business. That's the way kids wear it these days, isn't it? It actually is very cute on you now that I think about it. I shouldn't have said anything to try to change you."

"I know, and I'll try to forgive you for that someday."

"All right. Well, you two be nice to each other. I'll be making my evening tea if you need me."

"Steep that beast to perfection, Grammy. Remember what I taught you."

Ricky heard the footsteps of somebody leaving down the hallway before hearing the quiet words of his sister say, "Really wish *that* happened first..."

"*What* happens?"

"This thing! Duh! If I knew Grandma was gonna be so cool about it, I could've said no to this bullshit braid."

"Yeah. I know what you mean."

"No, you really don't."

Returning to his rituals when hushed tones started to replace booming banter and all was well, Ricky was satisfied with the lack of ridicule directed his way and ignored the increasingly indistinct chatter of his brother and sister waiting their turn in line as he rolled up the sleeves of his white martial arts gi. The left sleeve, as it typically did, unrolled almost immediately.

Decidedly, he allowed it and grabbed the only container of toothpaste visible. The tube, though gratuitously large, was almost completely empty. He held the brush and paste in close proximity to each other, straining to extract the remnants of the used vile. With one final pinch, a geyser of greenish white goo shot forth from the applicator held in his right hand, covering his other arm in the viscous paste. His once-white sleeve was now a multicolored mess. "Can't blame that one on Lou..."

He collected as much of the toothpaste from his clothing as was necessary on his new toothbrush and cleaned his teeth. When that was finished, he used toilet paper to remove any excess substance from his rapidly changing wardrobe. The stain that remained was far from inconspicuous; his grandmother would no doubt notice it and force him to remove the jacket in an attempt to wash it, and he felt no desire to go on an undesirable hike in the morning wearing only her sweatpants and his skintight, sleeveless undershirt. In an extremely rare stroke of luck, he spotted a few safety pins scattered over the counter. Ricky triple-rolled each sleeve for symmetry and double-pinned the rolls to reduce the likelihood of an unfurling incident, hiding the pins in the thick fabric and out of sight.

Feeling as reasonably comfortable as he could be, he grabbed the doorknob. With one final glance at his copy in the wall, he noticed his hair had lost some of its volume, giving him his first objective in the morning: retrieval of his secret styling reserve to salvage his visage. As he twisted the knob on the exit, a fresh tube of toothpaste at the back of the counter caught his eye. "Awesome..." He swung open the door, surprisingly caught off guard by the irritated faces of his brother and sister glaring up at him, and jumped.

"Did you have fun?" Leunga teased as Ricky slinked past them.

"It's my turn now," Sydney stated. She darted for the door, just as her older brother did the same.

"Nuh-uh. You're gonna take forever!" he said while gripping his younger sister's shoulder, attempting to force her into the hallway, unsuccessfully.

Sydney pushed against his face with an outreached arm. "No I won't! Let go!"

"You already get to sleep in the real bed tonight, let me go first! I gotta pee my ass off really bad!"

"I'm younger, that means I need the bathroom more than you."

Leunga paused, completely unsure if the statement was true or not. And if true, he was almost afraid to find out what she could have possibly meant by it, causing him to back down a bit.

Feeling her stoner sibling release his hold on her, the middle child rushed into the bathroom alone. "I'm just gonna take a shower!" The door flew shut and the knob clicked. It was likely the sound of the door locking.

Leunga's emotions flared red-hot. "Gaw!" And right then and there, he vowed to get even with his little sister by hiring his kung fu-ing kid brother to beat her up. For no more than two American dollars. I doubt he'll do it for anything less than three. "I also need to shit!"

Locked, Out of Stock, and Barrel Roll

Every agonizing second introduced further pain. Leunga writhed and twisted, unable to free himself from his metal tormentor. He shifted into every imaginable arrangement, finding no relief. The battle proceeded well into the night.

The sofa bed, now consisting mostly of bed, came equipped with strategically positioned support struts, designed for maximum comfort and stability. Leunga was grappling with one such strut when he finally decided to destroy some silence. "Hey! Richie!" he whispered directly next to his brother's ear. "Are you still awake?"

Ricky, desperately trying to ignore his older brother's actions, found it unavoidable. "Yeah...why?"

"This bar is—this is—how are you not annoyed with this bed?"

The younger one turned around, coming face-to-face with Leunga. "The bar? I can barely feel it."

"This thing is digging into my fucking spine! Trade places with me."

"No. I'm not trading spots again."

"Goddamn, if I wake up tomorrow and I'm paralyzed it'll be all your fault. Seriously."

Ricky wriggled under the sheets to his previous position and made a slumbersome suggestion. "Try sleeping on your side. The bar goes between my ribs and hip."

"I'll never fall asleep on my damn side. I can only sleep faceup." Supine. Leunga squirmed up the bed toward the last remaining portion that still resembled a couch and sat upright, legs outstretched. The room around him was pitch-black, yet his eyes were adjusted enough to notice the tall teen's legs dangling off the end of the miniscule mattress. He looked to his own feet, using them to aggressively search for his alloy antagonist, inadvertently kicking his brother in the back. Really, really hard.

Ricky groaned. "Go to sleep..."

With a sigh for himself and no one else, Leunga remained upright, surveying his surroundings. The darkness did little to thwart his vision, other than spotting fine detail. He noticed the grand prize he discovered the previous afternoon, leaning against the back door, and his mind raced with questions to ask his grandfather—about the sword's age, design, attack power, bonus stats, monetary value, and unequivocally most of all, its mysterious origin. The next morning would begin with a renewal of the epic quest's purpose, commencing a new adventure in the party's log. Day one: looking for a grandpa. Wow. Sounds boring. As he let his brain bounce between subjects, he leaned his head back, resting it over the top of the sofa backboard. Staring at the ceiling, he whispered to his bed partner, "Are you excited about going hiking?"

Ricky breathed slowly.

"Are you awake?"

"No," he stated with indifference.

"Is that 'no' to hiking excitement, or 'no' to awake?"

The room was silent.

Determining that there might have been little to no significance in that response, a busy-brained Leunga closed his eyes in the hope to, at some point, fall asleep, yet his mind continued thinking about the sword and the haunting tale his grandmother wove earlier that night. Obviously. After all, he was the resident geek.

•   •   •

A sudden crash sent Leunga's eyelids darting open; his fully dilated pupils contracted in the blinding sunlight of the early morn. The day he had waited almost twelve hours for had finally arrived. Stretching out his legs, he rubbed his eyes with both hands, relieved to have full dexterity of his limbs. He jerked his head forward to see if his bed partner was still asleep, only to receive a massive, sharp pain throughout his neck. "Oh shit me," he stammered after realizing he had fallen asleep while sitting up. While Leunga spent the time massaging his tender neck with every hand he had, he noticed his brother's half of the bed was entirely deserted, and he was instantly perplexed, but not for the right reasons.

"I better go wake your brother," the increasingly familiar voice of his grandmother said as she approached from the kitchen. "You'll need to head out soon if you want to find a good campsite—Oh! Good, you *are* awake. I made pancakes and huevos rancheros with some of my homemade salsa picante." She smiled and retreated toward the clatter of cutlery against dishware. "Come have some before your brother finishes them all."

Doing as he was told in the haze of his otherwise disobedient mind, Leunga sleepily arose at the order while gripping his aching neck to keep it stable as he made his way into the brand-new day. He cornered the kitchen archway and with sleep-drenched eyes discovered what appeared to be his siblings sitting on stools at a now-overcrowded kitchen island with Ricky plunging into a pile of pancakes the size of the moon and Sydney peeling, and subsequently eating, grapefruit while handling a giant knife. Carefully and carelessly, the eldest sibling shuffled over to his youngest companion and put his arm across his brother's back, staring at his large stack of pancakes. An epic breakfast to mark the continuation of an epic quest. All the components for the start of an epic day. Epic.

Ricky stopped chewing momentarily. "Can I help you?"

"Every damn time. *No.* I'm just looking."

"Would you like something to drink?" their grandmother asked and pulled a juice glass from the cupboard before Leunga had a chance to respond.

"Yeah," he accepted and knew exactly what he wanted. "Hi, I'll have a grande double-shot espresso latte with soy milk and no foam. Please and thank you."

"I don't quite know if I have any of that..." replied the impromptu barista hesitantly as her elderly fingers traded the juice glass for a coffee mug. "But there is a pot of fresh coffee here if you'd like."

"That's what I said."

Hurriedly swallowing his third to last enormous mouthful of pancakes before someone short had a chance to start taking his fair share, a boy on his best behavior smiled. "These are way good, Grammy. Can I have another, please?"

Their grandmother smiled in return as a family matron often does when providing for the children—even if the children are, or in some sense nearly are, adults. "For you, hermoso, I added real cinnamon," she informed as she readied to maneuver another mouthwatering morsel over to the young man's almost-empty dish. "I saw it on that cooking show with the woman who came in second place on *Sous Chef Maestros All-Star* season three." And then she slid the pancake onto his plate. "Did you watch the finale? I wanted Terry to win."

Ricky shoved a gargantuan bite of crispy dough into his face and agreed with whatever his grandmother had just said. "Mm-hmm."

Leunga rested his head against his brother's occupied arm and answered the question that was not asked of him more than minutes ago. "I take my coffee black...with tons of cream and sugar."

"Not supposed to drink caffeine, it'll stunt your growth," Sydney snickered with a mouthful of raw fruit.

"If I knew where you were right now, I'd slap you in the face."

"Louie, I don't want any of that talk here." Their grandmother poured the hot beverage into her grandson's mug and set the cup, along with the jug of creamer, down within Leunga's limited reach.

"Yeah, *Louie*, you're not supposed to hit girls," said Sydney before she peered around the teenage obstacle at her side and watched for her other brother's response.

"And I don't, but that means I could still hit *you* then."

She narrowed her newly makeup-shrouded eyes at him and scowled.

Releasing Ricky's back, Leunga used his freshly freed arm to drown his coffee in chilled creamer, generously overflowing the cup's contents and spilling everything over its side. He drew the mug up to his lips and blew over the surface of the lukewarm brew before taking a sip. Through drowsy eyes he noticed the digital display on the microwave and nearly lost the liquid through his nose. "Abuela, is that clock right?!"

Their grandmother turned and read it silently. She nodded to her grandson. "Yes, sleepyhead, it's almost nine."

Leunga felt a sudden bout of dizziness. Nine a.m. in the morning. He shouldn't have even been waking up for another four to six hours. He staggered to the last remaining stool next to his sister and sat, resting his head on the granite counter before him. It was all too much to handle at once, and he needed time to recuperate. With the knowledge that he was nowhere near his full strength, as anyone might imagine, he shut his weary eyelids and just listened to the symphony of the breakfast scuttle. Perhaps it was the strange atmosphere of the room or the mild warmth of the coffee travelling toward his stomach, but it was then that Leunga fell fast asleep in the midst of the mist at the dawn of this epic new era for what would surely be a full ten hours of uninterrupted rest.

Unaccommodating as ever, Sydney repeatedly poked her older brother's ribs with her outstretched pinky. "Your freakish hair is in the eggs." *Pelo rancheros.*

·   ·   ·

"Do you have everything you need?"

Ricky stood idly by, knowing full well they didn't have everything, while waiting for the second strangest camping trip he had ever taken to begin, yet he chose to remain silent and hoped his grandmother would make the realization herself.

"I would've made you kids more sandwiches, but I couldn't find the peanut butter I bought last week..."

"Probably organic anyway..."

"Oh! I also threw in a handful of the protein bars your grandfather takes with him on his hunting trips." Handful in this case meaning three or four dozen—maybe even *five*. "And you should take this little pot. In case you need to boil water or something," she added and gingerly forced the cookware into the overstuffed navy blue duffel bag Ricky once considered to belong to himself. "I hope that's enough..."

It certainly should be. To the dude's duffel she donated two canteens, fifteen bottled waters, a durably resealable bag of two-and-a-half-dozen chocolate chip cookies, five chicken salad sandwiches, five mustard and cheese sandwiches, three peanut butter jelly sandwiches without peanut butter, two jelly sandwiches, three new toothbrushes that were on sale, zero toothpaste, a travel size bottle of shampoo, seven small yellow towels, an unopened stick of women's deodorant, a lightly used stick of men's deodorant with a bunch of hair on it, sunscreen, an official trail map, a mostly full two-hundred-count box of matches, some environmentally safe mosquito repellant, an energy-efficient windup flashlight with a supposedly charged capacitor, one miniature collapsible shovel of mediocre craftsmanship, a "handful" of protein bars, a small pot, and a bunch of other stuff.

Sydney looked down her chin into the bag. "I also put in some supplies." I have no idea where she found room for anything.

"And you should also take these," their grandmother insisted before she examined the immediate area. "Wait...where are they?"

As the elderly woman searched the room, Ricky felt optimistic she would remember something else she promised she would get for him that morning.

"I must've left them downstairs," said the senior, ceasing her inspection of the living room as she headed for the staircase. "I'll be back soon."

Ricky's heart sank. He inhaled quickly to speak.

"Oh, and I'll get your pants from the dryer, hermoso."

And then he exhaled in a sigh of relief.

Leunga equipped the sword and sheath. "Oh man, this is so fucking awesome. I didn't think this epic quest was going to be so fucking epic!" He quickly cleaned his chin of slobber using his long, mostly white sleeve and moved right along to the jittery jumping in place that the anticipation forced him to annoy everyone with. "Fuck!"

Sydney smiled. "It is kind of exciting." She was much more excited about the aspect of observing wildlife being wild than finding their grandfather and a rusty sword. "The camping part might actually be fun."

"If you say so, dude..." Ricky picked up the loaded luggage and looped it over his left shoulder and neck. "Oomph," he grunted as the collective weight of all of the junk his grandmother threw into his bag caused a momentary loss of balance. He stumbled a bit and regained most of his equilibrium, but he was using so many of his muscles to keep himself from flipping over that you could tell he wasn't walking anywhere anytime soon, like a perfectly packed, strained statue entitled "The Ricky."

"Try keeping the bag behind you. It'll be out of your way and you won't be all lopsided."

"What, like—you mean like this?" Ricky shuffled the duffel so that one strap was over his shoulder and the bag itself was vertically aligned with his torso.

Sydney shook her head and pointed. "No, put it the way you had before, but keep the bag part over your butt."

The full fellow followed her instructions, looping the strap over one shoulder and across his chest while letting the duffel rest easily behind him. "Oh yeah, that is bett—" He tripped backward a few feet before catching himself. "That was close. Gonna take some getting used to," he stated as he started to take a step forward, but he began falling backward again, stumbling into his grandmother's decorative end table and sending a valuable porcelain vase careening to the floor. Hundreds of glass particles filled the area as the vase lost most of its value. "Aw, no...again?"

"Are you kids okay up here?" asked a loud voice as it travelled up the staircase, followed by their grandmother. Entering the living room while carrying three tightly coiled sleeping bags and a dazzlingly clean pair of pants, she then said, "I heard a crash."

Ricky looked up with eyes wide. "I'm so sorry! I tripped and it was there," he explained, pointing, "and then it fell. I'll pay for it." He really regretted saying that last part. He had no idea how he was going to pay for it. And neither do I.

"That's all right, hermoso, it gives me an excuse to buy a new one." She let the bedroll bundles fall to the floor as she unfolded her grandson's pants. "Here. You can go change in the other room."

Ricky snatched the pants from his grandmother without making eye contact. "Thank you," he spoke timidly. He managed to walk several steps before stopping as suddenly as his bagged burden would permit. Something was off. Something other than everything else that was wrong with that picture. Lifting his martial arts pants up to eye level and stumbling briefly, he made a disappointing discovery. His perfect pants were perfectly shrunk; small enough to never fit him again. Cancelling his trip, he incidentally displayed that dwindled fact for all to see when he turned in disappointment toward his family with britches unfurled. I said *britches*...

"Cools, can I have them?"

"Oh! I'm sorry, hermoso... I should have read the label."

"It's okay." He carelessly rolled up the pants and found a pouch to place them in, assuring, "I have more at home." The final word of his sentence stimulated a longing to return to his upstairs bedroom and don his comfortable clothing, but I have no idea why.

"Will you be okay wearing my sweatpants?" That is a ludicrous question.

"He's fine with it." Joining his sister in her acceptance of their elder's offerings, Leunga too picked up one of the sleeping bags and noticed a long strip of fabric attached to either side of the roll. Upon its discovery, he promptly ripped it off.

Sydney nodded slowly. "That was a shoulder strap."

Her older brother studiously studied the frayed strand in his hand and agreed. "Too bad." Dropping the ruined roll, he picked up a different one, this time utilizing the shoulder strap almost exactly as it was intended—if it were attached to the back of a fanny pack.

"Well, if you're all set, then go have some fun, kids!" the elderly woman affirmed as she gave a great big hug to her willing granddaughter and gazed out the back door behind her eldest grandson, surveying the trees with a smile. "I think you'll have a very nice time. The weather should be beautiful, but don't stay out there for too long. I'll get worried."

"Yeah, Grammy, you will. And thanks for all the crap to carry."

She squeezed what she could out of the youngest member of the expedition in an embrace and gave a kind reply to his elder brother. "You're very welcome. Be sure to be nice to each other and have a good time together."

"We'll try to try," pledged a young lady who knew better than to promise the impossible, urging her brother onward with a flick of her bangs and braid. And the reignition of the confounding quest was well underway.

With sword and bedroll outfitted, a brave-looking Leunga was more than prepared for his arduous journey into the epic unknown. Siblings waiting in the wings were hungry for his leadership, so he threw open the large screen door and drew in a deep breath of the thick forest air. "Well, this be it. Let forth the bellow of awesome be known, and this I say unto us all: let the good times roll!" And after another silent tooting of his own horrendous horn, he took an overly dramatic, extra-large stride and fell down the patio stairs.

Spreading Solstice

A warm, sweetly humid, estival breeze drifted through a plethora of pines and imposing oaks, a guiding gust that left a euphoric feeling with each brief embrace. Leaves chattered unremittingly, signifying the arrival of each squall. An orchestral avian collection conversed in singsong melodies high above, discussing daily discoveries and disappointments. The rabble of a babbling brook cracked the stress of life and filled the area with soothing ambient noise. The sights and smells beneath the leafy canopy were reminiscent of a storybook tale. The natural shades of vibrant green and subtle brown all around easily overwhelmed the senses with woodland extravagance. Utter tranquility. Welcome to paradise.

"God this is...sucks!" Leunga groaned with the forced sensation of every step, feeling all of the muscles he never knew existed, and sensing some of the ones that never did.

"But we just left," reminded Ricky as he followed closely behind his brother in single file, trailed by his sister. "It's kind of..." He shrugged, surveying his surroundings while adjusting his duffel bag. "Nice."

"You don't know nice," Sydney informed her little brother. "This right here is damn-ass awesome. This is exactly what summer is supposed to feel like. It's perfect. It's not hotter than hell yet, the air smells naturey, there's no clouds today, and there's lots of shaded sunny-shine. Appreciate it, turdburger." Odd behavior for a girl who makes a habit of dressing like it's the end of the world. A little *too* odd.

"Yeah, it should make for a nice, blinding walk." The eldest proceeded to craft a pair of fully formed hand binoculars—seeing as how the brim of the driving hat that mysteriously materialized atop his head seconds after saying good-bye to his grandmother did little to shade his squint—and placed his creation against his face to shield his eyes from the remorseless, and beautiful, sun. He stumbled along the path while attempting to become accustomed to his new eyewear and noted, "It was supposed to rain today."

"Um... I think that was yesterday. And it didn't." Ricky staggered behind Leunga, trying to avoid stomping on his brother's heels as they frantically darted left and right in an inebriated fashion; although, in his defense, the stoner was probably sober. Checking the position of his satchel behind him, the laden lad happened to glance back and noticed that his sister stopped along the path a couple hundred feet behind and was staring into the trees in a daydream manner, while his brother before him continued tripping over his own ineptitude. Truly the makings of a fine family vacation.

"Shit! We should've brought me some sunglasses."

Ricky slowed his own pace to allow the guiding guy more room to thrash around. A follow-up question came to mind. "Didn't Grammy have any you could *steal*?" But as soon as he said that, he quickly harbored a small amount of guilt for calling attention to his brother's recent crime spree—the blatant query slipped out of his mouth, which tends to happen when it's the truth. Leunga stopped dead in his tracks, causing the younger boy to halt in fear of retaliation for the comment. Ricky held back his duffel to keep it from shifting in front of him as the bedroll positioned insecurely atop the bag fell to the ground.

Whipping around as haphazardly as he could, Leunga glared up at his younger brother through the lenses of his handnoculars. His eyes narrowed with rage—or possibly bewilderment; it's hard to tell—and he replied, "Couldn't find any I liked." He stood staring at his svelte sibling, awaiting the continuance of their fascinating conversation. "Maybe if she had some disposable sunglasses, I would've taken those." I hope such a thing does not exist.

Feeling more than a little uncomfortable with the grave glares of his big brother, the teen looked away, once again at their sister. "Um...yeah. Maybe we should wait for her."

"Who?"

The taller guy glanced into his brother's concealed eyes, his own expression conveying concern. "Syd? She's, like, way far away." Crouching quickly while attempting to hold his disobedient bag in one place, Ricky swiftly bent his way over toward the bedding by his toes, when suddenly, he froze. The sweatpants he wore nearly stretched to a point of catastrophic destruction—had he reached down any further, they most likely would have ripped, so when it took him over a minute to maneuver in a way that left his leggings unfettered while he proceeded to pick up his tightly coiled sleeping bag, it made total sense. The constriction of his pants reminded him of his desire to avoid being seen by all humans—and some of the more prejudiced animals. "I'm okay with waiting here..." Out of sight. "You know, 'cause shouldn't we let her catch up?"

"You mean to tell me that we *haven't* been following her?!" To the eldest's great amazement, there was indeed no one leading their group. Sidestepping Ricky, he observed the path they travelled in alarm. Leunga utilized the zoom feature of his fleshy binoculars, spied on his sister some great distance away, and then made a command decision. "She's lost to the ages. Fallen behind like so many wounded soldiers... Fuck her, let's go." And with that, he returned to not following any leader along the path.

Through no small feat of agility, Ricky replaced his bedroll on its perch above his duffel bag and followed. "I would really feel better if we waited for her," he said, stalling for time to avoid entering the inevitable search for their grandfather, possibly near people. "If we don't, uh, she'll probably be super pissed when she catches us." Gawking back to check on their sister, he saw that she had yet to move from her post. He briefly considered hollering to her but decided it would attract far too much unwanted attention to himself.

"You mean *if* she catches us. In the middle of the forest, surrounded by the same scenery on all fronts, and no compass to speak of. We'll be long lost before she finds us."

"That's...good."

Very abruptly, Leunga removed his binoculars and played a drum roll with his hands against his stomach. "I'm hungry. Toss me one of them sambwidges."

"What?" Ricky sighed at the thought of searching for one of the sandwiches in his overstuffed pack. "Dude...we just ate breakfast like an hour ago."

"Yeah, and the sambwidge will be a delightful continuation of said breakfast."

"It would be nice to take a little break..." Sydney agreed calmly from a few feet behind her younger sibling.

"Oh my god—jeez!" Ricky yelped, startled, as he lost the load of his sleeping arrangements for the second time that second. I very much doubt he won't do it again.

"But we should wait until we find a camp," she added and patted the bedroll resting beside her hip. "That way we can get rid of this shit too."

"Fine," Leunga exhaled in total acceptance of her terms. "But when I die of starvation, don't just bury me out here. It's gotta be a Viking-style funeral fire, or nothing. I'm too precious to settle for anything less."

Watching her younger sibling struggling to retrieve the lost roll on rigid legs after she already started trekking away with the other brother, Sydney forced herself to wait for him as she shook her head over her shoulder and frowned. "This is just sad. Leunga, get his sleeping bag and carry it for him before I burst into tears."

To which a bewildered brunet stopped and replied, "Me carry it for him?! I'm already carrying all of my own! Why don't you do it?"

"*I'm* already carrying all of my own too, and you're the one who ripped off the strappy thing on his anyway, so you pretty much deserve it."

"There is no convincible way you can ever prove that to me and you know it, so it doesn't count. In your face."

"Okay...well, I already did more than my fair share of the work today, so that lets me off the hook forever," she informed her smaller sibling while the grunts of a guy gathering his goods continued to fill the air. "Unlike you I was an essential part of the packing process for the trip you decided to make us take. If you had helped out even a little bit, we probably would've been able to leave early enough to be at a camp by now, but you didn't, so good job."

"Um. I don't really think that's true, dude. It took long enough the way it was..."

The sambwidge solicitor was stunned. "What the hell are you talking about?! I did help! I helped so very much!"

"Bullshit. When?"

"I refilled my flask for us." He helped himself.

The statement confused Sydney. "Ho—where?"

"While you two were stuffing sacks and breakin' vases, I found Grampy's stash." Leunga shoved his hand deep within the reaches of his right cargo pocket, searching for his stainless steel cask. While he was wasting time trying to find the visual aid for his useless demonstration, his feet began stepping in an obscure direction by themselves. Because they were acting on their own volition, this caused Leunga to miss noticing a large tree root on the path, and he tripped on it. Flying backward—or forward depending on your perspective—a losery lad landed with great force on his back. The fall would have been far worse had his bedroll been cushioning his head rather than his lower lumbar as the sword positioned diagonally across his back kept his spine nice and rigid. The tumbled twenty-something forcedly removed the sleeping bag from beneath his posterior and sat up, quickly shooting to a standing position once more by himself as if nothing happened.

Leunga dusted himself off and pleaded, "Look, let's not fight about it just yet. I'm still on a high from escaping that boredom factory we was just in, and I'd rather you didn't drag me down to your level. That was straight up unpleasant having to be all censoring myself and shit for that old lady whom I love so very much. Saying things like darn, crap, heck, fuck, shucks, frickin', and fudge. Sucked."

Having finally secured his belongings to their rightful place on his personage without me noticing, a kid cracked a frown as he stopped taking the lead along the path and stalled long enough for one of his partners to steal it from him. "You just said the F-word."

"No, but I wanted to!"

A tomboyish teen nodded as she too began walking the way of the beaten dirt and raised her eyebrows. "I know, right? I almost said *shit* right in front of Grandma!"

"Also, you flipped off Grammy with both hands yesterday."

Leunga glanced back at his sister as he passed her and asked, "Why can't everybody just swear when they want to, and nobody would care?"

"They're fun to say because they have some power," she suggested. "I think the words lose their power if you say them too much."

"Good fuckin' point."

Okay. Let me stop right there. Before these two find out that they need to be any more generous with the casual obscenities, I would like to point out that the liberal use of profanity is not atypical behavior for their age bracket. Freewheeling expletives are commonplace among the youthy people of whatever today is. An all-too-common characteristic of young adults all throughout history—a secret language hidden right under the surface, used almost exclusively among groups commonly considered to be peers as defined by relative age—it seems to be a means of separation from their domineering elders. Escalating levels of vulgarity becoming progressively intensified as generations accumulate. The youth of the world spreading their linguistic disease in the absence of authority—or, as in occasional cases, within the presence of it. And in the future, communication will likely consist of nothing but words about feces, private body parts, and alphabetic letters turned into bombs, all stringed together to form some semblance of a language. Personally, I can't wait.

The three siblings travelled along the trail, past innumerable trees and below countless chirps. Leunga drew in a deep breath and sighed. "What the hell are we doing out here in the forest anyway?"

"Camping trip?"

Ricky was losing patience, of which he has an almost infinite supply. "Looking for Grampy..."

"Oh my god! You're right, I forgot about that." The slacker scanned the surrounding wilderness and repeated, "Maybe we should hurry this up then."

Someone in sweats was overjoyed by the idea. "Okay! Please! Whatever!" He was anxious to sit down somewhere out of sight as he pulled at the edges of his grandmother's turquoise tights. "As long as we get away from other people."

Leunga laughed lightly. "Relaxify yourself. It's almost the end of June and the weather is glorious. No one will be outside." Neither Ricky nor Sydney knew whether or not his comment was sarcastic. It was executed so deadpan that I'm not so sure myself.

Placing her hand beneath her abundant bangs and over her brow palm down, Sydney shaded her already-shaded eyes, because through the dense cluster of trees, she thought she spotted something unusual. A squint was all it took, and a burgundy object off the path about forty-four-and-a-half yards away became all the clearer. "Hey, look over there." She pointed with her other hand. "That sign says 'campground'...or 'rumpround.'"

"Perfect. Either way it sounds good to me."

Her loftier little brother pointed in the opposite direction for obvious reasons and said, "Wouldn't it be better to camp over there...near the—" But Leunga and Sydney had already jutted from the path and entered the unscathed soil between them and the rumpround by the time he began. With a sigh directed at his inability to communicate any cohesive argument for his case in the half second he was allotted, Ricky regretfully followed the two, noticing numerous cars parked in a gravel lot not too far from the sign. Someone was sure to notice his situation. As they approached the developed area of the campground, the sound of laughter and conversation filled the air. A myriad of recreational vehicles seemed to sprout through the trees like, well, *trees*, and the voices that went with them became louder—it was also evident that securing an empty campsite in that vicinity would be a difficult task. Ricky darted his eyes around as they entered the dirt road of the recreational acres, mentioning, "Gonna be hard to find a spot."

"Yeah, too many other idiots here."

They walked along the drive, observing each numbered site, all of which were occupied by some form of dwelling, be it tent or trailer. Oddly enough, after scanning most of the area and continually hearing the echo of enjoyment, they had yet to see another person. "Where the hell is everyone?"

Leunga faced Sydney for a split second that lasted five seconds too long. "Where the hell is an open spot is what I want to know."

Ricky's nerves were running high as each new campsite could lead to somebody catching a glimpse of his unfortunate wardrobe. His big brother's desire to be discovered perplexed the teen, considering that other youngish man was also bedecked in unusual garb—that, and he had a hazardous weapon harnessed to his back like a lunatic. Allowing himself to assess his own attire situation while his brother and sister wasted their time seeking a site they would probably never find, he glanced down at his pants, or more accurately, his grandmother's pants, worn comfortably around his waist and reaching midcalf down his long legs. Still wearing his typical socks—long and white with the gold heel—he was thankful that those illustrious heels full of holes were still covered by his mostly black sneakers. His gaze moved up to his karate gi, now worn with the sleeves rolled up to his elbows, held securely in place by the safety pins he discovered in his grandmother's guest bathroom as you may recall, with the gi itself worn openly, revealing the white sleeveless T-shirt he wore underneath. And finally, his belt, used to tie the gi shut, was entirely missing.

He stopped in his tracks and made some awfully audible thoughts. "Dude. Where's the belt?"

Sydney turned. "What?"

"My belt is gone..."

Leunga turned as well. "You mean the one you left on Grampy's drawer thing? I always thought you did that on purpose."

The mindful martial artist had completely forgotten. Before removing his actual pants, he untied the belt and set it next to his grandfather's collection of creepy porcelain dogs atop the dresser in their grandparents' bedroom. "Great..." He considered his recent bout of luck. "Grammy probably poured acid all over it by now." Gi flapping openly in the warm wind, he was sorely sunk. Now on top of everything else wrong with the last few days, he was destined to hike as an incomplete karate movie cliché.

His sister smiled warmly and said, "You can use my belt if you want. I don't really need it anyway; it's just for show." Which is odd because it's always concealed by the lower ridge of her black T-shirts.

Ricky pictured the metal-studded band of pleather around Sydney's waist and frowned. "Uh...no, that's okay. You can keep it."

Acting in a way that was almost helpful, Leunga gave great consideration to his companion's complication and tried to make the best of a bad situation. "Doesn't those sweatpants have a drawstring or som—I am not seeing a goddamn open spot in this whole goddamn place...and where the goddamn is everyone?!" Totally saw that turnaround coming.

"That's not really what the belt is for..."

Folding her arms, a sister sibling followed her sights down the unpaved road. "Only three more spots we haven't checked...and they look full from here."

Ignoring his clothing situation for a moment, Ricky had a thought. "Grampy is hunting, right?"

Sydney nodded her head in disgust.

"Then he's probably not camping around the other people." Ricky was on a roll; he just wished he had thought of this before they entered the campgrounds. "So maybe we should camp closer to where he is...like, away from the people."

Leunga stroked his cheek in deep contemplation. "My word...the child is right..."

Gazing down at his older brother, the child was content in his response. "Should we, like, go back to that path we were on then?"

The adolescent anarchist girl began walking the dirt road back the way they came and agreed. "Might as well. It's not even noon. We have a lot of time before it gets dark." A very rough estimate of the current time—though surprisingly accurate.

So the three siblings trekked toward their previous path, ever vigilant for other people along their journey. Fortune smiled, and Ricky managed to avoid unnecessary human contact, for the moment. Perhaps his luck was changing, and in turn he was starting to feel as though the day could only get better from there.

Suddenly, Leunga faced his younger brother with compact eyes and issued a warning of immeasurable magnitude, bringing the brawling boy back to the depths of defeat. "I still want that sambwidge now, goddamn it."

Don't Panic

Sword in hand and held ready to strike, the sentinel sibling felt a chill run up his spine as his head whipped this way and that. He could sense it from all around. He could taste its presence in every breath. He could hear it watching him from afar. An ancient evil was out there, lurking in the shadows where it reigned, waiting for the perfect moment to pounce. As his survivalist sights soared through the scenery in search, a wild-eyed Leunga tightened his grip around the hilt of his blade and swallowed back the fear eating him alive, allowing every little feral inclination to take hold of his heart at once and elevate his perceptions to their limit. Suddenly, he stopped—spinning his face and falling into a spell of distraction at the odd angle he abruptly beheld. Standing over his brother, he watched Ricky dig through the garbled contents of the duffel bag set on the ground, and, for the first time in a long time, he found himself staring down at the top of his golden follicles in utter awe and wonder. Such a rare thing it was to be so high above his brother's head that he saw the sight as somewhat more than mesmerizing. Lost in a sense of hypnosis, Leunga slowly reached out, fingers spread wide, and moved his hand gently along the firm ridge of Ricky's hair.

The teen ducked out of his sibling's range quickly. "Hey!"

"Wasn't me!" Leunga raised his hands shoulder high in a gesture of innocence. "I'm far too busy defending your ass right now."

Brow brimming with suspicion, the sandwich searcher glared up through the lustrous fuzz right above his brown eyes and held up a paper-wrapped brick for the sandwich seeker. "This one says 'chicken salad.'"

"Gross!" He gagged immediately. "Are you trying to make me die?!"

"Dude, Syd can't have those, so you and I have to eat them."

"You mean *you* have to eat them."

Ricky put the item back in his bag and began searching for another type. "So all of the chicken salads are mine."

Leunga scowled. "Whoa! Says who?!"

Meanwhile, relaxing on a rock big enough for two while lying practically flat on her inclined back, just off the beaten path with her shredded jean-clad knees aimed skyward, their sister tapped the touch pad of her cell phone, silently communicating to a different world while simultaneously ignoring the real one all around her—very wisely, if you ask me—deeming the distraction to be a necessity as soon as her partners in the pines insisted on grinding their miniscule amount of progress to a halt somewhat far from the prying eyes of the happy campers, who were no less than ten solid minutes of walking away. Like a head without a body, the device hovered above her face, leering at her as she awaited a response to her message; suddenly, a dark void enveloped the screen. Sydney held the power button, but the phone wouldn't reactivate. "Damn it." She sat up and interjected, "My fucking phone died. Piece of shit." Facing her brothers, she stood and insisted, "Let me borrow one of you guys'."

Leunga visibly ignored the request of his sibling, looking around at the treetops quickly to avoid catching her eyes.

"You could have mine if I knew where it was."

"Man. You guys suck."

Agreeing, Ricky continued his search for his brother's extra breakfast, with the added objective of finding his wishfully unused telephone. He pulled out another paper-wrapped snack and said, "Cheese and mustard."

Leunga was baffled. "What? What are you giving that to me for? We don't have any time for that now. I just noticed that we're completely stopped in the middle of some nowhere place for no reason when we should be walking to find that son of a bitch camp thing we kept going on and on about already! Come on." The once-demanding hiker grabbed the sandwich and threw it back into the bag. "You can eat that later. We gotta go."

The youngest very delicately got up off the ground to avoid spoiling his slacks, nearly annoyed by the waste of his efforts but eager to get to a campsite to unload his treasury. Calming down a bit before thinking his thoughts, the taller teen pictured the contents of his duffel bag smashed together in an orgy of toiletries and foodstuffs—not to neglect the few remains of his martial arts gear trapped at the bottom—and he was pleased by the idea of loosing—and losing—his load of excess junk. With one arm he firmly gripped his heavy bag's handle and swung it around the side of his neck, causing the bulk of the contents to spill out of the unzipped bag. Immediately forgetting all concerns concerning the possible tearing of his turquoise track trousers, he happily let the frustration of the moment dictate his actions and knelt neglectfully, grunting angrily. "Son of a butt...!" Luckily for him, his newish knickers needed no special treatment whatsoever because they're obviously indestructible.

Sydney squatted beside him. "Here, let me get that for you."

"Thanks."

She swiftly picked up his cell phone and turned it on, only to pause. "Wait, I don't remember her number..."

Straining to reach a few things just out of range, Ricky submitted to the fact that he needed a helping hand and beseeched their brother, "Dude, can you hand me that stuff by your feet?"

Leunga visibly ignored the request of his sibling, looking around at the treetops quickly to avoid catching his eyes.

Rather than picking his battles poorly, Ricky simply sighed with all his might and carelessly crawled to the collection of scattered energy bars by his sibling's soles and gathered them up without a physical fuss. Disheartened, the solo member of the trio grumpily threw all of the misplaced contents back to their original overloaded container the best he could, remembering this time to zip the bag shut. As he stood again, Sydney held out his phone, which he promptly snatched from her and dropped into a side pocket of the duffel before heaving it behind him again—only to knock his bedroll off of its precarious perch, narrowly catching it clumsily in midair to the sound of a heavily relieved sigh. I told you that would happen again.

Without a wish to delay the end of their day any further, the pack mule complied with the unspoken instructions of the collective and followed his suddenly strolling siblings, stabilizing his heavy freight as they went. The gravity-greedy gifts attempting to leap from his possession at all times made him think of the grandparent who gave him so many wondrous things to drop, which immediately led to the reminder of his obtrusive troop's actual elderly objective—up until that point, he had been entirely preoccupied with his self-image. He *is* a teenager after all. Looking forward, he directed his words toward his brother at the head of the beast with an inquiry. "Hey Lou, if we find Grampy—"

"When we…"

"*When* we find Grampy, what are we gonna do then? Like, are we supposed to start doing what he's doing with him after you ask him all of your questions or whatever, or can we go do what we actually want to do instead? Whatever that is…"

One young man took a moment to assess the question. He hadn't actually planned that far ahead. There was much he wanted to ask a geezer, but he only really needed to find out where the other sword was located, a task he could have easily achieved over the phone. Glancing around as they trekked the trampled trail, Leunga carefully evaluated their current situation and calculated their next move. No clear answers came to his mind, and in the emptiness of ideas he made a grievous realization. "Wait, how are we ever gonna find Grampy out here? This is smack dab in the middle of nowhere…"

"Dude…shouldn't you have thought about that before we spent the whole night at Grammy's house just for this…?"

"Yes! I mean, no! I dunno! Maybe. Shut up! I'm thinking." Leunga raised his fist to teeth and bit down on his knuckle, gnawing for a few minutes while he searched his empty thoughts for an obvious solution. A simple solution. So simple it would be obvious. A large portion of the trail below their feet passed by him unnoticed. He unclenched his bloody knuckle and came to a decision. "Okay. I say we keep following this trail."

"Man, I could've told you that—"

"And after that!" he yelled at the pines, to which they replied with tensed silence. He had no follow-up to his point.

And that's when Sydney had an idea. "I have an idea." With her hands she created a tube around her mouth and shouted as loud as she could. "Grandpa!"

The chirping of the birds stopped momentarily as her voice travelled through the trees. A faint call returned shortly after her cry. "Yes?"

"Found him!" Sydney grinned. "That was easy!"

And that's when Leunga was unconvinced. "I am unconvinced." He repeated her action and shouted, "Is your name *Leunga*?"

An extensive bout of silence followed, broken by the same elderly man returning the howl. "Is that a real name?"

"Leave us alone, please," the young man of the same name replied before waiting for additional responses from the old guy. His voice returned to a reasonable volume to say, "I think he'll leave—"

"Okay, but if you kids need anything, just holler!"

Unlike anything I've ever seen before, Leunga waited tolerantly for any more comments that may journey their way—a unique feat for the dubious dork. No more than a minute passed before he was satisfied with the lack of continuance. "Let's—"

"Did you say something?" the same withered voice echoed.

"Mother fuck!"

Sydney shouted in reply, "We're okay now, thank you!"

Leunga sighed with exasperation and lowered his voice secretively. "Gonna be a lot harder to find Grampy than that, Syd."

"Shut up, Ricky."

Ricky reacted. "Man, that didn't sound anything like me..."

"It was you. Don't lie. We don't have time for it anyway," his older brother covered as he continued along the path. "We gotta get out of here before any more old farts decide to disturb our peaceful frolicking and shit."

After almost several minutes of welcome silence during the stroll, someone sniffed. "I smell smoke."

The young lady joined her younger brother and drew in short breaths through her nose. "Smells like a campfire."

Leunga darted his eyes back and forth from the lowest vantage point of the group and noticed a plume of gray gas rising from the trees in the distance. "There it is."

Sydney whacked the back of her hand against her older brother's arm and said, "Maybe it's Grandpa."

"You two go ahead and see if it is... I can't really go fast with all this stuff."

"Come on, ya big sack of crap," the eldest replied to the youngest. "It can't be that heavy. You're just being a big sack of crap."

Suddenly, their middle sibling jogged down the path in the direction of the smoke and insisted, "Race!"

The impromptu contest caught the shorter guy off guard. "Shit!" He tripped over his own boot but managed to maintain a standing position and ran after his sister, leaving Ricky in the dust. Leunga's sprinting capacity was minimal without the proper motivation, but defeating his younger, athletic sister in a footrace appeared to be all the incentive required. So, running at top speed toward the dark fog, he sped after a sylph sibling in haste. The surrounding trees flew past him in a blur. He could scarcely hear his footsteps as he focused on that win; however, despite his blinding velocity, he was rapidly losing ground on the first-place contestant.

Sydney continued to jog leisurely down the trail, her braided hair bouncing side to side with each step while her airy, unparted bangs held their position fragilely above her left eye. She glanced back at Leunga with a smirk and sneered, "Oh, come on! Are you serious right now? You can't possibly beat me, so why even try?"

A slacker saw the smug face of his sister gloating in his near future. Desperately wanting to avoid such a situation, he dug deep and juiced up his afterburner. A second wind filled his heart as he began gaining ground at a steady pace. For him, the race was far from over—but not for her, for she was already stopped at the finish. He dashed past her and touched the bark of the first wide pine he could find. "This tree is the finish line. I win."

"Sure you do," said Sydney, slowly observing the source of the campfire from a safe, and hidden, distance.

The winning loser panted heavily and gripped his ribs. "You almost had it at the end but it just wasn't meant to be. It came down to a photo finish...oh god."

"At least you beat me," congratulated Ricky as he walked to them steadily and stood next to his brother with a water bottle in his extended hand.

"Yes I did." Leunga grabbed the offering and drenched his face with the entire contents of the plastic container, letting nary a drop touch his tongue.

Sydney looked back at her brothers and reported, "I don't see Grandpa. Or anyone actually." She returned to her study of the campsite. It appeared to be deserted, with the exception of the smoldering embers in the fire pit.

An older boy wiped his face on his sleeve and shouted, "Grampy? Is that your camp we're looking at?" He then looked at Ricky quickly and added in a quiet tone, "If that other fucker answers I'm gonna go berserk..."

Ricky nodded, deeply concerned. Luckily for everyone involved, there was no response.

One hiker took the lead and crept cautiously toward the camp, overhauling her big brother's important question by transforming it into a form that was more manageable when she was sure there would be no answer. "Hello? Anyone here?"

A chill ran down someone's spine. Eyes widened by superfluousness, a pothead said, "I just got the craziest feeling that this is all an elaborate trap we are very nearly about to be walking into, but then it went away the very second I started talking, which might mean I should shut up by now, so I did."

Ricky nodded in agreement with his small sibling and whispered, "I know what you mean."

Put at ease by the fact that the site had obviously been abandoned, Sydney entered the area without worry—until she noticed how horrific it actually was. The place was a mess: food wrappers strewn about, empty cans, glass bottles, and, for whatever reason, magazines. Sydney sighed in disgust. "Uch. Total shithole."

Her younger brother followed warily. "Maybe a bear did this."

She picked up one of the magazines and immediately dropped it. "Ew! I don't think bears would need this much porn..."

Leunga perked up and scurried into the camp. He bent down and began gathering the periodicals into a stack, stating, "I'll just get these cleaned up..." After assembling every visible piece of his new collection, he stood and turned to Ricky, in hopes of making the workhorse carry the treasures, but he was intercepted by his sister, who seized them and dropped the hoard into the defunct fire. As the glossy pages unexpectedly burst into flames, Leunga silently raised his fists into the air and looked to the sky, falling to his knees and quietly mourning his loss.

Intrigued by something she saw soon after that, Sydney lifted a lightweight, oddly shaped bundle of green fabric and declared, "Hey, somebody left a pop tent." Right away, she jiggled the object in the space before her face to see if it would activate, but it remained inert. "Should we take this? I doubt anyone is coming back to this dump."

Ricky investigated the unexplored portion of the site. "There's a cooler over here," he informed and flicked it open with his foot, momentarily losing his equilibrium. Regaining his balance, he peeked into the coffer. "All it has is beer."

Leunga perked up and scurried over to the cooler. Without a word he began loading the icy beverages into his beige cargo pants until they were filled. "Why would someone leave all this deliciousness?"

"It's inconsiderate is what it is," his sister said and struggled with the issue of how to secure their new tent to her sleeping bag shoulder strap.

"So true," he agreed, gripping the last two beers that refused to fit in his shorts, and attempting to decide which one to open first. The chilled cans numbed his fingers while he examined the labels of each. They appeared to be identical, but he wasn't entirely convinced. The cool condensation on the left hand can—mixed with the lost dexterity of his frozen fingers—caused him to inadvertently release the object. It soared to the ground, smacking against a jagged rock. The pressurized contents exploded in a fountain of fermentation.

Sydney had to hop away from the oncoming torrential rain in haste, yelling, "Jackass, you got beer juice all over my leg!" And while wiping her calf clean on a boulder she felt the urge to add, "Dumb dick bastard..."

Leunga cracked open the remaining can and shrugged. Gathering the second biggest mouthful of the bitter nectar that he could fit in his face, he took a long guzzle of the grog before exhaling emphatically with exaggerated satisfaction. "You're welcome."

Ricky tapped a glass bottle with his foot and walked to a flat rock nearby. As he sat, the colossal weight pulling against his chest and neck lifted. And that's when he realized he found exactly what he was looking for all along. A camp no one would ever want to find. It was the perfect place to preserve his people-free preference. There was no one else within earshot of their current position, and it was likely to stay that way. In relief he sighed and watched a small stream in the distance flowing and came to a decision he hoped everyone would join in on. "Dude, I was just thinking about it. We should just, like, make *this* our camp. Yeah? I mean, we're already here."

"Whoa! Rick! That is so crazy that you just said that. I was barely starting to think the exact same thing. Right? I mean, this place is so perfect it makes me want to grow a beard about it. We are officially home away from home!"

Sydney paused her undertaking and glanced at the surrounding clutter. "In the middle of a garbage dump? I don't know about you, but I'm not really in the mood to clean up a ton of other people's shit."

"Whoa! Rick! Let me get this straight. You want us to set up camp *here*?! But there's huge amounts of trash everywhere! Admit it, everything would be better than this."

Realizing his mistake almost immediately after coming to the concise conclusion that it was a good idea and all, the taller teen surrendered to his siblings. "Oh, right. Yeah, okay..." The epic quest to find their grandfather was unquestionably taking its toll on the young man sorely seeking cessation; his strained muscles pulsed without the added weight restricting them, knowing full well that at the drop of a hat, they may need to bear the burden of the bulge once more, keeping them tense and unable to truly relax. And yet, despite his downtrodden demeanor, Ricky was still thrilled to have this opportunity to rest, no matter how temporary it may be. Oddly enough, it was even starting to feel like he could be having a good time. I think all that heavy lifting has done something to his head.

Leunga sucked out the last remains of his alcoholic refreshment and dropped the aluminum in line with the rest scattered along the ground, taking another from his front pocket and gingerly cracking open the second can of ale. "Boy howdy. How great is this adventure so far? Really makes you wonder, doesn't it? About who or what I have no idea, but at least it's a yes. No wonder Grampy comes out here all the time. If I knew there was gonna be free beer, I never would have told everyone I've ever met about how much I hate real-life forests. It won't be long now, and I'll be wasted. Thanks, trees!"

"I guess if you keep helping us look for a place to put our stuff and don't make us stop every five minutes to wait while you barf, that's good..."

"It's great!" And he gurgled out another gaseous cloud of vapor. "Greater, even."

Grimacing, Sydney wondered, "And exactly how many more of those would it take to make you and your mouth pass out for the rest of the day?"

"Maybe ten. Why?"

"Just checking." Leunga's younger sister quickly added an optional collection contingency to their quest as the search for many things continued. "Be on the lookout for more of those abandoned campsites, guys. We need to find eleven more beers."

"Agreed! Meaning, we best be on our way. No, time to lose!" he said incorrectly. "We ride!" And once again the trek was on its way back onto their former trail.

The center sibling managed to fasten the green package to the base of her bedroll shoulder strap and glanced at her older brother. "Uh-huh." Holding her expanded equipment behind her with both arms, she walked briskly toward Leunga. Without acknowledging her younger cohort visually, she raised her voice and ordered, "Come on, Ricky. Time to go."

Taking one last look at the serenity of the distant brook, the young man with the many demands made against him carefully arose and once again adjusted his cargo. The small respite granted by the makeshift bench was just enough to keep him going. Barely. So he casually followed behind his siblings without a peep, allowing his long strides to compensate for his slow pace, and not long after leaving the deserted campsite, he caught up with Leunga and Sydney. Smells of pine sap and dirt filled his nose as several moments quietly passed along the trail, and Ricky had even forgot his dread about being seen by someone not within his own bloodline. It was going to be a good day after all.

A sudden cry for help resonated through the trees. "Who the fuck stole my shit?!"

"Did ya hear that?" Sydney glanced around behind them for the source of the investigation while keeping their speed and said to her older brother, "Hey, quest-nerd. You should go help him. That's all they do in video games, right? Going around, helping random losers with the shit they're too lazy to do for themselves. Now you can do it for real, as if it's not the creepiest thing ever."

The quest-nerd couldn't erase the disgust from his face. "Cripes, keep it in your pants, lady. I'll not allow you to put this thing on pause while you go hit on some cheese-squeezer. Guy sounds like a douche anyways. Probably wearing a backwards hat and $300 sunglasses." I feel that I should apologize for Leunga's previous comment—wearing a baseball cap in reverse accompanied with overpriced designer sunglasses does not a *douche* create, but it's a start. "No more stalling. Not like it's our problem; we didn't do anything."

"I think we stole his stuff."

Sydney scoffed with frustration and spoke to her older sibling. "Fucking idiot. I said *you* should go help him. I'm not gonna help him. Why would I? That'd be so stupid. Besides, whoever stole his stuff is probably miles away by now, so shut up."

Ricky warily glanced back at the travelled trail, anticipating, but not hoping, an irate camper would appear to rightfully accuse their group of unlawfully removing his belongings. The unusually dressed dude's uneasiness about being seen had been trumped by his desire to be free from the world of unwanted human confrontation, and all of his nerve-numbing fears came back with a vengeance, but what else is new? As the accidental thieves rounded an increasing number of corners, and an incredible number of seconds passed, the only aware boy of the bungling bunch became slightly less concerned about unnecessary trouble and refocused his uneasy attention forward through the pines, but it was pretty clear what remained ever-present in his head. The pleasant thought of breaking away from his malarkey-magnetized associates and being alone to have some much-needed time to himself danced through his mind as he watched the back of his companions' oblivious brains. Already, he was formulating a foolproof wish to go back home. Let's hope it doesn't come true.

Two for One Tuesdays

Rife with rejuvenation, air-conditioned breeze beat the back of his neck—a refreshing break from the unruly estival heat just outside. He closed his eyes and lost all focus of his immediate goal. Nothing else mattered at that point, only the cool movement flowing around the ample body of his fauxhawk. That stiff, sunny yellow hair of his went sweeping through the wind like a rudder on a barge sailing on a direct course through calm seas, and it soothed the world. His loose-fitting, lime green, short-sleeved, collared shirt waved freely in the gale above his olive green cargo shorts. More than enough green for one outfit. And although the mechanical hum was deafening, he barely heard it in his trance—a trance that was easily broken by the jabbing hand of his older sister nudging his elbow.

"Shit...I am freezing my goddamn ass off," she informed her brother as well as a decent portion of the deli line in front of her while she kept her arms tightly folded around her ribs to ward off her shivers. "Hold our spot; I gotta go look at something," commanded a suddenly distracted Sydney as she broke away from the slightly taller teen standing at her side and walked across the fluorescent lit linoleum floor swiftly, safely away from the direct blast of the arctic zephyr.

Ricky watched her weave through the awkward display stands of the small grocery store on an indirect path to a place that meant little to him. He knew it was impossible to go anywhere with his older sister without losing her down some aisle as her curiosity got wind of something of mild interest, but the boy was confidentially counting on that trait. He sought the obvious solitude she obliviously offered during the beginning of what would surely be a relaxing summer break. Now with no one around to bother him—only the silent strangers standing in a row with their backs to him—he was invisible. Alone at last. With six customers in front of him in the deli line, he knew it would be a while before he had to worry about ordering his double-decker club sandwich, allowing him to float freely back to his happy place. And with no one behind him at the moment, he could truly be at peace.

The drumming of the cool air kept his mind in a state of pure relaxation, a rare feeling for him, but as with everything peaceful in his life, it was not meant to last. A tin can filled with food, or something else edible, rolled along the ground in a rumbling clatter on a steady course, coming to an abrupt stop only when it came into contact with a size thirteen black sneaker. Shaken loose by the tap of a small cylindrical distraction, Ricky opened his eyes discouragingly, glanced down at the rolling receptacle of sliced peaches, and immediately wondered what it was doing at his foot and what it wanted from him. He bent down cautiously to avoid destroying any part of his carefully crafted appearance and picked up the can. With the sweet stainless steel in his grip, he investigated the out-of-place nature of his interruption briefly before quickly noticing a kindly faced old woman flank him from the left with a smile in his direction.

Realizing that the foodstuff in his palm must belong to the invading geriatric shuffling his way—or surely would belong to her as soon as she hopefully paid for the dented goods—Ricky held out the pantry-perfect package as an offering with a bashfully gentle grin.

Slowly grabbing the dastardly droppable metal, the elderly woman expressed her gratitude to her hero. "Why, thank you young m—Stephen!"

Ricky's expression quickly curled as he glanced around curiously. "H—me?"

"Oh my goodness! It's so nice to see you again, Stephen! Oh my, it must be almost three years since I last saw you. Are you still playing the piano I hope?"

Seeing as how this particular young man had never touched an actual piano in his entire life—with the sole exception of his grandmother's that one time when he broke three of the keys while catching himself from the slightest of stumbles—this woman was certainly identity mistaken, but instead of risking the torture of discomfiture with something as silly as telling the truth, Ricky reverted to his usual cast of characters to find his substitute for the remainder of this wishfully short, awkward encounter. "Uh...sometimes..."

"You were such a talented student. I was sure sorry when you stopped coming by for lessons."

"Sorry about that. I...guess I just got busy with other things." Clearly, some people are not the type to make corrections of another's inaccuracies, and that goes double for the teen in green; he would rather allow everyone to think what they want and avoid the embarrassment of embarrassing them entirely. However, the woman *was* obviously inaccurate. Anyone could plainly see that Ricky was not Stephen, and Stephen was not Ricky... At least, that's what I assume. Come to think of it, I've never actually met Stephen. I suppose he or she could potentially look something close to Ricky, but the odds of that happening are so far beyond the realm of possibility that it would be miraculous. Or not... I have no idea. That's why I'm still rambling until somebody decides to stop me. And on that thought, what is the truth if not the most recent set of perceived facts? I mean, whether it's conceivable or not, if it can be believed to be the truth, then what's the harm? And I would love to dissect this topic further, but I'm kind of in the middle of telling a story here, so can I please continue? Thank you.

"Mmm..." the elderly lady continued after a review of her limited memory. "You must still be in high school. Is that right?"

Unfortunately, yes. Stephen was all too familiar with the nuances of senior high life. "Um...yeah," he said. "I just finished my sophomore year last week." Huh, I guess he felt one little truth couldn't hurt.

"Really? I thought for sure you would be on your way to being a senior by now."

"Oh! Right!" Stephen chuckled nervously. "That's what I meant..." Huh, I guess it *could* hurt after all.

"Well, I'm sure you've been studying hard for college! And what a handsome young man you've become. My husband looked a lot like you when he was young."

Stephen smiled at her and shrugged, not really sure how to react. "Thank you..."

"All the girls in your class must really like you. I hope you don't break too many hearts!"

"I try not to!" replied an ostensibly embarrassed teen accompanied by a meek nod. Finally something he could honestly hope to achieve.

"I'm very sure you do." His harasser grinned. When it was clear that no one else was clamoring to keep the conversation alive, she said, "Well, I wish I could stay and chat some more, but I should get going. I have a lot to do today. First I had to take care of the shopping, you know. Then I have to take the cat to the vet because she's been having a little breathing problem lately, so we're going to go to the doctor to find out if it's serious. You remember Copernicus, don't you? Well, she's getting on in years, and I get very worried about her. Oh, and after the vet, I need to take my wool cardigan to the dry cleaner to get that stain out. It's been there for weeks! They did such a wonderful job with my pullover that I think they'll be able to clean out a little jam. And I *still* haven't picked up my prescription from the pharmacy from yesterday! I hope they won't be mad... I can't believe I forgot. I can be such a scatterbrain sometimes!" Sometimes.

With a blare of his eyes, Stephen winced and hopped in with a courteous remark in hopes of curtailing the chance of listening to any more of the relentlessly friendly woman's plans for the coming months. "Sounds busy!"

"*Very* busy," she agreed with a boisterous eye roll. Stephen's plan apparently worked, for his former piano professor began to show indicative signs of attempting to make a run for it, and that was just fine. "Anyway, I'm glad I got to see you again. What a wonderful surprise this has been to bump into you here. I normally don't come to this store because it's so small, and they don't carry the brand of toilet tissue that I like."

"Hmm," hummed Stephen as he gave a discreetly disgusted nod.

"Now don't you be a stranger, y'hear? You can come visit us anytime you want for some cake and coffee." That sounds tempting...I wonder where she lives.

"Okay."

Turning back toward her little shopping cart with an almost-forgotten can of sugary peach meat in her hand, the woman smiled before abruptly looking back at the boy when she realized she had forgotten to make a request. "Oh, and say hello to your mother for me!"

Standing in line with his attention on sandwiches and dill pickles destroyed, a thoroughly conflicted Stephen promised, "I will."

"And have a wonderful summer!" she added as the wobbly cart in her grip led her on a course to the cashier, chalked up as just one more incongruity in that long line of unwarranted civil distractions our friend the handsome young gentleman could have done without.

"You too..." replied Ricky, hoping Sydney hadn't seen any of that transaction. With a sly look over his right shoulder, the pretty boy spied on the sister he lost and quickly realized she was far too consumed with her own interests to care, or notice, anything he had done, permitting him to sigh silently in relief and return to a now steadily unsteady out-of-body state, where at least it was quiet for the moment.

Another slow drumming of the cooler above invited him to cease his thoughts and seal his eyes shut, allowing his lazy urges to take over as he drifted downstream in vacant vacation relaxation for a minute of nothingness. He opened his eyes for a second to check the line's progress. No movement. He closed them again to focus his senses on the feeling of the arctic wind. Minor numbness in the extremities, a sensation of stillness, no audible dialect; this was truly summer. Ricky let himself lose track of time; after all, he had nearly three full months to waste away, and hopefully with as little outside interference as possible. At least five minutes passed before he instinctively opened his eyes once more to check on the line. This time there had been movement. In fact, there was someone new in front of him.

A midteen boy just about the same age as Ricky stood right before him in the line as if he had always been there. Somewhere in the range of six feet tall, he was just slightly shorter than the boy behind him, less the taller's impressive crest of gold. With his daze completely shattered, Ricky stared at the back of this new head of hair—a strangely familiar hairdo constructed of intricately woven columns of darkness, resembling subsidized crop fields—and a swift sensation of defeat attacked his nerves all at once. The inevitable had happened; a friend had him cornered—Ricky had only hoped it wouldn't have been so soon. He forced a smirk and said, "Hey, Hunter."

The young man in front of him slowly looked back over his shoulder, sporting a large grin as he did so. "Hey man, what's up?"

Already, one lad couldn't wait to be alone again. He saw the proceedings marching his way and it tired him out just thinking about it. Every little social thing that seemed to drift in his direction demanded his time, speeding his responses by neglecting his opportunity to think everything out before his reaction, forcing him into places with people he never thought imaginable or desirable, but such was life for Ricky. "Nothing much."

Hunter turned and faced his friend. "I've been trying to call you all day. Where's your phone at?"

The blond pretended to pat himself down in search of the very basic cell phone in his right front pants pocket and apologized. "Oh, I think I left it at home, dude..."

"It's cool, man. I'm glad I caught you though..."

Ricky could sense the demolition of his peaceful day approaching swiftly.

"Later on, me and the guys are gonna go meet a bunch of girls at the movies. Seth says he's finally gonna try to hook up with Bobbi Mitchell, and we all wanna be there when he fails. Hard."

"Cool..." Easily seeing where the conversation was heading, the taller teen attempted to derail it. "By the way, how did you even know I was here? Are you, like, stalking me now or something?" he jested.

"Ha!" Hunter chuckled cheerily for less than a syllable before he shook his head and said, "Hell no, dude. This right here was destiny working its magic on you. We were on our way over to your house, and I saw your car outside. The one with the badass skull decal." It was actually Sydney's car, but whatever. "We were going to ask you if you wanted to go. You in?"

Naturally, it was Ricky's original intention to avoid any unnecessary social situations for at least a week after school let out for the summer, but having come face-to-face with the very circumstance he wished to evade, he saw little alternative in the matter. Because of that reprehensible amiability of his, Ricky was always extremely careful with his use of the word *no*—overuse of the negativity will alienate any relation, desirable or not, but contrariwise, underuse leads to something far more destructive. Of course, he only saw the former half of the danger. As long as he perpetuated that attitude toward himself, his happiness would always come last—something he wished he could change, but for that he needed help. Help he could never seek, because he didn't know how to put into words the things he felt, but like, what teenager *does*? Right? And it was then that he began to wonder if Stephen had the same social ordeals that he did, while also wondering if it were possible to trade lives. "Um...what movie is it?"

"Dunno, but it's gonna be lousy with hotties there, and you *know* they're all gonna wonder where you are. You gotta come, dude. It's gonna be sick." Hunter saw the instant indecision in his friend's wandering eyes and decided to sweeten the deal, adding, "Also, I think *Becky* might be there," which caused his eyebrows to raise in anticipation of his bud's response.

The name conjured a churning of one boy's stomach: the awkward silences, sweaty palms, shortness of breath, and the uncomfortable eye contact. Ricky began feeling the symptoms just thinking about her. She was a slightly older high school girl with a knack for misunderstanding—

misinterpreting the smallest signals, intentional or not. Jokes whiz right over her head without hesitation, no matter how hilarious they may seem to the people around her. The girl with whom Ricky shared an awkward secret. Like, *super* awkward. Nevertheless, for reasons he didn't understand or accept personally, he looked to Hunter and nodded. "Okay. I'll be there." A wave of disappointment pulsated through his chilled frame as he forced another smile.

"Hells yeah," hailed Hunter as he held out an open palm perpendicular to his torso. Ricky grabbed his friend's hand, and they commenced an intricate form of handshake that would be far too difficult to describe with mere words. "Ten o'clock at Sequoia Cinema."

"Okay."

During their interaction, something caught hunting Hunter's eye. He turned his attention down one of the aisles of the small, and vastly unoccupied, grocery store. "Whoa, damn." On the other side of the market, a woman stood with her entire left side facing the deli line at a section of personal hygiene products, perusing the quaint grocery's limited makeup selection. Particularly the eyeliner. She had a definite tomboy vibe; the type of girl who would never wear hot pink lip gloss or rouge. Far across the linoleum she stood, balanced on one leg with her uninhibited foot coiled around the back of her immobilized ankle, slightly rotating back and forth while she placed her index finger against her chin in a thoughtful way. Hunter tapped his comrade's arm and demanded, "Check out the bimb."

I would like to take a moment to alleviate some potential confusion and define the term young Hunter has just articulated in the spirit he has intended:

Bimb: Noun. A term of endearment for a physically attractive young woman, typically intelligent and frequently found alone; designated by the acronym for a Beautiful Independent Modern Babe. Not to be confused with the notoriously derogatory term *bimbo*; bimb has only positive connotations.
Synonyms: beauty, gorgeous, lovely, etc.
Example: *"Whoa, damn, check out the bimb."*
Related forms: *Bimby*. Adj. *Bimbly*. Adv. *Bimbed*. Verb. Etc.

Doing as he was instructed like always, Ricky followed Hunter's stares and looked down the particular aisle, where he too noticed a young woman with sprightly straight hair loosely arranged in an alternative rock genre sort of way that went into jagged ends down the back just past her shoulder line—contrasted by shorter, fluffier spikes of golden hair that swept across her forehead in an intense assemblage of bangs, edged to blend with the rest of her choppy mess of a mane and roguishly draped above one eye. She wore a gray pair of high-tops—retro basketball sneakers with a white soles and toe area—and had lean wrists decorated in an array of treacherous bracelets, dark jeans with shredded cuffs dangling below her knees, and a faded black slim-fit T-shirt worn with a Union Jack spaghetti strap tank top as a cover shirt... Ricky immediately turned toward his friend, taken aback. "Dude, that's my sister!"

Hunter laughed. "Oho damn! Dude, I didn't recognize her." He popped his fist into Ricky's shoulder as a gesture of repentance while his eyes remained fastened to the teenage woman. "Hey! Introduce me to her."

"Duh, you two have met a bunch of times, dude. She already knows your name. Remember? She used to drive you home, like, *all* the time."

"Right...right..." he reminisced. "You'd think I would remember someone like her." Hunter and Ricky watched the blond girl from afar as she accidentally dropped the nail polish bottle in her hand and cringed as it bounced along the floor. Luckily for her it didn't break. "What grade is she in again?"

"She just graduated last week, man. She's goin' to college."

"Fuck damn. Are you sure that's Syd? What about that girl you were with when I was at your house like, I dunno, two months ago?" One month. "How many sisters do you actually have?" Hunter teased. "Seriously though, did she get a haircut or something? I thought your sister had black hair."

Already disliking the direction of their discussion, the caboose glanced over at his friend wearily as Hunter gawked at his only sister with a disturbing stare. Ricky could tell that his longtime school chum was clearly not interested in any responses to his previous questions, obviously preoccupied with his fascination. The droning of the swamp cooler filled the gaps in their conversation with incessant chatter, cooling the merchandise. Other than the fact that Hunter was obsessed with his older sister at the moment, the quiet association was nice—a quaint reminder of how life used to be before high school began, when Ricky, Hunter, and that long-lost funny girl—the one who now lived mainly in his memories with her dark hair and the cute laugh—used to enjoy being in each other's company without the need for constant input from one another for entertainment. Wondering why Hunter suddenly found his lanky sister to be so enchanting after all these years, Ricky opted to join his current line companion in his quest for answers and looked in the direction of the nigh nonexistent makeup selection once again.

Far away where she stood alone, Sydney's conscience got the best of her. Deciding not to pretend she wasn't the one who dropped the makeup in the first place, she bent over with a roll of her eyes and a sigh to pick up the bottle of lacquer she had secretly kicked under the deep cavern of the shelf. With the seat of her derelict pants aimed at the deli counter toward the back of the store, she knelt on the slick, speckled floor and laboriously wrenched her arm under the confining space filled with dust and hair in search of the damned—a compromising position to take considering the teenage boy interested in examining her at that very moment. An unintended gift for the young man in cornrows.

With rapidly widening eyes, Ricky immediately turned to Hunter in defense of his sister, not wanting to know what his friend was thinking at that moment but certainly wanting to put an end to it. Upon noticing his peer's unabashed, blank stare coupled with brow heightened in arousal, he felt the sudden need to stop his pal's tactless ogling. With an expression expressing his detestation of Hunter's conduct, Ricky threw him a quick, angered glare and a light shove of the shoulder. "Hey! Come on, dude..."

Hunter snapped back to attention and took the hint. "Sorry! Don't need to kill me, I'll stop!" he said before gradually returning his eyes to the bimb across the store to enjoy his public peep show.

Strangely, Ricky was not in the mood to play his standard part; the role of the accommodating best friend. Something in Hunter's attitude struck him as especially off-putting, and he frowned. "It's not me you have to worry about. If Syd catches you staring at her like a freak she's gonna be pissed...mostly at me for not stopping you, and I gotta ride home with her, man. And that's *after* she kicks both our asses." He said asses.

Eyes still fixed on Sydney, the dark-haired teen agreed with whatever. "Yeah...shit, dude, you gotta invite me over more often." The next boy to say *dude* is getting a smack.

Nerves nearly on edge as he found himself wishing his sister was suddenly struck blind before she could notice any gawking guys staring in her direction, Ricky instantly felt that he was already allowing his friends to visit his house an appropriate amount and caught himself thinking that that fact should have been apparent to all. Without a warning, another bout of stillness presented itself in their exchange, and odd as it was, their momentary lapses in conversation were far less awkward than they normally would have been; it felt almost peaceful to Ricky, despite feeling like he had to be a barrier to separate Hunter from Sydney. Protective needs aside, the area was once again beset by chilling serenity as the machine above their heads continued with its task of filling the empty void with the sound of nothing. He took a moment to enjoy the silence in the presence of potential chatter. Alone at last. If only this amount of tranquility was commonplace in their mutated association, but all good things must end. "Ten o'clock, Sequoia Cinema?"

Continuing his review of his good friend's sibling, Hunter nodded. "Yeah. So uh, does she have a...*boyfriend* or anything?" Suddenly, he stopped his stare and gritted his teeth. "Aw shit, I forgot!" Quickly he began hustling to the large wooden door of the market and explained, "I got people waiting. Remember, ten o'clock, Sequoia Cinema! See ya later, man. Damn it!"

"Bye," Ricky said with a sigh aimed at the lack of sparked conflict between himself and Sydney as he watched Hunter's braided cornrows pass through the chiming doorway, once again allowing him to enjoy the accompanied solitude of the sandwich counter line. In the absence of thought, the freezing air against his back returned him to the trance. Alone at last. The plans he made for later took a backseat in his mind and he focused his senses on that feeling flowing over his fauxhawk and around his neck. One satisfied customer left the line, pulling the chain forward with the exception of the last link.

Ricky opened his eyes and stared skyward; trees on all sides. A large fern stood next to him as he finished his lavatory business. Retying the drawstring of his newly acquired sweatpants and rinsing his hands in the bubbling brook nearby, he wondered if it was the same stream he saw an hour or so earlier. He stretched his back, free from the burden of the weighty duffel bag that he left in the care of his brother and sister some few dozen yards away. Alone at last. Standing back, he took stock of their current situation: wandering aimlessly through the dense tree line, looking for a man who has miles of forest in which to hide, and no discernable means of finding their way home. A bit bleak, but Ricky found solace in the fact that they had yet to find another human being during the increasing number of hours spent on a supposedly busy trail. Perhaps the search would be cut short due to lack of probability. And perhaps not.

Indistinct arguing boomed through the pines, like a cannon shot distorting the sound of the stream and ruining the moment for good. Ricky glanced in the general direction of the squabble with full knowledge of the participants involved. Though their voices were vague, he clearly heard the abundantly exasperating tones of his brother and sister, locked in a brawl of words. At that point, he chose to remain where he was, enjoying the calmness of the rivulet, but he was finding it difficult to concentrate on anything other than the quarrel filling the trees. The burbling splashes of the chilly water were no match for the ever-present echoes of his family. Regretfully, Ricky walked back slowly toward the kerfuffle to see if he could stop it.

As he edged closer to the path, the voices around him were becoming comprehensible. His brother was the first to be heard. "You don't know what you're talking about. That panda was a fuckin' hot ass!"

"That doesn't even matter. Mom made me get rid of it because of *you*."

"Are you even listening to yourself? You're not making any sense anymore."

"Tough shit!"

Anxiously approaching the maelstrom, Ricky's siblings' glares were suddenly directed right at him. He paused, feeling the palpable malice in the situation. Pretty much right away he had the sudden urge to flee, and at the risk of being labeled a coward, he began backing up with the hope that he was never seen.

"Come here." Sydney's eyes were locked on her younger brother as she then addressed Leunga, insisting, "Let's ask Ricky."

"Whatever."

The youngest camper cringed while awaiting the question. If only he had stayed by the brook and delayed his return until the end of their argument, the target wouldn't be all over his handsome face. "What...?" he asked cautiously.

Sydney shrugged. "You heard what we were talking about. Who do you think is right?"

Even if he was inclined to take anyone's side, Ricky knew better than to get between his brother and sister on any matter—including ones where he could actually have an opinion—and his eyes quickly locked onto the ground, unwilling to step to the rescue of either of them; and if he wasn't pining for some permanent alone-time before, he certainly was after that. "I think...I don't...want...not going to..."

"Aha! See, stupid? Rickins agrees with me."

Sydney was noticeably appalled and her voice broke. "Ricky?!"

"Wait, I'm not—"

"You know what? Shut up. You guys are jerks." Sydney dropped her equipment on the dirt path in a huff and demanded, "Don't leave without me." Storming off in the opposite direction her kid brother had come from, she muttered something as she left.

Leunga sighed as he watched his sister leave the group, apparently traumatized by the proceedings. He stood, facing away from his younger brother and inhaled deeply. "Why is she always so mean...?"

Ricky could tell that his brother was distraught over the recent exchange of words he and their sister were having before the younger male entered the conversation. With a hand reaching over to the little brunet man, he made a rare attempt at some consoling contact. At first, Ricky's gauche maneuver hesitated, until he surrendered to the moment and placed a caring hand gently on a short shoulder to comfort his older brother. Leunga reciprocated the gesture by softly grabbing the teen's hand with his own. They stood like this, both staring in the same direction, for at least four minutes. The taller one felt extremely uncomfortable with his brother's tender grip. Leunga slowly picked up the bigger boy's hand and began caressing his own cheek with the back of his younger brother's knuckle. Ricky withdrew his hand almost immediately.

Wandering over to his sibling's navy blue luggage, Leunga promptly sat on top of it, causing crunches and pops from within. Ricky fretfully listened to the destruction of their supplies before beseeching, "Uh...dude? Would you mind not sitting on that?"

"Just need a sec..." the eldest answered, placing a hand over his mouth and squinting blankly into the trees.

As quietly as could be, Ricky collected their sister's gear to keep the dirt off of it like he knew she would probably want. Despite feeling like her temporary enemy for whatever reason, he still felt obligated to take care of her things, urged with the desire to bypass her mood and preserve her sensitive feelings no matter what the situation called for; even if he was the younger sibling, he was always able to maintain an insight into the delicate workings of his sister over the years—a link drawing back to the days when he and she were inseparable so long ago—though as of late, his connection with her had been slipping, unable to read her at times as she was becoming increasingly distant toward him for reasons he couldn't decipher. Dusting off his sibling's sleeping bag roll, Ricky watched Leunga's vacant statuesque pose compressing their victuals, and as luck would have it, the peculiar sensation of peace in the face of chaos returned to him in the silence of his brother's absent presence, and so the tired teen allowed time to pass by unrestricted, enjoying the tense moment for what it was. Alone at last.

Minutes later, his older brother finally punctured the peace. "Where the *hell* is she?"

"Hey, buttheads," a disembodied female voice sounded from close by. "I found a fuckin' camp."

United Bastards

While waiting for one of her siblings to hurry his business up, Sydney stood beside her older brother with her hands stuffed into her back pockets beneath the bedroll resting against her pants, watching as Ricky staggered over the roots scattered along the forest floor—unfamiliar with his equilibrium sans the duffel bag, much like an infant learning to walk—and she snickered as she caught a better glimpse of the turquoise sweatpants from behind. "Maybe we should tell him."

Laughing lightly, Leunga shook his head. "No, we shan't. Not ever."

"It's my turn next when he gets back."

"Hell, just go now. I know how to wait alone."

Raising her left eyebrow while simultaneously lowering her right—her often overused expression of skepticism and disbelief, exaggerated greatly by the volume and intensity of her family's dark eyebrows—she supplied the scenery with a signature stare and said, "Sure...and then when I get back, all of our stuff is gone and you have absolutely no idea where you hid it."

"Anything is possible."

Quickly jerking her head to the side to remove her bundled bangs from obstructing her eyes as much as she could, Sydney let her mug-masking hair rest in its customary location diagonally covering her forehead while dropped just over the edge of her left eyebrow—still the only portion of her hair not trapped in a tight braid. She felt the strange sensation of being watched and glanced to the right to see if her present pest was trying to bug her by making a game of staring at her when she wasn't looking; however, that was discovered to be an ideal scenario when compared to what was actually happening, because Leunga was found picking at the inside of his ear, studying each expedition afterward to check his results quietly to himself. Unfortunately, Sydney was trapped, watching him in disgust and unable to look away.

He flicked a fleck of ear dust into the ether when he noticed her sickened grimace. "What?"

She was finally able to look away and whined, "That's so gross."

"Oh! But when *you* do it, that makes it okay!"

Sydney elevated her voice to match her brother's increasing volume. "Because I don't use my fingers, *and* I do it alone in a bathroom."

Leunga scoffed and shook his head at her. "Such a bogus liar. I just saw you do it at Grammy's house yesterday and you smeared it all over the walls."

"No I didn't."

"Yes."

"No."

"Yes."

Sydney fell silent, knowing that if she kept calm she could easily win any argument with Leunga.

"Yes."

She rolled her eyes and ignored the incessant insect accompanying her. Just then, a pleasantly warm breeze floated across the path, propelling her substantial bangs over her eyesight yet again. Unwilling to remove her hands from their mysteriously comfortable position in the pants pockets behind her, she waited for the wind to die off rather than blocking the bluster with her palms, and threw her head to the left once more, removing the blond bouquet from most of her vision.

"Yes. Hey, that reminds me," Leunga remarked and rested his entire left elbow on his sister's shoulder—an unnatural position considering she's easily eight or nine inches taller than him—and leaned in close to question, "Do you remember that show you used to watch with all the animal-human hybrids?"

Sydney scooted her head away from her brother's nauseating breath and kept her cool, decidedly not reacting to his unwarranted physical contact. "They were only animals," she clarified. "They just kind of looked like real people. Oh my god..."

"Yeah that's the one. Do you know where that toy you had of the panda is? I kind of need to know."

Rapidly losing her patience, she answered between bouts of holding her breath. "No, not anymore."

"Oh come on! You do know and you want to keep it all to yourself," Leunga practically shouted into the side of her head.

Sydney turned her face away and inhaled. "Why would I do that?!"

"Quit lying and just tell me where you keep it." His words pierced the surrounding stillness, especially near the sister's ear.

She ducked away from her bothersome brother, evading his elbow as she increased the outrage of her attitude and escalated the force of her reactions to combat her kin—quite justifiably if you ask me. "Oh my shit! Brush your fucking teeth!"

"That panda is as much mine as it is anyone's."

"Have you been eating garbage?! Jesus!"

Leunga reached out and grabbed her bicep, snarling, "This doesn't have to end badly for you," his eyes growing wider with each word he spoke.

"Seriously, I don't even have it anymore! You're *drunk*, aren't you?"

Her big brother began squeezing her lean muscle in short intervals, having just then realized she was potentially stronger than he anticipated. "I'm willing to fight you...in rock-paper-scissors for it."

Sydney wrenched her limb away from Leunga's grip, miraculously retaining her pocketed position. "Why the hell do you even want it anyway? The panda was the dumbest ass of a character!"

Leunga tightened his lips and glared at her. "You don't know what you're talking about. That panda was a fuckin' hot ass!"

"That doesn't even matter. Mom made me get rid of it because of *you*."

"Are you even listening to yourself? You're not making any sense anymore."

"Tough shit!" said Sydney just before she heard rustling off of the path and looked, catching Ricky's anxious eyes. She had become exhausted with the constant badgering of her big brother and knew she could rely on the younger to end the argument in her favor. As her off side sibling began backing up slowly, she beckoned him calmly. "Come here." Holding her sights on the complimentary brother, she suggested something to Leunga. "Let's ask Ricky."

"Whatever."

Ricky winced. "What...?"

His older sister shrugged her occupied arms. "You heard what we were talking about. Who do you think is right?"

Unexpectedly, the taller sibling stared at the path, plagued with some sort of hesitancy. "I think...I don't...want...not going to..."

"Aha! See, stupid? Rickins agrees with me."

Sydney was shocked; it was supposed to be common knowledge that her little brother always took her side during Leunga's tirades. Betrayed in a blindside by the boy, his name cracked in her throat as she spoke. "Ricky?!"

"Wait, I'm not—"

"You know what? Shut up." Struck by sudden opposition, the outnumbered young woman removed her hands from her pockets and lifted the shoulder strap of her cargo over her head in a huff and informed her brothers, "You guys are jerks." After she angrily tossed her things onto the trail, she told them, "Don't leave without me." Storming away as anyone would expect, she exited the area on the contradictory course Ricky had recently arrived from, and as she left she muttered, "Stupid shitheads. Why are boys such assholes?!"

What had started out as an unusual day—considering the fact that they had never before eaten breakfast in their mother's parents' house, nor slept there—was becoming increasingly troublesome. Despite many things, Sydney had given the aspect of finding her grandfather much of her recent attention, and after no time at all, she was supremely doubtful it could be done. Choosing then to forgo aiding her brothers in the search, she altered her outlook and focused on nature instead, but was finding that too to be difficult under the strange circumstances—especially when her older sibling still insisted on testing her tolerance for his senseless sixth sense when it comes to finding the perfect combination of things to say in order to ruin his sister's mood in a matter of milliseconds, regardless of his incredible age advantage and the maturity that should have come with it. Their casual hike had turned into a real downer for one damsel in despair.

As she trampled the fallen pine needles and heavy undergrowth of the forest, she happened to recall the source of her misery and gave it the cursing it had coming. "Stupid-ass bastard crap sword. What a piece of shit." Continuing her mindless walk, her brain was buzzing with frustration as she gazed only at the ground beneath her feet, letting the existence of her clomping flops be the only thing she allowed her head to hold onto. Boyfriend. She paused, wondering why that word decided to reappear in her thoughts, and then she looked up. Sydney was surrounded by an unusual sight for a densely forested area: an open clearing the size of a regulation softball stadium field bereft of any of the coniferous clutter you might come to expect. At the tips of her toes, she found ground, flat and ready to be ruined by a concrete creation. Above her bang-buried brow, she watched birds dancing with each other in the sky. On the opposite end of the opening, she could see a larger-than-average pond, complete with tranquil waterfall and gentle stream, and all at once, it drew her in completely.

She walked out into the wide-open wilderness. Glancing around she saw no discernable manmade trail to speak of, only an uncharted section of the woods no foot had yet dared to touch. This was a prime location for the interruptive activities of the populous, yet it appeared relatively untainted. Making her way toward the tall wall of water rushing from the rocks above, Sydney saw that the area was much like a grotto—a recess in the body of water surrounded by small trees, concealing and safe—and she was in awe of what she witnessed. Not far from the waterfall, a collection of boulders and upturned logs sat in a large semicircle facing the pond while producing a protective shield, as if placed by an ancient culture that revered well-positioned campsites. Her incidental discovery was almost too good to be true.

Sydney studied the area carefully and deemed it perfect for their excursion—quite possibly the only potential campsite she could ever lend her seal of approval to, as far as wild sites were concerned—but she was feeling mighty apprehensive about telling the other two about the camp, reminding herself of the way they ganged up against her again and again. If the group was unable to find a camp, they would be forced to return home where she could be rid of the boyish brats for good and go about her life as usual, but her primary reason for putting up with the hike in the first place was to be a finale to her generally untroubled, and worry-free, youth—and also as a means to forget recent heartaches. It was a difficult decision she felt unwilling to make for herself.

She placed her hands into her back pockets and stared out over the glistening pool. The sun warmed her face as she listened to the chirping in the trees. It was like it was meant to be—an ideal vacation spot, too perfect to pass up. With everything that could go wrong, and probably would go wrong, there was also a chance she might actually have fun—maybe even see some of the local wildlife. Wouldn't that be nice? And in all honesty, she wasn't all that upset about her abrupt exclusion from the mentality of the pack when she fully considered that the only alternative was to be like one of those brothers of hers; after all, she was used to her spot in the social minority—and more to the point, she really did enjoy her outcast existence, because she understood that it ultimately meant she was utterly unlike the rest, and that could never be a bad thing in her book. In an act of goodwill, she set aside her petty squabble with Leunga and took her rightful place as the bigger person, both figuratively and literally. Somewhat reluctantly, she made her way back along the makeshift path she created and called out to her brothers, "Hey, buttheads. I found a fuckin' camp."

Mission Accomplished

Leunga stared into the bright eyes looking up at him; irises of a vibrant green as vivid as a newborn leaf glowing in the sun pierced his mind. Picking at the lengthy brunet hooks protruding under his black wool hat and brushing them off to the side, he saw that his reflected image was surprisingly clear in the crystal pond, most likely due to the cloudless nature of the midday sky. The rustling of his siblings behind him went unnoticed as he splashed large handfuls of water on his face, soaking his skin and the sleeves of his long-sleeved T-shirt, as well as a decent portion of his short-sleeved polo cover shirt. The miniscule man stood, drenched in fresh water like the victim of a water balloon onslaught, and turned to his sister, who, at the time, was inspecting her new tent for a possible method of making it open. In light of their recent quarrel, he took this opportunity to peer out from his dripping driving cap and offer a few kind words. "Good job finding a camp, Syddles."

Knowing that his vaguely insincere comment would be the closest thing to a full apology she could ever hope for, Sydney accepted. "Thank you." Oldest brother and only sister were now suddenly on good terms with each other. Yay.

"This is cool!" proclaimed another. Ricky was less impressed with the secluded scenery than he was with the absolute lack of potential people. "It's like our secret hideout," he commented and continued to take account of their abundant inventory, removing one or two items from their luggage at a time and setting them on one of the large rocks auspiciously shaped like a shelf. Taking sole responsibility of the unpacking project for his family, he was happy to do so until he came across a sandwich marked "chicken salad." Presumably delicious. I wouldn't know. With the knowledge that his sister would never eat one, and after considering the fact that his brother sort of had an adverse reaction to the specific variety, Ricky knelt down next to his duffel bag and quietly unwrapped the sandwich stealthily, taking a large bite. He chewed the mouthful slowly, savoring the feast. A drop of water splashed against his bare arm, and he instantly looked to the sky to check for rain but instead found his brother hovering over him, staring at the sandwich.

"You know, I asked for one of those like two hours ago."

Ricky swallowed; the large lump of shredded chicken and indeterminate sauce seemed to be caught in his throat. "Okay, you want this one?" he asked and held up the unbitten half of his secret snack while struggling to force the wad in his neck down along its path to his stomach.

Leunga shook his furry head, water droplets dashing everywhere, flicking without remorse from his long shag. "No, give me that one." He pointed into the duffel bag at a sandwich labeled "PBJ-PB." "Yours looks horrendously gross."

Widely unnoticed where she was—standing, like, ten feet away— Sydney stretched the light green fabric of her encased shelter, pulling on what she assumed were support rods within the bundle. With her right arm outstretched, she wrenched her left arm back, much like a bow and arrow. She held this position, gritting her teeth, until her right thumb slipped out from beneath the coiled pole, sending the tent shrieking into her face. Her instinctive reaction to the impact was to protect the affected area from further destruction, so her free hand flew upward to the base of her nose, slamming against her mouth with a slap while simultaneously jamming her teeth into her lips again. Can't fight nature. Despite the added pain her palm supplied while attempting to protect her valiantly, she continued to press it against her mouth in mortification, concealing any superficial damage she may have sustained, along with her humiliated expression. Her embarrassment subsided when she noticed her brothers hadn't seen the incident, seeing as how they were preoccupied with the objects in Ricky's bag and crumpling paper or something. Steadily, she released her lip grip and tapped her mouth with her fingertips to check for blood, and upon seeing a clean hand she returned to her task of unraveling her nemesis.

"Is this mold?" wondered Ricky as he held up his chicken salad wedge for his brother to inspect.

Leunga took another exceedingly large bite of his peanut butter-less sandwich before edging closer to his little brother's hand. He noticed an almost microscopic speck of green dust along the crust of the sourdough bread. "Hmmm, could be. What does mold look like?"

"Like this, I guess..."

"Here we go." The eldest, and by far the *wisest*, sibling reached over and pinched off the edge of his consuming companion's sandwich, leaving the remaining bread soggy with pond water. He held the crust close to his face for further analysis and proudly announced, "I got it."

Ricky stared at his ruined sandwich and said, "Thank you..." Slowly he placed it to his mouth and took a careful bite, unsure if it was still edible. Dysentery.

Shoving another mammoth bite into his own face as he watched his sibling slowly devour the soured sandwich, Leunga was forced to realize just how long it had been since he studied Ricky at their grandmother's breakfast counter that morning. Filled with the urge to uncover what time and relative dimension in space it was at that very moment, he looked to the sky, staring at the sun for almost one full second before he determined that it had probably moved since he last noticed it hours ago. He pushed the contents of his mouth to one side, enabling him to speak. "Goddamn, it seems like we've been awake forever. This day just won't end." Swallowing his remaining snack, he glanced over his shoulder at his sister and said, "Hey, Syddy, what time is it?"

Placing the folded tent under her armpit as she ceased her endeavor, Sydney held up her forearms vertically in front of her face and answered, "I'm not wearing a watch, dink." Although her wrists were vastly covered in an array of morosely colored wristbands, some with sharp metal studs, none of the objects appeared to be any form of timepiece, be it digital, mechanical, or even atomic sundial.

Ricky finished his squalid sandwich and shuddered. He looked to Leunga with a pertinent question. "Uh, hey, why did Grammy wrap these up all weird?" Noticing the strangely familiar fashion of the deli method their grandmother employed for containing their sandwiches as a way of forgetting other things, the teen boy expressed his confusion regarding the wax paper wrapper he was now having trouble finding a refuse bin for. "It's...weird. She way should have just used those baggies I saw in her pantry. She had tons."

"Oh, yeah, I made her do that," Leunga replied.

His brother stopped stocking their new rock shelf with provisions immediately after having begun the task again. "Why?"

And the eldest shrugged back. "Why not?"

Ricky had to think about it for no time at all. "Good point."

From her seat out of earshot of her brothers' mumbled conversation, Sydney stretched her head their way to try and hear anything she could, attempting to feel a little more included on their neat little vacation. "What are you guys talking about?"

"Nothing," someone said. "Shut up."

"You shut up."

"No, you shut up."

Seeing as how it was way past their lunchtime, according to his desire to eat another helping of their rapidly dwindling rations, Ricky spoke to Sydney without looking. "Dude, do you want one of the sandwiches? They're way good." And in quick anticipation of her presumed reply, he began digging into his duffel for one untainted by animal flesh.

"Yeah, okay, give me a peanut butter one," she stated somewhat sullenly. She sat on an overturned log—a wooden seat of the simplest construction placed in propinquity to the fire pit they began preparing earlier that afternoon before it became too tedious and they all stopped digging—and furrowed her brow in thought. Annoyed with the lack of progress she made with her tent situation, Sydney silently gave up and set the green bundle down next to her on the lumber, resting her chin on a strut created by her right arm while she awaited her lunch and deliberated on her dire distaste for her compounding camp-wise conundrums without so much as a twist on her slightly swelling lips.

A very investigational little Leunga stood next to his squatting sibling in secrecy and whispered, "Hey, do you have a watch?"

Ricky paused his search and glanced up at his brother's face before directing his gaze at his very visible wristwatch: a large silver analog timepiece with a secondary digital display he received many birthdays earlier, held stationary along his arm by a navy blue sweatband worn underneath the watch band. "Um... *Yes*?"

"Good."

The younger one waited an extended moment before asking, "Do you, uh, want to know the time?"

Leunga mulled over the question, carefully analyzing each of the many layers buried within the syntax of his brother's words. "Sure, why the hell not."

Ricky performed a motion he was well acquainted with, flicking his right wrist toward his face. The hands of the clock had long since stopped moving; however, the digital portion functioned flawlessly. "It is...a little after one o'clock."

"The chrono mage hath spokened."

Sydney pivoted her head against her hand and looked over at her elder brother. "So that means you are officially late for work now. Good job."

Leunga glanced at his younger sister. "I'm late every day, and I told you a thousand times already, I got somebody to cover for me."

She shot him a puzzled expression and expressed, "I don't think you ever said that."

"I did." At no point in the last thirty-seven hours did Leunga utter any combination of those words in the same sentence. "Maybe you just weren't there when I did."

"Hmm. Maybe." Dropping her sights to the unfinished pit taunting her tootsies, the young maiden mulled over the amount of effort it would take on her behalf to convince her brothers to complete the excavation without her help, when suddenly, in one fluid motion, Ricky pulled out a paper-wrapped snack food from his cargo, turned, and tossed it at Sydney. Without effort or forethought she easily picked it out of the air with her unoccupied hand as it closed in on her face, never letting her gaze leave the partial pit. "Thanks."

Leunga left his post next to Ricky, moving swiftly to a site a few feet behind his sister, eyeing her lime green companion on the pristinely debarked log and sorely distraught by what he witnessed. The tent clearly should have been opened by then. Aghast by the incompetence of this supposedly adult adolescent, the most aged member of the immediate family figured his sister hadn't attempted the task yet, leaving him no other option than to take matters into his own hands. He placed an extended middle finger against the tip of his chin, planning out his next move. Confident in the fact that Sydney was almost definitely unable to see him maybe, the slacker sibling slowly stretched out toward the tent, keeping his feet stationary while not allowing a sound to escape his perimeter. With his extended digits, he cautiously pinched the outer ring and pulled the tent to himself, amazingly without anyone noticing the movement—aside from us.

As his sister peeled the sourdough slices apart to check the innards, she passed a touching tongue over her fattening lip and accurately observed, "Goddamn, camping sucks turds."

"Yep," Ricky replied.

Sydney went on to explain her well-thought-out opinion on the matter, though it was entirely unnecessary because everyone already agreed. "I'm okay with hiking and looking around at shit, but this here is stupid without Dad doing everything for us."

"I know. It's like...uh...yeah."

No one the wiser, the master tent blaster pulled at the edges of the green disc with all of his upper body strength, but it was to no avail. He paused to check and see if Sydney was in any way interested in glancing back at his pursuit, but she appeared to be engrossed with her lunch, taking annoyingly tiny nibbles. Leunga squinted at Ricky to see if his young brother had noticed her maddening behavior as well, but the boy had already returned to removing his luggage onto the accompanying rock and was verily ignored after that. Gripping the green ring with both hands, the eldest shook it back and forth while quietly muttering to himself, "Some kind of bastard sorcerer crafted this beast." With his left arm outstretched, he wrenched his right arm back, much like a bow and arrow—and much like a mirror of his sister's previous attempt. He held this position, gritting his teeth, until his right hand inadvertently released its grip on the slick fabric, flipping the tent into the back of Sydney's head.

As the flexible carbon tubing within the material came into contact with her oblivious cranium, a thunderous crack stilled the air. The abrupt impact forced her face to jerk forward, causing her to cough out the food in her mouth. In that brief moment of shock, Sydney released the gentle grasp she had on her sandwich, sending it bouncing across the dirt and into the unfinished fire pit. She cleared her throat, jumping up from her seat and twirling around, snatching the tent from her older brother's hand. "Assface, you made me drop my sandwich!"

Leunga quickly spread his feet apart and bent his knees into an attack position. Raising his fists close to his chest in preparation to block her accurate punches, he began ducking and weaving in place, keeping his eyes locked on his sister.

Sydney glowered at the floating, stinging nuisance in her face before checking the tent for any damage he may have caused to it. She was deeply frustrated with the discus and with the dingus for obvious reasons, which quickly manifested in her aggressive flicking of the broad board off in the direction of the nearby body of water. As it majestically glided toward a watery grave, the tent popped open, slowing its flight considerably and creating a fully functional refuge from all manner of insect and pest alike, landing upright with the door facing the center of their campsite magically. Sydney laughed triumphantly at the eventual ease of its construction. "Fuckin' finally!"

"I loosened it for you."

"I'm pretty sure my *skull* loosened it." Twice, but her brothers didn't need to know that. "Dick-ass." As she rubbed the sore contact point on the back of her head, her fingers ran over a French braid that had been created in spite of her unvocalized wishes. To her surprise, she could scarcely notice it anymore—most likely because she was largely unaccustomed to her somewhat recent habit of allowing the hair to hang freely—however, the fact remained that she felt ridiculous and uncomfortable and needed to restore balance to the world. Before completely obliterating her grandmother's work of art, Sydney considered the fact that their group would most likely travel back to the elderly woman's house when the woodland debacle was finished, and she had absolutely no desire to hurt the feelings of her grandmother. But she insisted on removing the ever-present reminder of that destructive conversation from the previous day nevertheless. Boyfriend. She faced Ricky, gripping the intertwined blond collection in her left hand, and said, "Hey, do either of you guys know how to braid hair?"

Her younger brother continued lining the rock with foodstuffs and replied without looking at her. "You're looking at me, aren't you? Why would I possibly know how to do that?"

"I can't make it as tight as it is by myself."

Astonished by the ever-hasty change of events, Leunga suddenly noticed he wasn't being pummeled to death by heavy metal accessories for some snapping action he accidentally unleashed against the back of some girl's noggin. His sister was far less angry with the situation than she should've been. It was confusing. Leunga warily relaxed his guard and answered her previous inquiry. "Yeah, I do."

"Are you sure?" Sydney confirmed and grabbed the upper elastic, rolling it down to the end of her braid in anticipation of his response. Logically, Leunga could have learned the skill at some point, but fully trusting the words of her older brother was not an easy task.

"Abso-cutely! It'll look even better after I style it up," he said at an acceptable decibel before lowering his voice to a whisper. "Promise."

Sydney looked down at her smaller sibling's face, carefully studying his expression, which happened to be completely blank. She unrolled the remaining elastic from the tip of her black-tipped, blond braid, and with spread fingers she accepted his offer halfheartedly, combing her way down through the shimmering golden lines, unlocking her conditioned mane, and lumping it to one side over her left shoulder for inspection—almost as if she couldn't tease her tresses back to a tousled comfort fast enough. She examined the bent and curled nature of her normally straight hairs with her left hand and grunted in protest.

An older guy gasped and clutched his throat. "Oh, wait! Stop! Fuck! Nope! Never mind. It's dreadlocks I know how to do. Definitely not braiding, are you kidding me?! You'll just have to avoid washing it for a while." He eyed his sister's long and somewhat messy locks and added, "That should be easy for you."

Sydney tilted her head back while closing her umbrageous eyelids and slapped her leg in aggravation. "Fuck!"

Leunga rapidly returned to his attack position at the sudden outburst of his sister. "Whoa now. I thought you hated braids." He waited, poised, ready for her to strike at any moment, and prepared to use anything in his surroundings as a possible weapon—although the thought of using the oxidized blade harnessed to his back didn't occur to him, which is a good thing. "You would look..." he started before he stopped. Suddenly struggling to finish his thought, he couldn't bear giving an actual compliment to his sister about her appearance, so he simply blurted the first few words that came to mind as uncreepily as he possibly could. "*Nice*, with dreadlocks." What a creepy thing to say.

Noticing her brother's awkward stance, Sydney scoffed. "Easy, killer." She shook her hair to its neutral position across her back, reestablishing her choppy, asymmetrical, alternative fashion in order to maintain her nonconformist-in-a-conformist-sort-of-way style and explained, "I'll just teach you—teach *Ricky* how to braid it before we go back to Grandma's."

Ricky's heart sank. "Do we have to?"

"It'll be easy." She nudged an elbow in her other brother's direction. "We can practice on Greasy."

Leunga thought briefly of his wild, extra-large brunet curls and wondered if they were long enough to be braided. Maybe, maybe not. "Like hell you will."

"Don't worry. You'll be asleep."

"I will...*never* be asleep."

Hoping that a change of subject might change his sister's mind about subjecting him to her lessons, Ricky stood and dusted off his turquoise sweatpants, content with his completion of setting up their camping pantry. He carefully arranged the items according to type and urgency of use, placing the perishables closer to the front and leaving some unnecessary items, like his martial arts weaponry, in the duffel bag set off to the side of the rock. Feeling like he had accomplished something truly useful to the group, he nodded. "So, yeah. I'm done now."

With the day somewhat back on track, Sydney strolled over to her taller brother and gave the guy an actual pat on the back that didn't embarrass her briefly at all. At first, Ricky thought it was Leunga. Side-by-side with her young sibling, the middle sister joined him in the admiration of his display. "It looks...*nice*." She reached out and grabbed a new sandwich with the hope that she would be able to eat it uninterrupted. "You know we have to pack up this stuff at night so bears don't come and kill us though, right?"

Ricky felt the presence of a person leave his side as he stared blankly at the exhibit. "Glad I only spent forty minutes on this…" Suddenly, learning to make a braid didn't seem like such a terrible thing to live through after all.

Leunga poked his face out of the zipped doorway of the lime green tent he was suddenly occupying and shook his head. "This is never gonna be big enough for all three of us. You two would be better off sleeping outside," he added, retracting back into the safety of the microfiber cage and completing the zipper seal.

"Holy hell!" In her haste, Sydney carefully set down her second sandwich and rushed over to the tent. "I'm the one that found it and brought it all the way out here! It's mine!" she said and searched for the outer zipper handle, but found that Leunga had hidden it within the enclosure. Pinching the corner of the doorway, she could tell that its inhabitant was holding the zipper shut, preventing her possible ingress. "Come on… Leunga, open the door," she griped and gripped the support strut, shaking the entire structure briefly.

"I can't."

Sydney jiggled the tent some more. "Yes you can. I just want to see how big it is inside." That, and forcibly remove the usurper. A moment later, she stopped rattling the cage to listen for her brother's next quip, but he was unpredictably quiet. She stood by, perfectly still, paying close attention to the mild rustling emanating from within the green pyramid. The crackling of the canvas steadily moved around to the opposite end. Slowly, Sydney positioned herself next to the source, just as something round pressed against the wall, stretching the fabric outward. She quietly squatted next to the object, careful not to let any part of her cleanish pants touch the dirt floor of the forest. Moving her face close to the protrusion, she checked her bracelets to make sure they wouldn't fall off before raising her open palm above her head.

A coy voice emitted from the entity. "Are you there?"

Her hand dropped, striking the side of the tent with a dull slap.

The construction quaked with the sudden erratic movement of its occupant, tumbling over in the process. Leunga squealed, "Holy bejeezus! Stop, you swine! Stop it! Okay, I'm out!" The zipper tore open, releasing the prized pothead within. "This thing is like an oven anyway..."

Next to his duffel and bedroll, a deeply dejected Ricky sat on the soil with his knees at his chest. He stared into the void of the bag that would need to be refilled, disconsolate, before turning his attention to his older siblings for what he hoped would be a beaming distraction from his dilemma. And lucky for him, he was correct for once.

Leunga reached an arm out of the entrance of the toppled tent and slithered out along the earthen floor, spreading a cloud of dust as he wriggled his way to freedom. "You didn't have to beat me senseless, you thug."

Standing, Sydney corrected her overturned tent. "Get up. I barely touched you." A generous act if true. With full consideration aimed at the small lump forming on the back of her head, she was entitled to use as much force as she deemed necessary, which, as it turns out, may not have been that much.

"People go to jail for defacing priceless art. You realize that?!" Leunga slid along the ground, crawling on his belly, creating ample space between himself and the green kiln; however, his heightened temperature problem seemed to continue well away from the tent. He squirmed closer to the core of the camp, effectively coating himself in a fair amount of filth, and grumbled, "Godfrey, it must be at least three hundred degrees out *here* too!"

Ricky rocked back and forth on the ground, watching Leunga slink toward the center of the site. "Dude, then why don't you take off the long-sleeve shirt?"

"I would, but I think it's gonna rain today."

"I'm almost positive...well, like, *pretty sure* that was supposed to be yesterday, and it didn't. Still." Abruptly realizing where he was and what he wasn't doing while remaining seated on the warmed earth, Ricky removed his borrowed bedroll from its inconvenient storage spot between the large rocks neighboring his duffel and fluffed it accordingly. Making sure not to let the part of the roll where his head would be later that night touch the ground, he positioned it parallel to his torso and leaned along the soft cushion. Then and only then, the fellow with the fauxhawk folded his arms and forced his head to flop back, basking in the sociable sun kissing his lightly tanned skin without the impediment of the foliage, allowing his eyes to close and letting his mind relax for a bit. Almost alone at last.

Sydney opened the flap of the tent and peaked in to assess the damage. "Ahhh...gross bastard, you dripped water everywhere."

Picking up and eating an unattended sandwich lying on a nearby log, Leunga quietly watched as his sister fixed the positioning of the shelter. As she shifted the lightweight haven, he noticed that she too was wearing multiple layers, but with far fewer sleeves—the entirety of her clothing, on the other hand, was significantly darker, and therefore, dangerous. "Hey," he hollered. "Why aren't *you* boiling in your beans?"

After making some final adjustments—and without looking at Leunga at all—Sydney somehow knew he was speaking to her. "Who says I'm not?" She's not.

"What the hell does that mean?" Leunga frowned as he glanced at his little brother, taking a swipe at the air toward Ricky. "Pay attention!"

Shoving her hands into her pockets—the front pockets, not the back ones...actually, it doesn't matter, either way works—their sylph sibling snickered as she searched for a snappy response. "Well, for one thing, it means I'm not a whiny little bitch like you."

Leunga took another bite of the puzzlingly placed sandwich and agreed. "You're very right. It means you're a whiny *big* bitch like you."

Sydney furrowed her brow and closed her eyes, frowning—not in aggravation at her kin's comment, but in disappointment with herself for setting up such an obvious zinger. "Shut up. Get the camp ready."

"Ready?"

As he continued to recline against the tightly coiled sleeping bag, Ricky momentarily extended one arm, pulling at the cuff of the oddly breathable greenish sweatpants resting at the base of his knees, and opting to form an out-of-the-blue opinion aloud. "You know, I like, hate these pants—*so much*—but they are surprisingly cool and comfortable." Facing his brother, he saw an opportunity to rid himself of his torment. "If you're overheating, we can trade shorts for a little while, man." Like, at least until the end of the camping trip.

"Huge new rule: no bastard boots allowed in my goddamn tent."

Leunga crumpled the empty sandwich wrapper in his hands and tossed it at his brother's duffel bag, missing it completely, of course. He looked over at Ricky and, with teeth clenched, he inhaled sharply, saying, "I can't. See, if I change one piece it would compromise the overall quality of the ensemble. You understand."

Ricky unfolded his arms and entwined his fingers behind his firm fauxhawk, supporting the weight of his head as he closed his eyes and sighed contentedly, deciding to ignore the declination of his proposal. "That does make sense."

With her tent entrance—or tentrance—left open to dry it out, Sydney looked over at her brothers. Leunga, plastered with a thin layer of mud, was recumbent in the unfinished fire pit and staring at the bench-shaped log above his head, while Ricky appeared to be dozing on top of his rolled sleeping bag. Surprised to see such a sedated scene after assuming her big brother had pertinent objectives he wished to accomplish, she began walking toward the kernel of their comfort-conducive site and soured her words with a frown. "Lazy asses." As she reached her older brother's feet, she stopped. "Is this all you guys are going to do today?"

"Tired."

Sydney tapped Leunga's oversized work boots with her own thin-layered sneaker. "Come on, dink, we gotta start looking for Grandpa while it's still sunny." She then glanced around the camp suddenly. "Where is my sandwich...?"

Ricky shook his head, shaking his entire balanced torso in the process, and grunted. "Please. Let's just not for right now, man. Please."

Leunga kicked blindly at his sister's foot in retaliation. "I'm with Ricks. You can go look for him solo a minute. Have fun and be merry. Wonderful time."

Sydney's head swiftly slumped at their response—a generous helping of her freshly free-flowing follicles falling forward to veil her very annoyed face. "Duh. Like I care if we ever find him...but something better happen soon. So far this plot has been all kinds of boring—I mean, the hike...has." Nice.

"This is gonna be a long vacation if you keep trying to make us do stuff."

"Quest."

"Whatever," Sydney said indifferently. "I just want us to stop wasting everybody's time."

Shortly after succumbing to his desires, Leunga reached over his own face and stroked the smooth bark of the log next to his head and cooed. That information will come in handy never. "Don't worry," he guaranteed in a strange voice that was very identical to his own, addressing the still-standing portion of the party. "I have a feeling something exhilarating and shocking is going to happen soon. Maybe even right...now."

It's Not Haunting without S'mores

Nothing happened for the next eight hours.

After only one full day of hardly working at it, their camp was practically complete. Just about. Actually, not at all. As the sluggish summer sun began to set in the fiery sky, Sydney was growing concerned over the lack of progress the group had made with their still-unfinished means of warmth and protection for the night. She knelt on the tough soil, hacking at the fire pit with the collapsible shovel provided to them by their grandmother, attempting to make the chasm a suitable depth for the miniature bonfire she had planned. A bead of sweat rolled down her forehead, collecting with the prior drops in the dark seclusion of her thicker-than-average eyebrows. Pausing to wipe her brow with her grime-covered hands, Sydney streaked dirt across her face, muchly in addition to the previous smudges she compiled during the twenty minutes she had already spent chipping away at the pit. By the way, it was a great day.

"You should really be seeing this sunset," Leunga strongly suggested, standing atop the tallest rock surrounding their camp and gazing through a small break in the tree line at the smoky sun setting over the horizon. His right hand sank deep within his pocket as he placed his flask to his lips with his free hand, wobbling from side to side due to the noxious fluid comingling with his blood. "All that pollution really adds to the effect. You know what would make this better?"

Sydney gave an annoyed grunt and looked up at him through dusty bangs. "Drugs?!"

"That too, but I was thinking of mi querida by my side."

His sister returned to her undertaking, mumbling to herself. "*Querida.* Am I supposed to know what that means, you stupid bastard, letting me dig this whole damn thing alone..."

"What?"

"What?"

Leunga swallowed a fairly decent swig of liquor and coughed. "I thought I heard you say something."

"Nope." Sydney tossed a pile of dirt aside, closing in on the completion of the pit. She glanced into the trees behind her, wondering if Ricky had become lost. After sending him and their older brother out to gather firewood, the boys entered the nearby trees in search of kindling and appropriate fire logs. As of yet, only one of them had returned—and without any pyre fuel, no less. Only about fifteen minutes had passed, but it was becoming dark rapidly. Just as she was considering forming a search party, she saw her tall, younger brother in the corner of her eye emerging from the trees on the opposite side of the large pond, and it instantly caused her to raise her head and shout, "Hey, why are you over there?"

A distant voice echoed over the calm water. "I, um...don't know. I never crossed the river..." In addition to the serene waterfall created from an elevated stream, the pond also emptied into a much wider tributary heading in the direction of the ocean, creating a protective wall of water along the south side of their camp. "That's kinda...I dunno. Stuff."

Sydney stood, satisfied with her accomplishment—or at least, the amount of accomplishment she could accomplish. She dropped the shovel in the direction of her brother's duffel and shouted once again across the pond. "Just hurry back. We need to start the fire soon." Shaking the surplus dirt from her hands, she glanced down at the fire pit, coming face-to-face with a surprise Leunga, startling her excessively.

Her sneaking sibling stared down at the pit he was standing in and complimented, "This is lovely, but it's still five hundred degrees out here.

Why would we need a huge fire?" The pit was hardly huge, though it could have been if anyone else had helped.

Calming her nerves, the woman walked to the body of water and replied, "Buttface, it's to scare off bears, wolves, big deers, cougars, and whatever else is out here." All animals she wished to see but not come into contact with. Sydney squatted by the warmed water and gently splashed cleansing handfuls over her forearms and face, carefully avoiding her thick eyeliner. "Plus, we need some light for when it gets dark, duh."

"Scaring animals you say? Well hell. We could've just used the flares Grammy gave us." Leunga sat on one of the camp's log benches and began invading the side pouches of their younger brother's luggage. "I know I saw some in here."

Sydney dried her arms against the lower inches of her lavender camisole cover shirt while carefully avoiding the faded black T-shirt underneath. Squinting at her brother, she questioned the accuracy of his recent statement. "She did not," she stated with certitude—although there was a moment during the great packing of that morning during which the middle sister was absent and collecting other beneficial camptastic items of fundamental function from other areas of the house. "Did she?"

Leunga went wild with delight at the sight of a black tube in the trove hidden away at the bottom of the bag—an item a little more than a foot long and just a tad wider than the narrow handle of a baseball bat, or common house broom. "Hah! See? I told you!" He snatched up the cylindrical object from its hideaway in a hurry, until he noticed an identical piece rise as well, connected to the first by six inches of heavy-duty nylon cable sprouting from a single tip of each cylinder, and he went wild with disappointment when he recognized what it really was. "Shit. Never mind, this is Pretty Boy's nunchaku."

Grabbing the martial arts tool from her brother's intoxicated grip without asking, Sydney held the weapon with her left hand and instinctively began swinging it slowly, hypnotized by the swirl of the shiny black item glistening in the light of the disappearing sun. "Kinda cool," she remarked. "Wonder how it's supposed to cause damage..." Guessing correctly quickly as she lost a little control and felt it smack into her knuckle, she restarted the steady twirling of the baton and glanced at the back of her brother's unsuspecting head—who remained preoccupied with his search—but decided not to test the bludgeoning power of the club just yet.

"Here we go." Leunga held up a stylish silver item, clearly having no resemblance to any form of chemical flare. "I founded it."

Sydney watched her careful swinging of the pendulous nunchaku, mouth agape, before looking at her older brother's hand for a second and returning her gaze to the black cudgel. "That's a flashlight."

In his mildly drunken stupor, the stoner realized what he was holding and raised his eyebrows in amazed alarm. "Ooh! It's one of those stupid rechargeable windup flashlights! I love these stupid things!" As soon as his fingers would let him, he spun his black felt driving hat around, brim facing backward, indicating the importance of his following actions, and commenced a sequence that would surely be a gift to the world. Holding the device close to his chest, he gripped the bulk of it tightly with his left hand while pinching the crank gingerly with his right. He began cranking slowly but rapidly built up a decent amount of speed. It broke almost immediately. The reckless wrecker held out the separated pieces in each hand for all to see and added, "That was fun!"

In predictable fashion, his sister stopped spinning the taller teen's treacherous baton and allowed it to forcefully collide against her arm before she snatched the lamp from Leunga to prevent any more damage from being wrought upon it and to check the amount of power he had accumulated by turning it on. The light it produced was weak and dissipated less than a foot after leaving the mechanism. Shining the light instinctively in her older brother's eyes, Sydney was saddened, but not surprised. "Now we really gotta make a fire before it gets dark."

Just in time to see none of it, Ricky arrived silently behind them, his arms loaded with a wide variety of logs. Panting and attempting to catch his breath, he checked his right shoe, which was sopping wet—his left foot, however, was reasonably dry. He sighed with relief before noticing his sibling raiding his belongings. "Uh, here's the wood..." he informed warily, dropping the shipment and scattering the firewood beside his feet.

Sydney turned to her younger brother, hiding his nunchaku behind her back as she shined the delicate beam of light in his face. "Thanks, friend."

"Sure." The new arrival wiped his forehead with the rolled sleeve of his gi just as he saw his sister nonchalantly drop something behind her into his duffel bag, but he decided it was more prudent to rest his fatigued feet instead of finding out what it was.

As the martial arts weaponry dashed past his face into the cavity, Leunga looked to the sky frantically. "What the hell was that?!"

Happy enough to see someone had done what he said he would, Sydney kicked at the logs gathered by her brother and noticed a common characteristic: greenish tinge and stringy endings. "Wait..." she questioned cautiously, "are all of these alive?"

Dryly, Ricky swallowed. "Yeah. I had to, like, break them off the trees. It sucked."

The pervasive darkness encompassing them hastened one sibling's actions. She picked up a few of the branches and studied them. "Shite," she winced. "I don't think these will burn..." Gathering the smallest twigs together to form the tinder for the blaze, she dropped them into the pit along with some pine needles she discovered earlier that day near the encircling trees. "Throw me some matches," she ordered, looking to Leunga and holding out her hand—but only because he was closest to their junk.

The lad by the luggage took his gaze off of the sky to see if she meant for him to do it. She did indeed. Straining to grab the large box of matches on the rock shelf from his seat, he flicked at the edge of the cardboard with his outstretched fingers, barely catching the corner of it just right and forcing it to fall to the ground and slide to his foot. Leunga lazily lifted the container, not realizing it was partially opened by its collision with the ground, and shouted, "Incoming!" Lobbing the box with about as little effort and accuracy as anyone could manage, he sent it wobbling through the wind to his sister, where the cardboard drawer dizzily slid out of its shell, effectively releasing its chemical cargo in midair. The perfect pitch.

With her dominant hand held in front of her face ready to catch an easy pop fly, she clutched down on a handful of strike-anywhere sticks as the rest were scattered about in the darkening dust beside her. Sydney opened her paw, finding at least a dozen matches, and thanked him. "Nice throw. Dumbfuck."

Earning it without much question, Ricky rested on the nearest log, quietly keeping to himself after an ordeal of a solo search he would rather not discuss with us. Ignoring his cynical sister's criticism of his coniferous collection, he removed the drenched sneaker of his right foot, having slipped off of a stepping stone and landing knee-deep in the cool water of the westward rivulet. Shaking the soaked shoe toward the wide-open wilderness behind him, he watched while Sydney hunkered down, shielding the fledgling flames of each match she lit in an attempt to ignite the kindling beneath the twigs—matches, I might add, that his sister lit dangerously close to her profuse, loose hair—and it was all he could care to do in the decaying light of his summer day misspent far away from home.

Match after match burned out before Sydney could manage to light the dry pine needles, and perhaps it was the sweet humidity of the twilight air or an extremely inopportune bout of misfortune, but she had exhausted her handheld supply without so much as a smoking spark. Exhaling noisily, she leaned away from the pit, closing her eyes and kneeling in a circle of matches strewn across the floor. "Anyone else wanna try?"

Accepting the challenge before this so-called "anyone else"—possibly to prove his pruned pines had potential—Ricky restored his soggy sneaker to its rightful right-foot place and moved in next to Sydney, careful to avoid crushing any wayward matches beneath his gigantic feet. As he fell to one knee, the male teen looked at the fiery options available to him, but rather than using any of the dozens of readily available matches scattered neatly across the ground, he went for the only one that didn't have any dirt on it yet, which just happened to be stuck in his sister's hair.

Like the pedestal for an impossible prize, and looking like a vivid representation of a singed matchstick itself, Sydney's floppy tresses held the closest chemical-tipped stick in her younger brother's perception; thus, he promptly scooped it out without her detection and grabbed the matchbox sleeve in her extended hand. The fire-starter was dragged over the coarse edge of the cardboard, where it burst into a quick flame. Ricky held the lit stick in the core of the pit. Within seconds the tinder ignited, chaining to the kindling as it crackled into light, and the handsome hero saved the day. Or night.

Smelling something close to smoke, Sydney opened her eyes, shocked to see an active fire. "Whoa, shit. That was lucky!" She glanced back as her svelte sibling stood and stooped back to his seat a few feet behind her, saying, "Good job."

Ricky wearily forced a smile, fully prepared to end his dreadful day.

Leunga gawked hypnotically at the growing flame as his brother sat near their sister and handed Sydney log after log to fuel the blaze. He quickly abandoned his search for a phantom flare and edged closer to the bonfire begging for his attention. The twilight quickly wound down as the comforting heat of the roast replaced the swelter of the early-summer daylight. The warmth embraced him, soothing as it caressed his clothing, dancing across his spellbound expression over emerald eyes, and caressing his cares away. "If I wasn't so sure that fires sucked at saying me stuff in English, I'd swear this thing just told me to go fuck myself."

"Jesus!" Sydney screamed. "I just got hit in the face by a big-ass spark! Holy hell. That freaked me out."

With a mighty look of boredom on his face, Ricky passed more wood and wondered, "Fire much?"

"No kidding. By the time it gets dark, this thing is either gonna burn out already or burn down half the forest for us."

"Well," Leunga said, wiping the drool from his face, "as long as it's not our half of the forest, then I think we'll be just fine."

•   •   •

The violent blaze illuminated their allotted area of the wicked wilderness. The gentle, smoky summer smell of burning bark filled the night air with serenity. As the waxing moon was replacing the setting sun—and after dodging a few dozen more gigantic sparks—the siblings each situated their nocturnal nests along the open-ended center of the camp, completing the circle started by the partial ring of rocks and benches. They claimed their own personal spaces in order of shortest to tallest—or oldest to youngest; it's the same either way. When that situation deeply upset Leunga—who expressed his aversion to being anywhere near his sister's tent over and over again—Ricky took the middle. After preparing their sleeping bags in the moonlit dusk, the three sat around the fire, staring at the ballet of glowing sparks shooting skyward in a vain attempt to join the stars.

"Has the smoke killed any of us yet?"

"Don't think so," Sydney yawned. "So what's next on your *epic quest* itinerary?"

Leunga shook his head and narrowed his sights at his younger sister. "Such a rotten mouth on this one..."

She wiped her humid eyes while looking off into the invisible tree line. "It means, what do you have planned for us next, dipshit."

Her brother grinned in disbelief and said, "Plan? Damn, man, this is the plan! Hanging out and having a good time in the woods." He reached out and patted someone on the shoulder. "Right, Rick?"

Ricky jabbed the fire with a long twig. "I'm not."

And the eldest nodded, persuading, "See? Nothin' doin'." But then, he suddenly realized he could no longer feel his tongue, or his teeth, and became extremely alarmed momentarily.

Unwillingly forced into a leadership role for the night, Sydney began a more constructive conversation. "Okay. For tomorrow, we need a plan—"

Leunga leaned a little closer and whispered loudly, "Okay, tomorrow."

"Yeah, we should make a plan for finding Grandpa, or for sight-seeing. Whatever... Either one. I don't care."

He leaned a little more. "*Plan.*"

"...Right. Maybe we should leave the sleeping bags here and make our way back to that path we were on and follow it until it ends. Um...we'll take the canteens and some protein bars—"

He leaned a little less. "A plan."

"Shut the hell up!" Sydney exclaimed as her eyes widened with frustration; the glow of the flame reflected off of her glossy brown irises furiously. Super scary.

Leunga held out his hands palm-down and fanned the air slowly in an attempt to lower the volume of the room while he searched for his teeth. "Okay, okay. Here's the plan." He paused, gliding his tongue along the outer stratum of his dentin. Relieved with the rediscovery, he continued. "We go to bed right now and then make a plan when we wake up tomorrow at noon."

Ricky's eyelids drooped again. He glanced at the watch on his right arm. I think it read five minutes to eleven. That's a sensible hour to call it a night. "I'm with that."

Relinquishing her very temporary spot in the leadership limelight, Sydney complied with the wills of her brothers—as she often did—and shrugged. "Sure. Whatever."

Inside the instant it took for his big sister to gift him her permission, the youngest stood up, anxious to enter the comfort of the dream world waiting within his weary head. Staggering sleepily to his sleeping bag, he prepared it for his imminent access, unzipping the edge and folding back the flap. He sat on the open comforter, carefully keeping his dust-covered shoes off of the plush fabric interior, and without untying them, he pushed his sneakers off with a controlled flick of each foot pressed against the back of the opposite heel. Ricky removed the damp sock from his right pedal and slid his long legs into the cool embrace of his sleeping bag, very ready to close his eyes in the comfort of the summer moonshine and enter his well-earned slumber.

"But, I'm not tired yet," informed a fully-formed Leunga as he tapped his chin with the tips of his right hand's fingers.

Sydney stared at the inferno before her, clawing under her tight pleather neckwear to alleviate her chafing skin. "Me either. We should play a game."

"On *what*? There's not even a decent TV out here."

"Fair enough."

Suddenly, Leunga slapped his knees twice in quick succession and loudly announced, "Oh! Guess what? I just barely thought of a real thing that we can actually do! Let's go full out cliché and tell horror stories around the fire!"

Sydney smiled at the suggestion, raising her left eyebrow in response. "Oh, I'm going first. I know a really good one! Addy made it up and it scared me shitless."

The eldest was intrigued, and so am I. "Don't keep us all waiting!"

Wasting no time readjusting herself for suspense's sake, a sister sibling leaned toward her brothers, Leunga more so than Ricky, and began. "Okay. Once—"

"Hey, kids!" interrupted a very jovial voice that came soaring forth from the surrounding darkness. "Nice camp!"

Sydney released a short scream at an ear-splitting pitch she had not reached in almost a decade. She quickly balled her fists inches in front of her angered face, and fired an equally angry-sounding noise from her nostrils.

Leunga clutched his chest and began burping heavily. "Oh god!" he panted and reached a hand toward the round, pale moon. "I'm way too beautiful to die! Good story! Good shit!"

Ricky calmly rolled over in his sleeping bag and opened his eyes.

An elderly man wearing earthy camping attire materialized as he approached the campfire; a few inches taller than Leunga, but burly in build and tan, his light gray hair was lengthy, many inches longer than Sydney's, and was tied back in a ponytail of split ends draped over a backpack designed with only one diagonal strap to be worn in the same fashion as Ricky's dark blue duffel in recent occurrences of camp-wise carrying. Of course, no woodland grandfather would be complete without a thick goatee groomed over many decades. The visitor eagerly wandered forward into their camp with a large grin garnishing his wrinkled visage—he had a gruffness in his voice as he spoke, a gift of his years. "Whoa, far out! What the hell are you three doing here in the forest, man?"

Leunga lowered his outstretched arm and released his maroon polo shirt. "Oh, it's just Grampy." He lost interest in the new arrival very quickly.

Sydney sighed with relief. "You scared us."

"Bummer." Their grandfather showed grave concern over his impressive entrance. "Didn't mean to."

Ricky lifted his head sleepily and greeted him with a quick, "Hi, Grampy," and then dropped his cheek back onto the soft cushioning of his bedding, golden hair jostling stiffly.

The old man faced his youngest grandchild and waved. "Hello, Junior!" He then lowered his voice and leaned to Leunga to ask, "People still call him that, right?"

His grandson nodded. "All the time." And he was, as usual, lying.

"This is so crazy," Sydney's surprise stated. "We were just about to look for you tomorrow. Leunga has something he wants to ask—"

"Whew!" The elderly man interrupted his granddaughter, powerfully thumping a hand on her shoulder. "Sounds like I got here just in time, man.

But let's save that stuff for tomorrow. I've been walking these woods all day, and I just ate some more magic mushrooms a few minutes ago that should be kicking in soon, and I don't want to be busy when that happens, if you know what I mean..."

Leunga gained interest in the new arrival very quickly. "Have any more?"

The Cursiness of Questages

The sound of metal colliding with stone resonated through his skull, welcoming him to the new morning. For the second time in as many days, the sun's radiated waves crashed against his luminous green eyes as he was so rudely awakened. With a raucous, groaning gurgle, Leunga writhed on the forest floor, infuriated by the life-sustaining fire in the sky. His hat, having fallen off in the middle of the night, sat readily at his fingertips. Realizing such, he sat up quickly and ran a hand through his mangy curls, checking the form and style his hair had forged itself into during the night; as it turns out, his brunet mane actually looked more presentable after seven hours pressed against the ground, but he threw the cap on anyway. Lazily looking to the empty bedroll of his brother at his right, he slowly swiveled to the filled sleeping bag of his grandfather at his left. A secondary ruckus sounded from the rocky ridge of the camp, forcing Leunga to squint in the direction of the source.

Ricky lowered his head, whispering, "Shhh! Grampy and Lou are still asleep."

Trying to remain feminine under the circumstances, Sydney sat, perched on one of the larger rocks, clutching a recently used eyeliner kit and a permanent marker she always kept with her, coloring her fingernails and watching a pool of water slowly crawl toward the long since extinguished fire pit. "*Sorry!*" she hissed. "I didn't know the pot was there. Why the hell did you put it down right behind me anyway?"

"Dude, I put it there *before* you sat down..."

"We still have a bunch of bottled waters. You didn't need to fill the damn pot, dummy."

The younger shrugged. "I thought we could use it to, uh, you know, rinse our hands and stuff so we didn't have to go all the way to the freakin' pond." Rinsing off his hair gel-shrouded hands in particular.

"Huh. That's actually a good idea. I'll go refill it then." Sydney hopped down, squishing the mud below her skidding descent while swiping the cookware she gathered all by herself from the firm floor. She was heading in the direction of the camp's freshwater supply when she noticed a typically unusual, although recently common, sight. Her older brother stared at her through sleep-drenched eyes, awoken at an extremely abnormal hour for him—about eight o'clock in the morning. Sydney turned to her other brother while she continued to travel to the pond and whispered, "Leunga's up."

Ricky closed his eyes in disappointment. It would seem that his Monday morning would be ruined extra early. "Dang it."

Unwelcomed by everyone and everything and full of a superior sense of ill humor, Leunga curled forward, burying his exhausted face in his hands as he sat with legs folded under the cover of his comforter. He rotated his lower jaw while tasting the filth covering his tongue and teeth. The early-morning chirping of the treetops ricocheted through his hungover headache. A foul tongue stuck to the back of his bite as he stretched his limited reach forward along the sleeping bag exterior—a stretch that inspired him to yawn, revealing the discolored interior of his mouth and expelling his rancid breath across the clearing. I'd say he clearly forgot to brush his teeth last night— unless, of course, he didn't actually forget. Leunga squinted at Ricky, contemplating whether or not to go back to sleep for the rest of the week. "Hey, Finny, what time is it?"

"*Dude!*" his brother whispered with emphasis. "Don't call me that...It's bad enough that Grampy still calls me *Junior.*" Flicking his wrist up, Ricky quickly answered, "Eight fifteen."

"Ante meridiem?"

The youngest sibling faced the oldest, clearly confused. "What's that mean?"

Leunga raised his eyebrows and stared at the dirt. "Don't know." His gaze travelled a little further, locking on the elderly man sleeping nearby with his mouth open, snoring robustly. Awake and ready to share that misery with the world, the elder grandson reached out his palm to wake the old man with a vigorous shaking of the torso, but was stopped suddenly by a hand with freshly blackened fingernails gripping his wrist.

Sydney shook her head, keeping her voice low, and insisted, "Let him sleep."

Unaware of her reasoning for the pot of water in her grip, or the possible intentions with said liquid, Leunga looked into her face and widened his eyes for an instant as if to say "Whatever, kid," before he ripped his arm away from hers, smacking himself in the chest with a thud.

At the exact same moment, Ricky found the object he had been spending most of the morning looking for: the heavy-duty deodorant their grandmother had kindly packed for them. And since she had so kindly given them only one for him and his brother to share, Ricky wanted to be the first to use the purportedly new stick. Cautiously waiting until his siblings weren't looking, he popped off the top, raising the chalky, cerulean blue pillar out of its shell while keeping a watchful eye on his family. He turned his back to them, and in the privacy of their presence, he pulled his short canvas robe open wide with one arm and quickly applied the antiperspirant to his armpit—the first time during their vacation that he felt lucky to have worn a sleeveless undershirt. Glancing over his shoulder before repeating the action on his other armpit, he was certainly satisfied that the plan worked perfectly—with the exception of the few gray hairs he saw embedded in the business end of the bar, which he failed to notice before applying the sporty scent. "Ewww!"

Leunga rubbed his eyes rigorously with the base of his palms, trying in vain to allay his prevailing sense of exhaustion, but it was totally useless. Recognizing the horrifying fact that he was definitely up for good that morning, he decided to alleviate another pestering sensation. He stood shakily and shuffled south to the clear pool, realizing then that he had slept in his oversized shoes. With tan work boots partially submerged in the cool water, Leunga grappled with the large metal fastener of his khakis, and, after many furious attempts, his petite fingers freed the button from its imprisonment and he began unzipping his cargo shorts; although, for the record, they were certainly loose enough to pull down without undoing the button or zipper.

"Whoa! Idiot, what are you doing?" Sydney whispered forcefully, jogging up behind him with a hand blocking her view. She had absolutely no intention, or desire, to allow her eyes to get anywhere near what her brother may have been handling. In fact, I think it's safe to say that nobody wants their eyes to suffer through that.

Leunga zipped his fly halfway up and turned, noticeably annoyed. "I'm gonna take a piss. What does it look like?"

"Don't!" she demanded, adamant about blocking the view of him with her hand. "We use that pond for washing hands, and for drinking if we run out of bottled water."

"Fish whiz in the water all the time and we drink that."

Sydney entreated an ordinance of hygiene in their camp, choosing a more considerate tone to express that wish—borderline begging, really. "Please! Go pee near the trees. Please..."

Holding up his unbuttoned pants up with one hand, the would-be whizzer was feeling mighty generous for a groggy grump and splashed his way down the shore obediently to the nearest tree, which was pretty far away. "Whatever Princess wants..."

She sighed with relief as she lowered her blinder; the mere thought of being anywhere near her brother's excretions made her shudder. Actually, it's making me kind of sick too. Sydney returned to camp, calmed, and amazed, by her older brother's reasonability over the matter. Matter of the bladder. Sorry. She sat next to Ricky, who appeared distraught about something. "What's wrong?"

Ricky's face was frozen—and his thoughts were locked on a few gray hairs—with his giant, dark eyebrows raised extra-high, his eyes narrowed to a soured squint, and his lips frowning extra-hard. Slowly, he faced his sister, and his mug returned to its normal worried state. "Uh, it's nothing..." he mumbled and looked at the probable culprit of his distress just as the old man began to stir in his sleeping bag. "Just...stuff."

Their grandfather lazily raised his head and yawned noisily. "Mornin', kids!" Much unlike the love of his life, his many years did little to hinder his movements, so he quickly sprang up, performed some light stretches, and spryly hopped over to the body of water, where he proceeded to unzip his forest green shorts. Slowly the sound of liquid splashing against liquid filled the air as the chirping birds and rustling trees added to this overture of nature.

Sydney tried not to listen as she made a defeated and disgusted whimper.

Leunga entered the camp, shaking his damp hands after rinsing them in the stream. "Oh sure! *He* can pee in the lake, but *I* can't?! I hate this place."

The elderly man turned his head while continuing his restroom routine. "Whoa now, Louie." In the light of the early morning, he noticed something he failed to detect the night before. Their grandfather pointed at his grandson with a single jabbing finger and said, "That is a mighty fine shirt!"

Pulling at the edges of the striped polo, the complimented kid lost his very temporary hatred for his grandfather and played it cool. "Who? This old thing? You flatter me. This guy right here I am is flattered."

As he zipped his fly to the sky, their grandfather hopped up slightly and faced the camp, studying the sublime fashion sense of his grandson. "I have a shirt almost exactly like that one!" But not anymore. "And a hat like yours too." If the old man had bothered to take a peek at the back of Leunga's headwear, he would've seen his own monogrammed initials: LAM. "Whoa, it's like you copied my style." I would use the term *stole*. "Looks good on you, man." Trés chic for a thief!

Still reeling from the incident with the deodorant, Ricky cocked his head and shuddered. Eager to bring an end to the trip and to keep the topic of attire from catching fire and drifting over his way, he softly grumbled, "Couldn't we, like, not talk about Lou's stupid fashion sense until *after* we get back home?"

"I'd like to hear more about it now."

"Whoa! Wait a second!" their grandfather abruptly exclaimed in a great explosion of realization. "You kids said you wanted to ask me how to do something." The old man bent down, removing a filled plastic bag from the utility vest he wore every hunting trip in addition to his single-strap backpack. An overabundance of pockets to hide whatever needed the most hiding. He walked to the center of the site, holding the opened bag toward his grandchildren to treat them before their upcoming inquiry. "Anybody want some?"

Leunga enthusiastically peered into the sack. "Ooh! Are these the 'shrooms?"

Their grandfather was taken aback, not remembering ever telling the children about his stash. "Uh... What...? No, man, it's jerky. Deer or pig or something..." A growing concern consumed him as he wondered how his secret managed to escape.

Ricky was indeed considerably hungry. "Yes, please," he replied and gripped half a dozen large pieces from his grandfather's hand, his domineering stomach forcing him to abstain from helping direct the conversation to his brother's disruptive sword for the moment. "Thanks."

"Yeah, okay..." said the eldest sibling as he set aside his search for mind-expanding toadstools and grabbed a piece, shoving the entire thing in his mouth. During his struggle to bite down on the sinewy foodstuff, he paused, pulling a very long gray hair from his mouth. "God, Sydney... Come on!"

"Hey, man, dogs don't bark. Know what I mean?" Only his granddaughter knew what he meant. The elderly man turned to her, holding forth the dried animal tissue and asked, "None for you?"

Pulling away, the girl shook her head compactly at the offering.

Leunga chewed violently. "She don't eat meats."

"Vegetarian," Ricky added.

Leunga snickered. "*Vagi*-tarian."

Ricky giggled at her expense, for reasons he couldn't comprehend or explain, before abruptly stopping himself.

"Mmm!" Sydney grunted in supreme disapproval of her brotherly supplied embarrassment and spoke only to herself. "Right in front of Grandpa..."

Leaning closer to his older brother, the youngest's eyes widened as he whispered, "Shhh! I think she can hear us."

Their grandfather faced Sydney and smiled with wonder. "You are?" That seems like something he should have already known about his only granddaughter. "Right on! I'm a vegetarian too!"

His confession made no sense to her. "But you brought jerky...?"

"Ah, yeah, ya see, your grandmother still packs all of this stuff for me. Same care package every damn time for however many decades I've come out here." He looked to the surrounding trees, searching for his lost time, before reporting, "With updated organic brands though...so there's that at least."

"Grandma doesn't know you're a vegetarian?" Sydney asked, with her naturally occurring expression of disbelief—left eyebrow up and right down, of course.

"Well, I don't tell her *everything*."

Leunga nodded and leaned against the boy by his side, speaking softly to his younger brother. "As it should be."

Ricky breathed in at the most inopportune moment and caught a whiff of his older brother's putrid morning breath. "Oh god..."

"Well, anyway, I'd say that's about enough of my horsing off," said someone as he zipped the airtight seal on the plastic bag and threw it into his grandson's duffel. "Let's get down to business before I get sidetracked again." The old man walked to his pocket-ridden vest and put it on, blindly opening the largest pocket on the back and removing a granola bar he tossed to Sydney. "What do you kids need?"

"Nothin'. I don't ever need anything—" Leunga stopped midsentence as his sibling forcefully jabbed him in the ribs with his elbow. He turned to the teen and looked up, only inches away from his little brother's face. "*What?!*"

Like a kick to the chest, the palpable reek his older brother seemed to generate internally incapacitated Ricky. He broke eye contact with Leunga and faced their sister, desperately seeking some assistance, but found her far too focused on wrestling with the wrapper of her stubborn snack to notice his needs or care. With eyes focused forward, and away from his brother, he discreetly coughed and calmly asked, "Do you um, wanna ask Grampy about the sword?"

As if the sun had suddenly gone supernova and the earth was no more, their grandfather's face was overcome with horror at his grandson's request. "Junior, did you just say *sword?*"

"Oh!" Leunga slapped his thighs and recalled. "That's right. We wanted to ask you about my sword." Taking the chance to glance around the camp, he realized it must still be in his sleeping bag and requested, "Ricksauce, go get the sheath from my bed."

Once again, it was the duty of the compliant youngest family member to collect the often-forgotten blade. Ricky stood, overjoyed by the fact that he would be out of olfactory range of his brother, and walked to the sweaty bedroll to grab the black leather harness from within, taking it to its owner shortly after that.

"*And* the sword maybe? God..." Leunga showed his brother the empty chasm of the sheath and squinted. "Such an airhead sometimes." Quite a strong accusation, considering the source.

"Huh." Ricky returned to the previous location of the harness, quietly muttering, "You didn't say get the sword too, duh..." Unveiling the veiled innards of the sleeping bag, he was happy to find the rusted sword deep at the bottom, with the pointed end aiming toward the area where his brother's head would be, naturally. Ricky gripped it tightly in one hand by the handle, turning back in the direction of the center of camp, wondering if his sibling had slept with it there. As he passed his grandfather, he heard the elderly man utter something in astonishment.

"Holy shit..."

"Yeah, it's cool, huh?" Leunga took the sword from Ricky and tossed it around, demonstrating its heft and durability for the old man. "Got it for my birthday, back before I could remember stuff." So, any time before a month ago.

"Holy shit." Repeating his shock, their grandfather's eyes darted between the familiar sheath and weapon in his grandson's possession. So many years had passed since he last laid eyes on the pair. Overwhelmed by the reunion, he sat on the log behind him, vision locked on the sword. The item of his inquest was never lost, only misplaced. Mystification settled in his thoughts; decades had separated him from that awful day when he returned home, covered in his enemy's blood and etched with ancient symbols. He looked down at the backs of his shaky hands, faint scars still visible—a permanent reminder of the pact he made. Now, suddenly, after all those years of torment and nightmarish memories, he was once again face-to-face with the cause of his grief. The old man inhaled deeply. "You found it for me. And now it's all over!" He grinned wide and said, "Now I can finally hide it with the other one!" As he got to his feet to grab the weapon away from his family, their grandfather made another realization and paused with confusion. "Why do your pants say 'bootylicious'?"

Ricky quickly understood who the old man was talking to as his brother and sister began giggling. Pulling up the back edge of his karate gi, he looked over his shoulder at the turquoise sweats adorning his long legs, where he found an upside-down image of a phrase in large-print bubble-lettering. Bootylicious. Although relieved that no one outside of his family had seen the long shorts, the teen still whimpered at the discovery. Apparently, his wardrobe woe was far more dire than he had initially believed.

Leunga stopped laughing as he began to fully comprehend his grandfather's statement. "Wait, *hide* it?! What the fudge for?! I want the other one so I can display these bad boys to the world...in my room above my bed."

The elder gent shook his head. "No way, man. You do not want to be dealing with the heavy shit I went through." He walked up to his grandson with an outstretched hand and urged, "Give it to me so I can get rid of them forever."

Leunga clutched the sword and sheath close to his chest and leaned away from the demanding grasp of his grandfather. "Uh-uh. Not so fast, fella. Maybe you should start explaining why you need this so badly before you go all grabby with it." And then he called him a name under his breath. "Butt. Cheeks!"

A wrinkled hand dropped to the senior's side. Agreeing that some sort of explanation was in order, the old man stroked his long gray goatee and tried to decide something that was probably very important. "Okay then. Where do I begin...?"

•   •   •

The group sat in a large semicircle around the fireless pit creating the camp's core. The old man sat back and folded his muscled arms, addressing his grandchildren as a whole. "You probably know my grandfather came from Scotland, right? Well, after my dad was born, they decided to immigrate to the land of the free...so they did, leaving almost everything they had behind..." The elderly elder pointed at the blade lying across the log next to his grandson. "Except for this sword. He was so determined to sneak this damn thing into the country with him that he smuggled it, making my grandmother

hide it under a secret hatch he made in her luggage until they got off the boat.
As my dad got older, my grandfather passed it along to him with a warning.
He was told that the weapons were blessed and cursed. And I know this is
gonna sound like bullshit...but he said any man in our family who took a
sword in each hand would be locked into a contract with the blades. To
protect the land from evil. Binding him until death or substitution. And only
men of our bloodline could even handle both of them at the same time
without being killed—and when I say men, I mean males; no women were
allowed to make the pact."

Sydney snarled disgustedly, secretly pleased that she could finally use
that big word she learned. "Yippee. Who would've guessed we came from
misogynistic pigs?"

One boy whispered to his intrigued younger brother. "What is that?
Hawaiian? Hawaiian bacon? We should probably try some soon. It sounds
Hawaiian."

And that other boy went on to whisper to their scowling sister.
"There's that one Hawaiian barbeque place, like, *right* next to my dojo. I bet
we can get some there probably. Wait, why am I telling *you*?"

"I know, Sunflower," their grandfather continued to his
granddaughter. "Our ancestors weren't exactly the most enlightened bunch.
Anyway, after heeding this warning, my dad stored the blades in the same
trunk they were brought here in, where they sat for decades, gathering more
rust. When I was...eighteen or nineteen—I can't remember—he told me the
story of the magic swords and the horrible curse, but I was too busy thinking
about all of the various movements and rallies and marches and all that shit
going on back then to give a damn about what he said, so I ignored a lot of it.
After he died, his house and all of his junk passed to me, so I sold most of
what I could and moved out here and met your grandmother. A few years
later, I was studying at home and I discovered his trunk and the blades inside,
which is weird because I was so sure I traded the whole damn thing for some
hash—I mean cash. Anyway, I removed the holster and it reminded me of the

fragmented story my dad told me. I figured he was trying to play a joke, telling me about curses and magic, so I instinctively grabbed a sword in each hand..."

Ricky leaned closer, supporting his head with his hands. "Did anything happen?"

"Hell yes something happened! I can't describe for sure what it was, but my hands began shaking so fast I could barely see them while the blades stayed almost motionless. A moment later, some weird symbols started glowing dark red on the swords, and my vision narrowed to a point. All I could think was that I was about to die. Then, as quickly as it began, it was over. My vision returned, and I saw these." He held up his hands, displaying the scar tissue on the back of them. "Some kind of ancient writing burned a ring on each of my hands. Shit, man... I was shocked to find out my dad was telling the truth. I just wish I had listened to him better... Oh well. After that incident, I decided to hide them back in the attic, out of sight and out of mind, but...being apart from them, I could still feel them, like they were calling out to me. Under the guise of burning my hands on the stove, I hid the scars under bandages, hoping they would disappear over time. But, you know, they never did." Holding his canteen to his goatee, he took a swig.

"It was a few weeks later when I suddenly noticed something moving outside the window during dinner. Something big. It happened so long ago, but I can still picture it today, man. I thought it was a big-ass bear standing on its hind legs in the darkness. Then it got closer. It stood like us, but it way wasn't human. It had these huge bony spikes along its back; a thick, furry pelt covered in weird-ass markings; long pointy ears; a wide grin of huge, razor-sharp teeth below a flattened snout; large bowie knife-length claws; muscled arms that reached from its shoulders to its knees; and a pair of giant, glowing, gray eyes that seemed to be searching for something. At first I thought it might've been another acid trip, but it returned the next night, continuing its search, until it saw me through the window. It was enormous and really sluggish, but after it looked right at me, it turned and sprinted into the trees, undulating. Luckily, your grandmother wasn't home at the time. I watched the trees for half the night, and eventually I fell asleep on the couch. When I woke up the next morning, the thing was standing above me at the window, watching me sleep with its radiant eyes and jagged grin. I figured it was attracted to whatever I did when I activated the swords, like one of the monsters from my dad's stories. I ran into the kitchen and grabbed some pots to scare it off, but when I got back to the living room, it was already gone, so the next day I left with the blades, alone and frightened, but all I could think about was protecting my wife."

"Did you find the..." Sydney tried to think of a clever descriptive word for the beast her grandfather detailed. "Thing?"

He chuckled. "Bastard found *me*! I don't know why, but I had the weirdest urge to look for *something* I could never seem to describe just *pulling* me into the woods, like a serious addiction, man. I was just wandering around for a few days when I had a weird feeling I was being watched, and I swear I could hear voices calling out to me from some other world. I couldn't really understand what they were saying to me, man, but it did seem like they were saying something about monsters in the trees, so I looked over my shoulder and there it was—just standing there about fifty feet back, looking at me with those hollow eyes. Slowly I turned and faced the creature. The thing must've been at least seven feet tall and four feet wide at the shoulders. My hands started quaking with such a horrible fear as I reached over to my right and gripped the handles of those swords on my back. As soon as I pulled them out of the case, its eyes started glowing brighter and it wailed through its grin. It steadily trotted toward me with its gigantic claws spread wide and outstretched. The pounding of my heart was deafening as it closed in on me, ready to swipe my life away."

Leunga jumped back. "Whoa! Did you die?"

"All I could remember was holding the blades in front of my face for protection, and it was like they became weightless—like light as a feather. And it was weird, but they slowly started contorting my arms and moving up into a guarding kind of thing in front of me. I could barely feel it. The...uh...*troll* monster got closer and everything got a little hazy. Pretty sure the swords started dancing in my hands, creating a furious wall of metal when the troll's big claw came rushing at my face, man, but it got too heavy for me so I had my eyes closed. When I opened them, the creature was howling in pain, gripping its mangled arm, which was sliced in half like this." Their grandfather held up his left forearm and pointed down the length of it with his right hand, indicating a clean cut between the radius and ulna bones.

Ricky glanced at the sword by his brother's side, trying to imagine if anything his grandfather had just described could be possible. The story was so outlandish there was no way the old man could be telling the truth. Could he? Don't ask me.

"It just stood back for a second, stunned while its arm hung limply before it staggered toward me again, but this time I kept my eyes open. And I saw it. Like this little sunspot filling my eyes. Then it was like the blades in my hands knew it was time to strike. They pulled me forward, moving my legs toward the creature, even though I way didn't want to hurt it anymore, but before I could do anything to stop it"—the elderly man made a slicing noise—"both blades eviscerated the poor animal's midsection, causing its intestines to pour out onto the forest floor. My face was splashed with its hot, sticky blood as I just stood there, watching in horror as the swords sliced giant gashes in its defeated body. Totally vicious, man. After the troll fell to the ground, bleeding all over the place, it burst into a cloud of this really dark black mist. When the mist sank into the dirt below, I saw the creature for what it truly was. Just a small brown bear cub. Probably only a few months old..."

Sydney looked off toward the trees with distraught eyes. "That's horrible..."

"When I saw the aftermath of what I did, I fell to my knees and cried, howling like the living being I just killed." Their grandfather paused. His eyes were damp, and he placed the back of his hand against his mouth as the awful memories began flooding back. He inhaled and slowly began again. "After that, I knew I had to get rid of the horrible swords and quietly live with the guilt for the rest of my life. In a daze of remorse, I found a cave in the forest and I threw the swords into a small well I found inside, hoping they would be lost forever."

"So where did it come from?" Ricky asked suspiciously.

"Where did what come from, Junior?"

Leunga added, "The troll, son."

"Ah. Well, my dad said something about a sorcerer, or maybe a mage, I don't really remember, man. It was so long ago...but I know this: those swords were made to destroy the thing that caused me to kill an innocent animal. Like some kind of hypnosis, I returned home without realizing it, covered in baby brown bear blood. Your grandmother was so relieved that I was home she never even asked me what had happened out there, and I'm not sure if I would've even told her if she did. For the few nights that passed since the day I killed the bear, these horrible nightmares filled my sleep, and always with the same bald man talking to me. Also, I couldn't feel the presence of the blades anymore—only the quiet solitude of the guilt in my conscience." The elderly man slicked his hair back with one hand, checking the firmness of his ponytail. "I had a nagging feeling that I forgot something in that cave, so I went back the next week to check on the swords...but one of them was gone."

Leunga stared at the blade by his side. "This one?"

Their grandfather nodded. "Apparently, I only threw one of the swords into that well and mistakenly took the other home. I guess Gloria hid it from me out of love, but I wish she hadn't... I spent the last fifty years or so searching the forest for that goddamn thing! I though I dropped it somewhere."

"Grandma told us you would come out here to hunt," Sydney commented with concern.

"I told her that so she wouldn't think I was crazy or high for wandering around out here. And actually, the only time I ever caught something was a rabbit I accidentally stepped on my first day searching. Poor

little guy... You know, I don't think hunting is even allowed in this forest."
He's right. It's not.

Ricky glanced over his shoulder at their grandfather's supplies with a quandary. "How does Grammy think you hunt without a gun?"

"But I *do* have a gun! An old rifle that used to belong to my old man. It's right here—oh shit, where is it? Well, never mind. It doesn't matter. It's probably not loaded."

Leunga bit the tip of his tongue, pondering the probability of his grandfather's yarn. "Uh-huh... So the other sword might still be in that cave mayhaps?"

"It definitely is," he said, nodding. "I check on it every time I go hiking out here. No one ever goes in there. Just the bats, man."

Finally some progress on the wildlife front. A strong chance to observe some natural inhabitants of the forest. Sydney cheered up at the aspect of seeing a few of the cute pig-nosed aeronauts. "Can we go see the bats?"

"Yes," her older brother agreed, holding up the blade and gradually aiming it at his grandfather—possibly as a threat. "You will take us to this cave..." He squinted and moved his lips closer to his nose, dangling the point of his sword at the elderly man's face. "Or else." Yep. Definitely a threat.

Their grandfather was thrilled. His years of searching in vain were now coming to an end. "Of course! You kids get what you need and we'll get going." The elder stood up briskly and walked off in the direction of the pond, secretly removing a small amount of fungus from a hidden sandwich bag within his tactical vest and popping the psychedelic mushrooms into his mouth. "We launch in ten minutes!" Lowering his voice to a point that his grandchildren couldn't hear, he added, "And so do I."

"Shouldn't someone stay here and guard my—" Ricky interrupted himself to correct his sentence. "*Our* stuff?"

Sydney nodded to her younger sibling and praised, "Yeah, definitely. You should stay here and guard. Don't want anyone to take our camp."

"Leaving a child in charge?" The eldest's eyes glared wide with shock at his sister's incompetence. "Are you nuts?!"

"Duh, he can handle it. He's sixteen for fuck's sake."

Leunga performed some quick calculations. Somehow remembering that he was practically seven years old when his younger brother was born, he took into account his own perceived age, subtract practically seven, imaginary number, $2\pi r^2$, carry the one. "That can't be true. He's coming with me and Grampy. You can stay instead."

Sydney scowled. "No damn freakin' way! My hell, I wanna see the bat cave."

"I'm really okay with staying here..." Ricky pictured the lettering on his hindquarters. "Really. I uh...might think I might actually prefer it."

"Quit changing the subject, Rick. We'll need your wilderness expertise out there. And besides, you're a little more expendable than her and you know it."

"Syd knows way more than—wait, what?"

"Shut up."

"Degenerate perverts wandering around through the trees freely..." Sydney pictured the depraved contents of the campsite they attended the previous day, along with the kind of people who would inspire such a lewd mess. "At least Ricky knows karate!"

"Whoa! Where did *that* come from?" a shortish thing asked, blinded by disbelief. "Very uncalled for, those phrasings. And now I have to take full credit for that behavior because I'm the old one and I should've taught you way better by now, I'd think. Pervs can be people too, you know. I greatly recommend you leave the Hawaiian cows out of this! They've done nothing to you except for being beautiful and delicious. Apparently you've never seen your own reflection?! Yeah, I thought so."

Ricky leaned as close as he could to his brother without actually getting anywhere near him, sniffing the clouded air. "Wow...it's not even nine and you're *already* drunk."

Leunga wobbled in place. "No, just buzzed."

"You suck. I don't *have* to stay here, you know..."

"Hey lady, it's not like we have a choice here. I didn't seek this leadering role, it seeked me because I'm the best there is. I know—I'm perfect for the job, and I have your trust." For reasons we all know to be completely compulsory, it was then that the eldest brother took the time to bow graciously to his sister, slowly. "You believe in me and I thank you."

"Absolutely not!"

"You'll be fine here. We need you here. You're the only one who can do this...here." Leunga motioned for his supremely taller male sibling to follow, to which the teen obeyed, but mainly only because the eldest inclined against him and belched. "Come on, Rickage. We ride."

Holding his breath with the best of them, Ricky glanced back dejectedly and squeezed out the words, "Thanks for staying here with the stuff, Syd..."

Sydney folded her arms, locked in a dire struggle with her older sibling's reality while desperately desiring a simple glimpse at this supposed cavern. "Great idea, buttwad. Let a helpless young *lady* stay here *by herself* unprotected in the fucking forest for an undefined amount of time." She quickly lost what remained of her cool temper and vowed, "I'm gonna spit in your sleeping bag!"

Leunga tilted his head back as his shoulders slumped. Seeing that his brotherly talents for putting his sister at ease were needed more at that moment than ever before, he turned to her with a look of sincerity and reassured her worried heart. "You're going to be just fine, Sydney. I mean it. I would never do anything to put you in danger. I promise, nothing will ever happen to you. You just have to trust me on this. Please. For me." Slowly walking off in a wrong direction without thinking, the soon-to-be-lost young lad added, "And if you start to feel scared about being a girl again, go get one of Dick's weapons; otherwise, light every intruder on fire. Besides, you're already safe from all the pervert pigs. No one out here is going to think you're a woman anyway."

In absolute acceptance of his assessments and advice, his sister let her eyes drop to her shoes and started staring with a sigh. When her brother finally changed course and began heading more toward the place he originally meant to go, Sydney looked right at him, raised her voice, and asked, "Yours is the green sleeping bag, right?"

The Heart

Sydney sat silently. Anticipating. Preparing. Her legs bounced to an unnecessary extent—a true sign of wracked nerves. Were she not focused so intensely on the large glass doors up the path from her, she might've noticed this involuntary action. Her effects were light, exactly as she planned for what she saw coming—only a small purse and a notebook. The conversation replayed in her mind all day. She had no need to pay attention to anything else anymore.

"Oh, hi!"

"Hey, Sydney. I haven't talked to you in a long time. What's up?"

"Nothin'. Actually, I'm glad you're here. My brother needs to use my car today, and I can't find a ride... Would you mind?"

"Sure! I parked right over here."

"Thank you so much."

Sydney sat silently. She practiced the scene again and again until it was flawless. She was ready for whatever he might say. Every possible scenario was predetermined. All she had to do was wait for the moment when it would happen. While looking over the concrete tiles, her neck had become strained, but she could hardly care. Each time the large glass doors flew open, her heart leapt to her throat, but each time it did, her target was not among the crowd. She knew it could only be a matter of minutes—her severe anxiety was a telltale sign. For a moment, she broke her focus on the doorway and glanced at the clock on her fancy cellular phone. School had ended only fifty-three seconds ago. Returning her gaze to the glass, she was confident she hadn't missed him yet.

Sydney sat silently. For the entire day, she had honed in on that moment. During physics class, she spent lecture time deciding responses and considering worthy anecdotes. In study hall, she hid in the back of the room and wrote down a few scripts. At lunch, she abstained from eating in order to keep her deep focus. She even snuck out of art class early to reserve a front row seat at the east door. All of it would come down to what would take only thirty seconds, yet it felt like it was made to last forever.

Sydney sat silently. More than fifty faces had passed, but none belonged to her objective. On top of her anxiety over what she would say, she was beginning to grow even more worried that the worst had happened and she had missed him completely. Her knees continued to oscillate up and down in small, somewhat controlled movements as she glanced into the parking lot, away from the doors. The black pickup truck with radio station bumper stickers was still parked, empty. *His* truck. Relieved by the sight, Sydney swiveled her head toward the door, where her surprised eyes instantly widened. A rather tall boy with platinum blond hair exited the school, slightly taller than her, with a shoulder bag across his back. Suddenly Sydney's breathing quickened and her hands quivered in panic. Forcing herself into action, she slowly stood on quaking stilts to intercept her goal. She began to stride toward him as their eyes briefly met, causing her to stumble slightly. And though her confidence took an irreparable hit, Sydney regained much of her composure, stepped out in front of him, and brought his stroll to a stop.

"Hey, Darwin...!"

"Oh, hi, Cindy. How's it going?"

"Nothi—I mean...good...um, I was kind of wondering..." She blanked. Sydney couldn't remember what it was she wanted to say. She couldn't even remember what she wanted from him in the first place. "Um..." she stalled and sought to make eye contact with the boy of her dreams, but to her dismay, she found herself completely unable to force her eyes anywhere near his face. She was trying to stare at the sun. And to make matters worse, she was fairly sure he had just called her Cindy.

"Well... I should probably get going," Darwin said, bidding farewell by sidestepping her and walking to his truck. "It was nice seeing you."

Something he said triggered her memory. "Oh!" Catching up with the young man and walking at his side—not too long ago she wanted only to walk by his side—Sydney tried her hand at talking to him again. "Um, would it be okay if you gave me—I mean, if I could get a ride home with you?" She should have stopped there, but she didn't. "To my house, not yours...unless you wanted—I mean, since we live so close it would be easy. The ride I mean..." This was not on any of the scripts.

As she finished what I hesitate to describe as her request, they arrived at a large black truck parked under a fruit-bearing tree covered in small yellow orbs. Darwin tossed his shoulder bag into the truck bed and considered her request. "Well, I'm not going home right now, but I guess I could drop you off on the way."

Like a light shining on her skin, Sydney could sense his eyes directed at hers; however, when she tried again to make eye contact, her pupils still refused to obey, so she kept her focus on his casually worn dress shirt with the sleeves rolled up and blushed. "Thanks."

"Hop on in. There's some stuff on the seat, you can just throw it anywhere."

Sydney rounded the truck to the passenger side and heard the driver's door slam shut as she discovered the fruit tree parked beside it to be blocking her route. Not wanting to scratch the paint of the vehicle, she inched the door open slowly until the top rim came in contact with the leafy branches; an opening of less than a foot wide. Even with the door completely swung open, getting into the tall vehicle would be a challenge, but with only a partial passage, Sydney found it to be exceedingly difficult. She stuck her right leg through the fissure and established a proper footing on the running board. With a solid grip on the inner door alcove, she began hopping with her left foot and, with the right amount of momentum, threw her weight through the tiny opening and into the cab. Comforted by the fact that she made it inside his truck without incident, she flopped into the seat, sitting on, and thusly obliterating, half a bag of potato chips. "Ooh! Sorry about that..."

Darwin laughed briefly and shrugged it away. "It's okay." Turning the key in the ignition, the monster roared to life. Despite parking beneath the shadow of a tree, the interior of the truck was exceedingly hot. He cranked the air conditioner to the max, and a breath of fiery wind shot from the portals before gradually becoming cooler.

Removing the bag of crushed chips beneath her, Sydney adjusted herself into a neutral sitting position as much as she possibly could. The baked leather seat seared the bare underside of her legs, forcing her to keep her knees elevated by flexing her calf muscles; uncomfortable to say the least, but it was all for the greater good. She gently set the chip bag down at her feet as the boy sitting by her side clicked one of the many knobs dispersed along the dashboard and the speakers crackled with life. A very generic male rock band was in the middle of a ballad when the amplifiers flooded the warm interior of the truck with alto singing and synthetic guitar riffs. It was easily one of the worst songs she had ever heard. The greater good.

Upon hearing the radio, Darwin turned to Sydney and groaned with a grin. "Oh, I love this song!"

Needless to say, the genre was not exactly her favorite type of composition. Typically, she was more accustomed to thundering drums, hypnotic bass lines, lamenting lyrics, and gloomy guitar solos; in fact, it was the only thing she had in common with her older brother—according to her. Sydney smiled as he elevated the volume a minor amount, and lied, "Yeah...it's great." She didn't care if they were listening to a recording of baby screams and dentist drills as long she could listen to it with him.

"Totally." Darwin geared the truck into reverse and turned his attention to the rear window, throwing his right arm around the back of Sydney's seat. Her heart rate rapidly quickened before she realized he was only using her chair for leverage and her blood pressure returned to a lowered, but still unusually high, level. The truck crept out of its shadowy den and soared through the parking lot to the nearest exit, directly to the same outlet Sydney normally took.

To allow her temporary chauffeur easier visual access to the flowing traffic on the roadway past the school car lot, the girl leaned back against her leather throne; her head pressed against the headrest while she tilted toward her driver, stealing a glance of his eyes while he was preoccupied with the oncoming traffic before them. His eyes were as blue as a cloudless summer sky, with the clarity of a precious gem. Each time he looked past her to the passenger side window, she couldn't help but stare into those eyes, even if it wasn't the direct contact she had hoped for.

"It's like a constant stream of cars," the driver explained as he looked left and right repeatedly, until he saw their salvation. "Ah, here we go." Down the road, a small break in the flow of traffic appeared—though Sydney didn't notice. Darwin wheeled the truck onto the road and entered the torrent of vehicles. They were now a mere six minutes away from their destination—the young woman would have to act quickly to achieve the next phase of her intricate plan.

Houses zipped by on either side of the street. Chilled air swept across her face, shifting her hair. The radio resounded with another unappealing song. The girl gathered her nerves; she had made it this far; there was no reason to back out now. "I, uh..." She searched for an icebreaker. "I like your car."

"Thanks."

To her disappointment, the comment failed to spark a conversation. Next topic.

"So...are you planning on going to college in the fall?" she asked, even though she knew the answer already, having overheard Darwin speaking to his friends about his acceptance letter, but he didn't know that.

"Yeah, I got accepted at CSU. It's only like an hour away, and I get to live on campus. It's a nice place."

"Huh. That's cool." She feigned disinterest. "Actually, that's where I'm going too."

"Cool, maybe we'll see each other." Darwin turned to her and smiled.

Sydney smiled back, still unable to fully look at his face. "Yeah, that would be cool." Her heart began to beat gradually faster as she contemplated her next move—her whole reason for hitching a ride with him in the first place. She stared out the passenger window and gathered her nerve, inhaling slowly as she turned and began her question. "Are—"

Just as Darwin began his own. "Do—"

They both paused for the other to continue, but neither one did, causing them to laugh. It was awkward, and I want to get out.

"You go ahead," Sydney insisted since she lost her bravery and needed time to recoup.

"I was just gonna ask if you mind me changing the radio station."

Her nerves were slightly put at ease by his request. Perhaps now he would choose a more acceptable variety of music. She shrugged and said, "Sure!"

With her permission, Darwin held the button labeled *seek* down, searching for an appropriate substitute. The digital frequency landed in unfamiliar territory, so he waited for the radio display to notify him of the song name while he darted his eyes between the road and the stereo controls. Dangerously distracted driver. The silence became sound. Commercials. He tuned into the next listing and abruptly stopped his search, satisfied with his discovery. "This song kicks ass."

Sydney heard a mere three chords and recognized the melody immediately. Once again, she was sorely disappointed with the boy's musical insight, but it was nothing that couldn't be fixed.

"What were you going to say before I rudely interrupted?"

"Um..." She had yet to regain the courage, but finding herself locked into the situation, she decided to go ahead with her proposition. "I forgot." Never mind, I guess I was wrong.

"Happens to me all the time."

With her hands in her lap, Sydney fidgeted with her last remaining bracelet while staring out the window. Houses and trees passed by in flashes. Once again, she was incapable of acting—another discouraging event in a series of now-or-never situations revolving around the boy next door. This was it. She would never get another chance to tell him what she had felt since the day when their eyes first met while in the halls of their high school. The time for action was upon her, yet she couldn't bring herself to do anything; her window of opportunity was rapidly shutting, and she was allowing it. Disheartened by her lack of resolve, she gazed out at the familiar blurs passing by while trying to think of something interesting to say. To her surprise, she started to speak. "Prom is coming up soon." And her eyes grew wide as she heard the overt statement leave her mouth.

"Yeah, are you excited?"

Her excitement over the subject would strongly depend on his imminent answers. "Yeah." Having accidentally forced herself into this conversation, she chose to roll with it. "It's gonna be fun."

"Last year's was so awesome. I went with Laura Deakin. Who did you go with?"

Sydney briefly considered the idea of making up a name but decided against it at the last minute. "Ah, I couldn't go. I was...sick that week."

"That sucks."

"Yeah, but I *definitely* won't miss this year's..." Sensing that her moment of inquiry was approaching, she began twirling a small amount of hair around her index finger. The teenage girl glanced in Darwin's direction before redirecting her line of sight out the windshield. "So..." she began, as her blood immediately ran cold; it was the moment of truth, do or die—her heart was pounding so hard she could almost hear it. "Have *you* asked anyone yet?"

"Eh, kind of. I'm just going with my girlfriend."

The blurry world outside of the truck froze with the utterance of that final word. Sydney too ceased all movement. She hadn't known. Girlfriend. She sat staggered by that word. All at once, everything that would be, or could've been, exploded, bursting into a thousand pieces of soul-shattering agony.

"Anyone ask you yet?"

Slowly, her breathing returned. Her twirled hair released its grip on her index finger. The sound of another musical abomination echoed in the background of her thoughts. She mustered enough enthusiasm to appear social. "Not yet..."

"Don't worry, it's not for another three weeks anyway, right?"

Sydney sat silently. She fought back against the confusion and frustration evident in her welling eyes, turning her face away from Darwin. Involuntarily, she began chewing on her fluorescent pink index fingernail, lost and looking for someone to save her from the deluge of despair. Girlfriend. Sydney could picture her: a bleach-blond bimbo in a halter top with whale tail underwear on full display, shamelessly protruding above a denim miniskirt. In the crushing silence of her mind that followed, she made a distressing discovery. Sydney glanced down, noticing black elastic straps jutting out at the shoulder of her plain white, ribbed, cotton tank top. Her natural golden locks were primped and stylized into waves of curls for the first time ever. And her new pair of extraordinarily tiny, flannel board shorts were still revealing an embarrassing amount of her long legs. The only remnant of her former self was a wide plastic wristband covered in large metal studs forever worn on her wrist as a symbol of beautiful aspirations of anarchy—her final piece of the girl she used to know; the one who showed tradition no quarter and encased herself in metal to shun society's norms. During her quest for affection, she had been transformed into the very stereotype she used to mock. Seeing the persona she had become for *him* made his indirect rejection sting just a little more. She was out of place, awkward, and ugly.

Darwin stopped his truck behind a small green coupe at a stoplight and said, "Halfway home." Looking out the clean window on his left, the driver and his passenger both stared out of their respective portholes, one of them waiting for the other to speak.

Sydney sat silently. Wishing the light would turn green. She wanted so badly to hide in her dark room, safely away from people and pain. Secluded alongside her heart in her cell. She stared at the bright green light for the perpendicular traffic. The carefree people passing, relentlessly reveling in their relationships—something she may never know. Almost four misguided years of studying, planning, altering behavior, transforming, falsifying an obsession in a sport that mimicked his just to have common ground—and it was all spent for that single instant. For that word. Everything for a boy who would never see her as she saw him. Suddenly, her stomach began to growl with hunger—another reminder of the wasted sacrifices she made for him—and it temporarily brought her back to the land of the living. She could tell by his abruptly altered attitude that he most certainly noticed, but was being polite and ignored the sound. "That was my stomach."

He gave her an inconspicuous smile before bursting away the awkward moment when an auspicious reminder leapt into his head. "Damn, I almost forgot! I've been meaning to ask you something. My girlfriend was wondering"—there's that hellish word again—"who that one guy is you drive around all the time? She keeps wanting me to find out...you know, since me and you, like, live right next to each other and stuff."

"...That's my little brother. Richard."

"*That's* Little Rick?! Whoa, growth spurt much?" Darwin chuckled alone. Before them, the small coupe accelerated quickly at the sight of a green light across the intersection, followed closely by the large black truck. "I remember you used to always be the tall one. That seems so crazy now."

She nodded robustly to avoid the need to speak. Sydney felt absolutely no need to ask why Darwin needed that information. It didn't matter. Another two minutes and she would be home. Hundreds of trees garnished the remaining roadside between the vehicle and solitude. A topiary torrent of carefully pruned foliage flashed by in the midday sun. Sydney blankly watched the mayhem; she barely heard her peer fiddling with something on his portion of the cab. With the clicking of a button, the window to her right glided into the door. A surge of mild spring wind dried her eyes and abused her managed hair without warning or mercy. She recoiled and attempted to contain the situation as much as possible by gently holding her lengthy golden hair down with her palms. The blustery chaos made her feel the mournful need for an urgent appointment with her flatiron and a black scrunchie to correct her regretful mistake of making herself look the part of a desirable teenage woman. The words that echoed in her lungs bounced around the walls of her chest. She knew that her new memories would be a keepsake she would hold onto forever to remind her that her self-confidence was shot, and it flew out the window with the broken pieces of her heart. She'll swallow the pain and keep it locked away, let the secret grow in the dark, never to see the light of day—act like it never happened, and play make-believe with her heart for the rest of time. Her only hope was to refrain from adding to her heartache with any more words. Girlfriend.

Suddenly the glass sheet reverted to its raised position. Darwin cringed, embarrassed. "Ah! Sorry... I meant to just roll my window down."

Sydney slowly began reconstructing her hairdo without the use of a mirror and softly said, "It's okay..." Her palms concealed her distraught visage under the guise of readjusting her precious hairstyle. It was consoling. Taking all the time in the universe that she wanted before returning to the nebulous world whizzing by, she suddenly looked out the window and noticed a house, painted burgundy many years ago, ornamented with eggshell white trim and shutters, a dark roof in dire need of repair, and an open garage with a fire red jeep taking up both possible parking spots at once. She was home.

Darwin shifted his black truck into park. "Here we are."

There they were. In the absence of attentiveness, Sydney managed to collect her things quickly and opened the cumbersome door, shifting her knees into the tepid air. Almost there. She lunged forward, prepared to land on the sidewalk running—maybe running forever from there, never stopping and never looking back until the ache in her lungs went away—when she was stopped by something. The seatbelt. She always wore one, but in this particular instant, she couldn't recall putting it on. Her left hand wrestled with the device for an eternity. Finally there was a snap. The canvas creature withdrew, dragging its way across her face. She sat, motionless for a moment, consumed with irritation. Nary a hindrance to impede her path, she leapt from the cab and stumbled along the concrete.

Outside where she paused her retreat for the sake of saving face, she mustered the friendliest fake grin she could manage and turned toward the boy, still unable to meet his eyes. "Thanks for the ride!" Sydney stood at his truck, unfocused on her physical state. On the seat she left something precious and seemingly irreplaceable behind, but she couldn't take it with her; it still belonged to *him*, whether he wanted it or not. She looked blankly through the doorway, watching her fragile hold on his affection slip away. Close the door, Sydney. It's all gone now. She slammed his passenger door shut before hurrying across the front lawn to the doorstep where escape was only the twist of a knob away. Arrival.

"Hey, say hi to your brother for me!"

Standing halfway inside the screen door, Sydney placed her hand around the warm, metal orb with her key waiting patiently for a twist. Without looking directly at the boy, she could already feel her makeup begin to run as she glanced over her shoulder with gradually reddening eyes; she didn't want to associate his face with the despondency she felt, though it almost certainly already would. "Which one...?"

"Lou. I see him all the time over at the Coño Café." Darwin shifted into drive and crept forward. "See ya later!"

"See ya..." Sydney waited for the truck to leave earshot before carefully wiping her eyes with her bare fingers. Her left hand twisted the knob without her help, and the cherry red front door creaked open, granting her entrance to the living room. She passed through the makeshift hallway created by the half wall overlooking the unused dining room on her right and the oversized couch back at her left placed at a right angle from the door. The swamp cooler hummed in the adjacent corridor, casting a numbing chill throughout the area. Sydney stared dejectedly at the floor as she rounded the far end of the couch and slouched on the closest cushion, narrowly missing a pair of crimson-nailed feet. She quickly glanced over, noticing her older brother sitting at the opposite end of the sofa. A young woman with dark, spiked hair was lying face up on the couch, her head on Leunga's lap. The two appeared to be feeding each other cheese crackers.

"The hell are you wearing?" asked an eruption of crumbs that exploded from Leunga's lips, scattering orange flakes across his adjoining associate, but the young woman didn't seem to mind.

Coated in cheesy debris, she leaned her head forward a bit and greeted the girl with a grin. "Hi, Sydney. How was school?"

Directing her eyes away from the couple, Sydney shrugged. "It was okay, I guess..."

Leunga struggled to swallow his mouthful of jagged snack as he pointed to the front door with his thumb. "Who were you talking to out there?"

"Nobody..."

The bespectacled woman whose name escapes me at the moment asked Sydney with remorseful concern, pulsing with a level of empathy few people exude, "Bad day, huh?"

Sydney shrugged again in response, unwilling to look directly at her brother and his dear friend.

The black-haired woman, taking up an unfairly high number of the couch's cushions, asked, "Anything you want to talk about?"

Instinctively, Sydney considered spilling the beans and revealing her innermost secrets to her brother's girlfriend without hesitation right then and there before her heart locked away all of that anguish for her to hold alone, but an outside force forced her to stop, no matter how much she wished she could confide in her couch's confidant. Such was the nature of the girl using Leunga as a pillow, and the teen typically felt free to divulge every miniscule detail of every event leading up to the day that she was broken, to minimize her pain by spreading it out over any number of people she felt comfortable around—but with her older brother nearby, she could never say a word, so she shook her head quietly in dismay.

"Oh. I understand…" The lounging lady could sense that her boyfriend's presence was inhibiting the hurting young woman's response. "Maybe later on me and you can have a little girl talk."

Sydney sadly smiled silently at the thought of being able to open up to someone who respected her as a woman and not just a teenager. She nodded with suppressed joy and turned away again to hide her continuously distraught eyes.

"Can I come too?"

The dark-haired damsel returned to a more relaxed position, resting the full weight of her head on Leunga's leg. "By the way, Syddy. I don't think I've ever seen your hair like that before. It's very cute that way."

Pinching the lengthy blond tresses draped over her collarbone, Sydney let the unexpected compliment take over her senses in an aiding embrace of serendipitous support. Instead of twisting it into a bundled loop in the back as she always would, she let her hair down that morning, parting the majority of it off to the right so that her face would be more visible if she happened to be the passenger in a car. Despite having been partially destroyed by the wind, she managed to recreate the original style. "You don't think I look stupid…?"

"You look beautiful, but then again, you always are."

Sydney wanted to cry right away—not out of sorrow, but of gratitude for learning the truth she felt foolish for not knowing sooner. Throughout her body she felt a rush of acceptance and smiled meekly. "Thanks." A much-needed glimmer of hopefulness sprouted from her brother's dark-haired comrade in Sydney's otherwise gloomy world. A little black bandage on her cracking heart. Maybe it wasn't the worst day of her life after all.

Leunga carefully dropped a cheese cracker into the awaiting mouth of his couch companion and asked, "So why are you dressed like a Fashionista doll? Is it Halloween?!"

Sydney avoided his questions and posed her own. "Could you drive me to school?"

"You want to go *back* to school? Why? That place sucks."

"Yeah, but I left my car there...and Ricky."

"Come on, Syd," Ricky exclaimed as he came bounding out of the bordering backwoods. "Hurry!"

Sydney looked up. Her younger brother arrived, dashing past the camp's rock ring and hopping over the log opposite the one she was currently using. As he moved, his karate gi flew open like a cape, revealing his recently acquired sweatpants while creating a much more dramatic entrance. Magnificent. His seated sister leaned back a bit and tilted her neck upward to see his flushed face more directly to say, "Did you find the bat cave?"

"No," Ricky panted, now taking an opportunity to catch his breath. "But Lou did! It's cool! You should see it. We can leave the stuff here—it's not that far."

Motioning to his previous path with an upward-facing palm, adding a qualm-camouflaging smirk and a phony attitude to match—hoping wholeheartedly that the further she fled from her loneliness, the better she would be—she suggested pleasantly, "After you, sir."

Little Rick smiled and turned back the way he came.

Sydney stood silently. Her mind inescapably harkened back to that word her grandmother articulated so infamously, and as she and the other teen trounced through the dense woodland, she wondered why it wouldn't just leave her alone. A strange stroll through thick thicket. The birdsong melody from the treetops fell on deaf ears. A babbling creek nearby ran silent with the overwhelming thought skulking through her head. The crunching of the undergrowth beneath her feet was no match for the memory making a mess in her mind, and though she tried to forget the evil things spoiling her sunny summer day, they refused to leave her alone. Boyfriend.

Walking with the wish to feel the light on her shadow again, Sydney caught a fleeting glimpse of the phrase posted on Ricky's tail and couldn't help but grin.

Belly of the Beast

A swelling darkness surrounded him on all sides. Chilled rock walls pressed against his arms, constricting his movements. No drawstring to illuminate his environment. No stepstool necessary. Only the sound of his heartbeat pounded in his ears. He felt the gritty earth beneath his fingers as he slowly crawled forward into the shadowy void. Inching his way blindly through the rough terrain, he felt a snagging on his pants. After many furious attempts at dislodging the obstacle, Leunga made a realization. "Sweet shit... I'm stuck."

Stunted legs dangled in the open air, safely on the outside of the rocky ravine. The sun glinted off of the back of his exposed calves as the fabled blade sat in its sheath, leaning against the rock entrance he was trapped within. Violently, he began wriggling from side to side, trying to increase the size of the opening in the rock, but no such result could be produced. Exhausted by his predicament, he stopped to take a break while he awaited the return of his siblings. Though his senses were dulled by his isolation, Leunga felt the anticipated presence arrive behind him.

Sydney was more than a little disappointed. "*This* is the cave?" All she saw was a small outcropping of boulders arranged in such a way that there was a miniscule opening along the bottom. That's not a cave.

"Cave?" Leunga laughed, apparently talking with his legs like some people do with their hands. "Hells no. Grampy is waiting over near the real cave. I saw a lizzerd run in here and—"

Melancholy and still feeling like the ditched little sister with a chewed-up heart, Sydney kicked dejectedly at the duo of flailing feet, unintentionally making contact with her brother's shinbone, and striking with more force than she typically would have in comparable situations. She instantaneously clenched her teeth and cringed.

"Ow! What the fuck?!"

Sydney thought of an excuse quickly. "Uh, Ricky tripped on your leg..."

"You okay, big stuff?"

Leaning against one of the nearby boulders ornamenting the hillside, the kid in question held his aching ribs in one hand and nodded, unaware of their recent interaction. "Sure. Just need to catch my breath..."

"So anyway..." Leunga began, and promptly lost track of his thoughts. "What?"

Ricky controlled his breathing carefully to give the appearance that he was much less winded than he actually was. "Hey, you should tell her about the lizard you saw. That was awesome."

"Right! I saw a glorious lizzerd run into these rocks and I'm gonna catch it and keep it."

"Oh," said Sydney slowly as she pictured Leunga's only other pet—a box turtle named Alice—and the tormented expression on its corpse. No autopsy was ever performed, but the cause of death appeared to be a combination of smoke inhalation and being sat on one too many times. The teen tried not to imagine how something without a protective shell would fare against her brother and made a recommendation. "Um...maybe you should just let it go. I mean, you don't have anything to carry it in."

Leunga cocked his head to the side, which was difficult to achieve in his dilemma and unnoticeable by anyone other than himself. "Uh...I have pockets, duh."

"But that might crush it..." Visions of Alice—frozen in his final moments.

"Uh-uh. These pants are ultra-thick. It's like armor. Armour. That marvelous lizzerd would be safer in my pockets than anywhere else in the world!"

"Almost looks like it's on fire. It's got these reddy-orangey stripes down its side and a cool zebra tail," replied Ricky, returning to regaining his composure and panting silently to himself. "When you see it, you'll see."

As if waiting for its queue, a small camouflaged animal with a black-and-white-ringed tail was noticed by a stilled sibling, crawling along the side of the outcropping an oldish boy was encased in. It skittered across the white stone before jumping to the dirt below upon noticing a disembodied pair of legs near its home. The lizard scurried over to Sydney and paused on her old-fashioned sneaker, jerking its head side to side in search of danger. She held her breath and watched it motionlessly, trying not to scare it. It sat there on its gray canvas perch, assured that the possible threat had passed, and darted off into the underbrush. "It's cute."

"You kidding? It's ba'dass. I'm gonna name it something. And maybe introduce some radioactive waste to its diet and see if it goes all dinosaur on me."

Ricky faced the portion of the boulders in which he assumed his brother's head was located and stated, "Cool!"

"Yeah. Awesome..." Satisfied with the escape of her sibling's reptilian prey, Sydney felt a bit more included and began studying Leunga's situation. "So hey, do you need help?"

"If you could tell me if you see the glorious lizzerd, that would be great."

"I meant help getting out of *that*."

The voice of their grandfather danced through the trees. "Are you kids coming back or what?"

"Be right there!" Leunga shouted joyfully through the thick walls around him.

"Maybe if you hold still, we can pull you out." Sydney inched closer to her brother's wild wiggling with her arms extended in assistance. As she got within range, Leunga's large boot smacked against the back of her helping hand, causing her fingertips to smash into the adjacent boulder. "Ow, goddamn it!" In immediate retaliation, the sister stood back and kicked her older brother's shin again: same spot, striking with premeditated force, before whirling around and walking away in the direction of their grandfather's holler.

"Fuck..." a certain something exhaled in agony.

Sydney called back. "Ricky tripped!"

The stoner in the stones sighed, shaking away the pain before saying, "Rickers, when you're done tripping all over the place, tell me if you see anything on your end, 'kay?"

"Oh, okay. I just saw Syd let your lizard run near her feet, and she didn't do anything about it."

Leunga grunted angrily with another failed attempt at removing his elfin frame from its ensnared location. "Good detective work, son, but that also means you let my lizzerd get away too. If I ever get out of here, we'll discuss your punishment."

"*More* punishment?!"

•   •   •

Sydney stood at the jaws of the real cave, peeking in curiously with her mouth agape. A rush of chilly wind embraced the bare skin on her arms and calves, dying off momentarily before starting again, as if the entire chasm was breathing. She folded her arms to retain warmth for her shivering torso as she took a few steps inside. The walls surrounding her seemed to engender the drastic drop in temperature she noticed while exiting the summer swelter just outside of the darkness coiling around her. From somewhere past the shadow realm in front of her face, a series of clicks resonated through the chamber; certainly it was the sound of bats.

Stopping just at the lapse of light, Sydney twisted her head to the left quickly, tossing the obtrusive bangs away from her right eye. Quite possibly her best eye. She stood mindful of her footing while she strained her sights to catch a glimpse of any dark gliders. "Hello?" None of the bats answered. Standing perfectly still in the silence, she leaned forward a little more, listening closely for any clues of the bats' location; in fact, she leaned a little too far forward and lost her balance. Panicked by the pitch attempting to swallow her whole, she stumbled along the rocky darkness with greatly tensed muscles before stabilizing herself by gripping a concave opening in the wall. As she sighed with relief, the echoed clattering of a dislodged stone in front of her foot bounced down the slick rock into the blind shadow below.

Fluttering wings of fright resonated through the void, indicating an airborne colony moving in her direction, toward the exit. Instinctively she moved, squishing her back flat against the cold rock fortification, allowing any winged creature an easier passage along its flight path. Screeching bats rapidly approached as the entrance hall of the cavern filled with their dark silhouettes. Sydney smiled as she felt the shrieking breeze generated by dozens of charging wings flying in front of her astonished eyes. Lost in the moments of that awe-inspiring experience, she decided that the camping trip was suddenly worth all of the trouble.

"Holy bastard bats, man!" Leunga bounced around outside of the cave, waving his grandfather's hat in the air to deflect the oncoming torrent of cave dwellers. "Shit, dude, they're in your hair!"

Having helped his small sibling escape one peril only moments earlier, Ricky started running in circles around his brother, batting his crunchy coiffure with his palms. "Whoa! Whoa! Whoa! Aw crap, get it out!"

The elder continued to jump around in a tizzy until he had an idea and dropped the wool hat to grab the hilt of the weapon on his back with both hands, removing the rusted blade from its shelter and shouting, "I'll kill it to pieces!" He hopped up onto a small boulder in order to more clearly have a direct shot at the assailant atop his brawny baby brother and instructed, "Hold *very* still..."

Ricky wisely moved away from Leunga with words to emphasize his actions. "Wait! Wait...!" the younger man implored and ran open fingers along the rigid ridge of his golden fauxhawk, fondling the sheer crest symmetrically splitting his hair in two halves while checking for irregularities when he realized that his older brother was probably mistaken about the attacker in the first place. Finding the truth for himself, he assured, "I think I got it."

"Come closer. It might be hiding in that spiky area in the middle," suggested one brother to another. Lifting his weapon with all his might, the twenty-something man high above the earth prodded at the pretty boy just out of his dangerous range with his heavy metal menace. That's when Leunga froze and noticed something strange before he had a chance to decapitate his sibling. The sword with the machete-like quality in his hand was glowing faintly in vibrant red symbols etched in light along the blade. An ancient writing in incandescence, unfinished and waiting for its other half. Leunga studied the lettering in shock and shuddered. "Fuck me furiously..."

Sydney stood at the maw of the mammoth, peeking out in enthrallment at the colony of bats moving in a large globe of wings and fur through the sky before disappearing over the trees. With a warmed will, her eyes fell to her companions—and to the faint glow emanating from the weapon in Leunga's hand. A feeling of uncertainty swelled in her thoughts as she slowly discerned that the tall tale their grandfather illustrated that morning might actually have some merit. "That's unsettling."

Ricky looked up at the blade in his brother's hand with wonder. "What happened to it?"

Leunga stared at the weapon and shrugged, his face contorted with confusion in reply.

"Can I see it?" asked the handsome hunk, holding out his palm. Seeing with his hands. The sibling with the sword carefully set the handle in his brother's grip. Ricky held the symbols along the blade close to his face for further inspection. The radiance illuminated his stunned expression, reflecting indecipherable characters on his dark brown eyes under the mosaic shadow of the trees. "Maybe it's like glow-in-the-dark paint."

Furrowed brow, wide-eyed, slack jaw extended forward, nostrils flared, Leunga's face was frozen with a myriad of expressions—some good, others not so much. His gaze surged through the trees unwillingly while he searched for the appropriate terminology for their situation. Finally, he was able to articulate his intellectual emotions into easily understood words and held a single syllable continually for at least three minutes. "Uh..."

Sydney stared at her brothers in a trance. Sinking her hands into her back pockets, she leaned against the cavern wall. Without detection, rough igneous scuffed her upper arm as she gawked at the mystifying scene. The entire event seemed surreal, like something from a fantasy mural painted on the side of a heavily used microbus.

Leunga drew in a deep breath, never taking his sight off of the blade in his sibling's grip. Just then, he thought of something important to say. "Uh..." Once again holding that syllable for three minutes.

Pulling her attention away from the oddly glowing weapon in her younger brother's hand, Sydney scouted the trees and asked herself, "Where the hell is Grandpa?"

The elderly man patted his granddaughter's back heartily. "I'm right behind you!"

The pounding of his palm resonated through her chest as her heart jumped at his stealthy return. "Ow..."

"I just had a wild vision, man." He says *man* too much. "I went into the cave and then these demons were all around me poking my face with pitchforks." He pointed at the small puncture wounds along his forehead, which he was probably unaware of. "And then one landed on my hair, and it was like, whoa! And it started whispering secrets about how the government found a satellite orbiting Earth that was over two billion years old, and it has an American flag on the side. Glad you finally decided to come along with us, Sprout. I want all my grandkids to be here for this...so let's get going!"

The old man headed back into the shadow; Sydney's eyes narrowed when she saw a strange brown splotch dangling from her grandfather's ponytail. She strained her squint to see into the enveloping gloom absorbing the elderly man as the bat in her grandfather's dense hair turned and looked at her. "Grandpa, wait!"

He panicked, searching for the obscure beseeching of his granddaughter. "What'd you say, Sunflower?!"

Seeing that the old-timer was on the verge of a mondo freak-out triggered by just about anything she said, she course corrected. "Um...so can you tell us why the sword is kinda glowy now?"

"It'll go away," he ensured assuredly and kept on keeping on. "That's just another part of my wild hallucinations, man. Nobody can see it but me."

"Oh," she replied with a nod and wished what he said was true. "Good..."

•   •   •

Holding the weapon in front of him, Leunga took slow steps into the dissipating darkness, using the increasing glow of the sword as a makeshift torch. With his younger brother and sister in tow, they inched forward into a realm of both shadow and substance their grandfather was far too familiar with. Leading on, the eldest sibling heard the shuffling of the old man disappear from the reach of the red phosphorescence lighting their path. The intense drop in temperature was a welcome relief from the torrid estival weather outside—for some. Echoing drops of water pinged invisibly as Leunga felt the hand gripping his shoulder tighten.

Caught by a severe case of the shivers, Sydney vigilantly watched the narrow path in front of her brother's feet as she held the collar around the base of his neck for guidance. One misplaced step could be fatal in the blind chasm, and with her older brother's impressive record of clumsiness, the danger was amplified a thousandfold. The bright illumination of the lettering along the blade shed foreign light on the surrounding stalactites and stalagmites, innumerable rows of teeth along the fearsome jaws, and luckily, the grand exit of the colony some minutes ago left the chamber hollow and devoid of life, much like Leunga's head. "Ha-ha-ha!"

"What's so funny?"

Sydney snorted. "Nothing."

Ricky squinted in the darkness, gradually losing ground on his sister and brother as he continually wiped his forearms across his face. Loose wisps of dry thread assaulted his crisp hair and worried mug. Every few steps introduced several new strands to his already-altered appearance, collecting mainly around the eyes and nose. No matter how many times he wiped them away, more seemed to gather instantaneously where the previous group left off. Ricky exhaled quickly through his nostrils, temporarily eliminating the threat. He opened his lips to call out to his older siblings and was presented with a mouthful of deserted homes. "Ugh!"

Leunga looked past his occupied sister at the location of the disgusted cry. "What the hell, Rio? Stay with the group."

"I keep—" Ricky spat, attempting to remove the errant strand from the tip of his tongue, unsuccessfully. "I keep walking into spider webs. Pthht!"

"Really? I'm in the front, and I haven't seen any."

Touched by a need for distraction in the frigid tomb, Sydney glanced at their dim surroundings for a moment to take in some scenery and look for possible cobwebs, when she suddenly exclaimed, "Oh! You know what? This is too perfect. I just realized Grandpa got us to come all the way in here without his help just so he can jump out and scare us again." Hopefully without more of the playful abuse! "Goddamn it."

Leunga crept forward along the thin trail, keeping his eyes on the boy at the back. "Hunch on down and hurry up! Just keep your eyes open and—" The sound of a construction boot jamming into an abrupt upward step in the path thundered through the walls as its wearer flew forward, falling to the rocky floor with a slap. The sudden impact of his tan footwear crashing into the hidden stair caused him to release his grip on the mysteriously lit blade. As it soared into the darkness, the lettering along the side grew rapidly dimmer, losing all of its lustrous lighting abilities as the metal object clamored against the stone floor somewhere in the abyss. The darkness was instant, enclosing them in an unknown world, lost and without aid. To make matters worse, Sydney also tripped and slammed on top of Leunga.

A female groaned. "Oh shit..."

"Crap!" A distraught male asked, "What do we do?! Pthht!"

"Did either of you guys hear where it went?"

"No... Pthht!"

"Okay then... I guess I kind of did. What kind of dumbass magic sword loses its power when you don't touch it?!"

An injured male grunted. "I bet I could find it easy."

"You sure? It could've fallen down an infinite pit. Pthht!"

"Yeah. I gots this one."

"Just go really slow and be careful..."

"Well, maybe if you got the hell off of me I could start goin' all careful-like."

"Oh..."

A blind shuffling ensued—a gathering of noise reducing in size as the sound of skidding slid slowly along the rough ground. Inching along the path, the skidding was accompanied by a palm batting the cool base of the cave at random locations in proximity to the grinding slide. Very meticulously, the searching hand travelled with the skidding, away from the original position, moving slowly for a dozen feet or so until it abruptly stopped, clapping against something strange. "Ew—the what is this?! Ugh, it's all hairy and warm... I think it's alive!"

"That's my leg. Pthht!"

"You went the *wrong way*?!"

"Hell, I can't see shit! Wait, couldn't you *hear* me going the wrong way? And she says nothing of it. Lazy."

"I'm closer to it now. Let me try to get it." A secondary—and somewhat more confident—skidding began from the source location of the first, moving in the opposite direction at a quicker pace. The slapping of the cold stone floor from the newest recovery attempt was far more controlled and methodical, sweeping motions in a semicircle in front of the skidding. Moving steadily through the void, it sped until its progress was brought to a dead stop by instinct, sensing warmth and breathing from close by. The ambient cave sounds died off momentarily as the respiratory response to the skidding stopped. Silence stilled the air. "...Grandpa? No? Okay!" The skidding moved quicker, the clapping more rapid, when suddenly the sound of metal jingled against rock. The hand clapped along the blade in tepid relief. The weapon clattered with the floor as it was groped up to its hilt. The bright red lettering along the tarnished iron burned away the darkness as it was lifted from the floor with a metallic swish.

Sydney knelt on the cold ground, brandishing the blade high above her head, searching for whatever may be lurking in the shadows. She stood slowly and glanced in the perceived direction of her brothers. "You guys stay there. I'll come get you." Through the void a noisy rustling echoed around the teeth of the cavern, causing the swordswoman to face the source of the disturbance, aiming the tip of the hefty sword in its direction. As the rustling ceased, it was followed by a click accompanied by sparks.

Calmly, the clicking continued, along with the addition of more sparks emerging from the shadows. Another few clicks later, a flame appeared, illuminating Leunga's face. "Okay, we'll wait over here then."

"Pthht! You have a lighter?" Ricky asked and squatted next to his brother, admiring the large flame while peeling a web from his incredible eyebrows.

"Oh, hell yeah! See? It has the Admiral Amazingman symbol on the side."

"Cool."

Sydney relaxed her stance, lowering the heavy blade as she rolled her head back. "Oh my god...bastard ass."

As the youngest stood, he helped his brother up from his stony seat. The fire in Leunga's hand followed his face upward, keeping the ghostly image of his visage stationary against the flame. "Thank you, patsy." The torchbearer released his youngest sibling's helping hand and held the lighter closer to the median point between the two brothers' faces. As he moved the bright orange glow higher, the web-covered face of Ricky appeared more visibly, along with the floating head of their grandfather watching silently beside them. "Whoa! Shit!"

Ricky jumped back, startled. "Inhuman fiend!"

Sydney watched the apparition of the old man appear like a specter from the shadows near her brothers. "Ha! I knew that was gonna happen."

"Come on, kids! We're almost there!" The elderly man vigorously gripped his grandsons' shoulders and squeezed as hard as he could, lovingly. Leunga and Ricky winced at the gesture of adoration. The old gent moved confidently through the unlit expanse between the low light of the Admiral Amazingman flame of justice and the curious luminance of the sword. He reappeared next to Sydney, calling out to Leunga and Ricky as he walked right past the girl with the glow. "It's just around this corner." And once again he disappeared.

Making her way back to her big brother, the middle sibling handed him the weighty weapon as he shut his lighter cap, returning to her position behind him. "Watch out for the step this time, 'kay?"

"Muh! You too!" Decidedly without decision, Leunga took a far more casual approach to their spelunking upon seeing the geriatric move so swiftly through the halls, and he sprang forth with no delay. With the lit blade dangling by his side in a loose grip, he walked carelessly into the unknown.

A voiced boomed through the tunnel from somewhere up ahead. "Whoa, man! Wild! It's like I can feel the swords again...or maybe that's the psilocybin."

The leader glanced back at his sister, who was strangely struggling to keep up the pace. "Damn old man bogarting all those—"

"Keep your eyes forward, goddamn it! We're trying not to die here!"

"Pthht! Yeah!"

Instantly addressing the interruptive sister over his shoulder, someone said, "Rickwich is right. You need to chill it on ice. This ain't no thang—" Leunga stumbled forward, mildly tripping over another odd stair, but remaining upright all the same. "See? Nothin' doin'."

An unusually thick cluster of webbing collided with Ricky's eyes, impairing his vision. The giant karate-clad kid paused, whipping his hands furiously against his face in a grand gesture of overwhelming irritation. He ripped web after web from his irate eyes in the manifestation of his repressed aggression and persistent frustration with the family's relaxing camping holiday. Flicking his web-ridden wrists at the floor, he heard a low vibrating coming from his brother and sister and asked, "What was that?"

"Sounded like you slapping yourself silly."

"I think I heard it too." The pothead paused along the path, allowing his sister to bump into his back without reprisal. He searched the cavern with his ears, hoping to reencounter the odd droning, but there was nothing but the continual silence of the shadow. "Guess not." He took a quick step forward and it began again. "Guess yes!" An abnormal sensation followed. Leunga glanced at his right hand—the one lazily holding the sword—and noticed that the entire thing was jostling, causing an incremental humming sound as they moved closer to their grandfather's destination. With weapon held in both hands, he became consumed with uncertainty. "Uh, didn't Grampy say these things can kill somebody who touches them?"

"Something close to that."

The eldest sibling turned to his sister, offering the vibrating blade. "Here, hold this. I think it's your turn now."

Sydney shook her head in shock. "No!"

"Big Rick? You wanna lead?"

"Pthht!"

"I'll take that as a yes, please."

Reassuring her brother with a hesitant shoulder shove, the girl guided. "You'll be fine! Grandpa said you have to hold both of them at the same time to die—or make a deal with them or whatever... I don't know, duh. So shut up and go."

Filled with his family's undoubted certainty, Leunga pursed his lips and nodded, accepting responsibility for showing his young squires the way along the path to the final encounter of the epic quest. He spun around, gripped the gyrating sword firmly in one hand, and held it high, pointing it heroically toward their destination. Drawing in an excessive breath, he lunged forward, walking with demonic speed into the awaiting heart of the beast. His legs carried him with verve, gliding along the path with ease.

"Slow down, idiot! We can't see—ow! Watch it."

"Sorry. Pthht!"

"What's this? Ugh! You got a damn spider web in my hair. And did you just spit on me?!"

"...No. Pthht!"

Leunga darted forward. Rounding a corner, he abruptly came face-to-face with his grandfather sitting off to the side of a wide-open room. Lowering the blade to his side, the vibrations became increasingly violent as he ignored the old man and edged closer to a pool of water across the way from his relative, who seemed to be enjoying himself at the time, so there was no need to bother him profusely. Slowly peeking his head over the edge of the rippling well, the sworded sibling saw nothing in the consuming darkness of the water. "You sure this is where it is?"

"Most definitely, man. It's down there for good, and soon they'll be together again."

Leunga placed his free hand around the rocky lip of the pool, staring through the bleak water. He held up the weapon at his right, shining its light over the calcified liquid, but was unable to penetrate the opaque fluid with illumination.

Suddenly, Sydney jumped around the corner of the room. "Boo!" she shouted and smiled at the elderly man, who seemed unfazed by her entrance and payback. "Nothing?"

As sad as it was, her grandfather shrugged at her and declined.

Appearing next from the gloom were Ricky, his face, and his hair, covered in countless cobwebs. The elderly man caught a brief glimpse of his grandson before freaking out. "Holy hell! What wild grotesquery is this, man? You demon stay back! I know all of your secrets already. You hold no power over me. I am the eternal!"

Shocked by his reaction, his granddaughter carefully eased over to the old man, placing her arm around his shoulders and calming him in a caring and reassuring tone. "Shhh...it's okay. It's just Ricky, Grandpa." A skill she learned while dealing with her stupid brother—the older one, of course—though in this instance, she was considerably nicer. "He's just uglier than usual, that's all."

The old man hesitantly trusted the words of the helpful cave sprite covered in explosive shadow and accepted the fluffy beast as his grandson. "Whew, bad trip, man. You look like some freaky cotton ball with giant ram horns and fiery eyes...and the demonic aura!"

Ricky felt his hair, checking for any possible bony growths. Sydney glanced at the dim image of her taller brother and saw no horns, but only the familiar blond fauxhawk covered in ancient spider strands. Out of the corner of her eye, she noticed Leunga gazing into a murky stew at the center of the chamber—a large room within the cave certainly containing the most stalactites—but the least stalagmites, oddly enough. "Is that really where the other sword is?" she asked immediately.

"Yep," the gray-haired guy answered. "And we can all split after Louie drops that bastard in."

"Wait," the woman interjected. "If he throws that in the water, we won't be able to see our way out of here."

Thoughtfully, Leunga placed a finger to his lower lip, holding the pulsating blade horizontally next to his chin. "That's easy. We tie Ricky's shirt to a stick, light it on fire with my lighter, and use it as a torch."

"That's idiotic! Where are we gonna find a *stick* in here?"

"Oh...you're right—Hey, hold on! I'm not throwing this masterpiece into anything!"

"It's for the best, man," an elder expressed. "For too long I've been haunted by this place. Tormented by the awful memories and pain caused by my hands. And now I'll finally have comfort in knowing that these evil tools will be lost forever, where no one can—wait, what the hell are you doing?!"

"One sec; I almost got it..." The water splashed across the rocky floor as Leunga searched blindly with his left arm shoulder deep in the well. "Maybe if it just—" He stopped talking shortly after he dove his head and much of his upper body into the filth, resurfacing a moment later. He took a breath and grinned. "I got it!" Out of the murky depths, he lifted an object, glowing in the same fashion as the identical one in his right hand. In an instant, the blade at his right stopped vibrating, and both swords extinguished in unison, returning the cave to darkness. "Um, I think they're broken."

A brilliant blast of light illuminated the chamber, filling the area with the luminosity of the summer sun. A thunderous rumbling resonated from the objects emitting the vibrant rays located in Leunga's awestruck hands. He stared down at the violently trembling blades and cringed as he watched the skin on the backs of his hands burn away, peeling back to reveal a twin pair of large symbols written in an unrecognizable language. In the echo of the tumultuous swords, he heard a faint whispering, as if originating from somewhere in his ears. He felt as if he were at the heart of a volcano, swallowing an ocean, burning the sky with his powerful breath, and invincible. As the thunder surrounding him continued, he was overcome with emotions. Inhaling deeply while looking to the ceiling, he let out a fearsome scream, powerful enough to rival that of the weapons'. The deafening sound of the swords abruptly died off, leaving only the mighty roar of Leunga to disrupt the natural cave setting. When he was finally out of breath, he paused to observe the damage on his hands: open gashes, many layers of skin deep, muscle and sinew burned by fire. He looked over at the horrified faces of Sydney and Ricky and clarified, "That didn't actually hurt. I just needed to scream."

"Aw, goddamn it, Louie! And I was in the middle of that speech too." The old man grabbed his suddenly struggling granddaughter by the tiny sleeves and pulled her in a little too close for comfort in order to explain, "I was practicing that all morning!"

The Sword and the Stoner

The force of the sun's fire pierced his wild green eyes as the family travelled out of the cave, blinding him momentarily. The trees above rustled furiously with the knowledge that something powerful had just happened in the neighboring den. A concentration of cosmic energy not meant to be handled by humanity was now unleashed. In the brightness of the June daylight, Leunga noticed the rust on his original blade had completely vanished, along with any oxidation the other may have sustained over the years. Studying his new weapons further, he noticed that the heft he once felt while holding his primary sword was gone; both blades were weightless in his grip. He crossed them above his head, sliding sheen metal against metal; the fiery glow of the lettering along the flat surfaces was now solid and ever-present, along with a sharp inch of light extending off the bladed edge of each sword. He lowered the items to eye level and placed them together, completing the set. Temporarily reforming them into one article, the sword-bearer smirked. "Cool, when you put them together this sword is a chub!" Each weapon's sharp edge faced away from its twin; the symbols along the sides became whole, as well as the rectangular hilt. Leunga stared at the writing, squinting hard to try and make it out. "Slip crow pain yo ho—oh wait, it's not in English."

"*And* they're safer than aspirin, man. Plus, totally nonaddictive."

"Really...?" Sydney nodded politely, and sincerely hoped the conversation would end there. Thrilled to be out of the unbearable chill of the cavern, she walked over to a patch of sunlight shining on a large flat rock and sat.

But the old man wasn't finished expanding her scope with his wisdom, so he followed his granddaughter, finding a seat extremely close to hers, same rock and everything. "I used to have this book that showed the types that were edible and where you could find everything, but now I can't find it anywhere." Maybe he ate it.

"Aw," sympathized the sister, swiftly becoming exhausted by the tedious toadstool tête-à-tête. She looked up at the trees, locked in yet another uncomfortable silence with one of her grandparents, praying that this one wouldn't bring up *that* word, especially in front of her brothers. Gazing at the wafting leaves, she chose to ignore the strange gnashing noises emanating from the elderly gentleman's mouth and kept her eyes skyward. At least the sunshine felt nice.

Ricky emerged slowly from the refreshing chill of the cavern, reentering the scorching summer sun. Pinching the last strand of webbing from his forehead, he squinted out at his brother swinging his newfound weapons wildly in the open path leading from the cave's entrance. The bright red glow that was once flickering faintly under the shadow of the trees was now continual and as bright as a full moon. Along with the shine of the ancient symbols, it was now apparent that the razor edges of each blade too were radiating a soft atmosphere of light—noticeable even in the bright, cloudless weather. Ricky's eyes were fixed on the swords as his mouth unmistakably asked, "Does this mean we can go home now?"

Leunga stopped and slowly turned his sights toward his brother. He grinned with the biggest, goofiest, stupidest smirk he could muster before redirecting his gaze at the twin weapons in his grip, saying, "So, Grampy, when can I start hacking and slashing some ancient monsters?" Awaiting the imminent response, he stabbed each sword into the dirt below him, narrowly missing his own feet. "I deserve to know."

The old man sighed. "Damn it, Louie! I told you to drop it into— we're not going to fight anything. Put them back into the holster; we need to find a new place to hide them. Damn kid. You're lucky to be alive, man."

"Why do we have to find a new place? You could just take them back into the cave, couldn't you?" speculated a svelte grandson as he folded his arms behind his back and leaned against the sun-heated outer wall of the cave, effectively concealing his bootylicious backside.

In reply, his grandfather shook his head. "That monster I told you about came after me for a reason, man, and it knew where to look." He paused, adjusting his position on the hard surface of his bench before explaining, "Louie was standing at the well when he *didn't listen to me* and made the swords his, so the dude probably knows they were there. It just *knows*, man. That's why I went back to check on 'em in the first place. They're way too harsh to just leave for something like that thing to find."

The youngest hiker glanced around at the tree line. "The warlock guy?" he asked very skeptically; although considering the recent events, it was becoming slightly more plausible.

"Yeah, hmmm..." The elderly man made some wavering hand gestures while trying to find the right terminology—probably indicating something, but it's definitely unclear. "What was that thing my dad called it? Christ, he said it to me at least a dozen times in the same sentence that day, man...you'd think I'd remember it—oh! *The Summoner.* That's what it was. Summoner...yeah, it makes sense now that I think about it. Summoner!" He readjusted himself again and said, "Summoner."

Sydney turned halfway toward her chair buddy, raising her left eyebrow to ask, "Did you ever see it? Or *him*? Or whatever it was?"

"I think so, but not in person," her grandfather guesstimated. "Like I said before, I kept having these nightmares after I ditched the sword in that cave there. Same bald guy. Tall, kinda buff, sort of tan, pointy braided beard of black hair, and he kept talking to me in my dreams. If I had to guess, I'd say that was him. Almost felt like he was really there too, man. It was wild."

The teen leaned forward on her seat, staring at her white, rubber-tipped gray shoes. "What kind of things did he say to—" She stopped midsentence as the man sitting at her side failed an attempted left-cheek-sneak and *accidentally* passed gas very audibly. Discreetly, she leaned back and looked away, placing a fist beneath her nose to block the passage of air.

Leunga grimaced at the trumpeting from the stone slab. "Ew! Sydney, that's gross! Apologize this instant!"

She quickly turned toward her brother and responded in a panicked whisper. "That wasn't me!"

"Ugh, I feel like I can already smell it. Pee-eww!"

Continuing her questioning with a roll of her eyes, someone asked the senior, "What kind of things did he say to you?"

"I mean, when a guy farts, it's funny, but when a girl lets a massive one rip like that—I mean, come on, what the hell? I am going to be violently sick over here."

The elderly man scratched his ample goatee and thought about the teenager's inquiry. "You know, it's weird. All he would say to me is that I was a nice guy and I gave it my best shot...almost like he was proud or somethin'."

"Huh." Ricky bounced his head against the rocky surface behind him and innocently assessed, "He doesn't really sound like a bad guy."

"Yeah, I guess not...but it still doesn't change the fact that he sent out a helpless baby bear in order to stop me."

Ricky continued to spring against the cave and remembered. "Oh yeah..."

"Actually, it's not even the smell. It's the *sound* of it. That's gonna be in my nightmares forever..."

Sydney removed the fist from her nostrils and said, "What would make him want to attack people? I mean—if he actually can—why doesn't the Summoner attack everybody? You said he's from Scotland, so why the hell would he travel thousands of miles just to attack you? Does he always just go after the person with the swords? Or is he just stupid like that?"

"Christ, that's a lot of questions, Sunflower. I don't know; maybe he's got a vendetta against our family. My dad told me that the Summoner was killed by the swords, but now I know that's bullshit; otherwise, I wouldn't have the memories that torment me, man. I guess he lost some of his confidence, because I heard he used to attack villages all the time. Maybe the swords have something to do with that..."

Ricky glanced at the weapons pierced into the earth—their gallant glow gone without the hands of Leunga to light them—and suddenly, a familiar sensation besieged him. Breathing in sharply many times in quick succession, he promptly set free a booming sneeze. He wiped his nose with his bare arm and asked, "What makes those swords glow?"

"Huh? Oh, right, yeah. I guess I forgot to tell that part. Okay, so, anyway, this is what I think my old man said." Beginning a barrage of information once again, the elderly man cleared this throat with words at the ready, as if he had been waiting to reveal a thousand secrets all at once his entire life. "Way long time ago, man, there was this blacksmith guy and his apprentice who wanted something to fight off the Summoner with, right? Well one day, they go up to the forest and meet this hermit guy who knows all kinds of old magic—even considered it old back then—and he says he can make a weapon able to defeat anything as long as it's created with a good heart, or something. So the blacksmith's apprentice makes those weapons over there and takes them back to the hermit guy who asks only for a drop of the apprentice's blood. The apprentice guy grabs his master's dagger and makes a wicked big slice in his hand, giving the hermit like a whole mug worth, man. So then, the hermit starts channeling his chi into the weapons and coats them with the young guy's juices before he takes the same dagger and cuts his own wrists, holding them like this over the swords. When the hermit guy died, they say the apprentice picked up the swords and they started glowing and now they can move without even trying."

"The guy *kills* himself just to make some stupid swords?! What an idiot."

Leunga stopped retching on all fours momentarily and looked up. "Hmm, 'stupid idiot blood swords.'" He stroked his chin. "That could be a great name for them. Not really, but it'll have to do."

"Well that's how I remember my dad's story," their grandfather said with a shrug. "Could've been exaggerated over the generations, man. It *was* like seven hundred years ago."

"Seven *hundred*?! This wizard guy has been alive for, like, seven hundred years?"

The elderly man nodded at Ricky. "At least that long, Junior."

"Yowza." Leunga sat back on the ground, legs stretched forward while propping himself up with stiff arms angled behind him. He stared at his new toys and got to thinking. "Hey, how do I make 'em do the things like you said?"

Their grandfather released an annoyed grunt and stood slowly, walking over to an object placed with care on the forest floor. "*You* don't," he replied, picking up the small item and tossing it to his granddaughter. "*They* do." Sydney caught the pinecone easily and shot him a confused glance. "Get up, Louie. Take a sword in each hand."

Compelled by the mysteriousness of his grandfather's actions, Leunga obliged him. Rolling onto his back and gaining some momentum, he tried to execute a jumping tactic to land upright on his feet without the use of his arms, but failed miserably. Five times. Before the sixth attempt, he bailed and stood up somewhat simply. Leunga travelled to the blades, still perforating the ground, and placed one hand around each incomplete handle, causing the fiery lettering to reappear instantly. With a firm grip, he jerked his lower back upward to remove the blades but couldn't get them to budge. "Gonna need a sec. I punched a hole in the planet."

Their grandfather turned to Sydney, saying, "Throw it at him."

She stood, poised, ready to release the ball in her hand—a familiar stance. Leunga watched as his sister rolled her left arm back, aiming her shot with the right. Without hesitation or emotion, Sydney complied with the request and threw the spiked globe with deadly accuracy and lethal force toward her brother's awaiting face. As she unleashed the pinecone, the boy between the blades stared at its entry into his personal space, fully expecting it to smack against his teeth and allow him a free counterattack against the girl, when he was surprised by the vision before his eyes. As if instantaneously, the swords in his hands sliced long gashes into the ground to ease their escape and flew up toward his chest, moving his arms like a furious gyroscope. They danced around in his tight grip, causing a symphony of polished metal gliding easily through the air, swishing and pinging against each other in a hasty ferocity he had no control over. The pinecone entered the fury of the storm and disappeared, blasting into a thousand pieces scattered along the ground. When the threat passed, Leunga's hands dropped to his side, once again leaving him in control. "Whoa! I got pinecone dust on my cheeks."

Sydney couldn't believe the sight and giggled. "Wow!"

Ricky was shocked. He chortled at the jaw-dropping speed and expert katana handling his brother had just performed. During his many years of martial arts tournaments and exhibitions, he had never seen someone move twin blades that fast. "Can you do it ag—"

A massive, low rumbling echoing in the distance far from their position outside of the cave interrupted the teen's request—a vaguely elemental droning, almost like a mountain grinding against a mountain. Roaring like perpetual thunder, it bellowed continuously, destroying the tranquility of the forest surrounding them as it lingered on and on. Its origin was impossible to pinpoint and continued to grow louder with each passing moment. Eight minutes later it came to a sudden stop, replaced by the sound of an immense chain falling. Each link clanged against another metal object as it quickened in pace upon exiting its housing. The event ended with a deafening thud somewhere in the distance.

"Well, what the hell was *that*?!" The old man looked around at the empty trees, unable to see the forest.

"*You* don't know?!" asked Ricky, panicked by the senior citizen's comment.

"Maybe a train got derailed?" Sydney suggested.

"I've never seen a train track around here, man."

Leunga quietly looked at the sky. For reasons unknown to anyone, he felt an overwhelming sense of peace and oneness with his surroundings. He and the swords stood solid as a single entity in the face of uncertainty, surging with an ancient force. Holding the blades chest-high, he looked down upon them with respect and appreciation and sensed what needed to happen next. There was no doubt in his mind that the quest was epic up to that point, but now the adjective seemed insufficient. Their epic quest was over; now it was the dawn of something more. "Grandiose. No, that's stupid..."

"What if a dam broke?"

"No dams around here for miles. It sounded like it was getting closer to us."

"Copacetic? I don't know what that one means..."

"I know! A cave collapsed."

"But it sounded like a machine. Or a pirate ship."

"Maybe it was...the guy?"

"*Legendary!*" That's the one.

"...Shit. Louie, we need to hide those *now!*"

Leunga took his eyes off of the weapons and looked to his family—each of them staring at him with differing emotions. Sydney appeared to be the calmest, not allowing the turbulence to shake her nerves, but still concerned. Ricky, on the other hand, was wide-eyed and twiddling his fingers, clearly fearful about the strange occurrence taking place far off—both of them looking to their older brother for a response. Leunga faced the mournful face of his grandfather, before looking again at the twin blades. The mirror-like quality of the refreshed metal reflected his determined green eyes back at themselves and he solemnly said, "We can't."

"Louie, very soon something is going to try to attack you, and you'll slaughter it horribly. It's heavy, man. Believe me, you do not wanna be living with that the rest of your life."

"I play Fantasy World every day. Trust me, I'm up to the task."

"I don't know what that means."

"It's a stupid online game he pays twenty-five dollars a month to play, and he only ever plays with one other person."

"Yeah sure, and like paying a hundred chungs for a new softball mitt *isn't* the dumbest thing to ever be."

"*Oh my god!* That was *two* years ago, and I actually needed it!"

"Needed it for *what?!*"

"Listen," their grandfather insisted, "killing an animal isn't a game, man. You'll be causing actual pain to an actual living thing. And it won't stop with just one. Unless you hide those things now, or somehow manage to stop that bastard making forest critters do his dirty work, then they'll just keep coming. I just know they will..."

"Well then, it's pretty obvious isn't it? We have to find the Summoner and put an end to his evil ways, preferably by the end of today." Ricky and Leunga glanced at each other before simultaneous staring at Sydney in bewilderment. Even their sister was shocked by her own statement. Her eyes darted between each brother before clarifying, "...Right? To keep the animals safe?" Makes sense to me.

Leunga reached back over his right shoulder and skillfully holstered the blades in the sheath harnessed to his back without looking. "Yes...Sypney is right for once. Weird."

The youngest quester was growing concerned at the aspect of spending further time in the wilderness, and the possibility of finding a troll in the middle of the forest. He walked over to his brother and leaned closer to inquire, "Wouldn't killing somebody be really illegal?"

Leunga reached up and gently squeezed his sibling's cheeks together with his dirt-covered hand and said, "Sweet, naïve Richard...everything I do is illegal. And it's only illegal if you get caught, otherwise it's fine, just like everything else."

Sydney felt electrified with a sense of duty, like a superheroine protecting the vulnerable from those that would exploit them, asking her grandfather, "How do we find the Summoner thing?"

"My guess is you look for whatever just made that big-ass noise out there, man."

Ricky glanced at the gray-haired guy with perplexity. "You aren't coming too?"

"I don't think so, Junior. I've already wasted too many years out here." The elderly man sighed heavily as he lifted his brownish bag over his long ponytail and set it on the rock beside him. "Here, you kids will need this more than me...I can't be of any help anymore anyway. I'd just slow you down." Inhaling deeply, he looked up the path at the awaiting jaws of the cave one final time and patted his abdomen. "I think it's about time this old bastard said good-bye to these woods. Time to go back to Gloria for good..." he told himself as quietly as he could. Turning to his family, he offered, "I'll be sure to tell your mom that you three are extending your relaxing vacation... Are you absolutely sure you want to do this...?"

Sydney stared at her brothers and nodded.

Leunga looked to his sister and then to his brother. "Totally."

Ricky recognized the hopeful eyes of his siblings and shrugged. "Sure..."

Though his concern for their safety still burned at the tip of his tongue, their grandfather gazed at the group with a smirk, for deep down in the pit of his heart, he knew that any one of these kids of his had the strength to do what he never could, and he wouldn't dare trust this task to anyone else. "Okay then. I hope you're ready. Bye-bye!" And then the geriatric man swiveled around and sprinted full speed down the path away from his grandchildren, disappearing from sight mere moments later.

Watching the elderly man dash away as he sniffled in protest of the pollen threatening his sinuses, Ricky remarked, "There's a bat in his ponytail."

"Hey! Hey, old man! You forgot your bag!" Leunga glanced at the backpack draped across the rock and laughed. "Idiot forgot his bag."

"He just said that we could have it, idiot."

"Whoa hell! I wonder if he hid any 'shrooms in there..."

Ricky's eyes hovered through the trees as he sighed. "So what should we do now?"

Searching for something inside the taupe treasure trove set upon the rock, Leunga stroked his coarse, stubble-covered chin, which was just enough hair on the end of his jaw to be lost in the hazy middle ground between a beard and whatever the opposite of a beard is—a limbo created by laziness and an unwillingness to shave more than once every couple of weeks—while he suggested, "We start looking for the Summoner, I reckon."

"Heh. Looks like your *epic quest* might actually be epic now." A sister smiled, placing a congratulatory pat on her older brother's shoulder.

"Nay, wench, this quest be *legendary* now."

Sydney quickly swatted the back of Leunga's hat, propelling it to the ground. "Wench?!"

LEGENDARY

Invite to Join Party

The woods echoed with a deafening stillness. Unknown dangers lurked around every perilous pine in the dense forest, far from the safety of the rock-walled campsite. Every slight shift of the wilderness was cause for alarm. Sydney and Ricky held an alert watch of their surroundings as they walked steadily along the only manmade path connected to the cave's trail, travelling away from their camp. They watched vigilantly for any sign of a colossal chain or standard troll, when suddenly, a large fern just off the path shook violently. The two siblings continued walking forward, merely glancing dismissively at its ferocious quaking. The seven-foot plant trembled wildly until their older brother emerged from it slowly.

"Stay on the damn path, damn it. You're gonna get a tick."

Leunga laughed boisterously, beating his chest with tight fists. "I am the energy of a thousand suns all thundering at once! A full tank, a new battery, someone has pulled my string, and I am living! Whew! It is really hot today... Really, really fucking hot. Pricky, can I ride on your back?"

Ricky inhaled unexpectedly, holding his breath for a moment before sneezing with a volume that would shatter rock. "I'm—I don't wanna...I just did, I'm not carrying you any more today..."

His older brother kindly added, "Do it and I won't attack your sack while you sleep."

"No."

"Oh my god," Sydney said, sickened by the gender-centric topics brought to light over the course of the day. "Quit talking about pevl—pubic par—*private* parts. There is a *lady* present, you dick. You can't talk that way around women."

Leunga stared at his ladylike sibling and had a thought. "Syddley, kneel down so I can get on your shoulders."

"Okay, sure! Right afta I punch-a you in da face. I'm not some little rideable *dinosaur* you can ditch down the road when it's convenient."

"Wh—whoa, what in the name of hell? You're not allowed to make things up. That's just amazing nonsense." Following closely behind Sydney while she trekked forth along the dusty trail, the shortest of the siblings suddenly had another massive thought. With all of those new superpowers his swords lent him, he didn't need his sister's help when it came to boosting his buns up for a lofty lift over the dirt, and so he reached up and gripped his hands firmly around her shoulders at the peak of the twin spaghetti straps over her faded black shirt and hopped with both feet—three, maybe five times—before lunging upward, wrapping his legs around the back of her waist. Surprise!

The girl stumbled forward, apparently astonished. "What the F?!"

Leunga folded his arms, encasing his little sister like a koala wrapped around a tree caught in a tornado, keeping his forearms around her slender neck—more neckwear to go with the subtle black choker he just noticed. "See? This is not so bad," he noted. Although a heavy portion of her teased tresses did dangle annoyingly in his face. Leunga blasted the floppy mane with his furious exhaling powers but was only able to move it slightly. "Onward, beast!"

Sydney laughed angrily. "Ohoho, little shit...you are so very dead..."

Chewing gently on an errant lock of her airy blond hair, the casual rider was careful to avoid the dark black area at the tip of the golden lines as he rested his chin on the long white sleeve of the undershirt covering his forearm. His eyes collapsed under the heavy weight of his heat-inspired drowsiness and he drifted off, listening to the calming chimes of the trees wafting in the warm summer breeze, until he realized he had something in his mouth and he spat in terror when he noticed what it was. "Ew, goddamn me! Now I want some cookies."

Sydney faced her back, and consequently her older-brother-backpack, toward a large pine tree and pounced backward, slamming Leunga into the trunk. Squish.

Instantly, he released his grip in horror, unaware of the events taking place, and slid down the rough bark, where he rolled into the dirt, defeated. "I am slain."

"Dude, at least he didn't jump into your arms like he did with me."

Massaging as much of her traumatized back as she could reach, his sister agreed with the other teen. "Yeah, but damn is he heavy. He seems like he doesn't have a lot of *mass*, but it's very *dense*." Physics class: B minus.

"Maybe he's supposed to have, like, the same weight as us, but his bones stopped growing for some reason, so it got all compacted up."

"That's probably it."

With his nose in the cool mixture of dry and strangely wet soil, the eldest coughed, blasting a shockwave of dust beneath his face and asked, "Are you two guys talking about *me*?!"

"Of course not."

"I don't think we were even talking."

Leunga smelled conspiracy...and whatever it was his nose was in at the moment.

Sydney readjusted her clothing as she turned around, looking down at her broken brother lying facedown in the dirt, surrounded by dozens of tiny fern sprouts like a giant sleeping among the trees. "You're super fine. Get up, please," she said with a slight sigh and spied the pines, checking the area for any actual giants before returning her attention to Leunga, who had yet to move. "Get up *faster* maybe? What the—" A patch of wet hair brushed against her cheek before she grabbed it to study the anomaly closer. "Fuck."

Ricky wiped his nose on his bicep, obstinately assaulted by the overpowering force of the milieu's mighty pollen. He sniffled, temporarily holding back his increasingly runny nose. Without forewarning, he sneezed twice in rapid succession, startling himself and his siblings.

"I think you made me deaf," Leunga remarked and rolled onto his back, staring across the path they had yet to travel in hopes of spotting the object of their inquest through the trees: the source of the thunderous grinding and the mysterious shackle. His search quickly faded as a vibrant object on the ground near his face caught his attention. Reaching over, he snapped it up, studying the orange item floating above his face—an almost-perfect specimen of a drinking straw, lost and found in the middle of the forest floor—and he was stunned. "Someone has lost the most magnificent beverage device I have ever seen. They must be looking everywhere for this. Jackpot, bitch."

Already knowing what the other boy was thinking, Ricky sniffled. "Um...hey, just—you know, don't use that until you wash it."

"Well, gee, Mom, you really think I shouldn't put the filthy ground-straw into my precious mouth?" Leunga inquired, scoffing and squinting over at his brother with a jutted upper lip.

"I dunno. I guess so."

"I'm obviously only taking it for the reward," the eldest explained as he placed it safely into his key item pouch next to his knobby left knee. "And maybe for some extra exp."

Upon hearing about the possibility of a reward, Ricky offered, "Want me to carry that for you, dude?"

And Leunga regretfully declined. "Never."

Meanwhile, an ominous cloud loitering in the not-so-distant sky, threatening to ruin their march with a downpour, caught a girl's eye. Sydney stood still, staring at the monstrosity of gray mist through the high-reaching pine needles as she gripped the damp hair in her fingers, figuring she found the source of the soak. She held an open palm up and tested the changing weather of the wilds, but sensed no direct rain. An attack of the frizzies was a possibility nonetheless. In the event of severe humidity or a cloudburst, Sydney opted to return her hairstyle to its former form—a comforting style widely unchanged for most of her senior high past. It was only somewhat recently that she overhauled her look and began to let her hair down for reasons only she would know. Seriously, I don't know.

Ricky glanced at his sister, noticing her attention directed at something in the sky. He followed her gaze and observed the looming darkness above the central trees. A visible vortex of swirling plumes. Something about the manner of the immense cumulous in the otherwise cloudless sky seemed unusual, somewhat malevolent, while at the same time, boring. Suddenly, Ricky sneezed.

Pulling the bulk of her decidedly jaunty mane into a temporary ponytail, Sydney wove the shiny new extremity into a loose whirled loop of a bun with inches of untamable, darkened endings darting off in whichever direction suited them best—like a stationary blond meteor frozen in perpetual free fall as it forever careens toward Earth with a trail of black tails following closely behind—an intentionally messy, and playfully feral, bun positioned at an area where it might be able to fit through that open hole on the back of a baseball cap—or softball cap—if she ever decided to wear one. No discrimination intended. Holding the bunch against the back of her head, she tied the bundle together with a few of her elastic jelly bracelets, performing the second nature styling so quickly and expertly that neither of her brothers witnessed the event. Like a ninja.

"What the hell are you looking at?" asked Leunga, turning his head to scope out his brother's point of interest. "Aw, yeah. See? I knew it was gonna rain. I totally told your ass."

A labored gust fought its way through the unbreakable shield of trees, knocking Sydney's unparted blond bangs out of place once more just as she finished her hairy business. Jerking her head to the left, she shifted her long, wispy wall to the side and looked at the storm cloud again. "We should really start moving. I don't really want to have to look out for monsters in the fucking rain."

Suddenly, an intense growl echoed from somewhere along the path.

"What the hell was that?!" Leunga shouted at an unnecessarily loud volume from his post amid the dirt. Immediately, he asked a line of follow-up questions, still shouting. "Bugbear? Owlbeast? Hawkbeast?!"

Answering, the youngest lowered his voice. "Me! That was my stomach. I'm really hungry."

The lounging loser in the mud patted his own forehead in adulation. "Aw, yeah. See? I knew it was a Fauxhawkbeast. I totally told your ass." Déjà vu.

Ricky glanced around, whispering, "Shouldn't we be a little more quiet? The, uh...*shouting* is kinda giving away our position a ton."

Leunga started shouting some more. "What did he say?!"

And Sydney leaned over her older brother, placing her hands around her mouth while she yelled down at his face. "He says all the shouting is giving away our position!"

"Hmm, is it? I always thought all his goddamn sneezing was doing that for us already."

"Dude," a dude said, "whatever happened to tectonic espionage and whatever?"

"It was tactical *and* it was action. *And* that was almost ten minutes ago. The times are a-changing, Rucky. Rocky. Ricky! There we go." Leunga reached up and grabbed his brother's offered hand, finally managing to get off the earthen floor with a little help. A lot of little help. He stood straight, fully prepared to return to the trek at hand in search of the bizarre hubbub, as was everyone else. With his right thumb and index finger, he pinched the orange straw suddenly in his grip again and raised it to his lips. Placing it against his tongue, he bit down while returning his hands to his pockets. "What are you so worried about, anyway? We've been walking for a half hour and seen nothin'." Instantly perplexed, the pothead took a double take at the sight of his sister. "What's different...?"

Sydney turned her head, pointing at the spiky, loose, twirled bun of blond and black hair displayed.

Leunga scowled. "You took off your jacket?!"

"Okay."

He rolled his eyes. "Well, whatever. Just don't lose it. It's the only one I've got."

Revisiting the concern he voiced only twenty minutes earlier, thinking everyone already forgot what he said, a boy abruptly blurted something that had been nagging at his nerves when the opportunity was just right. "There's been—uh...you know. Um. I was just thinking," their tallest brother started and scratched at the back of his blond crest. "Not that I actually believe it, but I guess I'm still just having a hard time with the whole...killing somebody thing." Ricky turned quickly, throwing his hand over his mouth, and sneezed.

"For the fiftieth fucking time, we're not going to *kill* anyone!" his sister the rebel reiterated. "We're just gonna go find the guy and tell him to fuck off and leave everyone alone. Quit worrying."

"But will that really work?"

"Probably not, but that's what we're gonna do."

Just wanting to make things as clear as he could, the brother pondered. "So...as soon as he gets mad at us for having the swords, you guys want to let him kill us all then, right?"

"Ricky, lighten up. Jesus. Nothing bad is going to happen to us. We just want to talk to the asshole."

The eldest agreed with his sister robustly. "And if the shit does go down, I slash his stupid head in half. No questions asked. Easy."

"Yeah—well, no. Actually, I don't know. Goddamn it, you guys are confusing me too much. Let's just wait until we get there to see if he's even human or not and then we can go from there...I sound like such a tool right now..."

"Uh...why wouldn't he be human...?" the looker of the bunch wondered.

Sydney stroked her ear and said, "Well...think of it this way. That guy—"

"Grampy," Leunga added.

"—said it was over *seven hundred* years old, right? So it can't possibly be human."

Leunga nodded. "Yeah. And that guy—"

"Grandpa," Sydney added.

"—said it's gonna try to attack *us* first, so *technically* it's self-defense. And no prison for us."

One sibling started to stare at the ground unexpectedly, gently tapping a baby fern with her foot. "Actually, that brings up something I wanted to ask..." she said, suddenly sounding unsure of herself. "If we do find some kind of troll or something out here, do you think we could possibly consider maybe not hurting it? Please?"

"Wh-hut?! Are we to just let it rend us to shreds instead?! From the stuff mushroom man says, these things sound damn vicious! If it tries to kill us, then we have little in the means of options, mademoiselle." Leunga struggled with the pronunciation of much of that sentence, except for the very last word, oddly enough.

Sydney whimpered quietly at the thought of bringing pain to a living creature. She suddenly found herself questioning her motives and reconsidering their plan. "Shit...maybe this whole thing was a bad idea after all..."

Inspired by the sound of her logic—the same logic he shared—her younger partner tilted his head back and moaned to himself in angst.

"Man, what a total downer you are. And I speak clearly of course to both of you," their brother belittled. "This is unproper attitude for my minions to be spewing at me from all sides. Would you two just relax? Grampy made it sound scarier than it actually will be, like all of his stupid gardening stories. Just calm your fool selves down, and let's just try to enjoy this time we have for what it should be." Leunga sighed contentedly as he glanced around, filled with a sense of sibling togetherness in the fading remains of a wild west. "Just me and my little peeps hanging out."

Ricky recoiled repugnantly. "We could've done that at home." He could see through his brother's excuse to the core of the eldest's argument: a naked desire to waste time seeking a fantasy dreamworld that could only exist in a juvenile psyche. Turning his focus away from Leunga's crispy, plantlike brunet curls, he murmured something that sounded like, "Butthead."

Leunga could swear he heard Ricky just refer to their sister as a *butthead*, but decided to keep it a secret and use it for extortion at a later date. To be determined.

Sydney fought her anxiety and chose to ignore her irksome need for wildlife preservation by focusing on her remaining summer and her time with her brothers, carefully saving her other thoughts for when and if the time would arrive. Her outlook brightened considerably as she smiled through her malaise. "You know, it has been kind of nice being with you guys. It's been so long since we all went camping out here together. A little bit more hectic and really stupid and weird this time, but—"

Leunga interrupted his sister, loudly. "Brothery sisterish freindshiping around the leumongous ginormumentalous trees! With bonus levels!"

Clearly annoyed at not being able to complete her sentiment, the young woman's mood took a U-turn at full speed. She exhaled angrily, saying, "You're an idiot. That's not how you spell friendshipping. Also, that's not a word. In fact, most of those aren't words."

Ricky sniffled. "Well then, what are they?"

"Mouth garbage."

Leunga was stunned, amazed by his recent discovery. "They aren't? Well then they is now, I coined it. And besides, I was using it as an analahjie. Analogy?" he asked his sister for clarification confirmation without hope for an answer before continuing right away. "So it doesn't count."

"Simile?"

Sydney shook her head. "That's not even close to an analogy. You don't know what an analogy is, boner-balls." She meant to say "boner-brain," but some things just have a way of slipping out when they're least expected. Or most expected.

After a healthy grimace and a sour scowl, Ricky was displeased to rediscover some of the more vulgar imagery his sister tends to supply as he scoffed silently and muttered, "Yeah, Syd, we gotta be careful with what we say around you. No talk about private parts. You're such a lady...real *ladylike*..."

Realizing her gross overstep in verbal promiscuity, Sydney tried to hide it under a quick retort. "Fuck you, Finnegan." The rapid hostility of it all! So much for freindshiping. Friendshipping?

Leunga's eyes grew wide. " *Whoa*! Do *not* call him that...he might kill us and use our bones as dumbbells!"

"You're a dumbbell, wordsmith," his sister added courteously. "You suck at talking."

"Oh, sure, yeah, yeah, uh-huh, right, yeah, and like you know what a metanalogy is?" Leunga growled. "You and your damn system of words..."

"Vocabulary," she suggested.

"Nerd," he suggested.

Ricky sneezed, thankfully bringing the argument to an earsplitting halt. Case closed. On to the next one.

"Okay, I've been completely silent about all the sneezing"—no he hasn't—"but come on, man! Do you really have to *scream* every fuckin' time you blast one?" shouted a shaken little Leunga. "Seriously, you blew out my eardrum."

"Sorry, it's my allergies." Ricky sniffled.

"What?!" Leunga shouted.

Sydney looked up at Ricky with mild contempt to calmly ask, "Don't you have pills for that, loudfuck?"

"What?!" Leunga shouted.

"Uh, yeah. I forgot to take them this morning. There should be some in my bag." The sneezer pictured the chaos his duffel endured during the packing shuffle, the pandemonium of his grandmother and sister displacing the carefully compiled contents of his martial arts satchel, and was a bit on edge all of a sudden. "I hope." Antihistamine necessitation. "Um, maybe we should go back to camp..."

"Hell no. How 'bout that?"

"I'm startin' to get a little worried about my stuff. *Our* stuff. We sorta just left it all out in the open... I didn't think this would take that long, man."

"Worry not, tall one," Leunga replied. "No one would dare touch our crap now that I'm immortal."

"They would if you weren't around..."

"Shit."

Leading the way along the path, Sydney walked onward, attempting to charge her very annoying brothers into action. "Come on, jerks. Let's get this travesty over with so we can go the hell home. I want to get back and tell Addy why I had to stop texting."

Leunga followed, accompanied by his giant brother. "Duh, just call her on your phone, dink." He swatted back toward Ricky's evading arm and added, "Like *Addy* even gives a shit. Am I right?! Yes, I am."

"My phone died yesterday...and you were there."

"My condolences. I am so sorry for your loss." Leunga swiped at her, attempting a consolation pat on the shoulder, but instead, he smacked her bare bicep with a singing slap. He cringed as she looked back. "That might have been an accident."

Ricky lifted the thick collar of his white karate gi to his face and wiped his nose again while he scowled. He poked Leunga between the shoulder blades and leaned closer in order to repeat his often-voiced opinion of their sister's best friend forever—BFF—to the usual recipient of the insight with an appropriate addendum to fit their current situation, whispering to his confidant, "She's too *creepy* to give a crap about us camping, anyway."

"No effin' way. You did not just say that again! Man! I told you a million times by now. All those alterna-punk girls are awesome, not 'creepy.' They are the best, simply put. They'll do things—" Leunga paused midsentence to check his grammar, for the first time ever, in fact, which caused him to forget much of his point. "So anyway, when I met April, she was way into garage bands and emo Goth stuff, wearing tons of black and metal-studded shit, and she would do this thing with her tongue ring—"

Sydney grimaced at the direction her brothers' discussion was taking and interrupted. "Ew, shut up!" Though she had no tongue piercing, the similarities between her and Leunga's girlfriend's former style were uncanny. She glanced down at the path below her feet, noticing her own fashion in the process. "You know I dress almost the exact same way, right?" Sydney is a punk rocker.

Leunga cringed. "Wh—come on, Symby...don't be so sickening. I'm not talking about *you*, I'm talking about women. And stay out of *our* conversation, please."

Sydney became taciturn, leading onward quietly in hopes that her brothers would change topics without her help.

The eldest waited for his sister to respond, but she didn't, so he chose to continue. "So anyway, Rick, I'm just saying you can't always just go for those nympho groceries. You gotta give the melancholy lovelies a chance! They're the ones that *really* get freaky."

"Don't corrupt him," a young lady exhaled.

"Like this one time—this one day—me and April, we were on the couch downstairs outside my room—"

"God! Stop it, ass!" Sydney exploded, glancing back with concern. She had no previous knowledge of her brother's assessment of her own choice in style—or the fact that other boys might see it the same way. Some girl willing to perform any nasty act. A repulsive revelation. Though it shouldn't have been that much of a surprise. Facing forward, she felt the blood drain from her arms at the thought of being stereotyped in such a manner, and she swiftly raised her shields to prevent any further blows to the comfort she found in her clothing. "Fuckin' hell."

"Fine! Whatever! All of you shut up! But later, Dick, you and me...talking. Wait! You gotta see this." Leunga fished his expensive cell phone from one of his khaki pockets. When it was all the way out in the open, he jerked his thumb down on the button located near the top as hard as he could and turned it on. Reaching his arm backward, he handed off the device to his younger brother without looking and instructed, "Check out my wallpaper." As he felt the object leave his hand, Leunga added, "That's me on the left, and that black-haired girl next to me is April. Her name is April."

Leunga's girlfriend's name is April, by the way.

Ricky held the phone up to eye level, ignoring the path his feet were travelling. He stared at the picture—immediately noticing that Leunga was actually on the right—and inspected the young woman on the left with her hand behind his brother's head, giving him the appearance of having horns. An about average young woman in her early to midtwenties with jet black hair and a loving smile who apparently enjoys food slightly more than most people and isn't afraid to admit it. Ricky raised his large obsidian eyebrows and said, "I have met her...so many times..."

"April."

"She *lives* at our house, dude. Like, literally."

"Buttface, you have your phone?!" Sydney looked back over her older brother at Ricky, extending an open hand, demanding the dunce's device. "Let me have it for a sec; I wanna email somebody." Three guesses at who she wants to contact. That's right. First try.

As Ricky held the phone forward—circumventing his brother and inching closer to their sister's hand—Leunga became fairly alarmed. The aspect of facing off against a mythical troll paled in comparison to the idea of his sister discovering his compromising Internet search history. "Whoa, hold on now, friend," he insisted and intercepted the gadget from his brother's hand. "I'll—uh—I'll get you to the site for you. What is it?"

Without stopping along the trail, Sydney twirled around and stole the phone out of her older sibling's grip. "Yoink!" She snorted. "I know how to use this better than you. It'll just take a sec." Her black-nailed thumbs flew over the touch pad with both speed and accuracy, conditioned by vast experience, as the group continued forward.

Leunga's nerves ran high, increasing each moment that his teenage sister used his device. He found himself unwittingly staring inattentively across the undergrowth, searching for nothing. Ricky sneezed rapidly, unable to cover his mouth in time, and inadvertently splashed his older brother with a fine mist. "Rickers! Now is not really the best time..." The geek's anxious trance broke as quickly as it began. Desperately searching for an issue to keep himself distracted, he muttered, "We need to stay alert."

"Since *when*?!"

Sydney walked forward along the narrow trail blindly, her sibling's cell phone holding all of her attention. "Uh-huh. Gotta find that noisy-ass machine. Or whatever..."

Instantly, Leunga seemed trapped in deep thought. "Ass machine, yes...large, round, smooth edges. Like a pearly white peach. Beautiful. I'm getting hungry..."

"What are you talking about...?"

The eldest camper could not hear the query of his young brother because he was lost—vanished in the images and recollections of a black-haired beauty forever etched in his mind. He held his fingertips against the left pocket of his baggy beige shorts and was reminded of a vivid memory—one of few for him; a sense of nostalgic fear and uncertainty in the face of a dilemma was never far from his thoughts. Leunga looked down his nose at the dusty orange cylinder protruding out of his mouth and instantly spit it out. "Ew! Mother fuck!"

Not far behind the group, a large bush momentarily jostled with life. Ricky glanced back slowly. "Okay...I hope everybody else heard that..."

Sydney continued typing. "Huh?"

Leunga spat some more, hitting his naked shin with a splash. "Heard?"

Fear and Loathing

Showdown. Face-to-face with a horrific entity of unquenchable hunger for a priceless commodity, Leunga's eyes watched carefully as the gluttonous fiend slowly gorged itself uncontrollably. Its narrow hands captured every precious piece of his verve and destroyed it little by little. Nothing could satisfy the beast's insatiable greed.

"Can I *please* get some service here?"

"Oh!" Leunga hopped over to a stack of plastic cups close behind him and removed the apex. With experienced skill to back him up, he scooped a decent sample from a large cask of ice nearby and threw it in a blender. From the countless times creating this concoction, he had no need to measure the proper amount of coffee to add. With all ingredients in place, the machine whirred to a torrent of noise. As the clamor died, he poured the contents of the pitcher into the anticipated plastic cup. Carefully he clicked a lid around the open end of the glass and plunged a straw into the top.

Leunga placed the straw between his lips and quickly drank a third of his beverage. He glanced at the customer on the other side of the counter and offered his cup. "Did you want some?"

"I have been waiting here for five minutes while you just stared at the clock. Didn't you hear me?! I want to speak with your manager. *Right now.*"

"Okay." Suddenly, Leunga paused when he noticed the front door of the café open. A young woman with jet black hair and deep magenta lipstick entered. She wore a striking crimson button-up top, long-sleeved with a collar, red-rimmed spectacles that signaled seductiveness, black nylon stockings, and a skirt so dark it swallowed the light. Leunga peered around the customer in front of him and demanded, "Move it or lose it!"

As the woman with black hair and a fair complexion travelled through the air-conditioned café, the mystified man absorbed her every movement, watching her every step, as he did every day. Entering a small access door to the counter, she walked up to her boyfriend with a smile. "Hi, handsome."

"Hey, baby." Leunga grinned as he placed an index finger against his cheek and leaned up toward the young woman. She pecked his offered cheek with a kiss, leaving a deep magenta apparition of her lips, proceeding to point her own index finger on her cheek. Leunga accepted her suggestion and kissed her, leaving no trace.

"*Excuse* me! What kind of business allows this behavior?! I want to speak with your manager."

"Okay, cliché," said Leunga, looking into the eyes of the young lady by his side, peering into her glassy orbs of a brown so light they appeared gold in the glow of the midday sunshine. "April, this guy wants to talk to you."

The customer gasped. "I am a woman, young man."

Leunga leaned against the counter and quietly studied. "Are you sure?"

"What seems to be the problem, ma'am?" April asked calmly.

"I have been waiting and waiting for this terrible employee to take my order, which he never did, and I want you to know I'm never coming here again."

April took a short breath to prepare for her prepared statement and started with a shimmering smile. "We're very sorry you feel that way. We hope that you find it in your heart to come back and visit us soon, because we would love to redeem ourselves and serve your needs again. Thank you for choosing Coño Café, and have a wonderful day." She makes it sound so sincere.

"Yeah, you just get the hell out," Leunga added politely. He also makes it sound so sincere.

Grumbling in an English too vile to hear, the woman spun around and stormed out of the building.

"I missed you so much," admitted the man as he held his love's hands in adoration when they were finally rid of the complication. "Can I have the rest of the day off?"

April freed her fingers lovingly, clutching a pair of napkins to wipe her mark from Leunga's face. "Oh..." She was unusually disappointed with this instance of his frequent request. "I was kind of hoping we could have a little discussion. Something has been bugging me for a while... I think we just need to talk about it."

"Ooh." He could tell from the tone in her voice that he should find a way to weasel out of the conversation. "Can we wait until tomorrow? We got the day off. We can do that maybe after we do something stupid like have a picnic in a park or pet dolphins. Both!"

"A picnic would be nice, but it's supposed to rain tomorrow."

Leunga smiled with freshly cleaned cheeks. "We all know humans can't predict the weather. That's just science faction. It's gonna be great!"

After several years of becoming intimately familiar with her lover's distinctive perspective, April surrendered to his wild will without protest. "Okay, I'll bring some food if you bring the umbrellas. We'll have a nice little picnic. And then I really need to ask you something..."

Her recent behavior over the past few weeks had become strange to say the least. She was typically relaxed and uncomplicated—for her to act so bizarrely was a new experience for Leunga—what with all of the confusing text messages about things he could swear he never said to her. Something was certainly amiss in their bliss. Never before had the world seemed so serious, and he really didn't like it that way. So, sidestepping what she just said with his words, he untied his mauve apron and sidestepped her in person all the same. "And we could do one of those giant tricycles on the water. Run over the dolphins..." As he slipped the article off, his hand brushed his left front pants pocket. His heart skipped as the small container housed within the pouch bounced against his sweaty palm. He stood frozen in place, breathless on shaky knees. His throat was dry and bitter, leaving an unpleasant taste in his mouth. His world turned a little slower and absorbed every instant. April's gentle grasp cancelled his trance.

"Did you forget something?"

"Huh?"

"You blanked out on me there." I'm not sure why she was surprised by that.

Leunga wrapped his apron across the back of his neck. "Nope. Just thinking about tomorrow." He looked into her compassionate golden eyes and wondered what she might want to talk about; and if he would—or should— ever have a chance to ask her something that's been on *his* mind too. "You said that I got the food and you have the...other things."

"Okay." She grinned—her boyfriend always felt slightly more at ease when she smiled. "Call me when you get up. I'll get the food *and* umbrellas, and you can come pick me up."

"Hells yeah. I'll see you tomorrow—"

"Um..." a man's voice interrupted from the other side of the counter. "Would it be okay if we ordered first?" he asked politely, pointing behind himself at the half dozen people waiting in line.

April nudged Leunga toward the exit. "I can handle this. Don't forget to call."

"I won't." A promise he frequently forgot to keep. Pushing past the counter's half door, he barely heard the incomprehensible order of the cyclist at the front of the line. His mind, as it often is, was elsewhere.

A somewhat familiar voice approached from his left. "Sorry, dude. That doesn't sound good."

Leunga paused and glanced at a platinum-haired teenager in line—the face was of someone he kind of knew. "What doesn't?"

Darwin shrugged. " *We need to talk?* That's like the classic breakup phrase, bro."

His eyes darted left and right continually while one corner of his mouth was pulled upward in confusion. "Do I know you?"

"I live across the street from you. And I come here, like, every day. Sorry about your girl, dude. She's hot."

Leunga scowled, feeling sour and polluted by his recent interaction with the boy from across the street. Breaking visual contact with the young man, he began walking again without a word of farewell, travelling ever closer to the exit. As he placed his hand on the large handle of the coffee shop door, he looked back and watched the activity behind the counter. Noticing his gaze, April smiled once more at her Leunga, and he reciprocated with unease.

The front door chimed open, releasing the climate-controlled air of the café into the mild vernal atmosphere. Leunga stepped through, considering the inconsiderate words of his apparent neighbor. He stared at his feet, passing over the sidewalk of the shop, and walking mindlessly while he analyzed April's motives and desires, suddenly self-conscious, wondering if he even deserved to be in her presence in the first place. Realizing he had travelled aimlessly around the coffee bar several times, he stopped abruptly and found himself standing at the back of the store in the employee parking area by his utility vehicle—a sporty means of transportation much more accustomed to skipping over sand dunes like a stone over water than to carting a young man home. "Oh! Nice!"

Leunga stood at the uninhibited opening of his ride—an aperture typically covered by thick canvas mixed with vinyl on vehicles of the same make—and stared at the building by the automobile behind him. Just on the other side of the chipped brick barrier, his past, present, and future coexisted as one entity, fulfilling the public's caffeinated beverage requirements. Placing a boot on the running board of his red vehicle, he gawked at the faded wall, knowing exactly where *she* stood, and ran his hand over his left pocket once more, just to feel that inebriating mixture of fear and excitement in the wake of his anxiety. Dazed in a world of hope, he was held hostage by his own desires, locked in a staring contest with the beige exterior of his place of employment. Slowly he reached a blind hand over to the steering wheel of the always-open car and took one last longing gaze through the building. Without watching where he was going, Leunga hopped up into the driver's seat of his safari-ready ride and smacked his shaggy head against the upper rim of the doorway with a loud thud that echoed through his skull well into the next five seconds, but was apparently unaffected by the collision.

Sitting between two guiding white lines against oil-stained concrete, he watched the shifting wall of juniper bushes through his windshield vacuously. His mind was racing, and before he knew it, the dark object housed within his pocket was suddenly situated in his sweaty palm, resting on his felt seat edge. Leunga lifted the box closer to eye level and glanced at its simplicity. One small object holding such immense, cataclysmic, and altering power— manifesting as a symbol of a never-ending beginning. With the item held gently between his thumb and middle finger, he was inundated with thoughts and possibilities, so much so that he became terrified. Quickly, Leunga threw his hand into the large cargo pocket at his left and buried the box out of sight and out of mind. As he removed his hand from the oversized storage compartment on his thigh, he slyly pulled out something else: a small white tube of paper pinched at one end, thicker than a pencil and as long as an index finger—a homemade cigarette rolled European-style. Professional Amsterdam. High-class. No amateur twists for this aficionado.

He sighed quietly to himself as he placed the paper-wrapped cylinder between his lips and grabbed an entirely ordinary gas station lighter from behind the dashboard compass. Glancing left through the vacant doorway of his car at the café, he snapped the lighter to life, holding the bright flame to the pinched-off end of his homemade smokable. After a momentary lapse of thought, he sucked carefully, scorching the tip of the tube with a temporarily glowing orange ring. As the end of the rolled flora smoldered persistently, he drew a deep breath through the cardboard mouthpiece of the cylinder and discarded the lighter. Soothing fumes filled his lungs as he held onto them before exploding into a burst of short coughs. Leunga closed his eyes and leaned his restless mind against the back of his seat, allowing the panacea to take over.

Rapture pulsed through his muscles like an electric current, surging and recharging as it drained him of his drive. Drifting away in a sea of silk and strawberries, he took a decent drag of the joint and blew a solid stream of smoke into the stratosphere. The stress of the day dripped off of his fingertips and soaked the floor mats, freeing him from the earthly shackles of indecision. Lying on a grassy hill, he began to slide up, frictionless, floating along the blades. He placed the burning stick between his lips and inhaled while the sun swirled in a ring around the clouds and dripped sweet starshine on the universe.

A car door in the adjacent parking spot slammed shut. The midday toker rolled his eyelids open slowly and glanced to the right as he was greeted by a familiar voice. "What's up, Lou?"

Leunga exuded a torrent of smoke and smiled. "Hey, man..."

"What are you doing out here? Aren't you working today?"

Seated nicely, he snickered. "On my way home right now. Just needed to burn a little." He took another breath of giddy exultation and offered it to his coworker. "Want a hit?"

The young man in the mauve apron shook his head and shrugged. "Naw, dude, April can always smell it on me..."

Leunga nodded as he blew twin jets of smoke from his nostrils. "True. That's true. I agree with that. It's true."

The car next to the jeep beeped, activating the alarm. "Well...drive carefully, yeah? See ya next Tuesday, maybe," his coworker said with a wave and walked off in the direction of the café. "Have a good weekend."

"Yeah. You too." With a yawn made mostly by his nostrils, Leunga sat up with his blunt resting between his lips tilted to the sky, keeping his precious embers secure. He threw his right arm over the passenger seat and looked back, slamming his foot on the accelerator. The engine roared with ferocity, yet the car remained motionless. Confused by his utter lack of progress, the dizzied driver faced the steering wheel and noticed the vehicle was still in park. "Duh!" With his left hand, he reached over and pulled the gearshift between the two front seats. Reverse. The car flew backward and stopped just before colliding with the brick wall of the coffee house. Leunga glanced above a dangling pair of twelve-sided, fuzzy red dice into the rearview mirror as he positioned himself forward in the vehicle; and though he couldn't see her, he knew April was behind that looking glass. Quickly shifting into gear without thinking, he made his way out of the parking lot, passing palm trees and pedestrians aplenty. "Intruders!" he whispered as he hid his eyes behind his steering wheel. "Lest not lest ye be judged..."

Another lungful of cannabis exited his throat while he watched the colorful cars and all the different people glide by from his place in the center lane on the public-owned street. He knew they could see that it was him in the automobile, but that didn't matter that much just yet. The lethargic pavement slid under his pacing mind. Black water melted over his every pore. His crimson utility vehicle blazed a trail of flames as he reached speeds of almost twenty miles per hour on the busy boulevard, soaring through lights of red and green alike. Despite his cautiously persistent calm, an increasing concern was developing in his mind. Tomorrow already seemed like a day he wished he could forget. Pavement pulsed by as the panic of paranoia settled in. April's possible questions gushed through his mind, collecting in the tiny spaces between his teeth and throughout his ample eyebrows. If only that rude boy from across the street hadn't contaminated Leunga's thoughts of her with those words, it would have been just another day off with his querida. "I still feel like these people can see me."

Leunga's ride hummed along the asphalt quietly while its captain stared expressionless out of the windshield, safely concealed by his controls. Just up the road a bit—right over there in the crosswalk—a man in a suit stepped out and paused in the road. The racer raised his head and his blood-engorged eyes focused on this mystifying stranger as the man began waving both arms slowly, streaking wonderful color across the sky. The unexpected friendliness of the stranger was enough to temporarily remove Leunga from his funk. He cooed and smiled wide, tipping his rapidly disappearing legal indiscretion at the man in the street cordially. As the red vehicle barreled down on the mysterious man in the suit, the pedestrian leapt toward the median like a star showering space with enchanting dust as it grants wishes in the night. Leunga leaned out of his unimpeded doorway and greeted the stranger as he zoomed by. "Hello to you, sir."

Swerving in order to maintain proper traffic codes, a pothead pulled himself back into his car, sliding over into his seat once again. He glanced down in order to remark, "Uh-oh. Seatbelt." Letting go of the wheel, he grabbed the metal fastener of his safety belt and carefully maneuvered it over his head as to avoid bumping his fine smokable. With a click he was secure—a necessity when a car has no solid doors. I would also like to mention that since his utility vehicle is bereft of barriers on both sides, he is exceedingly fortunate that his free-floating property within the car isn't stolen every single day, but I digress.

The sun above brushed against his face and forearms, slithering over his skin and hiding in the shadow. Dotted white lines rolled past the roaring tires of the vehicle. Leunga's hazy mind tried not to dwell on dread, but not even the purity of euphoria could rip his thoughts away from the nagging gnome chewing away at his nerves. Trapped at a place he had never been before, he could see himself tomorrow, slipping closer to the end of his bond. The bottom of his glass. He had taken it for granted and waited too long. April was moving on, and he would be left behind. That was all it could be. That was all he could expect. That was all they had left. And if that wasn't bad enough, on top of everything, he had a sneaking suspicion that the vice president of the United States was hiding in his backseat.

To his surprise, Leunga's left hand flipped the turn signal switch upward, indicating a right turn. He focused on the task at hand and followed his own directions, entering a well-maintained parking lot surrounded by a white picket fence. Cautiously, he pulled into the first-available parking spot

and shifted the car into park. With one final inhalation of his spliff, he flicked
the roach into the grass and leaned back in his seat, staring over at the quaint
building he immediately recognized as April's apartment complex, finding
himself fully ready to pick her up the next day for the last time. "What? Why
did I come *here*?" He reached into his right pocket and pulled out his car
keys. "And how?!"

"Here."

Leunga looked into the rearview mirror at the sound of another
somewhat familiar teenage voice. He was met with the ample eyebrows and
brooding brown eyes of his younger sister.

Sydney repeated her statement. "Here." And again with more force.
"Here!"

Leunga stared at the person in his backseat vacantly.

"Take your damn phone back, jackass," she instructed robustly and
held out her brother's expensive gadget as she walked backward while the
group trekked forth along the forest trail.

"Oh, yeah! Whoa, sorry about that. I'm all..." He searched for an
appropriate phrase in his vocabulary, grabbing the gizmo. "Space case today."

"Today?"

"For your information, it took a million years to send that email.
Your phone must be packed with crap. Gross search history by the way..."
Sydney snickered as she turned forward on the path. "Should I be washing my
hands after touching that thing?"

"Hmm. No. Just don't touch your face or eat anything until you get a
chance."

She held up her hands and stared at them in horror. "Oh god, I was
only kidding!"

Already lost once again in the uncomfortable comfort of his wayward
mind, Leunga leered at himself, frozen in a time of joy in the presence of
possibly the only person he cared about more than himself, behind the backlit
screen at his fingertips; but rather than seeing the phone's background image

for what it was, he couldn't help but look deeply into the moment surrounding the couple in the picture rather than the actual picture itself, like staring into some long-lost dimension where everything was nice and he still had some weed to spare. "I miss my bud..."

Ricky offered kind words of consolation, right after releasing another seismic sneeze. "I'm sure April misses you too."

Leunga smacked his forehead, narrowly missing his hat. "Oh yeah! And April too." With his thoughts astray, he gazed into the golden eyes by his side. He couldn't keep himself from smiling at the sight, until his mouth dropped out of place when he noticed the number in the corner of the screen indicating the amount of missed voice messages he had waiting for him. Twenty-three. Immediately, he knew which beautiful creature attempted to make contact with his hushed communicator so repetitiously, and it sent his knees quaking. A distant voice yearning to be heard, drawing him back to an uncertain reality he wasn't fully comfortable with any longer. He pressed a button and erased every message. "Shit! I didn't mean to *delete* them..."

"Uh...hey...do you think maybe you could help keeping watch? It seems like me and Syd are the only ones paying attention..." Even though Sydney was obviously preoccupied, Ricky chose to include his sister in his statement to avoid infuriating her in any way. A wise decision.

Leunga glanced an ear's edge back at his brother before trying to forcibly shake the anxiety from his head. "Everything 'round here looks the same. What's the point?"

"Dink, you're the one who forced us to go down this trail and look for that noisemaker. Ricky wanted to go back to camp and I wanted to stay at that bat cave some more..."

The eldest sibling stared at his sister's strangely altered appearance for the third time in as many seconds, warily puzzled. "Forced...?"

Sydney glared wide-eyed at the forest up ahead from the front of the line. "You threatened us with the swords."

Fidgeting with the cell phone in his hand as he tried to turn it off, Leunga thought carefully about her statement and stated, "I have no recollection of that...and it was more like a dangerous suggestion, not a threat. Besides, I dunno why, but, I just got, like, the weirdest urge to go deeper into the trees after we got out of that refrigerator. I can't help myself. I guess I'm just old-fashioned that way."

"Just keep an eye out..."

Leunga nodded, reminded by his brother that there was more to the trees than he could see—a secret menace that he found exhilarating, accompanied completely by a mystifying push brought on by his pact with the swords. A silent call drawing him toward an invisible entity he somehow knew was in the woods with them. The strangest yearning he ever had, beckoning him to search every inch of the forest for an answer to a question he didn't know how to ask. "Attentioning. What are *you* watching for?" he asked openly, blindly dropping his phone back into his large side pocket.

"Well, lots of things..." his brother revealed. "Wolves, cougars, bears, other people hiking..." Ricky's unfortunate attire was always on his mind. As the handsome teen maintained his role as the train's caboose, the springy, soft fabric embracing his posterior stretched tight around his form with each tread. He pictured the horrible phrase plastered across his cheeks and couldn't help but caress the raised lettering. Wonderfully crafted embroidery that truly complemented and accentuated his well-toned buttocks—but don't think about them for too long; he's still a minor.

"You look for deadly animals. I'll look for deadly chains."

"Actually, I think I heard the bushes moving around behind us a little while ago..."

Sydney scowled as she briefly directed her gaze back past her brothers over the group's faint tracks in the dry earth at the underbrush, and admonished the Adonis. "What?! Stupid, why didn't you say something?"

Leunga scoffed at his youngest sibling. "Nervous much? Come on! Grampy said we won't find anything until we want to."

Ricky frowned at the twisted excess of his eldest sibling's bedraggled brown hair and recalled, "Man, that's practically the opposite of what he said, but okay."

"He's right. If we're not careful we could get attacked by a bear," stated Sydney as her eyes returned to the trail at hand.

Leunga laughed. "A bear would be an easy deal. What we're gonna find is something way more intense and way tons more badass."

"Uh," Ricky shook his head tightly with stupefaction. "What could be worse than finding a bear?"

Sydney scratched her cheek and came up with the answer quickly. "A herd of bears."

"Man, listen this...a goddamn bear is not just gonna walk onto the path and swipe us. We're three people. A bear is just one person. We add them out by default."

"Okay! All I'm saying is that we need to watch out." *We* in this case meaning Leunga.

"We don't have to worry about anything." *We* in this case meaning Ricky. "You saw what these things can do," Leunga said while pointing to the blade hilts over his right shoulder. "I am a machine. An unstoppable force of valor. An unending fuego de libertad. Anything Grampy can do, I can do twice. I am the shit."

"A lot of his story didn't really make sense though." All of it, for instance. "He even thought I was a monster. Like, one of those one things...a, uh, phantom fairy tale acid trip, dude..." Ricky glanced at his brother and came to a simple conclusion. "Maybe he was just stoned!"

"So you're saying it was *me* making the swords glow and dice up that 'cone? I am fucking awesome!"

"Grandma also told us he came home covered in blood," another person added. "I really think he was telling the truth." It isn't often that Sydney would trust a mystical tale woven by a drug-addled mind and her little brother would remain skeptical, but there you go.

Ricky had forgotten the words of their grandmother; after all, he was much more focused on returning home at the time. Some things don't change. "Oh yeah...but Lou, do you really wanna kill...stuff?"

"Don't forget, Grandpa couldn't handle the tragedy," someone reminded distractedly. She wasn't sure if her heart could actually handle it either. While her morals clashed in her mind, Sydney took another glance eastward at the lingering rain cloud over the trees, squinting as she noticed strange movement around its rapidly shifting exterior—an overturned sea, churning in the sky. Imminent drizzle. Running her palm over the blond bunch at the back of her head, the young lady checked the construction and consistency of her new well-known hairdo. Nostalgia kicked in for an instant. Boyfriend. Her eyes went wide in terror when she realized she had just inadvertently touched her face and hair with her potentially tainted hand.

"I'm totally ready for everything always," assured an almost-poacher as he psyched himself up in spite of everything else going on around him. "And always keep in mind that we can't remember the future because we won't forget the past."

Ricky nodded. "I know, but, uh...shouldn't we learn from his mistakes or something? That's what normal people do, right?"

The eldest spoke with an unnecessary waving of his hands. "If there's one thing I myself have learned in how ever many years I've been alive it's this: you can't learn from the mistakes of others."

"Right, but can't we at least try? I was just thinking about it and...if Grampy was actually telling the truth, then maybe we should hide those." Motioning at the swords harnessed to his brother's back even though neither of his older siblings could see the gesture, the end piece of the party pleaded, "We should find a tree or whatever and bury them under it."

Leunga shook his head in great disappointment. "I don't get you sometimes..."

"Me either." Ricky agreed with his brother's sentiment as he scouted cautiously through the mighty pines. Their casual expedition to find their deeply misguided grandfather had taken a very unforeseeable turn. Seriously, I don't think any of them considered their hike would turn into an assassination attempt. Well, maybe Leunga did. In any case, Ricky's courage over the matter was visibly deteriorating. As the trio trekked the trail, a sudden skidding of the path sounded behind them, causing the youngest member of the misfits to throw his eyes over his shoulder, catching only the slightest sight of a wisp of dirt in the air just above the trail. "What was that...?"

Sydney finished wiping her hands on her jeans in disgust. "What was what?"

"Was what what?!"

"How could neither of you hear that noise?!"

"Nice try, Dickiness, but this place is as dead as something that's dead. Listen...see? The birds aren't even chirping."

The air was indeed still with an enduring sense of unsettling disquiet sprinkled through the trees. Looking around at the treetops while leading the troupe forward, Sydney repeated her big brother's observation, realizing he was correct. "The birds aren't chirping..."

"Yeah, I already know. I *just* said that!"

"Maybe it's a sign...a bad sign. What's that called? We should start heading back to our camp." Ricky held his hand a few inches in front of his mouth and sneezed, "Omen!"

Sydney moved forward along the walkway with her brothers in tow. Mute minutes passed while her eyes darted through the trees, searching for missing melodies. "It is kinda spooky... Once we reach the end–" She was stopped abruptly, blindly colliding with a solid metal post strategically placed in the center of the path for all hikers to observe and avoid. Most hikers. The blunt hindrance evaded her striding foot and crashed harshly right under her belt buckle with enough force to bring the nomads to a grinding halt.

Leunga hopped off to the side to avoid running into his sister. "Whoa! Please pay more attention to the path..." He snickered. "Damn,

Ricky, you just avoided catastrophic nut damage by letting her take the lead! Well done, sir."

"Ugh..." The girl buckled over, falling to her knees as she compressed her lower abdomen with both hands. "Fuck..."

Rucky—or is it Ricky? Anyway, Rocky glanced past his sister's weakened condition at the obstruction and observed, "I think this is the end of the trail."

Joining his brother, the slacker extraordinaire squinted at the waist-high, deep brown pole protruding skyward by three whole feet with faint yellow lettering drawing his eyes down vertically while he read aloud. "End...of...the...trail." Leunga turned to Ricky and nodded silently in concurrence. The trail's end. With one small corner of the wilderness inspected and secured by the vigilance of the group, it was time for them to head back to camp and recoup...as soon as Sydney was able to stand.

She spoke through clenched teeth. "Oh, god...why would they cement a metal pole in the middle of the suck-ass path and paint it the same color as the fucking dirt?! Goddamn. It slammed right into my zipper. Ow..." She hunched over and privately peeled up the bottom of her faded undershirt, pulling her black jeans outward and secretly assessing the injury. "Hope I'm not bleeding."

"Gross."

Ricky sneezed. "It's so rusty you can barely read it. Are you gonna be okay?"

Satisfied with her lack of lost blood and superficial damage, Sydney grunted, getting up slowly by gripping the same pole that caused her atrocity. "Yeah, I'll be—" She started speaking as swiftly as she stopped when she suddenly noticed something through the trees. Her pain subsided for the moment as she observed a small orange ball of fluff adjacent to a surprisingly quiet stream. Soon after that, she shoved her older brother out of the way and quietly skulked closer to the abnormality.

Leunga regained his balance before yelling, "Hey! I'm standing here! Make with the apologies before I beat them out of you with my butt!"

Sydney sidled up to a concealing fir and held a finger over her lips to quiet her brother's chatter, her full attention locked on the creature cautiously lapping up the rivulet. A shadowy fur of fire ran down its back to a large bushy tail. She knew it was a rare sight to see a fox in the forest, let alone a fox unconcealed and vulnerable, so the animal admirer held the tree by her side as she gazed adoringly at her new friend, once again contented with her decision to spend a portion of her precious summer among the trees.

Ricky watched with confusion at Sydney's instantly improved mood, when he noticed the small animal beyond the low ferns. Not exactly dangerous, but proof of the possibility. Carefully scouting the tree line, he caught eyes with his brother and sighed, hopelessly hoping Leunga would lose interest in their farcical cause and spontaneously order them to go back to camp to pack for home.

"Total bust! Nothing even *tried* to kill us," the eldest exclaimed in annoyance and leaned against a wide pine, exhaling his disappointment. As he stared at the ground, he folded his arms across his chest, wondering why the so-called Summoner wasn't enticed by such an easy target as their group. His grandfather's fantastic tale had inspired a sensation of elation at the aspect of a grand battle with an ancient evil, so much so that he sincerely hoped it was all true, but the quest was noticeably degrading, slowly losing its legendary status with each peaceful minute, and very soon, it ran the risk of becoming borderline boring—something he never thought possible with a pair of fluorescent swords strapped to his back. In fact, I don't think any of us did. If I knew it would be this dull, I never would have told this story in the first place. Sorry for the inconvenience.

Ricky quickly locked his hand over his mouth and quietly sneezed forcefully through his nose, expelling a translucent strand of mucus along his wrist.

"This sucks," Leunga announced. "Let's hurry back to camp. Rucky's about to explode and we gotta protect our effects. Rocky. Who knows what kind of deviantly deranged thieves could be lurking around this hole... Why, they could even be close by as we speak..." Closer than he realizes. "Ricky!"

Wiping his slickened hand against his sleeveless undershirt, he whispered in response. "What?! I'm right here..."

Leunga threw his weight forward and left his leisured stance, heading back toward the path. "Hurry up, Snydey. Stop eye-humping that cat and let's G-O!"

Again, the youngest could hold back no longer. The building force behind his sinuses had accumulated such a power that it had no other option than to be unleashed suddenly and without remorse. As he sneezed, a shockwave boomed quickly through the empty trees, causing the ground to quake.

The animal of the anarchist's affection sprang into alert mode, lifting its eyes and aiming its large, black-tipped ears toward the source of the disturbance, away from the stream and in the direction of a human female covered discreetly by a large tree. The fox stood motionless, studying the strange yellow-haired creature's motives.

Sydney smiled, careful not to bare her teeth, and waved at the fox. Perhaps she thought it would wave back. Unfortunately, it was unable to reciprocate the gesture, for at that very moment it began to convulse where it stood. Its fluffy face started to jerk to the side repeatedly with lightning speed, gradually quickening, and becoming an orange and black blur attached to its stationary body.

Ricky quietly joined his sister, adding to her confused and concerned expression with his own, unable to look away. As the fox shook its head violently, a thick fog as dense and as dark as an ocean tide formed beneath its frightened black paws. The smoke rose in little fingers crawling around the vulpine's rigid legs as it let out an echoing whine. Within an instant, the fog shot upward and swallowed the fox, covering it completely, where it then proceeded to swell, growing into an immense canine form.

Leunga stopped on the trail when he realized his younger siblings were not following his lead. He turned to call out to them, but before he could utter a single word, he caught a glimpse of the expanding malice through the thick underbrush. Leunga's jaw dropped. "Holy shat!" He turned to his flabbergasted siblings and shouted, "Do either of you see that thing?!"

Moonlight at the End of Days

Leunga, Sydney, and Ricky remained static, unable to take their eyes off of the sight. Where once there was a small adolescent fox now stood a horrifying beast coated in dense smoke. The creature stood nearly six feet high at the tips of its silhouetted shoulders and was easily fifteen feet long from its cloaked snout to the tip of its tail—and for metric measurements, please consult the handy conversion table I forgot to include. Visually horrifying, it had disproportionately large and muscular forelegs in comparison to its frail, wiry hindquarters, a stout chest giving it a sluggish pretense, and an oversized head that quite possibly could have outweighed a decent portion of the rest of its carriage with its immensity. Wide jaws snapped blindly as the ocean of haze expanded the monster's snout outward, making it capable of consuming its entire former fox form with ease. The stretching of its bones crackled under the thick fog as it continued to grow, slowly reaching its pinnacle shape.

The wild brute stood unfocused, drenched in smoke. Illuminated yellow globes appeared where eyes would be as it lifted its massive head and stared down the humans gawking at its transformed structure. As a dog would shake itself dry, so too did the dark monstrosity. With quick controlled movements, it jostled, flicking specks of shadow from its fur until its intended form was visible. A great white wolf with murderous intent grinned at the siblings across the underbrush. All along its immense body, electrified yellow runes pulsed in connected lines over its bone structure in large sections across its back and around its ribs, laterally down each leg. Several jagged crags were around its bushy foxlike tail, and individual markings flowed like tears from its eyes to each of its razor-sharp teeth. And finally, an especially large symbol on the beast's forehead finished off the effect of its incredible neon exoskeleton. Very scary, if you ask me.

FENRIR. Son of Loki, the Norse god of trickery, Fenrir is a mighty wolf of massive size and is the herald of the Ragnarok, the end of the world. Long ago, the Nordic gods of Asgard prophesied that during the final days, Fenrir would fight a fierce battle with Odin, king of the gods, and in turn kill him. To prevent this from ever happening, Tyr, the only god the powerful wolf trusted, agreed to place his arm in Fenrir's mouth while the other gods tied its legs with bindings, keeping it from growing too strong; however, when Fenrir realized the deceit that was happening, it snapped its massive jaws shut, biting off Tyr's arm. It is said that Fenrir's children Sköll and Hati persistently try to eat the sun and moon, respectively, chasing them across the sky each day and night. When Sköll and Hati ultimately accomplish their goal, they will plunge the planet into darkness and freeze all life, subsequently liberating their father and beginning Ragnarok. From the time of its leashing, Fenrir has remained dormant, waiting for the day of its freedom.

The great beast tilted its snout upward and gazed at the sky. Glows of a long-lost language echoed across its coarse fur as a sharp gust swept across its extra-large black ears—along with its big bushy tail, they were the only evidence that the transmogrified creature was once a timid fox. The bright white centers of its vibrant yellow eyes focused skyward, as if it were waiting patiently to see if Sköll succeeded in swallowing the sun. Fenrir sat obediently on stunted hind legs, watching the last remaining cloud drifting in the sky before sharply drawing in a breath and tilting back its ears. The air around its pursed lips vibrated as it let out a thunderous howl—the sound of a thousand lone wolves wailing in unison. Minutes passed as the trees far above its mammoth jaws quaked with the power of the monster's cry. As it eventually ran out of breath, Fenrir redirected its focus back to the spectators beyond the trees and waited for their reaction.

Ricky shook his unbelieving eyes. He had been tricked by the old man skipping through the trees on a path to safety. A rotten joke with no punch line. His unusual breakfast of dried animal muscle had clearly been tainted with some sort of mind-altering device. The thought of using drugs never appealed to Ricky, because he preferred his world to consist only of reality—that, and the rabid laws against such behavior—but by pure, uncut chance, it makes sense that his first, and only, *trip* would be an unpleasant one. He had already begun taking short, secretive steps backward when he announced, "I need to go lie down—" But a hand wrapped around his wrist and quickly pulled him away from the creature. Startled by the unexpected presence of his brother, Ricky jumped as he turned, noticing his older sister was already sprinting down the beaten path, indistinctly calling out for her siblings to follow.

"Come on, loser!" Leunga looked away from him as he hurriedly pursued the distant hollering of his younger sister. "Run already!"

Ricky took one last motivating glance toward the giant wolf grinning at their group and followed Leunga. The brothers bounded through the underbrush, hastily making their return to the trail in a vain attempt to catch up to their sister. Two pairs of shoes pounded against the hard dirt of the walkway as Ricky and Leunga made their escape. Rampant panting from each of them squelched any chance of hearing a stalker; both of them keeping their eyes locked forward, watching the black-and-purple-clad fugitive ahead disappear along the serpentine path. Ricky's heart beat with fear as he warily glanced back at the location of the wolf, hoping it had yet to move, but to his horror, Fenrir was already on their tail, trundling forth with hungry yellow globes bouncing up and down only a few hundred feet behind. He knew immediately that it was only a matter of time before the lumbering giant would catch them and turn them into portions for mutated foxes.

Leunga's scattered thoughts bounced against the trees and faded into the ether. As the brothers ran after their sister, the eldest unexpectedly darted off the trail into the underbrush by his side, shouting, "Follow me! We can hide in here!"

Ricky skittered across the dirt and blindly followed the young man bounding through the thick ferns, deeper into the forest. The sound of the wolf crunching through the plant life behind them gave them the strength and incentive to charge onward. Once the boys had made it through the concealing shrubs, they were faced with a barrage of tightly knit trees on all fronts. Leunga flipped a coin in his head and promptly decided to ignore it, running off to the right side instead. Just as they felt they found a proper moment to catch their breath, the panting of Fenrir behind them grew ever closer.

Leunga quickly snapped a small branch off a shallow tree as he and Ricky ran. He spun around for an instant and lobbed the stick in Fenrir's direction, yelling, "Fetch, fucker!" The perfect decoy. No mutt can resist the temptation of gathering thrown objects and returning the item to its careless owner. Drifting lazily through the sky before landing with a crack against the top of the wolf's cranium, the branch failed in its mission. The monster shook away the abrupt attack and roared with anger. Leunga glanced over his shoulder as he ran and scowled. "Oh what a stupid-ass dog!"

"Where are we going?!"

"There!" the leader shouted through bouts of wheezing, pointing between the trees at a massive boulder positioned next to the broad wall of a cliffside he just barely noticed. With a forceful shove, he pushed his younger brother in the direction of the great granite marble. The duo ran faster than either of them ever imagined they could, quickly reaching the refuge in a matter of seconds. Leunga ran ahead and squatted next to the immense stone, and entwining his fingers together, he created a booster stair for his younger brother. Ricky ran onward and placed his leaping sneaker into the awaiting hands. In one fluid motion, he was vaulted up by his oldest sibling, achieving higher ground with ease, where he then whirled around and reached down, firmly gripping Leunga's extended hand. Adrenaline coursed through them both like electric rivers as Ricky lifted his petite older brother up the rough rock just before Fenrir snapped at the eldest's feet. The Super Leunga Bros. leapt up the stony surface and climbed higher to the peak of the humongous boulder, where they sat, stunned by the events, with backs against the earthen cliff wall.

Ricky breathed heavily in relief as he glanced over to his brother, who was performing the same action. The two stared at each other in shock, when suddenly, the colossal teeth of Fenrir gnashed at the ledge of the rock as it jumped upward, unable to reach their location. "What does a drug trip feel like? 'Cause I'm—I think I'm seeing a really weird animal right now."

Leunga pointed at the wolf. "You mean that guy? That's not a trip, man. None of my trips are this organized."

"You see it too?!"

"Yeah, duh! Why the hell would I be running with my legs if I didn't have to?"

"It's real?!"

Spryly, the stoner reached over the side of the rock and slapped the leaping beast on its snout, surprising the wolf. "Obviously."

Ricky gasped tensely at his brother's haphazard behavior. Fortunately, no matter how hard it huffed and puffed, the monstrosity's efforts at attaining their height were ineffective. "I hope it can't get up here."

"P.S. What the fuck is *it*?!"

The teen tried his best to view the threat objectively. "A *really* big fox. But with a wolf nose. And a wolf mouth. And a wolf face. And a wolf body. And wolf legs... Maybe it's a wolf?"

Leunga furrowed his brow at the twisted form of the beast below. Deformed fangs gnashed in frustration as it investigated its possible options for retrieving its prey. Taking a moment to study its mismatched legs—brawny forelegs scraping at the rock face of the boulder, and the feeble rear limbs that seemed scrawny in comparison despite their enormous size—he wondered momentarily how it managed to remain upright on such gangly hind legs, until he recalled the lanky hind legs of his brother and sister and remembered that they both have the ability to stand as well. Leunga snorted at his brother's comment and agreed. "Weird-ass wolf..."

Ricky sat atop his roost, quietly waiting for something good to happen. Hoping for the world to reset. Expecting everything to return to normal, the tips of his fingers became raw with pain as he unknowingly dug his nails into the coarse granite, gripping the safety of his lofty seat. Unable to focus on anything other than his breathing pattern, the kid quietly choked on a lapse of bravery, feeling the fear growing in his chest. His eyes dropped to the edge of the giant boulder, and he found himself sincerely wishing that he and his brother had merely experienced a shared hallucination from eating their grandfather's nondescript jerky. As you might expect. "At least it can't climb rocks."

Quickly coming to terms with the accidental perfection of the fortuitous fortress he found in his fearful flight, a boisterous boy boasted, guffawing as he flipped off the pursuer. "Yeah-hah! That's right, bitch! In yo fuckin' face! See this? We're invincible up on this bitch, so that makes you a bitch! How do ya like that, b-b-b-bitch?!" *Bitch*—if you'll pardon my French—is a bit of an inaccurate statement. Though mythical, Fenrir is technically a male canine...or perhaps he meant the B-word as an insult. I take it back. Forget everything I just said. Not everything. "Bitch, we can live up here all *week* if we have to, so suck on that, bitch! Yeah."

"Yeah," Ricky reminded him, "but won't we, like, starve to death up here pretty soon?"

Realizing his brother was instantly correct, the eldest gazed blankly though the trees in horrified thought, until he stopped to stare the notorious neon nuisance in the eyes and yelled, "Bitch!"

The ferocious fenris wolf leapt against the upper hemisphere of the hideout with enough force to cause the rock to shift. Ricky could hear the increasing rapidity of his pulse with every second that passed. Consumed by panic and trepidation, the lad leaned forward to stare at the animal with his wary brown eyes unimpeded by their respective lids. Dumbstruck by lack of comprehension, he broke his own silence at some point minutes later. "What the *heck* do we do?!"

Leunga could sense the terror in his brother's words. "Hmm..." Leaning forward a bit to see the assaulting creature more clearly, he suddenly had a thought. "Oh!" He raised his voice to an empowered shout and suitably said, "Go away now! Leave our immediacy nary to return! Begone!" The giant beast was still as it sat obediently by the boulder, watching Leunga's unsuccessful attempts at driving it away. He growled, "I don't get it. That should've worked!"

Ricky sneezed. Sternutation. Hazily staring at the peak of the trees above, he viewed the top-heavy wolf in his thoughts waiting patiently to devour him and his brother. Wracked with nerves, he was reminded briefly of the metamorphosis that took place mere moments ago, and he attempted to take control of his fear by rationalizing the situation—to try to make sense of the nonsense. "Guh, this doesn't make any sense. How can an animal get all smoky and then...this. What do you think happened to it back there?"

"Sudden case of the rabies I would say." Leunga peeked over the edge of the rock again and nodded. "Yeah, that's what it is." He stared at the excruciatingly large skull and forelegs of the monstrous behemoth before him, professing, "I'm almost positive that's what rabies looks like." And I'm almost positive it's not. Leunga shrugged. "Or, you know, the Summoner guy did it..."

To his great disappointment, the handsome one had a grave realization with the help of his brother's frank statement. He swallowed as he too stared at the wolf attempting to kill them. "So that means Grampy really *wasn't* lying just to freak us...?"

A sibling stroked his chin and belched, "Yep."

Ricky twisted his sights upward, glancing above his head toward the earthen cliffside at his back as tiny flakes of dirt fell like rain into his eyes. He shook his blurred vision wildly and grimaced. "Man! We are *so* trapped right now. I don't think we can climb this wall. Ugh. How are we ever gonna get away from this thing?"

Leunga creased his face and shrugged without apprehension.

Turning to his wise older brother for advice, the teen wondered, "What should we do, Lou?"

"We should do a...what the hell is the word I'm looking for? A diversion? No, that's not it." That is it.

"You're right! We need something to scare it away with." Ricky's nerves were slowly returning to a much more controlled place as he took his mind off the impossibility of the situation. He glanced around at the area, assessing their options. "But...how?"

"Ooh, I know. Throw something at it!"

Hastily removing his new backpack—his grandfather's former rucksack, which, by contrast to his usual accessory, was so agonizingly comfortable that it was entirely unimportant to mention until this point—Ricky lifted it easily over his head and threw the entire pack at Fenrir. The knapsack flew with great force right into its snapping oversized jaws. The great beast shook its head from side to side before throwing the projectile angrily off to the side with a flick of its massive cranium.

"Dumb, ass! You threw the *whole* effin' bag?!"

"Well, you said to throw something!"

"Yeah, like a piece of food from inside it, jackwad!"

"You should probably start saying what you mean, dude..."

Leunga's mind surged with a contemptible idea. "Right now isn't the best time for things. I just got the best idea. We use my new *armaments*! It's so stupid it's obvious!" And so obvious it's stupid. "Swords is how it is these days anyways. Okay. I'm gonna need you to jump down on top of that guy and hold it still, then *I* jump down and stab at it thusly." Teamwork.

Ricky tittered nervously in disbelief and shook his head. "I'm not gonna touch that thing!" In his current condition, the karate connoisseur could imagine no feasible reason to ever leave the security of his elevated state. The dirt below might as well have been made of molten lava as long as that monster roamed the Earth. "Get someone else to do it."

"Hmmm..." This new development forced Leunga to reformulate his well-designed plan. "This is tricky..."

"Leave us alone! There's food right there in that bag!"

"It's not going to listen to reason. I think we're gonna have to hurt it."

Ricky rolled his eyes. "Uh...duh!" he replied in a tone of tremendous mockery. "Ya think?!"

Leunga thought of a way to salvage the tattered remains of his plan. "Okay, I got it. You take the swords—are you getting all of this? Then I—*I*— jump down and grab its tail while you follow closely and slice off its giant head. Okay, get ready."

"I'm not gonna use the swords. They're your swords. You use the swords."

Once again, his baby brother had destroyed his master plan. Leunga buried his head in his hands and burst. "All right, fine! When they write stories about all of this, I'm gonna get all the glory and any subsequent ass that goes with it."

"Uh...why would anyone write a story about *this*?!" Why indeed.

While ignoring his younger brother's statement, Leunga came to a carefully crafted decision. "Okay then, I jump down solo, straddle it solo, and poke it solo. Bastard."

"All by yourself?!" Ricky grew concerned over the probability of the execution of his older brother's plan. "Are you sure that'll be enough to kill it?"

"Uh, what the hell, kid? Do you have a better idea?"

"Not yet, but I think anything would top that."

"Maybe you can pummel it into submission by throwing more backpacks at it." Leunga was hemorrhaging patience. His work boots bounced against the rock beneath his toes anxiously while he dove back into the deep reaches of his mind—as well as digging through the mind of his sibling, and anyone else within reach.

Ricky listened to the depth of his own breaths, unaware of his older brother's mental excavation or of the persistent tapping on his boulder. Despite the danger far below his feet, he could no longer focus on anything other than the sound of air rushing in and out of his lungs, as if every breath was sacred. The brothers sat back and cloistered themselves in the darkness of their own bleak worlds, each of them desperate for an escape from their dire situation.

Gawking through the trees some more, Leunga took a hiatus from his cerebral adventure. "Gosh, I hope Sydney got away. That lanky blond bimbo—not you, the other one. What's-her-name just leaves us to be ripped apart by this asshole..." He leaned forward and glared at the ground below. Fenrir sat staring at its prey, tauntingly perched just out of reach as it snarled in protest. "Yes, that means you, asshole." Leunga returned to his post against the protective cliffside at his back to reunite with his thoughts. Caught off guard by the specter of his sister echoing in his mind, he suddenly found himself honestly craving her wisdom for the first time in his life. Gazing across the leafy clutter at the unseen path, he jested, "As fast as she was going, she's probably home by now..."

Ricky sighed, his nerves continually pulsing in waves of panic as thoughts of uncertainty rolled over the wrinkles of his mind. "Wish *I* was home by now..."

This was news to Leunga. "This is news to me. Are you saying you don't want to be here?"

His brother chortled as the wolf just over the edge growled once again. "Is it that obvious?!"

"Good hell. This is a free country. You didn't have to come with us if you didn't want to. Christ almightiness. And Buddha too."

A sense of relief and hope inundated the young combatant. "So...after we get away from this...I can go home?"

"My *what*?! Where did that come from?! You're gonna pull a Sydney and run away from us? How could you betray the quest like that? I think I might cry."

"No! No... I'm not—I didn't mean it." But of course he really did mean it. "No I didn't..." An awkward silence ensued, immediately followed by another awkward silence. The brothers rested against each other and fell into thoughts of flight: Ricky with his lips nervously between his teeth and Leunga with his pinky finger shoved up his nose. Equally sharing a common goal. Epic escape.

"I keep coming up with the same idea. Do you have anything yet?"

The younger boy breathed in sharply and shouted at the top of his lungs. "Help!" Then he sneezed.

Only slightly deafened by the abrupt explosion taking place very near his jolting ear, Leunga admired Ricky's attempt at securing their rescue and gave it the adulation it so rightfully deserved—even though it failed to produce results right away like everyone expected it to. "That works too."

"Hopefully somebody heard that," remarked Ricky, wiping his nose dry against his mostly clean, rolled karate gi sleeve. Actually, I take back the *mostly clean* comment...

Coming up with another plan some several dozen silent seconds later, the stoner said, "I wish we had a gun..."

"I wish we had bullets for that gun."

With a great big gasp of realization, Leunga ripped his hand out of his nose and gripped his brother's upper thigh. "Wait! I am a gun!"

Ricky glanced at the guy's groping hand and ordered, "Explain."

"Think about it, man! All that bullshit I said earlier is true! I really *am* the energy of a trillion suns! Look how high we are right now! I practically tossed you up here, and I'm like half your size!"

Ricky looked surprised. He hadn't realized that fact. "That's true!"

"My reflexes are probably so extremely sharp and kick-ass that I'd be, like, all zooming around and shit and nothing would be able to touch me! I can just run around until this guy gets dizzy and then blast him in the balls to bits! Maybe you really *can* be as worthless as you are right now after all!"

"Awesome!"

"Okay! New plan! We're going back to the old plan and we're calling it 'plan C.'" Minor adjustments to the same basic plan do not constitute a title reclassification, so it's still plan A. "C, but instead, I'm actually gonna do it this time."

The taller fellow felt a series of encouraging boons shower over him as Leunga leisurely transformed into a hero. He smiled nervously at his brother—hopefully it wouldn't be the last time he could do so—and said, "Good luck."

"No thanks. I never use it anyway." Leunga wiped his hand on Ricky's ostentatious pants as he released his grip, discreetly leaving something behind. The hero stood carefully, smashing his head against the overhanging cliff wall at his back before he slowly inched his way over to the portion of their hideout directly above the assailing monster. In preparation for his dazzling attack, he needed to correct for the wind beforehand. Leunga stuck his entire middle finger into his mouth and generously coated it in saliva. Slowly removing the digit from its oral den, he held the bird high in the air for all to see. "Wow. That tasted *really* bad." The eldest loser stood there and checked for changes in the stagnant climate for a full minute before realizing the air was still and evil. Cautiously, Leunga turned his back to the wolf and began to do some mild stretching—vain attempts at touching his toes and the like.

"Uh...aren't you gonna take the swords out of the case before you jump?"

"And risk killing myself on the way down?! I think not, young one." I admit, I'm surprised by this discovery. I had no idea Leunga was capable of that level of self-awareness and concern for his own welfare—or his ability of foresight for that matter; however, jumping into jeopardy with no prepared means of protection is incredibly dangerous.

"That's incredibly smart," Ricky said with a sincere smile. He was well acquainted with his brother's shady history of heights and sharp objects; after all, how else would Ricky have acquired that long scar on his neck running from behind his ear down to his shoulder? I did already mention his scar, I'm sure of it. A bit of safety originating from Leunga was a welcome and refreshing astonishment to the youngest hiker. It still doesn't change the fact that he's planning on jumping onto an enormous, and eager, wild animal, though.

The sheathed swordsman continued to roll his crackling spine around and rotated his ribs. With a loud popping of his hip joints, he nodded. "Remember, it's always a good idea to stretch before any strenuous exercise." Good advice. For more information, consult a trained professional or use basic common sense.

Ricky's dread began to bloom again as he listened to the repulsive sounds of his brother preparing to leap from their extreme height, realizing that Leunga was actually going to go through with it. "Wait a sec," he started slowly, "is this actually going to be a good idea to do or are we just being really dumb right now...?"

"What do you mean?"

"Well, now I'm not so sure about this. I mean, what if you miss it completely? You could like, twist your ankle or land on your tailbone. And then you get eaten right away."

"That won't happen."

Haunted by the vision of their grandfather's ravaged backpack appearing at the forefront of his concern, Ricky suggested, "Um, we should probably distract it with something so it doesn't bite you in half on the way down." A necessary addition to ensure a successful operation.

"Got it. I'll do an amazing ninja flip to stun it with brilliance."

The younger sibling struggled with disbelief over his brother's—"Do you even know how to do a flip, dude?!"—acrobatic capacity. Rude boy. "You should just keep it simple, man..."

The leaper reassured himself—out loud, for some reason. "Don't let him psyche you out. He's just a stupid kid."

"Hey! All I'm saying is I don't want you to get hurt."

Leunga smiled wide—really more of a giant grin. "Hey, thanks man! I don't wanna have to hurt you, either." He reached both hands to the sky, stretching every muscle he could find. Unbeknownst to the young man, he began to gradually tilt backward—a severe loss of balance—on a one-way trip to the beast below, no less. Ricky noticed almost immediately and swiftly snagged his brother by the shirt between the straps of the harness across the adult's abdomen, carefully pulling him closer and restoring him to an upright and locked position. Leunga glanced down at his scarlet polo with a question coming to mind. "Was there something on my shirt?"

As he leaned back in temporary relief, Ricky was horribly startled when a fibrous root reached out of the earthen wall and grabbed his hair from behind. He ducked away and yelped before turning to face the demon. At the discovery of an idea, he quietly gave a command to his brother as he yanked at the dry plant in its earthen home. "Hey, Lou, give me the lighter for a sec."

"We're gonna start a fire? I know it's tempting to reshape the world, but now is no time to daydream! We'll do it later."

"No!" Ricky wrestled with the fibrous corpse at his back, twisting around in his seat, suggesting, "We can use this to get rid of it. Animals are afraid of fire." So am I, but don't tell anyone.

Nodding quickly and quietly, Leunga whipped out the flame bringer and tossed it over to his little brother. Ricky ripped the root out finally and turned his attention away from the cliff just as a lighter flew at him. Surprised by the flying ambush, he clumsily attempted to pinch it from the sky, but it was far too late. The lighter bounced off his sleeve and clattered its way across the boulder to the dirt a dozen feet below. The brothers silently stared into each other's eyes. Leunga was the first to blink. "Forget the fire. After I do an aerial barrel roll, this guy won't know what hit him."

Giving up and giving in, Ricky threw his idea off the opposite side of the hideout and said, "Sure. Just don't die."

"I almost never do. Just let me just find my center...feel the chi." The stoner closed his eyes and cleared his mind—actually, he only needed to close his eyes. In one majestic vault, he would perform a perfect backflip and land squarely on the monster's spine, straddling it just out of reach of its snapping jaws, nextly removing the blades harnessed to his back, and finally plunging the mystic weapons into the cold heart of the assaulting wolf. A tactical maneuver that demanded his full attention. Leunga released a controlled breath, focusing his energy onto the moment at hand, mere seconds away from the instant of attack.

Through the trees in the direction of the beaten trail, a faint call of concern caught the immediate awareness of Ricky and Fenrir. The sound of Sydney echoed easily over the tense tranquility. "Guys? Are you okay? Guys...?"

One brother's anxious eyes darted toward the monster. Its radiant gaze was directed in the bearing of their sister with a look of encouragement. The wolf's wild grin grew greater as it gradually stood up, focused on her location. Ricky cringed. "No! What is she doing?! Why is she shouting?!"

It was time. Sinewy muscles contracted, sending the blade-clad warrior soaring to the heavens. Heavy work boots flew backward off the rock platform thirteen feet above solid earth with aim so accurate their target stood little chance. While gliding through the atmosphere, Leunga commenced what he hoped would be the best flip ever, but turned instead into a wild flailing in the sky as he quickly realized he lacked the necessary conditioning to perform a tactic he had never executed before. The launching loser plummeted to the ground like a thrashing snowflake as Fenrir ran off in the direction of Sydney. With a thunderous thump against the dirt, Leunga twisted his ankle on a protruding stone jutting from the luscious land. From the overpowering momentum of leaping off a giant boulder, along with the weakened state of his left leg, he fell back and landed squarely on his tailbone.

Coccyx crush. After a short backward somersault, he eventually came to a stop and wheezed. "Oh fuck! The various pains!" he screamed and rolled forward to kneel in the grime, rubbing his very sore butt crack in anguish. He cringed, massaging the pain in his ass before watching the other pain in his ass run off in the direction of his sister. Upon taking a deep breath, Leunga shouted an advantageous warning to Sydney. "Watch it, Blondie, that big bastard is coming for you." And then he looked up at the perch from which he leapt and calmly commented to his brother. "I guess it didn't see my flip."

Ricky leaned over the top of the boulder with deep concern for his older brother's well-being. "Get Grampy's backpack while you're down there."

The geek grunted as he slowly staggered up. With a soothing hand placed against his lower back, Leunga limped lethargically to the bag and picked it up, slowly making his way back to the boulder, where he held it up as an offering to his youngest sibling and politely pronounced, "Fuck you. Here you go."

Ricky reached down to the pack and lifted it back up to his roost. He noticed massive punctures lining the outer edges as he opened the main compartment to assess the condition of the sack's contents. He chose to take a moment to conduct inventory of their new supplies, checking if anything had slipped out of a large tooth hole. In the absence of evil, a thought occurred. Ricky's attention was helplessly locked on the perishables in the pack as he addressed his brother. "I think I have a plan now if you want to hear it."

Leunga was delighted. "Enlighten me now!"

The rucksack seemed to contain all of its original supplies: a dozen protein bars, a dozen granola bars, more raw fruit than anyone would ever need, something fairly large made of plastic that would later be determined by Sydney to be a slightly used water filtration kit, two flattened rolls of extra-soft toilet paper that would later be determined by Leunga to be required that afternoon, one tiny towel, a clear plastic bag filled with garbage of all sorts, and an empty pill bottle prescribed to an unfamiliar name. Nothing can stop him now. Ricky chose his words carefully, deciding to remain high until a full consensus on an escape could be reached. "Okay, um, while that big piece of crap is gone, we get the ass out of here and meet Syd back at camp." Due to existing mayhem, Ricky's strict inner censorship had clearly begun to lapse—that, and spending so much excessive time around his foul-mouthed brother and sister doesn't exactly help with the situation either; as you may not have noticed, not so long ago he was horrendously careful about controlling the escape of the casual cussing common among his family, but not so much anymore. Too bad. So sad. "Is that good with you?"

"Best idea I've ever heard. Should we go tell Syddley?"

Fenrir howled once again with the tone of a thousand wolves echoing at the moon hovering above the tundra. Leunga and Ricky threw their focus to the sound as they grew concerned with the overzealous cry of victory coming from the distant trees, far from sight. The eldest brother glanced at his young companion perched atop the stone haven. Ricky chewed vigorously at his lower lip, suddenly worried about the state of their sister's safety. Leunga saw once again the fear in his sibling's expression, and he made a reluctant decision. "Ugh...wait here..." He gripped the blades across his back and violently drew them from their sheath. The ancient weapons burst alive at his touch and shone with the light of a full red moon in the soft shade of the cliff at their back as another plan went right down the drain. "I'll go get Sygvey."

"Okay. Be care—" A brother began before sneezing once again.

Leunga could see he had one last task before his glorious battle with evil to save his sister: a little slice of brotherly advice. "Shut. The. Hell. Up."

"I want to, but I can't."

The slacker scarcely believed his brother's level of naïveté. "Dude, when you're about to sneeze, pinch that nerve under your nose. Everyone everywhere knows that. Come on!"

Ricky cleaned his snout with a quick wipe of the back of his hand. "Pinch the nerve? Where? What nerve?" He has a lot of nerve asking that question.

"Yeah, you go like this and press your lip against your teeth." Leunga held a sword to his face, carefully utilizing one free finger, constricting his zygomatic nerve above his upper lip and just below his nose. "It should stop a sneeze instantaneously." The most advanced sneeze prevention technique ever devised. Use as directed.

"Okay, I'll—" Ricky stopped abruptly, squinting as he inhaled in short intervals.

Leunga recognized his young brother's behavior as an impending outburst and exclaimed, "Be preemptive! Do it now! Act upon it!"

The pretty boy placed his index finger against his upper lip as the sensation of the sneeze climaxed. To his surprise, it worked. No sneeze. He has the magic. "That is awesome! Oh my god, the wolf is right behind you!"

The blades in Leunga's grip instantaneously jolted his arms up and shot over his shoulders, creating an X behind his back just as Fenrir charged through the trees, massive mouth agape. Closing in on the weaponized waif, the beast clamped its grisly fangs shut, catching the twin swords between its teeth. Leunga looked back as much as he could as he felt a mild jerking of the weapons in his hands. "What's happening?" he asked and attempted to shift his body around to face his foe but found that his legs wouldn't listen. "I can't see!"

Ricky watched as the great white wolf tugged violently at the weapons in his brother's grip. Its entire body jerked away from Leunga with no progress, seemingly unable to move the rigid warrior or his trusty weapons. "I think the wolf is, uh...trying to take the swords from you, dude."

Leunga laughed heartily. "Over my teeth-marked dead body!" His arms flicked outward to the sides uncontrollably, consequently propelling the beast back before he whirled around, coming face-to-face with the monster. Fenrir lunged forward with a charging head-butt as the swords slashed toward it in order to protect their master from the attack. Mystic metal and furry flesh were held together by nothing but uninhibited enmity. The knight and the nightmare held their standoff position for longer than either would have wanted. The young swordsman leaned into the blades digging into the wolf's fuzzy forehead, noticing a drastic change in temperature. "Whoa! This beastie is freezing fucking cold! If I wasn't about to die it would be kinda nice..." Ruthlessly refreshing.

The monster shed its metal tormentor, ripping itself away from Leunga's shield. Before the warrior had a chance to strike, the wolf leapt backward, away from its bladed prey. Landing in thunder, its mighty paws skidded to a halt along the dirt as it hunched its body closer to the earthen floor, entering an aggressive stance while it growled angrily. Leunga's eyes shot in the direction of Fenrir's forehead in search of damage. To his horror, the beast remained pristine despite having razor-sharp iron burrowing into its skull; however, the large neon marking above its eyes was flickering sporadically, unlike the solid yellow lights etched over the rest of its body. Puzzlement accumulated as something caught Leunga's peripheral attention. His focus dropped to his hands, where he noticed that the burned markings on the exterior of his grips were suddenly glowing with a flat fire as red as blood. As he was about to comment on the abnormality searing his skin, the weapons controlling his movements flew forward to block another vicious assault of infinite loathing from the hindered fiend.

Ricky clutched the edge of the rock with muscles tensed. His large brown eyes barely sneaking a peek over the coarse lip of the boulder, secretly and unseen—with the exception of his crunchy crest of golden hair, which was largely visible to all and still magnificently crafted. Shining silver steel clanged against enormous enamel after each snapping misery. With every one of the wolf's brutal blows deflected, Ricky, the combat art aficionado, frantically wondered why his brother refused to act more aggressively.

Leunga proficiently defended every attack with ease, without thought or reaction on his part, but quickly learned that he was unable to go on the offensive. With each lunge of the massive jaws blocked, it became less evident that the twin blades would be making a counterattack on their own accord. Gradually, he became cornered by the safe haven of the boulder, backing

away from Fenrir until the cool rock base grazed his bare calf, leaving behind
a smear of abraded skin. During his persistent defense, Leunga determined
that their grandfather must have left out a crucial element in his assessment of
how the weapons react. The bladed boy lost himself in hazy memories of that
morning while he was protected by the ancient magic in his palms. "Okay,
let's see... He said that he cut off its something and then it blew up, or he
popped it in its wang maybe." Leunga attempted to command the swords into
action, but found that they were in total control. "That lying old fucker! I can't
even do anything!" Suffering from an utter lack of necessary information—a
status that occurs more often than it should—he bit his lip and watched
helplessly as he was cosseted by the swords sheltering him from the relentless
assault without any idea to be had in his entire head. He was trapped.

Studying his brother's endless struggle with the horror, Ricky realized
the element that was lacking from their dire situation: a basis in reality. It was
all so unreal: magic weapons, mystic monsters, thundering chains, ancient
wizards, insufferable narration, and the fact that Leunga was outdoors.
Something within him snapped. Broken free to weave through space with the
sound of the sun, his panic subsided, replaced by relief and jubilation. As he
gawked at the gyrating metal pinging against jagged fangs, Ricky burst into a
short explosion of hysterical laughter, and then he sneezed without covering
his mouth. Manners.

"Well, sir, I'm glad you think this is so fucking funny..."

Ricky tilted his head back while it swam with understanding. Staring
skyward at the stirring cumulus waiting in the blue, he calmly declared, "It's a
dream. No wonder this day has been so stupid. I haven't woken up yet." He
smiled at the sky. "We still haven't gone to that spider web cave." Taking in
the scenery, he was awash in vivid pines and accurate forest clutter; a memory
of his sister and him, made into fantasy—climbing rocks among the trees when
he would look up to her as a best friend so very many summers ago—returning
to him as the basis of a nightmare. Ricky turned sharply, fully expecting to
suddenly see Sydney by his side, or one of his annoying high school friends,

maybe even Becky, but he would prefer someone more meaningful like the girl from his past whose laughter was irreplaceable. Sadly, no one was waiting at either side. Just a dream—obviously another in a continuing series of nightmares he had experienced recently. Too much caffeine. He had suffered through a heap of fretting in the face of the beast for no real reason, but it didn't matter because the worst of it was over. Casually throwing the bitten bag over one shoulder, his attention returned to the battle below. "Dude! I hope I can remember all of this when I get up so I can tell you guys all about it. I better not wake up before it's over..."

"Shut up! I'm trying to think!" As we all know, Leunga typically required silence while lost in contemplation. As he struggled with thoughts of helplessness and confusion, his beltless pants slowly, but surely, slid down his legs and collected in a crumpled pile around his ankles. He felt the chilly aura of Fenrir grope its way into his boxers and shuddered. "Freestyle!" Out of control and exposed, Leunga reviewed the inaccuracies in his grandfather's story and panicked as he addressed the swords in his hands. "Hum! What the hell are you waiting for?! Kill it already!"

Fortunately, Ricky mistook his brother's complaint as a call to arms. Liberated in his dreaming state, he felt obliged to win the moment and save his family from harm. Unlike most of his dreams, here he felt in control and powerful. Standing tall, he gave the task little forethought and dropped with maximum power. His solid, blond fauxhawk sliced through the stale air as he leapt from his perch with accuracy and might, striking the wolf with the full force of 187 pounds of lean, teenage muscle. Ricky's bubble gum-cushioned heel bent the beast's neck backward on impact, contorting its stance and ceasing its attack against his brother. Hopping along its ample spine, the master martial artist landed safely on the ground behind its bushy tail, where the ride came to a full, and complete, stop.

A line of runic symbols along the wolf's back burst into a cascading shower of flightless fireflies that faded before falling to the ground. The beast stood dazed by the onslaught; its mouth hung open, slack. Leunga peered into the abyssal cavern and noticed a small glint of light at the back of its throat. From what he could tell, the glow was similar to the large markings covering the rest of its frame, but was pure white in color. Time slowed as his wild eyes met with the radiance inside his opponent. He felt a heart spark ignite his every muscle. Surged with an arcane instinct, Leunga was compelled to strike. Bathed in bloodlust like a barbaric warrior charging over a battlefield, he was urged to rush toward the incapacitated animal.

Astray in a frenzied mindset, Leunga stepped out of his khaki heap and held a stabbing blade forth. His heavy boots pounded against the dry dirt with each step as his mostly nude legs brought him closer to his prey. The pointed spike entered the behemoth's maw and drove onward without a loss of momentum. Leunga uncontrollably stretched his arm forward between the beast's staggered fangs, puncturing the light at the back of its throat with full force. Through the base of Fenrir's cranium, the moonlit blade pierced the exterior of its furry hide from within, extending far beyond the point of safety. A flood of warmth drenched over Leunga's concealed hand as he slowly regained control over his movements. The blade in his grip slipped out of the wolf's fleshy gullet, freeing his blood-covered arm from its clutches.

Leunga watched the beast's last moments in awe, unable to take his wide eyes off the sight. Fenrir tumbled into a daze as its body systematically began to lose power. Shutting down. The behemoth released one final gurgled howl in its foreplay with death while its nose dropped heavily to the ground, dragging along, and spilling the crimson tide collected in its jaws across the forest. Sorrow covered the monstrosity's appearance as the weight of its failing body grew too great for its legs to abide, causing it to fall into a defeated mountain of fur and muscle. Foaming blood seeped through its teeth as the runic symbols encasing its frame, as well as its round eyes, lost their luminosity and forever faded to black.

Standing in the expanding pool of blood, Leunga stared at the corpse of his victim, confused and regretful. The life-force dripping off the murder weapon in his trembling hand splashed against the puddle, collecting with the rest of its kind. Within moments of the creature's demise, a hollow voice clapped against the trees and echoed a haunting hymn repeatedly from afar, until suddenly, the body of Fenrir exploded in a rain of thick, gloomy mist— the same substance that took control of the powerless animal minutes ago— showering over Ricky and Leunga in an impenetrable cloud of darkness much too large to see through, before slowly dissipating into the ground from whence it came. All that remained of the unfathomable horror was a lake of blood and the broken body of a helpless young fox.

Slowly making her way through the underbrush, the mysterious and elusive Sydney returned to the group with mud covering much of her face, arms, and a decent portion of her abdomen. Leunga looked over at his crud-caked sister and spoke with a shaky voice drenched in adrenaline. "Oh, there you are."

Magic Lightning, Tragic Thunder

Fenrir let forth its deafening howl, reverberating through the trees. The shock of the sound wave broke Sydney's awestruck trance induced by its transformation, forcing her into action. She turned to her taller brother by her side and noticed his dumbfounded stare. "Ricky! We have to get out of here!" she shouted, finding that her own words were nearly inaudible against the powerful blast of the wolf fifty feet away. She reached out and shook his shoulder forcefully, but did little to break him away from the mystifying scene. "Come on!"

As the wolf continued to wail into the sky, Sydney took quick steps away from the animal, passing Leunga on her way back to the trail. "Let's run!"

Though the girl could barely hear the voice of her older brother, she knew what he was saying. "You want we should leave Ricky?!"

Still unable to hear herself speak, she assured her partner, "He'll catch up! Let's go already!" And with that command, she began sprinting down the path, away from the terrible cry of the beast. Soon after she charged off, the dreadful howl of Fenrir faded out, forcing her to glance back once more, seeing her statuesque siblings, and offered a shouted suggestion—an audible one. "What the hell are you waiting for?! Go! Now!" As Sydney placed increasing distance between her and the massive monstrosity, she turned back once or twice, calling out to her dawdling brothers. "Hurry up! Damn it!"

Over the beaten path, her high-top sneakers glided on wings made of shadow, fleeing the peril in order to grant the group a chance to figure out what needed to be done. Surprised by her brothers' ability to follow so silently, Sydney ran onward at full speed, focused solely on the path ahead. As she wound around the pines, her mind raced with puzzlement and scheming; the odd arrival of the nightmare had effectively brought devastating mental chaos to the march.

The wild blur of black and violet went streaking through the trees with a fixed banner of gold rushing high above. Her long legs were carrying her quickly and quietly along the path with ease, until a nagging force began to pull at her ears, begging her to look back. Sydney glanced over her shoulder and noticed the absence of her brothers, along with the dearth of the mighty wolf. Sprinting along the trail, she abruptly paused, planting her feet firmly on the path and skidding to a sudden stop. "Holy crap," she said, scouring the path she so recently traversed, searching for any signs of her supremely slothful teammates. Minutes passed and she saw nothing of a sibling sort. "Where the hell are they?!"

Broken ranks. Sydney mumbled, "You slow bastards," as she waited for a moment in order to give them an opportunity to catch up. Regrettably, too much time had elapsed without a sign of progress in that area. In the interest of keeping her family intact, she reluctantly chose to return to the scene of unimaginable confusion to find some answers for her sudden solitude. Slowly backtracking along the trail, she opened her senses wide in the inert atmosphere of the silenced trees. The whereabouts of her misplaced brothers or the transmogrified fox remained a mystery as she listened intently for any evidence of their existence. Her steps slid across the soil, spreading tiny plumes of dust on her way back to their last known location, when she was caught by the abrupt realization of being truly alone in the world.

Out of concern for her own well-being, she remained quiet for most of her trek. Minutes that felt like eons passed by without a sign of hope for finding her hiking buddies. As the serpentine trail slithered back and forth through the enormous conifers, her heart grew more and more anxious about a surprise horror appearing around every turn. As time bred, her chances of finding something she didn't want to witness increased exponentially. Her mind conjured gruesome thoughts she desperately tried to block as she noticed something familiar through the trees. Sydney ceased her cautious walk and jogged along the path to the object of merciless harm. She stared at the wide metal tube, indicative of an ending course, and noticed something new. The pole that had so kindly jammed itself against her pelvis was twisted and bent, as if something very large had stepped through it, like a blade of long grass. Next to the curled metal along the trail, she detected the faint flying footprints of her brothers as well as the pursuing paw prints of the beast, and she began to follow them.

The phantom footsteps led partially down the path she had already travelled too many times before, abruptly changing course, perhaps due to a scuffle, and disappearing forever into the thick underbrush, where a valley of broken branches cut through to the heart of the forest. She squinted through the trees, when she was shocked by the sound of her baby brother shouting at the top of his lungs. "Help!" she heard him say as her ears perked up, awaiting the next cry for assistance so that she might be able to pinpoint their location; however, more than enough time elapsed without additional pleas, and she became overly concerned that the worst had already happened.

Sydney crept through the deep, jagged gash throughout the shrubbery, leading her slowly past the pines while her eyes scoured the area. Not long after entering the leafy chasm, it ceased and she found herself surrounded by a dense and naked tree line, obstructing her chances of tracking her family—hopefully only temporarily. The ground before her was bare of life and of markings, and so she stood at a crossroads, unable to determine the correct path to find Leunga and Ricky for lack of substantial trace. Idly waiting at her junction, Sydney studied all potential pathways and chose to take the route on the left. Carefully, she made her way around the maze of trees until she was stopped by a strange sight she clearly did not expect—a thirty-foot-tall earthen wall stretching around the clutter of short foliage in a large arcing crescent, but no sign of anyone. She lost her patience and felt the urge to call for her brothers, hoping desperately to hear their possible response. Sydney cupped her hands against the sides of her lips and yelled, "Guys? Are you okay? Guys...?"

Her hands noisily dropped to her sides as she awaited the sound of another person in the midst of her lonely wilderness. Moments later, Sydney sighed nervously as she reluctantly began to return to her former path, when suddenly, she heard a mysterious thumping echo over the roots. An injured Leunga could be heard over the tumultuous tumbling, warning, "Watch it, Blondie, that big bastard is coming for you."

The relieving voice of her brother was quickly overshadowed by the terror peeking past the pines. The unyielding shadow of makeup around her eyes went wide with horror as her glossy brown peepers darted in the direction of the noise along the base of the cliff wall. Galumphing between the trees, rows of jagged yellow fangs blared below a pair of hungry glowing eyes on their way to her location. Fenrir found the perfect prey.

Thinking quickly, Sydney spun around and sprinted toward the closest climbable oak she could find. With a running jump, she kicked off the bark of the forest dweller and wrapped her hands around a low-hanging branch, launching herself over the strut with ease and climbing her way up the steep wooden slope, well out of reach long before the wolf got anywhere near her. She watched carefully as the beast ran onward with great momentum before sliding to stop in a cloud of dust. Its frightening eyes glared at her as her frightened eyes stared at it; and while its mouth cheerfully wore an obtuse grin, its radiant sights conveyed agony and fear. It was a tortured expression of misery and jubilation; and even though she sensed great danger in the air, Sydney couldn't help but feel a deep sense of pity for the poor animal.

Her sympathy trembled back and forth as the giant wolf gazed at her perch high in the tree. Unsure of what to do in life-or-death situations regarding mythical titans, Sydney coolly shook her head and utilized some very, *very* worn-out clichés. "Nice doggy! Good boy! Be a good boy!" Pointing directly at the canine's cranium with one dominating digit, she laced her quaking words with authority and said, "Sit...! Stay...! Um...roll over, I guess? Fuck if *I* know. Just don't kill me!"

Unmoved by Sydney's perfectly executed commands, Fenrir ignored her orders and quickly lunged its full weight against her hideout, crashing its brow against the bark and shaking the entire tree. Sydney held on for dear life as her feet slipped from their post, leaving only her gripping arms around the trunk to support her. Terrified by the villain's strength, she panicked and couldn't reset her somewhat safely placed sneakers to their former roost. As she struggled to replace her stepping stool, Fenrir cracked its skull against her high hideout once more, ensuring her descent. The rough skin of the tree slipped through her clutches with the damaging force of its vibration. In that moment of shock, her vision was filled with a rapid upward cascade of flora. Sydney had no time to think or react—all she could do was fall, dropping like a ripened fruit from on high.

With a splash, she plunged face first into a very poorly placed puddle of dark brown liquid. Sydney removed her face as quickly as she possibly could and gasped for air, breathing heavily as she glanced down at her ruined outfit; to her dismay, she had effectively filthified both of her tops—wait, is filthified a word? Never mind, I don't care. As the grime rolled down her forehead and cheeks, she stared into the muck and groaned. "I hope this is mud..." A shifting of the forest nabbed her immediate attention and reminded her why it was that she was kneeling over a gross pool of slime. Slowly allowing her eyes to move up, she caught a glimpse of a pair of absurdly large paws standing at the edge of her puddle, only a few feet away. At the sight of the massive claws, her glance shot skyward and met with the glowing globes of the wolf.

The gruesome grin of Fenrir was aimed squarely at the smudged Sydney. In a hollow, almost metallic voice, the wolf leaned closer to her and whispered with an interesting accent—labored linguistics struggling to annunciate every pain-filled syllable. "*Scream...for...me.*"

Sydney stared at the beast, astonished. The deep colors in her eyes were amplified by the contrasting filth surrounding them as they grew wider with each passing moment. Surely her mind was playing a trick, because animals don't talk. Animals also don't morph into different animals dozens of times larger and neon, but the proof of the impossible stood before her, smiling like an idiot. She furrowed her grime-coated brow and narrowed her eyes with a small twist of her head, posing a question for the talking animal. "No?"

In the same haunting tone as before, Fenrir chuckled at her insolence. The great beast turned its mighty attention away from her for a moment, looking off in the distance at the place from which it had cornered the other humans, possibly waiting for them to come to the woman's rescue. With a sharp inhalation, the wolf launched its head back once again and released a wailing siren to draw the boys out into the open.

Sydney threw herself backward along the ground, sliding by the seat of her pants away from the obnoxiously loud screaming of the monster. Seeing as how she had accidently sat on the soil and therefore may have ruined her jeans, she lifted her shredded pants off the ground and crab-crawled her way across the forest floor in rapid retreat until she bashed the cushioned twist of hair at the back of her head against a tree with a thud. She immediately cringed at the impact and lost her desire to keep what remained of her outfit spotless, using her hands to massage her scalp.

As the cry of the wolf died off, its focus returned to the path it travelled to reach Sydney, searching for the swordsman and the pugilist. Noticing the inattentive monster's temporary lack of interest, the girl groped her propinquity in need of protection should the wolf attempt to attack her in her defenseless state. Off to her side, she spotted a large rock, but not too large that it couldn't be thrown at a damaging velocity when the moment called for it. Carefully reaching for the stone, her eyes were locked on Fenrir, hoping that it wouldn't notice her outstretched arm dangling toward her means of escape. Her fingers carefully wrapped around the smooth bludgeon and lifted it without a sound while the beast's mind was elsewhere. Sydney's fastened gaze remained steadfast, vigilantly tracking Fenrir's every move as she pulled the stone closer to her chest, looking for the right moment to strike.

The demon huffed in aggravation at not being able to summon the young men; it would seem that the nemesis needed to increase its assault against the helpless woman in order to call out its other victims.

It was time. Sydney's aim locked on her target as her conditioned arm muscles silently reeled back and snapped forward, releasing the projectile with power and accuracy—a deadly combination in any case. Just as the wolf turned its attention back to its mud-covered prey, it caught a decent sized rock to its face, forcing its head to recoil in surprise.

"Sorry!" Sydney cringed and felt remorse as she realized she had just thrown an object of harm at her fox—that is, until it laughed at her again. Fueled by the frustration of its failure to flush the female's family out of hiding, Fenrir began to sidestep the viscous puddle of indeterminate fluid and gradually drew closer to its seated attacker, when suddenly, its entire body froze in place. All along its massive frame, the lit markings burned brighter and much more solid, glowing like the sun. The wolf's mouth dropped open with an overload of energy as its eyes blazed with white-hot color. Sydney winced while she anticipated the monster's inevitable attack, shielding her face with her dangerous bracelets, but nothing happened. Through the break between her forearms, she peeked at the behemoth in time to witness it bounding away, back to where the voice of Leunga sprouted from before.

Her window was open. Sydney sprang up and hastily dusted the dry dirt from her clothing, leaving the puddle gunk where it was for the time being. She watched Fenrir trudging past trees, ramming against a few of them and causing large cracks along their bark. The rumbling sound of impressive paws quickly shrank away until they were gone, and she gave a much appreciated sigh of relief. But the threat was far from over; she and her brothers were still in danger so long as the creature could discern that they were trespassing in its land. Coming to the conclusion that the monster knew exactly where to find Leunga and Ricky, Sydney decided to subtly follow the wolf's lead and headed back into the bundled trees.

•   •   •

As Sydney cautiously trailed in Fenrir's footsteps, she could feel the grunge coating her face and forearms begin to dry, pulling at her skin and clumping in her hair, but luckily only in her bangs. How fortunate for her that she tied the rest of it back. Safely out of the wolf's sensory range, she attempted to clean her precious black shirt and camisole, grabbing handfuls of disgusting sludge and throwing them against the trees while paw prints the size of dinner plates cut a perfect path through the maze—the magnitude of her own feet paled in comparison as she walked in line with Fenrir's tracks. Not far from where she chose to take the left-side path, she saw a cloud of dust floating in the distance and she knew she was close. With one final ball of muck chucked against an unsuspecting pine, she heard the sound of singing metal colliding with something strong, and her concern was replaced with bewilderment.

Through the thicket she rushed onward, closing in on the symphony of battle. Standing tall on a very large boulder, Ricky stared down at his brother deflecting Fenrir's gnashing teeth without control. Sydney stopped to watch from a secure distance, holding a nearby tree for cover, when suddenly, she witnessed her younger teenage sibling leap from his settlement with one jabbing heel aimed squarely at the monster's neck below. The young lady was taken aback as Ricky landed a brutal blow against the wolf, causing it to bend its head back in response while the martial artist stepped across its spine to safety, landing behind it with one knee carefully touching the ground. Subsequent to her bigger brother's descent, a long line of fervent symbols along the creature's back exploded into tiny lights. Sydney's vexed attention turned immediately to a different creature before her—a monster shaped like her older brother, but with hands of fire and a bloodthirsty stare.

Within seconds of Ricky's successful melee, Leunga shot forward, sprinting and stepping away from his pants with one blade aimed into the wolf's yawning jaws. Sydney's heart skipped as she watched her bladed brother thrust the weapon into the open maw without mercy. Shining with victory, the sword tip pierced through the back of the fox's throat; the sister gasped at the sight. She couldn't believe the vicious nature of her weaponized sibling and her spirit sank. As if her heart could handle any more damage.

The blade receded, leaving the gaping wound and exiting the monster's mouth. Sydney watched as it gurgled one final howl before dragging its weary snout across the ground, releasing a deluge of blood. Unable to take her sorrowful eyes off the horrific sight, she managed to catch one last fleeting glimpse into the restraint and anguish evident in Fenrir's fading yellow eyes before the entire beast collapsed. A mysterious metallic voice similar to the one the wolf used minutes earlier bounced through the area, seemingly originating from alternating sources in a giant carousel around the campers, chanting in an ancient language impossible to understand. Not long after the mantra began, Fenrir burst into an enormous cloud of black vapor that swallowed both of her brothers whole before sinking peacefully back into the dirt. As the voice faded, the smoke cleared and she saw her fox, lying motionless on the soggy ground.

From out of the safety of the shadows, Sydney involuntarily stepped forth to rejoin her lost partners. Under the cool darkness of the cliff wall, she crept slowly to the small pile of fur in the center of the sea. With each step across the crimson dirt, the flat soles of her shoes squished through the humid juice, bringing her closer to the departed.

Welcoming her back to the family in a voice that was battered by the shock his shaking knees were not helping him hide, Leunga said, "Oh, there you are."

Ricky turned to see the person his brother was speaking to, but was disappointed and mildly confused by the sight of their soiled sibling. "Huh, I was kinda hoping it was someone else."

Leunga addressed the distressed Sydney as he rolled his head back and closed his eyes. "Feel free to ignore Rickwich. He just needs a good hard slap."

Ricky was bowled over by his dream's audacity. "Woohaw. How dare—hey, I could shatter you like glass, so watch it with the words."

Meanwhile, at the exact same time and place, Leunga decided to take Leunga's advice and ignored Ricky. He looked once again at the weapons in his hands; though the sword in his right grasp had recently punctured living flesh, the blade itself was suddenly spotless and continually glowing in the secluded shade engulfing the group. The same could not be said of the eldest's arm. In his clenched grip, the deep red fluid ran around his knuckles and began to coagulate as his hand gradually became one with the sticky hilt of the blade. Realizing that the danger was over for the time being, the swordsman placed the twin weapons back into their sheath and shook his blood-caked arm toward the ground, sprinkling the puddle with tiny droplets. "That was a lot more terrifying than I imagined it would be..." Apparently, all of Leunga's artificial video game experience was no match for the real thing. "Who else is hungry?"

Ricky shrugged. "I'm not starving anymore, but I could eat. Wait...how can I feel hungry in a dream? Dude, this is so...*something*! I can feel almost everything, but what does it all mean?"

Leunga wiped the sweat from his brow with his cleanest sleeve and stared over the fresh corpse of the fox at the distraught and muddied face of his sister gawking at the ground. He turned to Ricky with a direct order, finding that, of the three siblings, he was currently the most rational despite having just killed something the size of a sedan. "Hey, crazy train, give Syddy something to clean herself with." Filled with concern over the young woman's troubled stare, her big brother looked up at her and inquired about her condition. "You look like shit. Are you okay?"

Sydney remained reticent—afraid that if she opened her mouth to speak, the tears she held back would escape.

Retrieving their grandfather's towel from within the damaged knapsack, Ricky went along with the performance and handed it over to Sydney, who blindly took it without so much as a thank-you. With her stare fastened on the tiny body by her feet, she squatted by its side, gazing into its lifeless eyes, feeling uneased by the bizarre series of events leading up to its needless death. Slowly and gently, she stroked the orange fur down its back, granting its lifeless form one brief glimpse at the power of human compassion. Out of respect, she took the towel in her hands and carefully wrapped the limp remains of her new friend within it and held the frail little beast to her heart, intending to give the animal a burial later at the campsite.

Saddened by the actions he felt forced into taking, Leunga realized what the woman needed to do and chose not to comment about her misuse of the towel. With his bloodied hand held at eye level, he watched streams of life run down his forearm and collect as giant streaks all along the once-white sleeve of his long-sleeved shirt with a crease of his sorrow-filled brow. Sydney stood slowly, encircled by the massacre while causing her older brother to redirect his attention to her. Leunga glanced at the petite package in her grasp before letting his eyes drop to the ground where the pool of blood had spread at least ten feet across. "How did such a tiny little animal make such a big—" He stopped abruptly as he noticed what his words were doing to his sister's fragile state. "Let's just go. No reason to stay here..." Leunga sloshed across the lake of blood with Sydney following quietly, the beaten foe cradled in her arms like a newborn.

As the illusion of his older siblings passed before him, Ricky looked onward at their *filthified* nature and grimaced. "I think I'll leave out the part about Syd being covered in crap..."

Living the Dream

The air throughout the campsite was stifled and awkward. Nary a sound was to be heard in the expansive clearing—with the obvious exceptions of the muted cascade of a rivulet rejoining its sisters in the adjacent body of water, and the sound of gentle chatter coming from the pine needles as they mimicked the birds. A fever of serenity desperately attempted to spread over the infertile clearing, but all was not right with the woods. Something inexcusable had taken place. What should never have been awoken again was now freely roaming the golden land, trespassing on sacred ground and abducting the vulnerable for devious objectives, and the forest was aware of its heinous purpose. The campsite, which had been uproarious and enjoyable the night before, was now a blighted land of dread. Next to the familiar partial ring of large rocks, used sleeping bags remained strewn about and unkempt, left in a dire condition for lack of will and a cleanliness necessity. Significant moments in history arrived and left the stagnant area without so much as a nod to the irrelevant seconds trailing in their wake while the arrangement of benches and beds stood by and waited patiently for meaningful conversation to once again brighten their feeble existence.

Torpid and inert, the aura of the atmosphere dramatically shifted toward the walling trees to the west as the slow return of life crackled its way through the brush. Leunga stumbled vigorously over a wealth of roots as he exited the substantial wilderness and reentered the welcoming arms of the group's terrestrial housing, noticing that everything was exactly as it should be...physically. After tripping over his boots once more, he picked himself up again and dusted off his hands, sighing with relief as he gradually swaggered toward the cleansing force of the local pond. Reunited with the tentative security of their home away from home, Sydney took her hurting stare off of the treetops and momentarily glanced down at the swathed creature in her embrace. During the entire return trip, no one felt the urge to speak, including Ricky, who by that time was wondering when his dream would end so that he could recap the tale of horror to his sister and brother in full.

Leunga knelt by the glowing mirror of water and stared into the face of the cold-blooded warrior looking back at him. His sweat-covered bangs reached down like tentacles grabbing at his eyes from beneath his dusty driving hat. With his clean hand, he removed the black felt cap and shook his hair wildly, hoping to eliminate his uneasy thoughts under the guise of adjusting his appearance. Unable to rid himself of the recent memory of uncontrollable murder, he sank his encrusted hand into the summer pond, spreading the proof of his crime through the warm water. After removing his hand from the cleansing pool, he shook it dry and held it up for inspection; his palm shimmered with freshwater and nothing else, as if the event with the fox had never happened, but the evidence to the contrary was all around him. Blood slowly swelled across the bank of his bathwater, and the permanent stain of death and barbeque sauce remained along his sleeve, constant reminders of his guilt and sloppiness. With his skin purified, Leunga stood and slowly made his way to the center of camp to swim in a troubled mind and sit by his brother's side.

Sydney carefully set the recently deceased on top of the smallest boulder bordering their camp, glancing at the outline of the completely covered fox before turning to join her comrades around the unlit fire pit. The group's lengthy trek back to the clearing gave the girl the time she needed to reflect, and she chose not to dwell on the sorrow of the situation, viewing the critter's death as a quick end to its obvious suffering, but it still didn't keep her from feeling depressed. Sydney took a seat next to Leunga just as he sat on the center bench next to Ricky's luggage with his heavy mind propped up with both hands. Between glances at the older boy's perplexed expression and the younger one's calmly wandering stare, Sydney waited patiently for one of her brothers to shatter the awkward silence. Leunga glanced over at her, and the two eldest siblings locked eyes for a moment; Sydney smiled at him sadly to lighten the mood, but her eyes were filled with a sorrow that her grin was not.

Leunga broke off eye contact with his sister and sighed dejectedly as he caught a glimpse of his fallen foe on the rock behind her. "Well that sucked. How the hell are we supposed to find out what made that huge noise if we get attacked by weird crap?!"

Feeling generously rebellious, Ricky snapped at his accurately oblivious dreamworld brother. "Uh, duh! That's what you wanted though. Epic quest-haver. You were the one who took us out into the forest to live in stupid game land, so shut up."

"Whoa! Asshole!" Leunga scowled; his little brother was seemingly unscathed by the insult. "The fuck is wrong with you?! I just *killed* something! I'm physically traumatized over here."

"Yeah, I know. I was there, bonehead. I saved you from that thing because you wanted it *dead*, dude. And whose fault is it you had to fight it in the first place? Jerk."

"Ooh, I oughta punch your bootytastic ass so hard!"

"Idiot. I'm *bootylicious*. Duh." Ricky relaxed and reclined, realizing that the horrendous wording on his tail was most definitely a part of the dream too.

"Come on, guys. Please stop. The last thing we need right now is more fighting..." Sydney tried not to let her words bring out the sorrow in her heart, staring at the ground vacantly to reduce her chance of bawling in front of the boys, but it wasn't going well.

Leunga calmed his temper for his sister's sake. While glaring at Ricky and wondering what had caused the drastic lightening of his mood—how someone so squirrely could be so cool-headed after challenging a bestial behemoth was perplexing to say the least—he couldn't help but study the nonthreatening features of his brother's face: the gigantic, understanding eyebrows, compassionate brown eyes, those oh-so-sympathetic nostrils, and his wonderfully caring chin. The whole sight made Leunga's stomach churn. Noticing that Ricky was continually calm and collected about the entire situation, the eldest shook his head with disgust and commented, "Yeah, you just go ahead and feel great now, but then comes the crash. Boom." And then suddenly, Leunga screamed and jumped out of his seat, and then screamed again.

Sydney scooted away from the feral brunet hollering by her side. "What?! Why'd you yell?"

His green eyes darted around the camp. "Something just touched the skin on my beautiful leg!"

Allowing his golden crest to fall between the knees of his sweatpants, Ricky bounced his head against his legs and wondered how much more of his fantasy he would have to endure. Humming louder than anyone ever should, he slapped his calves in rhythm with whatever song that was, creating an annoying ambiance for his older brother.

Leunga rolled his cautious head around, and while searching for hidden haunts by his feet, he caught a fleeting hint of his brother's mad insanity and his sister's sad humanity. Disheartened by the sights, he sighed. "Perfect. Ricky's a wreck, Sydney is broken, and I'm can't remember the what I am..." A lethargic, narcissistic, impatient, addled, irresponsible, languorous, indecisive, bogarting, self-obsessed imbecile? "You forgot handsome."

Sydney looked around warily, asking Leunga, "Are you talking to me or are you talking to Ricky?"

"No."

Still staring into the soil, a sibling ceased his racket and shook his head, bouncing his face against his knees. "Dude, this has to be a record or something. None of my nightmares have ever lasted this long. Or maybe they have. I dunno now. When you wake up they, like, don't seem so long, but maybe they actually are. Like, everything gets squished down into little pieces as soon as you wake up, but in the dream it actually goes on for hours and hours. Oh crap. That was good. I hope I can remember that part too. Syd probably knows what I mean."

Glancing up at Leunga with mud and confusion covering her mug, Sydney inquired about Ricky's obscurity. "What does he mean by that?"

Fairly certain that whatever creature had grazed his leg was still in the perimeter, Leunga pointed to the broken fox and answered her without letting his defenses down. "He thinks all of the crazy shit going on is a dream. And we're in it. Gross, right?"

Sydney's sorrow snapped under the weight of her enormous little brother's carefree mindset, and she shot an infuriated stare at him right away. Jumping from her bench with haste, she lunged at the teenage man and pinched the back of his exposed neck just above his durable collar, squeezing a decent amount of his skin between her middle finger and thumb.

Ricky recoiled in shock at the amount of pain he was suddenly experiencing. Jolting upright in a furious wrenching of his lower back, he screamed, "Ow! Hey! Come on! Ow!"

Sydney shoved his shoulder. "Not a dream, buttface! This is real. Those fucking swords are actually glowing. That five-minute thunder through the trees? Yeah, that really happened!" Her instant anger was abruptly slowed to a simmer when her disobedient eyes decided to remind her of the wrapped object awaiting its burial, and heartbreak enveloped her senses yet again. "And she actually died... As stupid as it is," she began before pausing and gesturing at the bordering pines with both hands to add, "we're actually out here being hunted by an old bald wizard who'll probably end up just being a walking skeleton or some stupid shit—all because our ancestors sucked at everything and pissed him off a billion years ago. Treat it with respect."

Ricky stared with wide eyes filled with alarm at his big sister. He could clearly see the truthfulness in her concern as he warily rubbed the back of his very tender new injury—a wound he could only possibly sustain in the real world. "It's not a dream...?"

Sydney and Leunga each shook their head in response.

Ricky furrowed his brow. "So I can't wake up?"

"We *are* awake," Sydney replied in a disappointed, almost beaten tone.

Ricky's nerves began to tremble. "That stupid stuff that happened: Getting attacked by bats. Eating a bunch of spider webs by accident. Me jumping onto a wolf from a giant rock without, like, a padded landing zone. The fox..." He turned his head to view its remains more clearly. "Holy crap. It was all *real?*"

Leunga lisped, "Yesssss."

"Nuh-uh," Ricky rejected.

"Yuh-huh," he reaffirmed.

Ricky shook his head at Sydney. "No way."

She nodded. "Yes way."

As quickly as his mind had come to the conclusion that his combat world was an illusion, so too did Ricky realize the reality of his unfortunate visceral mistake and immediately understood the gravity of every action he and his family had taken. Bubble bursting like nobody's business, the boy blindly stuck an awestruck hand through his hair, destroying the perfect composition of his fauxhawk while he massaged his stumbling thoughts. Of course he wasn't dreaming; everything that happened seemed so realistic— much more than if it had been in an erratic nightmare. The bleak, cool breaths of the cave, the gripping sensation of webbing coating his face, the haunting feeling of being followed, and the undeniable fear in the face of evil he felt. His easy explanation for the impossible had shattered like a castle of sand under the swinging kicks of truth. He swallowed anxiously as he was suddenly flooded with the feeling of his nerves rising up his throat. Their grandfather's drug-fueled stories once again had the sudden eternal tinge of truth. Rapidly turning away from his siblings, Ricky spun around and vomited onto the dirt behind his seat, next to the rock shield protecting the camp from unwanted eyes. Total waste of summer. Bummer.

Sydney hopped back, colliding with an unwary Leunga. With a disgusted face, she griped, "Ew, god, why'd you puke?! Are you okay? That's sick. It's purple." She reached out and held her hand caringly against his heaving back, when she suddenly noticed the filthy nature of her fingers. Quickly realizing her mistake of accidentally leaving behind a perfect handprint made of mud and blood on his newly soiled karate top, she removed her touch and backed away from the brother immediately. Filled with a rush of embarrassment, she decided not to tell him about the stamp on his back until later. Maybe never.

Leunga gripped his sister's mostly bare arms from behind and glanced around her side at the grotesque sight of Ricky losing most of his breakfast. "I mean, what kind of mutant would dream about his own brother and sister...? Except for all those times I did—I didn't... I don't wanna talk about it anymore. What was that sound? Did you just barf?"

Ricky spit before sneezing onto his partially digested past. "I'm okay..." He turned slowly, feeling drained of his essence physically and psychologically. His perturbed mind wished to refuse the belief that what had happened could be real, yet he knew deep down the accuracy of his siblings' words. "I just need to rest for a second."

Entwining his hands together and wrapping his palms around the back of his shaggy skull, Leunga calmly walked around Sydney and stood in front of their little brother, large as the boy was. Seeing as how his hiking chum was finally coming to terms with the gravity of his monumental misperception, the eldest stared down at Ricky's worried expression and looked into the vacuum of courage behind the young man's dark brown eyes before slapping him across the face. Hard.

Ricky braced his neck as his sibling's surprised hand dragged across his cheek, and the teen's voice cracked under the confusion of his older brother's actions. "I'm sick!"

Leunga smiled and wandered off. "You earned it."

"I don't wanna believe it either, but it's not like we really have that much of a choice anymore." Thrown into reflection by her younger sibling's disturbing point of view, Sydney was inspired to convey her understanding of the day's events to the boys as she prodded her dirty chin with her dirty thumbnail and thought out loud—not only for her baby brother's benefit, but for her own as well. "I don't think the fox *wanted* to attack us. I could see it in its eyes. That poor little thing was just as confused and scared as us—maybe even more so. When I was away from you guys, I saw that *monster* for what it really was...just something cold and evil. It wasn't a helpless little woodland animal anymore. Something out there was controlling it—using it like a puppet to try and kill us for no fuckin' reason. Whatever happened to that little fox changed it into something wicked nasty with no remorse and no control. It wasn't an animal; it was just a nightmare come to life, and...she easily would have killed us if Leunga hadn't..." Sydney sighed as she returned to her previous bench and sat once again, using her palms to support the weight of her face. She needed to give herself a reason to continue more than anything. As hard as it seemed, she knew they needed to put an end to this evil before it wickedly used more innocent critters, and she felt the need to push the group forward so they could become the heroes they needed to be. "This sucks. Whatever fucking coward is out there right now spreading around that black fog needs to be stopped, even if that means we have to protect ourselves from another berserk animal..."

Leunga nodded respectfully from somewhere far across the camp. "We woke it up when we touched both of those swords. Now it's our duty to keep the forest safe and monster-free for all those geeks who want to walk around and stare at trees. And besides, I feel like I *need* to be here now, ya know? It's weird. So it's not a choice anymore. We *have* to destroy the Summoner. Oh my god! We are so lucky if he really is in America right now."

"It's not too late." Rubbing his tenderized skin, Ricky cleared his devastated throat, worried that his siblings were truly stern about heading back into battle at great danger to their own lives. For once, his priorities were not focused on hiding his feminine sweatpants. "There's nothing that says it has to be *us* who need to kill it. We can still stop and um...like, hide the swords for someone else to find. We could go home and try to forget about all this nonsense. Just like Grampy did."

Sydney shook her head. "No, Ricky. We can't. Whatever this sorcerer thing is, it has no respect for life. It has no place here. It has no right to do these things. It's something that doesn't belong in the world anymore, and we have this chance to stop it." She turned around on her chair for a moment and stared at Leunga before letting her haunted gaze return to the trees. "Anybody in our position would do the same; we just happen to be unlucky enough to be in our position."

Ricky spoke softly, showing his age in his response. "But not me and you. *We* don't need to be here." He looked to Leunga as his brother continued roving around the clearing to the other side out of earshot. "Lou is the only one who can use the swords. Like Grampy. He's really the only one of us who can do anything, isn't he? Maybe this is something he can only do alone..." He then sneezed.

She glanced at Leunga again and scowled at her other brother's impromptu immaturity, but she could understand where he was coming from. "We're all in this together, stupid." Sydney sighed and looked away as her older brother began to make his way back to the camp. "We gotta pretend that we all love each other and look out for one another like some kind of happy family. What if *he* got hurt out here and no one was around to help him? I mean, it's *him*. He's definitely gonna get hurt. We should be there for him, shouldn't we?"

Ricky nibbled his lip in response. Although he strongly disagreed with the logic behind her argument, she did present a very compelling case that required great contemplation on his behalf. She had never steered him wrong before—not with anything worth mentioning anyway. Knowing in some sense that Sydney was correct, he nodded slowly, right before he whirled around and vomited again. He wiped his chin and turned to his sulking sister, groaning. "Yeah, okay, but I hope he doesn't get too seriously injured. We're like a million miles away from everybody, and I don't want to have to carry him home."

Standing silently at his younger brother's side, Leunga shot a tested stare at Ricky and walked through the camp to sit beside their sister, reaching a consoling arm across her shoulders. He edged in close and let his eyes fall to their shoes to say, "Hey, you know I didn't want to hurt that fox, right?"

Sydney remained motionless, gazing blankly at the trees beyond.

"We were trapped! What else could I do?! I really didn't think it would actually die... I thought maybe—just maybe—I would be able to get rid of the magic crap and make it change it back to normal without hurting it... I dunno. I feel so bad about it all. I'm so sorry." It's all make-believe until somebody dies. "Can you ever forgive me?"

Sydney continued to stare off into the distance but smiled timidly to show her older brother that she knew he meant no harm.

"Don't give me that look. I said I was sorry! Doesn't that—no, you know what? Fuck you! You're not the boss of me."

Sydney furrowed her brow and looked at the side of the face of the tiny man with his arm across her back, noticing within seconds that Leunga was actually addressing a sizable moth on the ground in front of them—*very* large with brown and white bands all along its greasy wings and furry black antennae. The exact dimensions of an origami moth, depending on the size and color of the paper used to create its form. I prefer yellow, but whatever.

Leunga and his sister watched as the beast took flight, lilting through the air in a hazy launch, freeing itself from its worldly shackles. The tinier adult pointed an accusing finger at his lepidopteran rival and revealed, "You can hide, but you can't run! I know where you live, asshole!" Turning his attention away from the insect, he faced Sydney. Meeting eyes with her—a little more than a few inches from her dirtied face—Leunga continued to grip her shoulder as he leaned his head away from the uncomfortable proximity.

Staring at her with mass confusion, the warrior scowled. "What the hell happened to your hair?!"

Sydney leaned her head away from the uncomfortable proximity and grabbed the mud-filled bangs covering her left eye between her fingers. "What? It's only mud." That's what she thinks.

"No!" Leunga released his attached grip and flicked the twisted heap of hair looped at the back of her head with his middle finger. "I mean that!"

Crossing her eyes at him, she addressed the boy in a severely mocking manner, plainly in a language he might understand. "I thought it were gonna rain!"

Leunga glared at her through squinting peepers and observed the odd familiarity of his sister's former style reborn. Atavism intended. "At least you look more normal now, but something is still different about you..."

As time moved forward at a sturdy pace, the repartee was returning. With the group's understanding of their task ahead, Sydney steadily reeled her emotions back to a more controlled place, realizing that Leunga had already done the same. Back to a norm she was comfortable with in order to face any challenge directly.

Acting as the responsible and mature eldest sibling, Leunga nodded. "I think I might know what it is. Your face is still covered in shit...and I don't just mean the whole raccoon eyes thing. Go wash it off before you get pimples—more pimples." He then rustled his fingers under his hat and across the dark mess atop his head while fighting the urge to dowse his sister's face in a barrage of towels. "Hurry."

She smirked. "Yeah, okay. Maybe while I'm doing that you can put your pants on, freak."

Leunga glanced down at his bare boxers in shock. "But the air feels good on my garbage."

Shudder. "Great. Now *I'm* gonna throw up." Walking to the campsite's sole source of water and kneeling at its shore, the woman witnessed what it was her brunet brother spoke of, and it disturbed her deeply. The persistently calm state of the pool mirrored her grimy coat easily, allowing her a first look at her new face—a fusion of mud and eyeliner gave her a much more accurate raccoon-like appearance. "Holy crap, that's gross."

The air of the campsite drew closer to the status quo. Without heeding his sister's former fragile state, Leunga quickly quipped, "You mean your face? I've know that for years."

Sydney grinned to herself, pleased with the slow return of the hike's effervescent attitude. "That would be more meaningful if you weren't butt ugly yourself." As she rubbed her fingers over the crust around her eyes, something in the water caught her attention. A vision of torrential waves bounced off the surface of the peaceful pond and her focus flew skyward, seeing once again the type of cloud that had threatened a downpour over an hour ago. Another violent brew in the sky—quite possibly the same one that she noticed before. Ignoring the likelihood that her hair may once again be assaulted with actual rain, she returned to her task, throwing scoops of water against her face and arms, restoring some of her self-esteem.

Ricky rubbed his stomach as he sat ankle-deep in fear. His earthly plane was falling apart, being replaced by a monster's fantasy. His wandering eyes traveled over the trees as he looked for something indefinable to hold on to. Taking slow breaths through his mouth to fight his continuously unsettled nerves, he snagged a spotting of Leunga's psychotic stare, so he smiled weakly to his older brother reassuringly. "I think I'm okay now." While he watched the other boy slide his giant boots around the camp in search of a pair of pants—a feeling Ricky was all too familiar with—he sighed silently to himself, staring into the darkness at the backs of his eyelids. Trapped by the wishes of his brother and sister, he sat quietly, searching for the courage to say *no*. Ricky whipped around in his seat and threw up again.

Leunga was slowly rummaging through their grandfather's backpack in search of his pants when his face twisted with disgust at the sight of his brother retching over a purple puddle. "Cripes man, aren't you empty yet? How much of my food did you eat?!"

Unable to hear the inquiry of his older brother over the sounds of his bodily disaster, Ricky moaned, trying not to think about his overturned stomach. "How is any of this even possible?"

"You throwing up? I do not know."

"Not what I meant. This whole thing of...monsters and weapons. It's *so* stupid ridiculous..."

"What part of life *isn't* stupid ridiculous?" Leunga replied. "April used to say life was a chain of impossibilities linked together by the ordinary routine."

Sloshing water over her skin, Sydney listened from the pond and added, "Well, we hit the jackpot in the impossibility department shit for sure."

"None of this makes sense, but maybe it's not supposed to." Leunga raised his eyebrows and made a popping noise with his lips as he discovered his missing apparel in the pack.

Desperately trying to avoid looking directly at the boxers of his bottomless brother, Ricky sneezed at the ground and agreed. "Yeah, that's true, but I thought April only said life was a *crapshoot* and everybody should buy a poncho."

The eldest slipped on his khaki cargo shorts effortlessly and reassured Ricky. "Life is a lot of stupid things. Get used to it."

Gathering his bravery to deny his own participation in the upcoming battle with evil, Ricky quickly surrendered to the wavering nature of his resolve, waging a war no one would ever see. He looked out at his partners in crime under the cover of his hearty brow and asked, "So, what does all of this mean? What happens next?"

As if waiting for someone to finally ask that question, Leunga blurted out his prepared remarks. "We never found what made that grinding noise. I say we keep following us some random trails until we find out where it came from—or maybe we keep fighting crap until the wizard shows up all dramatic-like and we fight it in some sort of last boss showdown." He gently caressed the posterior of his own freshly returned pants and moaned. "Mmmm. Beautiful."

Sporting her newly cleansed expression, Sydney slid her hands into her pockets and kicked a stone near her shoes into the adjacent trees far away. "Okay, but let's wait for tomorrow. Getting chased around by a giant-ass dog really drained me. I'd rather just spend the rest of the day here next to the water." The returning thought of burying the fox caused her heart to slowly crawl back to a very dark place, despite her recent resurfacing happiness, pulling her lightened mood down into the abyss.

A wave of relief hit the youngest camper like a torrential rain. "I'm so glad you said it and not me. I was just thinking the same thing." Not the exact same thing, but something close enough. "Especially 'cause I'm starting to feel like I'm gonna blow chunks again," Ricky grunted while keeping a vigilant hand pressed against his abs.

Leunga squealed. "Isn't this wild?! How often do you get to fight a legendary battle using magic weapons? Outside of my drug frenzies."

"You never should. It's highly impossible."

Ricky groaned. "What about in video games?"

"Exactly wrong. This is what the fates have woven, and now it's up to all three of us to wear this itchy destiny without hesitation and march forward to victorious oblivion." Leunga hunched down and placed his palms on the ground in front of his feet. "What the hell am I even talking about?"

Sydney nodded glumly. "Fuck yeah. We gotta do this—even if it *is* a little bit extremely frightening. With all three of us working together, we could face anything that asshole Summoner wants to throw at us. I mean, if these things are going to be out there attacking us anyway—no matter what we do— we might as well stop them here. We beat that wolf without even trying. Think of how awesome we could be when we're focused. If there's anyone who could possibly stop this farce once and for all, it's us." She held up a pair of clenched fists shoulder-high with her pinkies and index fingers extended skyward, trying to lighten the serious nature of their new quest in a gritty voice that was not her own. "Because we obviously rock."

"Uh...what do you mean?" challenged Ricky as he cleared his throat and sneezed at his vomit pile again.

Leunga snapped back to what is tentatively called reality, having been staring blankly through his siblings in a stupor seconds earlier. "What? I wasn't listening. Somebody said the word *cowgirl* and then I just..." He trailed off as he returned to a trance at his own behest.

Sydney rolled her eyes. "Never mind."

The Courage

"I brought drinks!" hollered an overly-enthusiastic Leunga as he blasted through the screen door, stumbling into the living room of the burgundy house while holding a cardboard container of iced coffees behind his back. Carelessly wheeling them around in a large, swinging arc, he held the trio of large plastic cups over his head and smiled. "I don't remember which one is mine, so I've been drinking from all of them."

"Thanks." Sydney sat curled up against the closest end of the long, overstuffed couch nearest to the front door, already wearing her oh-so-cozy kitty-cat pajama pants in the middle of the weekday afternoon and typing up a storm on her phone. "You can put mine right in the trash."

Leunga grabbed a random triplet from his stock and took an overindulgent guzzle of the sugary brew before exhaling noisily. "Sure thing!" He turned toward the teenage boy across the room reading quietly in an easy chair under the direct stream of the air conditioner's cooling wind and asked, "Dicky, do you want yours in the kitchen, or are you gonna make me walk all the way over to you?" An entire ten-foot walk; four-fifths of half the distance to the kitchen table. Approximately.

Ricky blinked slowly, squinting constantly to keep his eyes from drying out from the air rustling over the pliable collar of his button-up shirt, tickling his neck with a soft touch each time the current faltered. Stiff blond stragglers bounced against his forehead while he attempted to read an arbitrary book from his father's collection, finding himself unable to focus on any of the individual words and reading entire paragraphs subconsciously, trying desperately to distract himself. He carefully glanced over to his brother's cool and refreshing offer of an icy, sweet beverage—a weekly tradition Leunga maintained by bringing his work home with him every Friday afternoon. The exact pick-me-up Ricky needed after an especially exasperating week of school as a sophomore, amplified by a tiresome ordeal he wished he could forget, but even as it was happening, he knew he never would.

Hours began to grow longer, stretching themselves to the point of madness while keeping his nerves on edge with each extended second. It was treacherously close to being too much to tolerate. Maybe he could find a way to take Monday off, start feigning illness on Saturday and work his way up. Something he could easily manage in order to give his nerves a much-needed break. He did find *some* solace that summer was only nineteen school days away—not including the final week of course; everyone knows those days don't count—and then it's vacation time. Three whole months of pure, uninterrupted relaxation. Ricky set aside his troubles from the previous day and grinned at his sibling's gift. "Thanks, Lou," he said as he quickly jumped out of the comforting seat. "I'll take it."

Leunga spun the roulette of drinks around and abruptly stopped. "Okay, take this one."

The tall teen moved quickly around the wooden table in the center of the sitting area obstructing his path, dashing to the other side of his older sister's extensive sofa space in order to obtain his award. Ricky had nearly accepted the drink from his sibling's carton when the room was frozen solid by a frightful sound. Ringing.

The brothers glanced at each other before slowly turning their collective attention to the phone, lit up like a devious lighthouse luring ships to crash on jagged cliffs. The boys turned back, once again meeting eyes. Leunga's face contorted with puzzlement. "Did *you* do that?"

Ricky's worst fear had come to life—maybe not his *worst*, but definitely up there on the list. His wide-eyed vision locked on the screaming demon beckoning him to respond despite his dread. Although he had been expecting the torment all day, he never thought in his wildest nightmares that someone in his family would be nearby to answer the phone. After having the tray of drinks warily shoved into his hands, Ricky watched his older brother edge closer to the dining room phone. The youngest's nerves burned brightly, and his heart leapt against his chest. "Don't pick it up!"

"Okay, I won't." The phone continued to ring endlessly. Leunga leaned in closely to read the name of the phantom visitor, speaking slowly as he read through his shaggy bangs. "Caller...unknown. You must try yourself harder, my plastic friend." Staring blankly at the chirping beast while it sounded three more times before inadvertently lifting the device from its cradle, the café connoisseur blindly put the speaker to his ear when ignorance and instinct demanded that he do so, and an incredibly unenthused word sprang from his mouth while he wasn't looking. "Hello?" he said just as it hit him. Instantly shocked by what his idle hands made him do, the smaller guy gasped at his own actions, forgetting to put his palm over the receiver as he rapidly pulled the phone from his face and admitted, "Oh shit! I wasn't supposed to answer it!" His alarm seemed genuine and sincere. Eventually surrendering to the situation within seconds, he shrugged. "Oh well... I guess now I should find out what it wants."

Ricky's breaths were quick and sharp. His eyes were growing with distress. With his eldest sibling's attention focused on him, he cautiously mouthed, "I'm not here!"

Leunga nodded, replacing the proper part of the device to his ear, and said, "Hello again?" There was a long pause as he listened to the caller on the other end. "Yeah, it is. No... I just said no! This is his brother. What is wrong with you?! I don't sound anything like him. Yeah...yeah, he's right here. Right now? Why? Uh-huh. Uh-huh... I see. Okay, sure. What?! Oh, right!" Leunga held the phone as an offering to Ricky. "Some girl wants to talk to you."

Sydney huffed in disapproval.

"She almost sounds legal."

With a dumbfounded look on his face, Ricky set the carousel of coffees on a conveniently placed end table next to the telephone and hesitantly grabbed the handset from his brother, feeling thwarted and betrayed. Standing next to Leunga, he observed the peak of their sister's blond head barely visible on the other side of the couch before redirecting his focus to his older brother. "Could I maybe get some privacy, please?"

Leunga nodded again, incredibly slowly, staring his little brother in the eyes with understanding and respect, but he continued to stay exactly where he was.

Sydney appeared not to care either way.

Recognizing that his siblings were static in their positions, Ricky's brow furrowed with worry. He knew he would be unable to speak on the phone in a calm and collected manner with his brother gawking at him like a statue and his sister eavesdropping on his every word; and with the droning of the air conditioner above his fauxhawk, he knew it would be far too difficult to speak with anyone on the telephone in that atmosphere, especially speaking with *her*.

Thinking of a way to gain some solitude, Ricky set forth a spontaneous plan—one that probably couldn't fail. With his hands gripping the source of his recent angst, adamantly blocking the passage of sound, he held forth the phone and asked Leunga for the most miniscule of favors. "Okay then... I'm—I'll just take it in the kitchen. Can you hang this up when I say so?"

His big brother took the phone and nodded once again, so much slower than before.

Attempting to allay his debilitating anxiety, Ricky sighed heavily. He walked down the hallway where portraits of his family watched him rush past a pair of short staircases sitting side by side while he made his way to the kitchen where he felt he would have the best chance at a private conversation. Lifting the cordless handset from its housing on the counter by the fridge, Ricky covered the mouthpiece quickly and quietly, calling through the hallway at his invisible brother beyond. "Okay, I got it!"

Involuntarily tearing small pieces of skin off his lips with his teeth as his nerves ran at full blast, he held the disruption of a peaceful week in the palms of his hands and drew in a deep breath, quickly plotting his conversation in advance. As he anticipated the beginning of his quest, his guts churned and twisted, tying into a labyrinth of stress—possible consumption of his brother's gift would be a challenge when and if he survived the upcoming chat. Ricky gathered his forces to brace his will against whatever he might do to himself next and nodded to psyche himself up. Deciding it would be best to dive right in headfirst and get it over with, the boy cautiously placed the device to his ear and began the countdown. "Hello?"

"Hi! Ricky?"

"This is...*him*?" The conversation he had desperately wanted to evade was already a roaring success.

"Um...hi, it's Becky. We talked at school yesterday?"

As if he could possibly forget the tense discomfort that filled his infamous Thursday afternoon. "Oh, yeah. How's it going?"

"Good... How are you?"

"I'm all right..." Except for the fact that his sweat-drenched hands were trembling, his knees were weakening at an alarming rate, and his muscles felt like they were being pulled to the ground by bungee cords. "I'm...uh, glad school is done for this week." Quickly, he wondered if any part of the thought he had just articulated made any sense.

Becky giggled a bit nervously. "Yeah, me too..."

There was a horrible pause of silence so thick that it clouded the land in a dense fog of awkwardness for eons to come. Neither one of them knew what to say next. Through his nerve-wracked state, Ricky noticed that the girl whose voice he was speaking with had lost most of her assertiveness prevalent the previous day in the school parking lot. Maybe the change in attitude had something to do with the lack of her wingwoman egging her on, or it could've been Leunga's abusive telephone etiquette. Her tone was gentler, somehow more considerate and sincere; she might even be someone he would want to get to know. Or not.

Ricky was so focused on trying not to sound like a babbling idiot that he could do nothing else. Teetering on shaky knees, he knew he needed to sit, but he didn't know where his legs were at the time. Feeling more and more like a fool in front of someone who might judge him by his actions—or find out what he really is—the blond boy had the sudden urge to avoid any more awkward pauses and fill the conversation with all things mundane. "So...uh...have you seen the new school mascot design?" New mascot?!

"Yeah, but I liked the old one more."

"Me too. The new one sucks."

Becky laughed. Ricky had no idea why, so he chose to join her in order to make the atmosphere more comfortable. She sighed pleasantly and asked, "Are you on any teams? I think you'd be really good at, like, basketball or football or something."

Like: misused staple of the teenage vernacular. One bite of this forbidden fruit can make, like, even the most intellectual person sound really unintelligent—wait! No! That one didn't count! I wasn't ready! My...credibility...

Ricky cleared his throat carefully to say, "Uh... I'm not on any teams right now, but I have some friends on the water polo team." And thankfully for him, they weren't there to witness his conversation.

"That's cool. I, like, *love* swimming, don't you?"

"Yeah, I—um...yeah..." Ricky's eyelids rolled shut in horror as he heard the odd combination of words slip through his teeth. Frantically searching for a means to salvage his self-respect, he moved the focus back to Becky, because as long as she was speaking, he wouldn't have to. "So...like, what are you gonna do this summer?"

"I dunno. I don't think I want to, like, get a job, but I might. I just want to maybe go to the beach or, like, hang out with someone new, you know?" Wow, subtle.

Of course, he *didn't* know. "Yeah."

"What about you? What do you want to do for summer?"

"Probably just try to relax and, like, not really do anything..."

Becky paused for a moment to draw in her powers. "Maybe *we* could, like, do something together..." Bull's-eye.

"Um, yeah, maybe." And there goes his relaxing summer. To hell with it; now he can spend every second of his free time wondering if she's going to call, or pondering the possibility that *she* is expecting *him* to call *her*. Too much for a sixteen-year-old boy to handle. Also texting.

"I got a car for my birthday, like, a couple months ago," she informed. "I drove my friend Vicki and her boyfriend to a campground, like, last week and it was *so* fun. Sometime we could all go swimming up at Lake Liddle or go hiking... Vicki and her boyfriend go up there a lot, and she says it's super private. Or maybe if you want, me and you could just take, like, a drive somewhere and find a place to...talk and stuff."

He bit his lip while trying to understand why the girl he was talking to was so determined to have him as an accomplice in some sort of teenage indiscretion. The conversation was moving too fast for him to consider the consequences of each individual word. In a clumsy attempt to direct their out-of-control discussion, Ricky tried to focus on something she said before the dam broke. "Cool, what—uh—what kind of car did you get?"

"Oh, it's a red convertible." The kind of car better suited to driving down the barren Mojave Desert highways at top speed to escape winged attackers while collecting speeding tickets. After all, it is bat country. But what do I know? I don't exist.

"Awesome."

"Yeah. It doesn't look that big, but..." Becky began to say something in an apparent effort to redirect the conversation back to the summer she aspired to spend claiming this new boy as her own, but she was finding it to be a bit difficult. In a mildly nervous voice, she continued with something her friend strongly recommended she mention, despite the girl's apparent uncertainty of saying such. "It's, like, really roomy—it can hold, like, a bunch of people, because it has this really nice backseat... It's, um, really cool."

If Ricky were older, or more adult-minded, he probably would have noticed the subtly obvious hints in her statement, but he didn't. "That's cool." His attitude proves that not all teenagers are innately pursuing that *one* thing—only the ones that are actually aware of what's going on around them are.

"I think it would be fun if we—" Becky stopped abruptly at the introduction of a very disturbing sound. Someone belched loudly into the telephone, sustaining the activity for nearly twenty seconds. Possibly from another receiver, but it's difficult to determine at this time.

Ricky panicked. "That wasn't me!"

"Wasn't me either..." Becky giggled suspiciously.

Leunga laughed as he hung up the phone in the dining room. "Perfect. Pay me, Syddles."

"Sorry..." Ricky frowned. "My brother is kind of..." He juggled a few adjectives around before landing on a very appropriate choice. "Stupid."

Becky grunted disgustedly. "Ugh, my sister is the exact same way. She's, like, thirteen. How old's your brother?"

Caught off guard, the teen had to take a moment to think. "Um...like, twenty...two...? No wait, twenty-three. His, like, birthday was like a month ago." Unfortunately, during the course of the phone call, Ricky seems to have become a victim of the teenage-tongue disease so much worse than usual. Poor thing. It's, like, highly infectious.

"Whoa! He's old."

"Yeah. *Way* old."

"So, um..." The boy on the phone listening intently sensed that the young woman speaking wanted to get to the grit and seal the deal, especially after she said, "Have you, like, thought about yesterday...?"

Only every agonizing second since they spoke by his sister's car. "Yeah, uh, about that..." Ricky paused to gather his words, trying to find a way to deny her expectations without hurting her feelings. As he anticipated his reply, his nerves cried out for help, but no one would answer the call; he knew he could never ask anyone for assistance, because there would be nothing they could do. He wanted to buy himself more time, maybe even ignore the upcoming question altogether, but her silence said everything; he knew that he would be unable to refuse her wishes, because opportunity had already knocked—Ricky needed to either fix his hair and reluctantly pretend like he wants to answer the door, or hide under the kitchen table and hope that it leaves. He chose something in between the two. "Would you...like to...go to the prom with me...?" He could taste the words as they rolled off his tongue. Bitter.

He heard the girl on the other end of the phone smile. "Okay."

Ricky took a deep breath. "Okay..."

She was audibly excited. "We can, like, talk about it some more at lunch someday at school—like what group we're gonna go with and stuff. I know where you guys, like, sit, so I'll like, come find you, okay?" Like...overload.

"Yeah, okay." The fact that Becky knew exactly where he and his friends sat during lunch should have made him apprehensive, but he was too preoccupied with trying to stop his body from shaking. "I'll, uh, see ya later then?"

"Okay! Bye, Ricky!"

"See ya, Becky..." He sighed with relief as he pulled the sweaty receiver from his ear. His trembling hand struggled to set the cordless handset back into its cradle as he replayed pieces of the conversation over in his head, feeling the devastating scorch of every small embarrassment burn into his memories to haunt him forever. He often wondered if everyone was the same way—a collective of recollections of humiliations that won't let go of anything— or was he just the lucky one? Regardless, Ricky tried to gather his poise enough to appear unshaken by the recent events and closed his eyes to exhale at the ceiling.

"Hello, Ricky."

"Whoa!" Startled by the surprise voice behind him, the youngling yelped as he jumped away from the sneaking attacker. He turned quickly and met eyes with the black-haired woman standing near the stove. Ricky sighed, letting his nerves begin to settle once again after completing the strenuous task of speaking with Becky over the phone. "Hi, April."

An expression of deep concern formed on April's ever-understanding face—a face filled with features that went well with her compassionate nature—as she looked up at Ricky's misery-stricken image. She apologized for her mistaken behavior, saying, "I didn't mean to listen in on your call... I tried not to pay attention. I'm sorry. My mouth was full when you came in so I couldn't warn you and then I just kinda stayed here in the corner. Who was that you were talking to? Unless it's private."

Still reeling from an abundance of stress, Ricky scratched the back of his crunchy blond head vacantly, keeping a steady stare at the linoleum floor. "Oh, uh, just some girl from school I met yesterday. She said that she and her friend had been, like, watching me for a while or something..."

April smiled, cooing softly in a way clearly indicating that she perceived the conduct as adorable. "Aw...that's so creepy. What did she want just now?"

"She wanted me to ask her to the prom..."

"Ah, I see." Her mildly bloodshot eyes lit up. "She probably felt like she had to move fast to get a cute guy like you. Isn't that, like, months and months and months away?" The pothead paused momentarily to speak to herself inside the bag of pretzels in her hand. "Wait...what month is it now...? Are we still in the month of me any longer she wondered aloud?"

Ricky could feel his face begin to blush. He turned away from the young woman to hide his burning embarrassment. "Yeah, I think it's like three weeks away or something."

April moved around to see Ricky's face more visibly. "Hmmm. Is she cute?"

He shrugged. "Well, technically yeah, she is."

"Do you like her?"

The teen bit at his bottom lip, tearing away another tiny piece of skin. "She's—I guess I don't really know. I never saw her before yesterday, you know?" He leaned his entire weight against the kitchen counter, resting his lower back on the hard surface just as April did the same right next to him. The two reclined silently while he pondered the question more carefully. He knew he had no real feelings for the girl, only an unwanted need to appease the people that find themselves inexplicably drawn to him, whether it was for his looks or his uncontrollable amicability; he felt forced to let everything take him and to give it all away. The aspect of always trying to make others happy at the cost of his own desires made him sick to his stomach, but there was obviously nothing he could do about it. "I guess I could..."

Clicking her teeth together for no reason, April tapped her chin with her fingertips before she said, "Something tells me you're not very happy about going to prom with this girl..."

Ricky glanced down at the woman by his side. Staring through her red-rimmed glasses, he witnessed the empathy in her enigmatic golden eyes and—for reasons he couldn't describe—it put his nerves at ease, if only for a moment. He nodded in response and replied, "But I already said that I would... I guess I better just go."

He felt a caring arm reach across his back as his gaze dropped back to the floor by his feet. April caressed the worried teenager sympathetically, trying to ease his apparent angst with a gentle touch. "You're such a nice person, Ricky. It makes me sad to see people take advantage of your considerate personality. I've never said this to you before, but I think you're a caring person with a big heart. You always seem to want to fulfill the desires of others before your own needs, and I wouldn't want anyone to hurt you because of that..."

With a flick of a switch, his secluded grotto lit up, and his hiding place was forever exposed. I see you. His innermost weakness was laid bare, and Leunga's girlfriend could see it so plainly. He had always been aware of his subconscious requirement to please, but finding out that *someone else* could see him for the cowardly monster he was shocked him to his core. He thought he hid it so well behind courtesy laughter and forced friendliness, but apparently his good-natured attitude had finally caught up with him, shaking his façade under the pressure of a hormone-fueled undertaking while simultaneously shattering his carefully placed defenses. A new era of complication was approaching, and the only thing Ricky could do was watch it swallow him whole.

"Well, when you think about it, it's just a dance, right? There's nothing that says you *have* to go. Or is it that maybe there's someone else you would rather go with?"

The face and the name popped into his head almost immediately. "I dunno..."

April snorted with laughter. "That's a *yes*. Who is she?"

"Well..." It was odd, the sensation of being forced to respond was nowhere to be found, yet he felt compelled to open up to her; after all, he was uninhibited when speaking with April, feeling that she was the only person he could trust to simply listen without judgment. He couldn't help but reveal his inner workings to her, because she clearly knew him and treated him like family. "There's a girl I sort of like, but...I used to be really good friends with her until we got to high school, then it just kinda ended."

"Aw, I'm sorry, Ricky. It's a sad thing when someone outgrows a relationship and goes off on their own while the other person gets left behind. That's what happened to me too. My friends started leaving one by one, joining other groups or going to different schools, until I was the only one left. I ate a lot of lunches alone for longer than I'd like to remember, but then one winter your brother came up and sat with me every day, and now he and I are best friends. I guess what I'm saying is that even if it's not what you always thought you wanted, at least it's better than nothing, and sometimes you get something better than you ever hoped for. Most things in life are just out of our control, but nothing lasts forever, right? So why not just try to enjoy what you have while it lasts?"

For a full minute, Ricky didn't know what to say. Drifting away in the words of the wise woman at his side, his wayward thoughts were fully fixated on his former friend, wondering if she felt the same way April did when she was abandoned. Despite his feelings over the matter those many months ago, his heart still sank at the idea of leaving one of his best friends in that condition after he foolishly clung on to his oldest acquaintance into the great unknown. Augmented by his amplified sense of humiliation, Ricky was ashamed of being an accomplice to such a heinous crime. His thoughts had switched tracks on him, changing the focus from his own troubles to worrying about the state of the girl whose laugh he could never forget, and wishing that he could go back to set everything right.

April burst into a short series of coughs that ended as abruptly as it began. Then she didn't even bother to clear her throat before going on to suggest, "You know...if you ever feel like you don't want to do something, you could always tell them you're busy. They would understand."

"I wish I could," Ricky said with a sigh. "But I can't think of stuff like that quick enough..."

"It's against your nature, isn't it?"

He nodded dejectedly.

"In a way, what you do for them is really brave. Sacrificing your own comfort to give them the friend they need, whether they deserve it or not." April rolled her lips between her teeth, entranced by the sensation of her new feelings of facial sensitivity. She repeatedly scrunched her face together before relaxing the muscles several times prior to returning to the discussion at hand. "They're very lucky to have you."

The thought had never occurred to Ricky. An observation that required a different set of eyes. He turned to her and asked, "Do you really think so?"

The dark-haired girl nodded, nuzzling her head against his upper arm. "The world needs more people like you."

With the help of her fresh perspective, he saw the spineless ogre in his reflection in a new light. Not as a beast to be despised, but as a selfless hero to be admired. Ricky smiled meekly, gaining a much-needed boost to his bravery. A stalwart shield for a timid little spirit. He only wished he could have heard those words long ago, before he chose to walk along the wrong path.

Possibly forgetting who she was talking to—or possibly not—April passionately groped her arms across the toned teen's midsection gradually and gave him a reassuring hug. Awkward!

Feeling robustly uncomfortable and justifiably confused by the unexpected embrace, Ricky reluctantly put one hand around her shoulder and swallowed nervously. Despite her noticeably drug-induced affection, he was happy to have her as a confidant after the tribulation with Becky. Of all the ridiculous mistakes that his older brother had made, April was the one shining success.

She smiled and whispered to his arm. "Don't ever change."

"...I won't," he quietly replied.

Leunga barged into the kitchen, wide-eyed and concerned. Ricky immediately removed the gentle grip he had on his brother's girlfriend. The eldest exclaimed, "Wait just a minute! April, if you're *here* then who's at the café watching the regist—" Interrupting himself, he abruptly sprinted out of the kitchen, passing through the hallway and living room on a direct course to the front door.

Looking through the wall at his older sibling's escape, Ricky timidly addressed the woman whose arm was still draped across his lower back. "Have you ever thought about firing him?"

April smiled and looked up at Ricky's focused stare. "I like having him around. He's cute and he makes a good decoration. And I like the drinks he makes. Well, actually, I am kinda worried he's gonna ask me—" Suddenly stopping her thought, there was a concealed scuffling of panicked shoes echoing from somewhere out the front of the house, causing a small cause for alarm.

The disembodied voice of Leunga shouted, "Impediments!"

A familiar voice apologized with sincerity from outside. "Sorry, dude!"

As Ricky recognized the sound of Hunter approach, his heart dropped into his stomach at the thought of explaining his recent interaction with the girl from school to his friends. More interruptions. He desperately needed a moment of solitude to reflect, an opportunity to resolidify, but it just wasn't in the cards that afternoon. He mumbled, "Here they come..." Perfect timing.

"Was that his brother?"

Hunter answered, still out of visual range, "Yeah, I think his name is Lewis." There was a mild tapping on the screen door before it squeaked open slowly. A clustering of footsteps entered the living room as Hunter addressed Ricky's sister invisibly. "Oh, *hey*. Um...is Ricky here?"

"Probably..." Sydney responded shyly, quietly slinking away and gliding up the small staircase in the hallway to the top floor of the house before her younger brother heard the unmistakable sound of her bedroom door slam shut.

One of the voices addressed the ringleader. "Fuck! Dude, she was *hot!* Who was that?!"

Hunter responded in the other room. "I dunno, maybe his cousin is staying with them—" He stopped himself as the group passed through the hallway and entered the kitchen in order to shout, "Rick-kay! Here you are." Hunter glanced at the black-haired woman by his friend's side and smiled with suppressed sincerity. "Hey, Sydney. Did you get my message?"

April smiled and shook her head. "Wrong girl...but she's here somewhere."

Hunter winced. "Oh, sorry! My bad. I thought you were Little Rick's sister..."

"Maybe someday," April answered with a snort and a full mouth as she clutched the bag of pretzels she had been snacking on tightly and carefully made her way through the sizable group of boys to the basement staircase. "I'll be downstairs if you need anything, Ricky. Have fun, guys." And with that, she tumbled down the carpeted staircase and disappeared into the shadow below.

"Cryptic!" Hunter snickered and smirked. "So did you call Becky yet?!"

Ricky smiled nervously. He had usually fared much better in one-on-one conversations with Hunter—or with anyone, really—than in a group setting, but in this case, he was trapped. Of course, he would prefer not to be the direct center of attention—something near the outer edges would be better—but Ricky was used to telling intimate details of his life to Hunter and the entourage of mid-to-tall high school boys with popped collars that seemed to follow. Finding himself awash in a social wasteland, he gave in and rolled with the tide. "I just got off the phone with her right before you guys came in."

"See?" Hunter addressed the rest of the group. "I told you my man would close the deal." Hip hip hooray. "What did you say to her?"

"You know...um...the usual stuff..." Although the conversation had taken place only minutes earlier, Ricky was having a hard time remembering any details that wouldn't seem infinitely embarrassing to mention. "We talked about summer coming up and...her new car..."

Hunter interjected, "And then you asked her out? Killer skills. Man, I wish we could've been here when it happened!" Anyone who truly knew Ricky would know that their potential observation of the telephonic conversation would have been his worst-case scenario.

One of the young men in the group grinned. "Ricky, you are the *shit*! Becky is, like, the hottest junior in school. Lucky much?!"

Some of the other members of the collective laughed, including Ricky, though his was forced.

"We need to get you situated with a tux, friendigo. Something with tons of class to make Becky want to get busy wit'cha in the limo." Ooh, a limo!

Ricky nodded as he noticed all of the blood draining from his extremities. The pressure to act eager was overwhelming. He wasn't sure when he would ever be ready to *get busy* with anyone anywhere, but the wave of opportunity was working against him, propelling him forward as he waded through his high school life.

Suddenly, without warning, a pair of Ricky's friends began looting through the refrigerator—uninvited as usual—and removed several cans of cola without asking, tossing them to some of the other high school kids and cracking them open. Ricky's high levels of affability enabled this type of entitled theft often, so he allowed the behavior to continue, because he had to.

"It's gonna be fuckin' *bad ass*." Hunter accepted a can of soda blindly as he inadvertently eyed his bud's martial arts gear by the screen door, inviting him to drop the discussion in favor of starting a new one so far away from the first without a care. He poked his chin toward the cavernous blue duffel and said, "Hey, that reminds me. How's it goin' in that new karate you're in? You said it was something like kung fu boxing, right?"

Ricky followed Hunter's eyes to the heap of equipment on the floor and was pleased to find a conversation he might actually have some control over. "Oh...yeah. It's like, something like that. I dunno, I guess I'm getting pretty good at it." Objectively better than *pretty good*.

"Damn, dude, you've been doing that shit for a long-ass time. You training to be an ass-kicking action hero or something?"

Ricky smirked, saying the first thing that came to his mind. "That's the idea."

"Fuckin' A!" someone said.

Hunter nodded with a grin plastered on his face. "Cool, man. Hey, you should be a cage fighter! Man, I bet those guys get so much pussy they don't know what to do with it!"

The boys laughed, hooted, pounded each other's knuckles, and agreed boisterously—mostly just to hide the top secret fact that none of them knew the actual logistics involved in those intimate implications from any firsthand experience, which I find statistically impossible for a bundle of teenage boys, but I'm not here to judge. Maybe they're all waiting for a certain friendigo to test the waters for them first.

Hunter turned back and addressed the collective. "Me and Ricky were in the same karate class for a while a long time ago, and *damn* he could kick the shit out of all the other kids! He couldn't lose." The kid in cornrows suddenly took a basic attack stance, keeping his drink open-end-up as he edged closer to his oldest friend, giving a few quick jabs at the boy's arm while the blond pretended to block each shot. "Right?! Right?!"

Ricky grinned against his will for the sake of appearances, breaking his own linguistic rule in the process. "Damn right!"

The group chuckled eerily.

"Hells yeah, man." Hunter took a swig of his drink and wiped his mouth on the back of his hand. "So Rick, what else are you doing today?"

And so ends the portion of the chat Ricky could hold some command over—not even worth mentioning, but there it is. He hadn't actually come up with an excuse for any activity Hunter and the entourage may want to include him in—his mind was scrubbed clean by the stressful phone call with Becky. Feeling each one of his friends' eyes looking at his own, Ricky began to feel a very familiar sensation of incompatibility.

He often wondered how and why he became such an integral part of the *cool kids*. All through high school, he never felt comfortable being clustered with the popular clique—he was an odd piece of their puzzle—but they obviously felt comfortable with him, seeking his company for practically everything. Ricky wanted so badly to stand against his oppressors, to rise up and say *no*—if only he knew how to sidestep his spirit. He shrugged, unable to quickly find a way to avoid being pulled into the tornado of high schoolers seeking his presence in whatever they may be scheming next. "I dunno."

One of the boys replied, "You should come with us to the Lemon." I know what that is—who said I didn't? It's some kind of open-air, outdoor mall officially known as the Tullin Lemon Garden, but the locals nicknamed it the Lemon—it's like a bazaar that only seems truly practical in places with warmer climates year-round such as theirs; complete with almost twenty-five retailers offering a slew of designer merchandise at unreasonable prices. Told you I knew what it was. "We're on our way over there right now."

"Yeah," a different boy added. "Gonna go check out the bimbs." No, I am not defining it again.

The perfect opportunity to use the kind advice April had bestowed upon him. *That sounds awesome, but I can't right now. I'm kind of busy today.* "Yeah, okay, I'll come..." Well, change is hard. Maybe he can try next time. Or not.

Another young man spoke, posing a loaded inquiry. "Hey Ricky, why don't you ask your cousin if she wants to go with us?"

Hunter squinted over the aluminum can inches from his lips at the questioner with derision. Like an alpha male defending his claim of dibs on a blond obsession currently hiding in her room, he playfully punched his friend in the arm roughly. "Nice, dude. Way to sound desperate."

Again, a few members of the assembly laughed.

Ricky furrowed his brow. "Which cousin?"

Hunter waved it away with his drink. "Forget about it. He's just being a retard." Leading the charge through the hallway, the guy guided the group to the front door. "Come on, Lucky. Let's get over there fast before all the girls get bored being there without us around and go home. Also, Seth just said he needs to bang one of those lingerie mannequins with the huge tits before he loses his boner."

"Fuck you, Hunter!" the boy snarled as his caring friends laughed at his expense.

"Hey, settle down, douche, or I'll sic Little Rick on you. His moves are nothin' nice. You'll be dead long before you know what happened."

Ricky chuckled vacantly, for his mind was elsewhere. His place in the pack was obvious to all but left him feeling at odds with the odd people who sought his friendship. At the moment, he only truly felt the desire to be alone. As he passed through the recognizable olive green hallway, he glanced at the sullen, solitary sibling portraits taken in protest the previous winter as a required gift to their mother. First walking by the morose pictures of his brother and sister and then past someone else he vaguely knew. Right away, he could tell that the frozen faces could see right through him, but they chose to say nothing about his noticeable cowardice. The private freedom of his quiet bedroom was just up the staircase to his left, yet it seemed so far away from his seat next to the moonlit campfire on his first night of active guard duty.

Disposable Summer Nights

The starry sky above existed unseen while Ricky's watchful stare was locked on the orange blaze before him. He allowed his worries to collect in neat little piles in the pit of his stomach where he could tend to them at the appropriate time. With his sister asleep in the tent across the fire and his brother out in the darkness, presumably abusing the tranquility in some way, Ricky could rest his qualms without their presence—let his mind wander where it wants while he kept his weary eyes on the crackling fire conversing with the stars. Alone at last.

Mere hours earlier, Leunga thought of an idea to ensure the group's security through the night he once saw in a video game, or so he thought: a rotating watch where one sibling would sleep throughout the night while the other two traded shifts at a halfway point of 4:20 a.m., thus giving everyone equal time as the group's guard during their camping trip...as long as they all stayed in the forest for a number of days divisible by three. Holy mustard! That's a long time. His intricate safety plan with its many unnecessary steps that need not be mentioned seemed to be centered around the fact that they most certainly needed to be on the lookout for any unwanted mythical visitors, and—according to Leunga—to guard against a vampire infestation, because once those suckers start nesting, it's damn near impossible to get rid of them. I'm sorry, but that was awful.

The siblings chose their order by a high-stakes tournament of rock-paper-scissors. Sydney won each round handily, awarding her the first full night's sleep in the newly deemed communal tent. Ladies first. Paper. It probably would have been the most beneficial for Ricky to take the night off to nurse his sour stomach, but equality is the main tenet of brothery sisterish friendshipping... I'm guessing. Either that, or he lacked the will to assert his feelings over the matter to the group. The whole thing is really very complicated. I wouldn't understand.

Ricky yawned to himself in the solitude of his night. He had an enormous amount of trouble keeping his eyelids from drooping uncontrollably as he tried to focus his blurry vision on his wristwatch, unable to get a clear reading. But surely—he thought—it was well after two in the morning. With a forlorn hand leaning against his face, he pondered his predicament, staining his mind with thoughts of escape as his weary spirit drifted in and out of hibernation like the tide sloshing against the hull of a ship. While searching for his place among the trees and tentative stillness, he could descry that he was trapped once again by the frailty of his bravery. Reluctantly, he saw no alternative to his present status other than his full cooperation in Leunga's legendary destruction of summer. One brother's quest is another brother's capitulation.

Just as the calm began to settle his nerves at the lack of danger, Ricky heard the sound of pine needles spreading along the ground among the trees. He whipped around, searching for the source of the disturbance, when he saw a disquieting sight. Off between the distant pines, a pair of glowing dots bounced up and down close to the ground, slowly weaving around the trees bordering the restful campsite. The blond's breathing quickened as he hesitated waking his sister at the vision of illuminated red speckles dancing in the clouded absence of the moonlight. He watched the lights attentively as he gripped the edge of his log, worrying about what this new monster would be and wondering why he couldn't see the rest of it in the form of a red exoskeleton.

The focus of the glowing orbs seemed to stay directed at the ground, until suddenly, they shot forward toward the camp. The teen's unblinking stare locked with the vicious illuminations, and the two remained motionless while they each assessed their opponent. Ricky and the eyes saw each other, one monster to another. Gradually, the luminous orbs moved closer to the camp, exiting the invisible tree line and moving steadily across the clearing. The night guard stood, taking a defensive stance against the oncoming fiend just before it could be revealed by the fire's light.

As the beast entered the radiance of the campfire, the eyes grew dim and its form began to take shape; it was a horrible sight to behold. Standing at a maximum height of just over five feet above the ground, it wore strange garments that seemed to serve only the most basic of purposes. Scrawny arms covered in a pliable material led down to its horrendously clawless fingers, gripping at the sides of its beige leggings, where it certainly must house its trickery. It carefully hid its elfin guise under a disastrous mess of awful brunet—oh, wait...it's Leunga.

The loser grinned. "I just stepped on, like, the biggest snail I've ever seen! Wait a minute!" Leunga noticed his brother's stance and glanced around quickly. "Are we under attack?! Is it the vampires? How long do we have until you change into one of them?! Get the stake!"

"Dude! Your eyes were...*glowing!*"

"Whoa, are you totally serious?! Were they *my* eyes?!"

"Yeah, man. I think so..."

"Neat! And very weird..."

Ricky rested his alerted status and rethought the phenomenon. "You know what? With all the other stupid stuff that's happened today, it's really not that weird anymore. It would be weirder if your eyes *weren't* glowing by now."

"Coinky-dinky indeedles. There must be some nuclearly charged air in this camp place here. That explains why no plants are growing..." Feeling fairly foolish, the older sibling ceased his assessment and shook his shaggy head with a light roll of his eyes and disagreed. "Hold on. That's stupid. If that was the truth, yours would be glowing right now too. Otherwise, no?"

"Yeah. Also, yours sort of stopped doing it when you were walking at me a second ago, so I dunno."

"They're gone?!" Leunga quickly became overly excitable at the news and held his hand in front of his face, checking for an absent glow. "Shit! I didn't even get to bask in the juice of my own awesomeness. Suck! Wonder how I make it go back..." While fuming with folded arms and glancing around the camp in considerable consideration, Leunga's gaze landed on the swords leaning against the largest rock. Raising his hands in shock before pointing loudly, he announced, "Oh! Those! That's the ones that did it!"

"Yeah, I kinda guessed that..."

"No! You don't! You *really* don't!"

"Shhh! Keep it down... Syd is trying to sleep."

Leunga nodded. "Oh, right...but I mean these!" He moved to the sheath and picked it up. "While I was out in the trees doing whatever I was doing, I kept feeling something holding my hand and pulling me somewhere. Like how Grampy was bitching about sensing the swords in his attic two hundred years ago. For some real reason, I could feel the camp wherever I went, and now I know I was just feeling the swords!" Another side effect of his pact with the blades of his ancestors—that growing power entrusted to him by the will of the fates, whether the choice was wise or not.

"Whoa."

"I know!"

"But wait." Never start a sentence with *but wait* unless it's for the good of humanity. "How come your eyes were glowing when you were far away from the swords, but Grampy's eyes never glowed at all when we were with him earlier?" Leunga, response?

"Man, how the fuck should I know? Maybe it's because he didn't touch the swords in forever, or because I just barely battled with a giant bastard and he didn't." Or perhaps the true reason was because their grandfather was close enough to the blades when they were reunited that the glow in his eyes was too faint to be seen, but I don't want to put words into anyone's mouth. "Maybe I'm just way more magical than him. Nope. Forget I said that. It sounded weird."

Ricky nodded inattentively as his brain began to lose power. He shook away the feeling to make a quick and simple request. "Can I go to bed? I'm way tired..."

Surprised by the off-topic remark, Leunga placed the sword by the rock and was speechless for an instant. He squinted at his sibling and said, "What?! No! You're the guard right now. Be guarding us."

"But you're awake right now too, and only one of us has to stay awake to guard, so..." Ricky's final word lingered in the air as it waited for his short partner to catch the hint.

But Leunga didn't catch it.

Returning to their previous discussion as if he hadn't attempted to gain access to his sleeping bag, the youngest camper continued, "So, uh...yeah. About your freak eyes—*freaky* eyes—what kind of superpower was it? I mean, could you see in the dark like it was night vision goggles or X-ray things?"

Leunga frowned. "No... Actually it wasn't anything. I didn't even know I had cool glowy eyes just now. I get these giant scars on my hands and monsters want me dead and I don't get any superhero abilities to go with it? What a fuckin' rip-off!"

"Dude, you still get to use those katana faster than anyone ever. That's a cool enough thing, right?"

"Yeah I guess, but now it seems incomplete without the X-ray vision... I could've been looking through the walls of girls' locker rooms while fighting off an undead swarm of zombies. Now all I have is the zombies...this sucks."

"Sorry."

"No fault here. Not now. But one of these days, I will find a way to see naked ladies in tantalizing scenarios. Today if at all possible. I promise you that."

"Can't use your phone for that...?"

"You need to call somebody? It's like three in the morning. Who do you know that's still awake right now?"

"I know you. You're still awake." The tuckered teenager smiled, wishing that he—or Leunga—was asleep. Preferably Ricky.

Leunga placed a hand on the boy's shoulder as his little brother sat patiently at their designated guard post and assured, "Yes, but you know I wouldn't answer the phone if you called."

"I know," Ricky yawned. "And I would happily do the same for you." He slumped over on his bench and felt the weight of his weary eyelids drag his mind into a wonderful dreamworld where his siblings never fought and ice cream sandwiches were always on sale. With a quick slap to the neck from his older brother, Ricky was pulled back to a dreary reality in which he had to stay up half the night. He tried once more to switch places with his partner in protection. "Hey, Lou. Since you're already awake and everything, how about you be the watchman, and I'll watch you from my sleeping bag?"

"No, because that wouldn't be fair to *you*."

Ricky stretched his lengthy arms and moaned in exhaustion. Grasping at straws, he attempted to trick his brother into pulling a double shift yet again. "I think you would really like being our guard all night long. The hero of the forest. Just you and the waterfall and the stars and—" He glanced skyward to see the moon, but was distracted by a blank spot in the sky. "That cloud."

Leunga shook his head, knowing it was the solitary purpose of his younger brother that night to be the first defender of his family's camp. "No way, Goldie. You can do this! I believe that very much! Staying awake all night long is easy. I've done it more times than I can possibly remember... Definitely less than ten, but more than two."

"If I fall asleep by accident, could you take over for me? And maybe try to get me into my bed, please?"

Startled by the request, Leunga jumped in front of Ricky and grabbed his brother by the biceps, shaking him wildly. "I won't let that happen! Do you hear me?! You will make it through this, and then when you have to do it again tomorrow it'll be way—" He was interrupted abruptly by a jarring event as he accidentally smacked his forehead against the forehead of the young man who he had been jostling violently. Leunga fell to the ground, holding his face with both hands and yelled, "Fuck!"

"Ow! Lou!" Ricky repeated his brother's actions—except without falling into the dust or cursing. Action. He rubbed his severely sore face with his palm and glanced at the very quiet tent sitting nearby. "We're really being way loud... Syd is asleep. Do you want her to wake up to the sound of us talking too loud?"

Leunga sat up rapidly. "Oh god no!"

"Then let's, uh, you know, not talk so loud."

"Right."

Wisely enough, the brothers decided to speak in hushed tones thereafter in order to avoid waking their sleeping sister, but little did they know that Sydney was silently listening to their every word as she sat wide-awake in the tent with her legs folded under the comfort of her bedroll.

"...Wait, Syd is still awake?"

"What?!" Leunga gasped.

Ricky furrowed his brow. "That's what the announcer lady just said." Oops...

Leunga addressed the tent, whispering loudly. "*Sydney?*"

"Yeah?" the tent replied.

"Go to sleep!"

"Okay..." Compliant for the moment, Sydney slowly sank into her sleeping bag, taking on her neutral sleeping position: lying on her stomach with arms folded under her face—an effective method for draining a trickle of drool—while keeping one leg out of the covers for temperature control. Of all the useless information. Though, despite her agreement with Leunga's suggestion, she remained alert, listening to the quieted chatter of her brothers as she replayed the horrors of the day in her head.

The sleepy voice of their sister reminded Ricky of the morose event that took place just before she won the grand prize in their tournament. A memento of her refreshed grief remained caked along the bottoms of his black sneakers. The coppery scent of blood was still fresh in his nose, even hours after his siblings and he had buried the fox on the outer ridge of the wall of rocks. He stared at the blood-soaked soles of his shoes and wondered if any more otherwise innocent animals would needlessly meet their end at the hand of his brother, his sister, or himself.

Leunga's wild-eyed stare locked on the faltering lids of his brother's eyes. The hero of the forest's unending gaze focused on the half-asleep watcher protecting his camp from surprises, and he became worried that Ricky would not be able to stay awake to the end of his shift. The changing of the guard. "Rickass!" Leunga jabbed his brother in the arm. "You *have* to stay awake! What if something decided to attack us right now? Who would warn me?! Stay up! For the good of the camp!"

Ricky nodded robustly. "Yeah, I know. Okay. I just need to rest my eyes for a little bit..." Taking his own suggestion to heart right away, he lowered his lids and his breathing pattern immediately resembled that of a person in the rapid eye movement cycle of sleep.

"I know exactly how to keep you awake," said the slacker as he stood quickly behind his little brother and began to give him an unexpected shoulder massage, smashing his fingers into the thick canvas robe. "I do this for April all the time. It always seems to get her w—I mean, it always makes her very sleepy. It's perfect for you."

Ricky snapped to attention, fairly alarmed. Though the rubdown was unwarranted, it felt amazing, so he allowed the activity to continue. As his big brother's fingers dug their way through the stress in his back, the kid commented on his sibling's ability to endure. "You're taking this whole situation really well." What did he really expect from Leunga? "I wish I could handle all of this as good as you do..."

"It's easy, I can teach it to you. It's all in the finger digits."

"I meant dealing with the existence of humongous dogs and stuff..."

"Oh! I know! Isn't it awesome? Just when you start thinking that—*okay, maybe magic really doesn't exist*—then boom, all of this stuff happens!" Leunga's grip on Ricky became progressively harsher as his mind began to wander. "This is a brand-new era, and it's exciting! Our world is different now, and we can never go back. The impossible has become our reality. It's so weird how easily our whole perception can be flipped upside-down and shaken so hard that we lose all balance and fall up to the edge of eternity and become one with nothingness. Doo-wop and toke a load of palisade before the decaying promenade." If any of that was supposed to mean something...it didn't. "Oh god, I wish I had a fatty right now, don't you?!"

Ricky winced as he felt his trapezius muscles realign to a more anatomically correct form. In the midst of his eldest sibling's overly jubilant outburst, he began questioning his own reality in the wake of witnessing an unimaginable wolf terrorize his camping companions. It was just a little more than he could bear. Too much for a midteen boy to handle. He tore himself away from Leunga's squeeze and got up abruptly, running into the darkness to the nearest tree, where he vomited quietly to himself. As he returned to his brother's side, Ricky cleared his throat. "I heaved. Big time."

"Christ hammer. Keep it together, barf bag!"

"Sorry... At least I really think I'm empty this time."

Leunga jumped up quickly and slapped his brother's forehead. "Shambazang! I need you hella focused, bitch. This quest shit just got killer serious."

With an exasperated sigh, Ricky groaned as he held a palm to his brow. "Ow. Okay...please stop slapping me."

"You don't seem to stop needing it. And you just hurt my hand, so I think you deserve it. I can't have some of my warriors taking breaks every five seconds to go blow chunks against the trees!"

"Yeah, I know, but like, I don't really think I can control it, man. Everything that happened today—or yesterday, or whatever—it's all too—" Ricky stopped immediately to grip his abdomen with both paws.

Leunga pursed his lips and shook his head at the towering boy. "Don't you dare do it."

Closing his eyes, Ricky stood completely still and waited for the agony to pass, but as long as he was trapped in the fantasy land of his inconceivable new existence, he would be forced to replay the nightmare over and over against the back of his eyelids, leading his stomach to tangle in a mess of disarranging disorientation as he could not picture ever feeling the way he used to again—even if he wanted to. "I kinda think we should let, like, the park rangers fix this. Don't you?"

"Have you listened to what you're talking about right now? Rangers don't use swords, man. They only prefer bows and arrows and dual-wielding daggers with ranged accuracy bonuses."

"Why can't they learn it, though?"

"It's a whole different job set. They'd have to start over from scratch and get totally new equipment and everything."

The boy whimpered dejectedly. "Oh..."

"Anyway, what are you so afraid of? The fact that we might actually have fun together beating monster ass? Or is it the whole idea that we have to *walk* everywhere with our own legs?"

Ricky whispered carefully, "I feel like you left out the part about the fear of us getting killed off of that list on purpose..."

Leunga stared up at the silent giant and was washed with what he perceived to be sympathetic concern. Ricky clearly didn't grasp the enormity of their duty and the gnarliness therein. Perhaps the kid just needed the secret, and Leunga had just the kindly advice to offer. "Look, man. I know you probably don't get this leveling up stuff and boss monster battles, but that's not *your* fault. You grew up in a different generation than me. I had to live off of video games and shit to survive, so I'm totally used to the whole warlock idea."

Breathing carefully through his nose, Ricky nodded in approval of his brother's continuance, barely able to listen to anything his shorter older sibling had to say.

"What ya need to do is D/C."

"Dee see?" the disturbed teen calmly asked.

"*Disconnect*, fool! Think of it as a game! That's what I normally do all the time anyway."

Ricky was very familiar with the concept; he had used the tactic many times before when dealing with life inside the walls of his senior high, but he had never done so on a scale of this magnitude. Carefully opening his eyes as the trauma subsided, the younger guy glanced down to the eager brunet standing below him with his hands on his hips, gazing high into the blond's brown eyes and giving the guardian a reassuring grin with his crooked mouth. Leunga was happy and he knowed it. His face surely showed it. Ricky could see the task suddenly set before them, handed down to them in a fiery fury during their humble little excursion to seek a lost old man by the deft hands of the fates; he began to understand everything that was happening around them from his eldest brother's point of view, and he didn't like it, but as long as the supposedly sleeping sister hiding in her tent was willing to play a role in the charade, Ricky was stuck tagging along for the ride, and maybe, just maybe, Leunga had a point. As stupid as it was, it just might help. "A video game. That seems dangerous..."

"Well, it ain't! It's the most undangerous thing ever, because you never die! And even if you do, you just come back right away if you have lives. Just keep your brain wide open and keep realizing how fucking radical it is that we get to do this! Nobody can—you know what?" And then for no real reason, Leunga stopped to rapidly clap a hand against the side of his combat brother's temple. "Just start doin' it already!"

Ricky recoiled, grimacing and shielding his pretty face from further swipes. "Yeah, dude, I get it! Disconnect! Whatever! You don't have to keep slapping me!"

"I really think I do."

"Are you okay, Ricky?" a canvas construction questioned with concern.

"My face *really* hurts..."

"Sydders!" a shocked Leunga blurted. "Go to bed! You are surely wasting your chance to sleep."

The tent scoffed. "So are you..."

Leunga laughed as he shouted at the stars, "How can you sleep on a night like this?!"

The truth was, she didn't believe she could, but for reasons far different than her big brother's. Laying under the comfort of her sleeping bag in an expressionless state, Sydney rested her thought-laden head against her arm-pillow, easily pushing the limit of all that she could take, and quietly trying to turn it all off. It was not going well.

More than half a minute later, and asking no one in particular, Leunga placed a thoughtful finger to his lips and noisily wondered, "What do you think it looks like?"

"What does who think that what looks like?" his brother yawned.

"You! And that thing that was able to make such a huge noise, of course!"

"I dunno." Ricky shrugged as he retook his post and alternated between rubbing his reddened forehead and throbbing sideburn. "Probably like a big metal turtle with a drill for a head and rockets for feet."

"Jesus, that sounds awesome! And so like, maybe the chain we heard was a leash? I was gonna say it was the big-ass trees talking to us or a flying fortress or something, but you definitely beat that! Rocket-powered metal turtle... That is music to my ass! Do you think we'll have to battle it?"

Ricky nodded in an attempt to allay his fatigue by continuing any conversation, no matter how very stupid. "Yep. Like you said, everything is possible now..."

"Wow. I am completely impressed."

"Yeah...me too." The youngest brother began to nod off once again, until an exceptionally loud snap from the inferno he was involuntarily leaning toward in a sleepy haze pulled him back to attention. Ricky rubbed his eyes simultaneously with one hand as he flicked his watch up with the other. The silhouette of his wrist blazed with a fiery aura, obstructing his reading once again. Twirling around to harness the power of nature's shine, he was thwarted by the burning light as its glare against the glass kept his sight safely away from finding out the hour, so he grumbled, "Hey Lou, what do you think time it is?" Almost a sentence. That one too.

With an inexplicable blade of long, dry grass dangling from his clenched lips, Leunga looked to the sky with wonder and shook his head. "I'll never know." Slowly moving to the smallest boulder, he hopped on it and reclined with his knees to the stars and his hands locked behind his head. The thoughts of possibilities skipped in large circles through his mind, making full laps around the track. He lost himself in a daze of wonderment and metacognition. Unwittingly, he began to hum a song that was at the same time familiar and indeterminate.

Ricky opened his eyes—having closed them to search for more stupid things to say—and looked to the sparks soaring above his head while the soothing melody filled his ears and opened his heart. As his brother continued the anthem on a constant loop, Ricky waited for the piece to restart before taking in a deep breath and softly singing along with the lyrics we all know so well. Feel free to sing along:

> *One morning we woke and began our lives anew.*
>> *The sun was shining on our hearts and one was made from two.*
> *So broken by loss, there's much we must undo.*
>> *We'll break the wake and make a place where all I'll have is you.*
> *There we'll stay. Where we can play. Walk by the blue.*

But in time, we'll grow distant. That's how it's meant to be.
'Cause love is just an island that sinks into the sea.
And if the waves come to swallow our last sweet memory.
I'll be sure to keep the bruises that you have left on me.
For the crime. I'll do our time. And then we'll see.
It was fun. But now it's done. Our fantasy.

In an opportune coincidence, the auspicious melody her brother broke into was one of Sydney's favorite songs. To forget about the day and prepare for whatever tomorrow may bring, she focused on listening to the boys' accidental, eurhythmic lullaby silently until her exhausted mind switched off, and she finally fell asleep.

Just before the chorus could come up, Leunga stopped humming abruptly. "What the hell song is this?" he asked his brother as the dry straw betwixt his teeth flailed about.

"'Under My Black Flame.' It's one of the only songs Syd ever listens to in her car. I used to hate it, but now I only *mostly* hate it. Don't ever tell her I said that. Holy crap, I hope she's asleep."

"Hmm... I think I hate it too. Should we keep going?"

Ricky placed a restful hand to the side of his face and yawned. "Why not?" And in the looming plague of responsibility that would follow them well into the new day, that's what the brothers did for the rest of the youngest's consciousness, which lasted almost five entire minutes. A new world record.

It's Barely Noticeable

The early morning took its time, arriving fashionably late, as it often does.

With the verbally amplified sounds of slices through the air, Sydney's eyes darted open to the sight of the sun bleeding through the canvas of her hideout. Awoken by the symphony of someone combating invisible ninjas, she groaned in exhaustion and slowly sat up. With one hand she checked the consistency of her twirled twist of hair—unaltered and undamaged, even after an almost full night of sleeping—good for keeping long hair neat or something—while she gripped her fragile new reality with the other hand. Freeing herself from the fire of her bedroll, she had the sudden realization that she was overheating in the oven that was the early morning tent, and mumbled, "Today is gonna suck." Desperate to escape the humid trap, she groggily crawled to the porthole and searched for the missing zipper to her way out. Sweat rolled down her cheek as she sighed with irritation when she noticed the door's key was on the other side of her exit. Batting at the tent entry, Sydney called out for assistance. "Excuse me, outside people, could you unzip this thing, pretty please?"

"You didn't say please!"

The zipper before her tore open quickly within an alarming instant, and she pulled the flap to one side to thank her aide, but no one was around. A drastic change in temperature cooled her quickly as Sydney poked out her head in search of her brothers, and was surprised to see at least one of them awake and active. Leunga stood near the edge of the rock ring and executed what he believed to be perfect tai chi movements, which he performed with a dismal lack of any skill for the ancient art. Oddly enough, he's actually quite good at pretending to do yoga. I have no idea why he didn't just showcase some of that instead. All the while, he seemed to be wearing an article of clothing that clearly belonged to Ricky due to its immensely oversized nature on the eldest brother's body, and its obvious function as combat armor. That gi really got to his head.

"G'day," Sydney greeted no one in particular and rubbed her exhausted face. "So did anything happen last night?"

Leunga shrugged. "I dunno, probably."

From his bed, where he was completely bewildered to be, Ricky looked up with dark rings under his eyes and moaned, "Didn't you stay up all night and watch?!"

Readjusting his new gi, the stoner stared at his sleeveless brother blankly. Suddenly, Leunga sneezed in terror. "Oh yeah! No, nothing killed us. My wicked moves saved us from all of the mountain cougars and lunar eclipses."

Ricky's fearful concern over his brother's reliability problem seemed to have immeasurable merit. He sat upright under the cover of his bedroll, half-asleep, and nodded. "Good. Can I have my coat back now?"

"Make me."

"Give him back his shirt, Leunga. Let's not start the day with a fight..."

"I oughta fight you for suggesting such a thing," one sibling replied to his younger sister.

Still sleepy, Sydney smiled kindly and implored, "Please?"

Leunga threw his arms in the air. "Whatever! It looks better on me anyway, but whatever." He carelessly removed the oversized robe and threw it to his brother's general area, unveiling the muddied, lavender, spaghetti strap tank top he had on underneath.

"What the *shit*?!" Sydney glanced down, only to find that her cover top was missing. All that remained was a lovingly faded, black, form-fitting T-shirt with a large silkscreen print of a crimson heart dripping with blood and a pair of flashy bat wings coming out of each side on the center of the dark material, along with a massive fissure down the side of the fabric underneath Sydney's undersleeve, revealing a bit too much of her skin and underwear—the latter being the primary reason why she wears the tank tops. Buy new shirts? How absurd. "You *snuck* into my tent last night and took off my clothes?!"

"Just this... I'm not a creep. Don't worry about it. I traded you my new hat for your dumb little tank top, so you don't owe me anything."

Shocked by his statement, Sydney angrily felt the top of her head, discovering a repulsive cap she had no idea she was wearing. "Ewww!" She ripped the item from her hair and threw it. "I don't want your disgusting grease trap! I want my shirt back!"

"No! I think this one actually does look better on *me*. It really brings out the color of my eyes," Leunga commented as he strolled around the camp in a dainty manner. Tiptoeing across the dust in his giant boots, he stepped up on one of the benches and did his best fashion model walk down the runway back and forth. "Sex-ay," he hissed seductively.

"You're gonna rip it! Take it off!"

On the catwalk, the camp's model citizen covered his nonexistent breasts with both hands and gasped. "I'm not a stripper for your twisted amusement! I'm a human being! I have standards," he belched as he continued to strut along the log. "Give me a dollar."

Properly prompt pandiculation, Ricky yawned profusely as he sleepily pulled his gi across his concealed legs into the comfort of the sleeping bag draped over his head. Beneath the soothing warmth of his bedcovers, he slowly got dressed in his previously stolen armor while he stared at his older siblings through his half-open eyes, bracing himself for an argument to start the brand-new day—the perfect complement to one of the worst yesterdays of his life.

Sydney used one hand to hold the hole along the side of her shirt shut and lunged out of the tent at her older brother. As she made her way around the lifeless fire pit, her prey quickly jumped over to the top of a boulder and bounced off to the opposite side.

Leunga poked his head over the igneous he was hiding behind with eyes wide and beseeched, "Come on, Sydkins. Let's not start the day with a fight."

"I will fucking kill you!" she growled and chased him around the grouping of rocks for several laps before grudgingly giving up. He proved to be too swift in her lackadaisical sleeplessness. Sydney closed her eyes groggily and groaned, "Goddamn it, Leunga. Why can't you just give it back nicely? It's not designed to be worn by little boys... I just woke up, and I'm already tired of talking you today..."

"Maybe you're right." Leunga tugged at the sides of his stylish new top and motioned around its upper edges, using his pointing hands with a snide smirk. "It's a little tight around the chest. You know what would fix that? Breasts. If only someone around here had some..."

That was uncalled for. It's not like Sydney ever made fun of him. Okay, she does that a lot, but never about his physique—no, wait, she does that too. Recently in fact. Regardless, he shouldn't have said anything. Actually, to be fair to Leunga—never mind, I'm not sure what to say. Yes, I'll be quiet.

Appropriately insulted by her brother's behavior, Sydney exhaled in simplified shock like she just had a tenth of the wind knocked out of her and leaned her tall hip against a boulder in her lingering fatigue. "Whatever." She ceased her desire to chase and falsely took on a cooler attitude to the situation. "Go ahead and be the biggest asshole in the world if you want. I don't care."

Taking her suggestion seriously, Leunga started prancing around with his hands around his waist, shaking his hips from side to side, and he followed her proposal with great gusto, transforming himself until he was very much ready to play the role of an A-hole—from his point of view. "Okay! Ooh, look.

I'm Sydney! I break windows and blame it on my brothers. I always go to college to get a masterette's degree in bitchology."

Caught off guard by the odd mockery, Sydney instinctively bent down to pick up her brother's sword sheath, slipping it on across her back in retaliation and dragging her feet around. Lowering her voice a little too much, she allowed her tongue to hang freely from her mouth and said, "Duh! I'm Leunga, duh! Mlah, I'm dubm. Duh...what duz inappropriate mean? I better gets a calculators to look it up after I fondle my fully grown sister in her sleep. Oh, wait! I finded a sword?! Activating world's geekiest loser. Let's go to have a epic quest. Mlah!"

"I'm sorry, did you say something? I couldn't hear you over the sound of my big butt."

"Oh no, I almost remembereded! I'm so high on farts all the time that I can't remember what I forgot to forget."

Leunga corrected his posture and took on a very strident tone. "Well, uh, I mean, uh, I'm Ricky... I'm boring and I want to go home."

Sydney corrected her posture and took on a very strident tone...didn't I just say that? "Um, yes, my favorite things are, like, karate and, like, pasta. Like. I broke my sister's nose when she was, like, twelve and she, like, went to the hospital... I mean, um, ummm. Barf!"

Leunga pointed an accusing finger at his sister while continuing his dreary tenor. "You uh, bring us dishonor...we need to fight, I mean, um, okay."

"Hmmm, sure, like, I mean, okay..." An alternative Ricky raised her fists and commenced the battle. Her rival Ricky and she briefly mocked hitting each other and added their own sound effects. And just like that, the animosity simmered. The white-hot antagonism common among family faltered—fickle anger that dissipates quickly in the absence of eggshells, where feelings are made to be broken without fear of ruining the relationship, experienced mainly by bonds like siblings who would never admit they were friends, as you know. "We're *not* friends."

"Oh this is such a dream right now. Pthhht!" Leunga spat wildly.

Real Ricky interjected, appearing suddenly by his brother's side with a spontaneously refreshed fauxhawk. "I got a good one, you guys! Here Lou, give me Syd's tank top for a sec."

"Let's have it," the eldest demanded as he slipped out of his final shirt of the moment, tossing it to his brother.

The taller teen took the article of clothing and handed it quietly to his big sister. "Here." Thus putting an end to their malarkey once and for all.

"Fuckin' finally!"

"I don't get it." Leunga gasped. "I'm nude!"

Sydney rolled her cover shirt on again and whined as she readjusted it. "Jackass, you stretched it." The word *scrawny* comes to mind when describing Leunga's build. In no way could he be illustrated as muscular to say the least, but in the spirit of impartiality, the tank top did seem a bit snug around his pectorals previously; not to say that it isn't snug on Sydney, but it's supposed to be. That's the point. Yes, I'll stop. "How the hell did *you* stretch out my top?"

"Woosh! Magic!"

"Oh shit! What the hell is that?!" Sydney abruptly asked as she innocently, and abhorrently, glanced at her shirtless brother.

"These are nipples."

At the call of his rumbling stomach, Ricky made his way to the duffel bag to scavenge for food while he grimaced at the disturbing behavior of his sister. "Uh...why are you checking him out...?"

Distracted by her discovery and nothing else, she sidestepped around the older young man to view his back, stating, "That is really, *really* gross..."

"What is?! I want to see it!" The slacker stretched his sight around in a vain attempt to check his back, crackling his neck joints in the process and screaming.

"This...*thing* on your back."

Leunga smiled and nodded with understanding. "Oh, you mean my tattoo! Cool, right? I calls it the skull-and-cross-bongs." He displayed his naked back to the collection of teenagers gathered by the boulders. With both hands he strained his arms back and pointed at the very large, circular tattoo in the middle of his spine. The ink stretched slightly as he lurched forward, warping the image of a bare, dark black, eyeless, human skull with some sort of flora on its forehead and an opened lower jaw as it hovered before a pair of paraphernalia made of classic blue glass situated in the shape of an X surrounded entirely by a swirling spiral tunnel made of wavy, woven wisps of cannabis smoke originating from each pipe's mouthpiece like chimneys leading away behind it. A very Jolly Roger indeed.

Leunga poked at the lumpy marking with his thumbs and grinned. "April has a matching tattoo of a skull-and-cross-beers on her shoulder...or at least she would've if I ever suggested it..."

"No."

"You already showed us that when you got it," Ricky remarked as he continued to keep his sight directed far away from his shirtless brother and scratched his head with exasperation. "Duh."

"I thought that was a henna tattoo. It's crooked."

Leunga groaned with remembrance. "Oh yeah, you guys already got to see my sweet tat. But why not gander again? Get a good hard stare going. But no photographs! I don't want there to be any hard evidence about my extra-curriculas activities. N'est-ce pas?"

"Man, I'm too tired to pretend like I care right now. Everyone in the universe can already tell that you smoke pot; you don't have to go around advertising it..."

"My word. A bug really crawled its way up your butt, didn't it, my darling?" replied Leunga to his brother's response. "And we were having such a wonderass time last night too."

"Goddamn it. Shut your mouth for a fucking second," Sydney interjected. "I wasn't talking about your 'I'm probably carrying—possession with intent to dumbass' cop signal. I meant that!" she exclaimed, pointing to the back of the lad lacking clothes in order to instruct Ricky to view what appeared to be an enormous series of runes across their older sibling's upper half. "It looks just like that shit on the back of your hands."

Ricky glanced momentarily and moaned in disgust before quickly looking away. "Ugh! That's sick..." He grimaced at the food he was suddenly having second thoughts about in his hand. "I was just about to start eating too..."

Jagged crags of open, split skin exposed the dried muscle and browning sinew beneath. Wrapped across his epidermis, tiny symbols of undoubtedly ancient script crawled their way toward Leunga's neck and around his ribs, connecting together in defined lines over his spine. There was something distinctly tribal about its design, yet at the same time, it seemed almost regal.

Sydney leaned in close in order to inspect the open fissures along his back, significantly grossed out at the ability to see her brother's bare ligaments, but entirely unable to look away. Entranced by the sight, she noticed something about its outer edges and frowned. "I think it's spreading," she noted and carefully touched the rim of the outermost symbol as it almost invisibly cracked his unbroken hide further. "But you're not bleeding. Does it hurt?"

"How can it hurt if I never even knew it was there? Hey!" Leunga whirled around and jumped out of her reach. "Don't touch me."

"Fine..." Worried about her sibling's excessive scar tissue, Sydney shuddered and turned away, finding herself hoping that after the vacation was over all wounds might fade away along with the memory of the epic quest. She knew when it began that morning that the day would be filled with adversity. The dawn of dark new era. As usual, she was right. "But if it starts to get worse, you'll tell us about it, right?"

"When what gets worse? Your breath? Oh, Sydney. Don't worry. I will."

"I know you will," she acknowledged vacantly and took a seat. "Really wish I didn't have to care so much about shit right about now."

"I know what you mean."

Doing his best at ignoring everyone, Ricky tore open his breakfast and began to grudgingly gnaw through the protein bar in his grip. Slowly chewing the sickening loaf of rice crisps and prune puree, he tried desperately to avoid looking his brother's shredded skin, but upon catching an uncontrollable, irresistible, momentary glimpse of the freshly scarred flesh, he winced. "Dude...gross...put your shirt back on."

"Must I?" whimpered Leunga before he reluctantly collected his clothing from wherever he was storing it and made his way to the campsite's local privacy station after no one begged him to stay topless for the rest of the day. "Well, if that's how you want to be, then go to hell, one and all. I'm gonna get dressed in the tent. I don't want any of you two watching me change..." he said with a squint as he mistrustfully backed his way into the humid room, only to reappear completely clothed seconds later.

Ricky took another resistant nibble of his disastrous breakfast and presented his brother with a timid, partial thumbs-up. Noticing the friendly gesture directed his way, Leunga flipped off his brother using both hands. Ricky instantaneously rotated his wrist 180 degrees groundward into a partial thumbs-down.

"You're right! Man, I'm super hungry," remarked Leunga at the sight of his brother's enticing meal. He began to sift through the contents of Ricky's duffel bag, when he stopped to ask, "Where be the sambwidges?"

"We ate 'em."

Leunga choked on his shock. "In two days?! That was our food!"

Ricky chewed, trying not to notice the similar resemblance of his meal to the twisted scars growing on Leunga's skin, and said, "Man, they don't last that long if you eat, like, three of them in one sitting..."

"Fair enough, but where the *fudge* are the rest of my cookies?"

"Oh..." The younger one began to fret for a second. "Were you saving those...?"

"Bichard?! Why?!"

"What...? They were tasty..."

"Yeah. They were. *Once.*" Reminiscing about the days when they had sandwiches and cookies to spare, Leunga took an arbitrary flavor of power bar from the assortment and grumbled, "This is just like that time you ate my last piece of Christmas pizza even though I sneezed all over it in the fridge." That last part was unknown to Ricky. "Dickhead."

"We still got tons and tons of protein bars here..." the youngest offered as a consolation prize and hoped that it would suffice. "You can have all of those ones you want." Carefully studying the miniscule print of the nutritional facts on his breakfast's wrapper as a necessary distraction from the disgustingness of the day—and to take his sibling's focus from the fact that he polished off three-fourths of their chocolate chip delicacies all by himself two nights before—Ricky announced his findings to anyone who would listen. "You know, they're not that bad when you finally get used to them...Plus, they're loaded with like a million vitamins. *Vitamin C: five thousand percent.* How is that possible?"

The other brother bit into his bar and quickly spit it out. "Ugh, these things taste like dog shit, but I heard somewhere that they're loaded with tons of vitamins and stuff."

"I *just* said that."

"And then so did I. Mine wins."

"So." Sydney suddenly snuck into the conversation with a quick query. "Is this really how we're going to spend all of our valuable time right now? Just sitting here and turding around?"

"Affirmatively. Why not?"

"Aside from being dumb as hell, it's not productive."

Ricky spoke through a full mouth in mild contempt. "I'm not turding around. I'm eating breakfast."

"I know. I can hear your gross little gooshing noises from way over here, doi." She's way over there. "Shouldn't we be talking about what we're going to do today? Where we're going to go? What the hell we're even gonna look for? *Anything*?"

Leunga looked to Ricky and then to Sydney and back to Ricky and then again to Sydney, and replied, "He's eating!"

"*But* we could be eating *and* making up plans. Get some structure into this ad hoc bullshit. I'm ready to get going and start kicking some magician ass already...goddamn it."

Pleased to discover that he wasn't the only one who was more than ready to get up with the get down, a numbskull nodded to her in agreement and danced for a bit in anticipation of the possible upcoming trials of the daily unknown. "Yeah, boi! We gots ta get this thang goin', yo! Tall shawty be all up over that quezt bidness! Know-what-I'm-sayin', yo?"

Surly, Sydney sneered, "Shut up, shorty."

"Yeah yeah! Totally. So's if you don't mind me asking, what do *you* want to do today?"

Ricky looked over at his brother, who was staring him at him eagerly and holding his entwined hands against his head as a suspended pillow in midair. The teenage guy glanced to their sister, only to see Sydney already staring at him and awaiting his response. The youngest hiker shrugged. "Um...well...we're still, uh...here to look for the sorcerer dude, right? I dunno. What else can we do except find some random trail and go hiking on it like you said yesterday...? Or we can go home."

"You know what? Dick Dick is right right."

Ricky looked to Leunga with surprise. "He *is is*?!"

"Entirely! I forgot about us trying to find that magician guy out here. We should just start doing that all over again today! Let's find ourselves on the first trail we find and hike the shit out of! It! That's the very best idea we could ever have." Aside from giving up and going home while they still had all of their body parts. "Very nicely worked. Five stars. I will definitely be recommending you to a friend."

A sister softly punched Ricky on the back to congratulate him on a day's goal well conceived. "See? Now this whole morning hasn't been a waste of everyone's time. If we keep being focused about it, we're bound to find the stupid-ass Summoner somewhere. Then we beat the shit out of him and save the animals."

"That's exactly the kind of sense it makes to me, old chum."

"While we're at it, we should also probably set up some safety rules—like what we should do if we can't find each other." Sydney went on to say, "*And* it would be a good idea if we made a strategy or something in case we run into some more crazy shit. Last time sucked."

Ricky slowly looked back and forth between the opposite side of their pond and his sibling's shoes. He hesitantly added to the conversation while his mind backtracked to the terror of the previous day. "I don't think anyone could've really prepared for anything that we saw yesterday, but yeah, the last time could have gone a lot better."

"To hell you go along with that commentary still lingering on your lips," blurted one brother to the other. "Yesterday was perfectly. How did you already forget about the extremely sophisticated backflip me and my swell swords did off the top of that large-ass rock and onto the back of that wolf almost? That just cost you a star. And you can forget about that decent review I was going to give you too."

Sydney chortled. "Are you serious?! You *flipped* from that rock?! By yourself?"

"Of course! I am the effigy of awesomeness."

"Huh. That's actually kinda cool." With the discovery of her brother's mystically etched hands and spine, his ability to flip from the top of a massive boulder was all the more believable. Wondering with awe what her brother was becoming, she was also worrying if he would ever be the same again.

Leunga nodded. "It was easily as amazing as you think it was. Times infinity." Plus one.

Ricky's face contorted with denial.

Sydney noticed the younger's twisted expression and asked, "What's with the dumb face?"

Her big brother backhanded her arm kindly and condemned, "You know very well he can't help it!"

"Well, actually, uh, Lou did *try* to do an amazing ninja flip, but he sussed it up."

Sydney scoffed, easily losing whatever amazed impression she just gained about her older sibling. "Ah. Yeah. That's more like it. I kinda figured he would suss a flip." I don't think the blond kids know what that word means.

Leunga growled, "Et tu, Ricardos? This is nice; the two tall freaks are conspiring against me. I knew it all along." He wiggled the fingers of one hand derisively at the pair. "You, hiding behind your puffy haircut with those shifty raccoon eyes, and you, pretending to be scared of every freaky noise we hear. First you tell people I didn't do a flip, but then what? What's next?! Telling them I shit my pants? And how can I prove that didn't happen, huh? Oh my god, how can I prove that didn't happen?!"

Sydney's expression lit up like the sun, smiling and scheming. "Hot beans, he's right!"

"Lou, I'm not gonna tell people you *S-ed* your pants..." Ricky reassured. "I'm just saying that your giant wolf story would be more believable without the flip."

"You'd like that, wouldn't you?! Don't act like you've never emblazoned a fable of your own life for your own profit!"

"I did what?"

"The buttbag means embellished."

Leunga held a fixed index finger in front of Sydney's face and warned, "You...correct me langwudge one more time and it's on, bitch."

"Oh my hell, calm down. I'm just trying to help get on with this shit. And you have to stop calling me derogatory names. It's debasing, very disrespectful, and not only is it insulting to *me*, but also my entire gender, you partially shaved ape."

"Fair enough," he agreed and extended his hand as an obligatory peace offering. "Truce?"

Sydney raised an eyebrow and accepted, so the two eldest siblings shook hands for some reason—side to side rather than vertically as per Leunga's typical fashion.

The smaller one retracted his grip quickly and cringed. "Ew! Your hand is *so* fucking sweaty! Why?!"

"Yeah, duh. They're always like that," she affirmed annoyingly and wiped her hand against her shredded jeans. "Why do you think I was the only girl on my team who *always* wore a batting glove *and* finger tape?"

"To look *awesome*? I don't know, you never let me go to your games." With one exception: her first softball game. Leunga arrived thirty minutes late, smelling of liquor long before noon—and half a dozen months or so shy of the magical age of twenty-one—and shouted demands that his little sister be allowed to play, only to find out that she was already on the field, to which he replied in a piercing alto, "Go Mustangs," causing half of the crowd to cheer.

Sydney suddenly became mildly distraught over the discovery that not every member of her family suffered similarly from her odd affliction—as if she never knew that before—questioning the restricted nature of her problem and wondering where it could have come from, realizing it would require further analysis at a future date. "Just ignore it," she suggested. "That's what I do."

Leunga was unable to follow her advice; he was fixated on her condition. "You should seriously get a doctor to check that shit out. It's gross. You're gross."

"You should seriously get a doctor to check for giant holes in your stupid fucking brain! And, oh my god. Once again, you've gotten us completely off track. Stop doing that!"

Shocked by his sister's insight, the brunet was stunned at the reminder. "That's what I'm saying! While we're here spending our wise time sitting around and twiddling our dinks, there's a wizard out there just waiting for us to find him and spank his ass raw until it glistens like an undercooked ham hock in the sun. At the very most, we could easily be multitasking this shite right now."

"Maybe we should just get back to making a battle plan already..." Ricky reinstated, rolling his eyes in aggravation aimed at the constant insults his ears were subjected to between those two adults of his after taking another huge bite of his unfortunate meal. "You guys can fight later." And then some saliva slipped from his lips while he rudely chewed with his mouth agape, which he unsuccessfully tried to salvage by slurping it back up noisily, but you didn't want to know that.

"What *plan*? As long as I whip out the swords when the fight starts, we're golden, right?!" Leunga glared at his brother, who was eating some stuff and inattentively pinching the sleeves of his gi in an attempt to correct its once-pristine condition that his older brother trashed. The twenty-something boy took a swing at him and said, "This is important, goddamn it!"

"Yeah, but what do me and Syd do? I'm starting to think it would be nice if we had, like, a strategy formation. Like one of you guys said."

"Syddoo... I like that."

"Oh! Like an RPG. I see..." Tapping his fingertips against his brain and stimulating the thought processes within, Leunga quickly lost his train of thought and ceased the activity, placing a hand on the back of Ricky's head just below the portion of his hair that becomes spiky and truly dangerous to touch. "Did you puke today?"

"Not yet."

He smiled consolingly and gasped, abruptly squeezing his sibling's spine. "I got it. While I have the swords out, you two stand by my side in a very lazy V-formation and—"

Ricky ignored the squishing of his skin and interrupted his brother with aptly fixed eyes directed ahead at the distant trees. "There's a guy over there."

Ladies and Gentlemen: Prepare for War

Sydney and Leunga turned in the direction of their brother's alerted stare and saw the man of Ricky's reference standing on the other side of the pond, looking directly at the three siblings. The mystifying man was tall, roughly the same height as Ricky if not taller. He wore clothing so dark it was difficult to discern from the camp's distance, but he appeared to have on baggy black jeans, black footwear, and a pocketed hoodie where he concealed his hands and kept the hood pulled over the top half of his face to shade his eyes, allowing only a fraction of his skin to show, along with a beard of black hair woven into a long braid with a metal ring holding it together at its base by the center of his collarbone. The man remained motionless, staring across the water at the trio without expression. Watching.

"Oh my *god*. Who knew they had such a supply of hunks in the worthless woods?! He is so hot!"

Sydney nodded vacantly. Her eyes were fixed on the mysteriously fascinated stranger. "Wh—um—huh..."

"I can't be totally sure, but I think I want him to be the father of my children. I bet he's like my age, maybe a little older. I have a very deceivingly youngish face. Should we talk to him?" Leunga asked eagerly.

Inattentively playing with a few of the lengthy rebellious hairs that slipped from the clutches of her loose bun at the side of her choker, the girl couldn't take her sights off the visitor, no matter how much she felt she needed to after the fact. The young man seemed very interested in observing the little camping pack from afar without so much as an expression. That's when Sydney secretly began to wonder if the handsome stranger was there because of *her*, and at that moment she began to feel a confusing loss of her motor skills as a steady panic settled in. "I thank—eeh, um... I think he's alone... I don't see anybody else."

Leunga waved his hands across the sky and shouted, "¡Oyé, amigo nuevo! ¿Como estais? Aý, estoy mas o menos. Estamos aquí para ir de excursión, pero estamos teniendo problemas." He pointed to his siblings. "Mi hermano y mi hermana son pendejos. ¿Tiene hermanos o hermanas? Si usted no, tienes suerte..." Leunga paused for a reply but was perplexed when the man remained silent. "¿Oyé, estabas aqui cuando que el trueno era todo? Eso fue raro. ¿Sabe usted de dónde viene?"

The man said nothing.

"¿Quieres unirte a nosotros? Nosotros no pican mucho."

The man said nothing.

Leunga scoffed and blared his eyes wide. "Wow, he and Rick-a-lick have a lot in common. You two would have plenty to *not* talk about."

The man said nothing.

The trees surrounding the clearing slowed their movement as Ricky felt the ground beneath his feet stop in concurrence with his beating heart. He swallowed dryly and couldn't believe the sight. Physically standing a mere pond length from the solitude of the tranquil camp stood a solemn individual wearing oddly modern clothing with a morose expression fitting the description of a dream his grandfather detailed the previous morning.

The Summoner said nothing.

"Hey! Are you even paying attention?" Leunga glared at Ricky, reminding, "I just made a hilariously soul-crushing joke at your grave expense. Make with the fuckin' yucks!"

Sydney shyly whispered a suggestion to her very vocal brother. "Ask him if he's seen anything that could've made that big noise yesterday."

"Don't breathe on me! And, stupid, I just barely said that exactly. Why don't *you* ask him?"

"Jackass, I took *French* in junior high. I don't know what the hell you just said! You could've been calling me a bitch again, or worse. Or told him that I think he's hot or something stupid like that..."

Leunga shouted, "My sister thinks you're hot!"

Sydney shoved her brother in the back as hard as she could. "You little shit!" Leunga turned and countered her attack with his own, reaching up and shoving her shoulders. She again pushed him, and the two continued in that manner for a childish amount of time.

While his siblings were quarrelling, Ricky panted in trepidation as he shakily grabbed the sheath with his brother's blades by the boulder behind him, turning then to face their foe, only to discover that the Summoner had vanished completely.

"Nice going, Sydness. You scared him off."

"Me?! He was probably offended that you would just assume he spoke Spanish based solely on his skin tone." That was Spanish? Wow, Leunga needs to work on all kinds of grammar.

"Racism? Are you kidding me?! Everyone speaks Spanish. ¡Español es la lengua de amor y fiestas!" Leunga explained as he walked to Ricky and took the swords from his little brother. "Muchos graciass. See?"

"It doesn't matter. We don't need his help anyway. We can find out where the Summoner is hiding by ourselves," she said with heart-lifting relief at the hopeful desertion of the man by the water. If a cute guy really was there just for her, she didn't want her brothers to be within a five-mile radius of her should the man dare the impossible and try to talk to her, as awkward as that would be to begin with. On a calming path back to the benches, Sydney stopped in her tracks abruptly and exclaimed, "Wait a sec!"

Ricky turned to his sister, expecting her to make the same realization that he had.

"Leunga still needs to finish the fucking strategy. What about the plan?"

A young man in sweatpants was crushed.

With a disappointed frown, Leunga began speaking at a leisurely pace, pausing every few words to ensure his idea was accurate to his desires. "Oh yeah, likes I was saying before everyone interrupted me, these giant monster things aren't very fast, so I think if youse guys just stay—"

Impatiently waiting for the words his brother was taking way too long to say—and greatly motivated when the isolation of being the only perceptive person in the entire camp crept up on him—Ricky stepped in and spoke with immeasurable speed. "Stay near you but not in front of you, maybe in, like, a big circle around the monster or behind you at all times, but not too close so we don't get hit with the glowing death razors and not attack the freak without you around and only get near it if we can somehow weaken it without getting killed ourselves. Got it."

"Near me...yeah." He looked across the pond at the deserted shore and whimpered sadly.

"That's a good plan, Lou..."

Sydney nodded. "Super. Now we're unstoppable."

Not only had the group just come into visual contact with the monstrous man without a conscience, but Ricky was clearly the only one who knew. The battle strategy that his big brother had created sat in his ears as he tried to regain his senses and pondered the aspect of telling his adult siblings whom they just saw. Ricky crumpled the empty wrapper in his fist and exhaled heavily. "So...are we *going* somewhere now? I'd kinda like to get out of this area as soon as possible, please."

"Oh my god!" Sydney stopped again in shock.

Ricky turned rapidly, eager to act surprised after his sister inevitably told them that the man they witnessed watching them like a statue was the Summoner. Artificial ignorance.

"I need a weapon to defend myself with."

No need to act, Ricky was sincerely surprised.

Leunga slowly locked eyes on the side of his brother's face in fear for their lives. "What for?"

Sydney shrugged in disbelief at the elder's ineptitude. "So I can protect myself if we get separated again, you hole."

"I thought you didn't want to hurt the precious little animals," Leunga mocked as he fastened the large, well-crafted metal buckles of the sheath's harness across his chest and upper waist, securing the danger to his back.

"I *don't!* But whatever that thing we saw yesterday was, it wasn't an animal. Animals don't talk."

Ricky furrowed his brow, forgetting about the Summoner's emergence at the discovery of this new information from his sister. "What?! It *talked* to you?"

"What the cheesy hell did it say?"

Seeing that her brothers were entranced by her anecdote, Sydney smirked. "Well, after it shook the shit out of the tree I was in, I fell into a puddle, right? Then when I was catching my breath, it leaned in real close to me..." She moved closer to Leunga and Ricky for effect, divulging, "And it literally told me to scream."

"Did you?"

Sydney scoffed, feeling like one of the guys. "Hell no. I'm not a *pussy.*"

Leunga was visibly repulsed by her sudden verbiage. "Ew! Ewww! Uncouth! Don't *ever* say that word to us again! Coming from your noise mouth it sounds like poison. I am going to have a very shitty day thanks to that."

"Way to overreact...goddamn. I was just saying—"

"Just saying a bunch of talking things about girl parts in front of little brothers. Yeah, I was there. It's okay to say it around other guys, but you cannot just spew that word so loudly. What if there was a girl around here, huh?! What then?!"

Sydney was understandably appalled and offended by the ludicrously lewd loser Leunga's obviously objectionable area of questioning and the blatant misunderstanding capabilities her older brother possessed—a very vulgar vocalization by a vagabond propagating a plume of perversion, and other appropriate alliterations. Although she clearly never meant anything along the lines of any literal slang translation, Sydney was far more pressed to dissect a few other things her brother just mentioned. "*Other* guys? What do you mean by *what if?*"

Her older brother sidestepped the quandary by ignoring it altogether. "This is all a life lesson to learn for you. You're almost a grown-up. There's stuff you should know by now. You should really be writing this down. This is the way the world works. Female types don't appreciate that word in public. If you want girls to like you, you can't go around blurting out the hard P-word, stupid. If a girl says it to you first, that makes it okay, but only certain types of girls do that. Wait, what type of girl were you looking for?"

Somewhere in her brother's noisy rant, she stammered, "Would you stop talking?! Why would I *ever* use *that* word in *that* way?! Especially in front of you two idiots. And, dumbshit, I *am* a girl!"

Leunga looked skeptical. "Are you absolutely sure? I wonder sometimes. You used to be a girl when you were a kid, but now...I don't know. Chicks don't usually swear as much as guys. Things may change. Maybe you megamorphosized. Ya just never know with these things. I guess your voice is kinda on the higher end of the stratosphere now that I think about it, and you look like you grow your hair on purpose. You might be a chick. Go over there and check. Chick check."

Sydney turned away and snarled at the irritatingly unwarranted discussion aimed at her gender. "Oh. My. God. Fucking...that is *so* inappropriate. Not kidding. What the fuck is wrong with your brain that makes you say that stuff?"

"WTF is wrong with *me?* You're the thing going around talking about her junk like we all have to hear about it. Wait, what was the question again?"

"I wanna beat you up," Leunga's sister snapped at him. "That's the level I'm at right now. Seriously. You're an assface. The point is, I didn't scream."

"Okay! Shut up already! I believe you. But you *are* a chick." The eldest eyed his sibling suspiciously. "Right? I mean, you do kinda dress like one..."

Sydney answered by firing an angered glare in her tormentor's direction.

Leunga abruptly panicked at her lack of definitive response. "*Right?!*"

"Yes!" she yelled immediately.

Cowering briefly at the sudden power of his sister's voice, Leunga calmly replied, "Okay. Whatever. Settle down...goddamn." I could be mistaken—it's rare, I know—but wasn't Leunga just making sport of his sister's girliness with a short skit involving her tank top or something only a few minutes ago? And now this. Maybe I'm just being stupid for trying to make sense of anything. "You don't have to roar at me, you monster."

"It's okay if you screamed, Syd. Lots of girls do that," Ricky added, trying to draw the conversation away from the extremely uncomfortable route it seemed to be taking.

Leunga continued to look at her with cynicism. "Yeah. That's what chicks do. They're great at it. Chicks are the best screamers. Chicks. That's fun to say."

"*Chicks...*" Ricky frowned after finishing the word. "Great, now I feel all weird..." A feeling commonly referred to as *guilt*.

Sydney snarled angrily and was quickly fed up with her brother's words for, like, the tenth time that day. And it was still so early too. She flicked her strongest finger against Leunga's forehead, thumping a black fingernail through his messy bangs against his skull.

He cringed. "Hey, that's my only face!"

"Quit saying shit like that! I told you not to make fun of my gender by calling me stuff like chick and bitch." She whispered irately through clenched teeth, "We shook on it!"

"Don't remind me..." Rubbing a few fingers over his indented skin, Leunga was fully ready to retaliate in some vastly necessary way, when something about his sister's sentiment suddenly struck a chord in his internal workings, and his attitude toward the situation instantly altered, as if her dinging digit just knocked loose a vital eye-opener he had been seeking his whole life. Taking on a tone of wonder and sincerity, he gasped. "Whoa. This is so crazy. I think I might've learned an actual lesson about respect today..."

"You did?" his brother asked in astonishment. That is quite alarming. Apparently, womankind had made a powerful ally.

"Yes. Don't call Sadney a chick because she'll bitch about it," Leunga spewed in acknowledgement. That is not quite as alarming. Lesson not learned. Apparently, womankind had kept a powerful enemy.

Sydney wisely chose to ignore her sibling's statement and returned to their previous discussion. "I still want a weapon."

Leunga nodded. "All right. That makes sense. As long as you're not still thinking of pounding me for no reason, then I concur. And just do it quick. I wanna take some time today to take a huge nap. I'm way tired for some reason."

"Yeah, so, weapon, please."

Fairly reassured that the great evil tormenting their group from across the pond was gone for the moment, Ricky could feel his nerves begin to cool. "Okay...um, I might have a sai or something," the fighter suggested as he scratched the back of his golden hair. "Or...uh...oh, I have some tonfa you can use. They're kinda like those billy clubs cops have except they're bigger."

"Hmm... I would rather have something sharp."

"Well, a sai is sharp." Ricky held up a hand with most of his fingers extended while curling his index and ring fingers down to mimic the shape of the weapon. He pointed to the end of his middle finger and added, "It's very pointy."

"Wait, no, never mind. I don't want to stab anything..." Dealing with a mild sense of conflicting needs, Sydney rethought her desire to wield a weapon against a living creature, when she remembered something mesmerizing from their first night with the forest. "Oh! How about the numb-chuck?"

"You mean *nunchaku*, ass bastard!" Her older brother was pleased to correct.

Sydney's face scrunched to one side and asked, "Does it matter?"

Leunga's face scrunched to the other side and replied, "No!"

"I'm not sure if I still have one in my bag..."

"Go check." Ricky's sister eyed her feet then looked to her martial artiste companion, knowing that he had the desired weapon in his satchel. "I'll help by waiting here."

The youngest rolled his lips between his teeth in thought, realizing that he too might need some form of defense against the wild. "Ye—m—uh...'kay, I'll try to get something you can use...one sec."

"I will assist," the eldest offered as he performed a lovely pirouette in place before stumbling after his larger little brother.

Sydney grabbed Leunga by the back of his polo shirt and jerked his lightweight body violently closer to her, choking him momentarily. "Wait, wait, wait, wait," she whispered.

Leunga readjusted his clothing while he waited to hear her excuse for returning him to his former spot, hoping she didn't notice the sound squeaking out of the back of his pants.

"I'm worried about Ricky," she confessed lowly. "I'm not sure if he understands why we're doing all of this. Sometimes it's easy to forget how young he is. Maybe we need to talk about it some more."

Silently standing as one in a two-person huddle for several prolonged minutes, each of the adults contemplated the woman's words.

"What the hell are you talking about?!" Leunga blurted a long time later. "I'm like *five years* older than you." More like fifty-six months.

"Ricky! I was *talking* about Ricky."

"Well, you should've said so in the first place!"

"Sorry! I meant to."

Noticing her need for some consoling, her small sibling set his hand up on her shoulder. "You're too focused on him, kid," he said sympathetically. "You're missing your own life. Try to think about something else..."

"Me being concerned about something is not a problem that needs a solution. I'm just getting kinda worried about our little brother. He was barfing *a lot* yesterday...."

Leunga yelled in her face as he shook the tall girl from side to side. "College!" Universe city.

"Um! I'd rather not."

Being the only sibling to experience any form of higher learning—no matter how brief—he felt obliged to disclose his knowledge. "You're gonna like it. The whole time it's like a big party where no one cares what you do and then you drop out."

She had hoped to avoid thinking about her educational progression during their excursion into the trees. Sydney attempted to interrupt her brother. "Sh—"

But Leunga was undeterred. "I had a killer time for that semester I had at community college, but—"

"Shut up."

"It would have been a lot better without going to classes every other day..."

"Shut up for a second."

"Oh! And the damn tests! All those goddamned tests. Seriously, it was like every month there was some class that had almost two whole tests about some stupid shit. And I swear, the teachers there—professors, they call it—they put so much emphasis on the tests, it's like having your entire grade depend on one piece of paper and fifty minutes."

"Please shut up," she begged as her nerves began to build, causing her to wrap her arms above the top of her head to cover her ears with her biceps while she contemplated silencing her sibling with violence.

"Plus, they put these questions on their tests that are so stupid impossible," Leunga continued uninterrupted as he casually wrapped his arms over the top of his head as a mirror tribute of his sister. "They go like:

> 21. Pneumonoultramicroscopicsilicovolcanoconiosis is a
> disease affecting what organ?
>
>> (A) Bone
>> (B) Three
>> (C) A
>> (D) None of the above
>> (E) All of the above."

"Stop it."

Leunga slapped his cheeks and howled, "Pencils down!"

"*Stop!*"

Pressing one index finger against his lips in a sign of silence, he pointed at Sydney and nodded. "You'll be fine. Just remember to always wear lots of sweatshirts with the school's logo on the front. Otherwise, college doesn't count."

"... Just help me watch him and make sure he doesn't have a nervous freak-out if we have to fight for our lives again."

"Who? Me?"

"Ricky..."

"Oh. Yes...he is the one who has serious potential to screw this whole thing up."

"One of the ones."

"Yeses."

Both eldest siblings turned their attention to their younger brother as Ricky delved into his duffel in search of a suitable weapon for Sydney. The teenage ninja paused for a moment during his search to vomit onto the ground by his luggage.

Leunga smiled. "See? He's fine. No need to worry about nothing."

Sydney gritted her teeth. "I'm not helping him bury any more barf."

Weapons of Less Destruction

"I'm really glad you're feeling better after what happened yesterday. Ya know? It's kinda...*nice* to see you happier again."

"Would you shut up already?!" Sydney replied to her younger brother as the twirling hazard flailed in her grip like a helicopter rotor before the free hand she held up to shield her face. "Just tell me what I have to do to stop this thing from spinning without breaking my nose!"

Ricky backed away from her a bit and instructed, "Just stop wiggling your hand and let it fall."

Sydney cringed as she held her outstretched arm still and allowed the swinging nunchaku to smack against her wrist, bouncing off her bracelets. "Okay I'm ready to start now. Let's knock this out. I can do it."

Preparing to teach his sister how to use a weapon that took him months—if not years—to get the hang of was a daunting task to accomplish in such little time, but with an exhale of nervous anticipation, Ricky was ready to give it a try. "It's gonna be hard to jam a bunch of lessons into one, but I think we can."

"Of course we can! Who said we can't?" His sister slowly started to rotate the nunchuck at her side once again until her brother shot out his hand and grabbed the baton in midair. She smiled embarrassingly and mumbled, "Oh right, sorry..."

"Let's start out easy. First thing you should do is hold the swingy part under your armpit when you're about to attack. Don't whip it around until you want to hit something."

Sydney placed the open baton under her arm. "It's cold. Now what?"

"Okay, when you have a target, flick your wrist outward and twirl the open end once or twice around the outer edge or your arm in a forward swing, then snap your elbow downward and swing it with all of your force at the thing you want to hit. And be careful, 'cause you could break a lot of bones."

"Isn't that the point?"

"I meant *your* bones."

"Ooh." Without a determined target—or a suggestion to attempt the technique from anyone—Sydney decidedly whipped the weaponry forward as per her brother's instructions to test his method so far, only to have the baton spin around too rapidly for her skill level and bash into her funny bone. "Oh goddamn it!"

Ricky winced before continuing his lesson without first checking to see if she was okay. "They work best if you keep them moving, but that can be dangerous if you start to feel like you're losing control. Try to keep them close to your body, like wrapping around your waist or going above your shoulder. Also try to avoid hitting your face. Believe me, it hurts."

"Yeah, I *bet*. This thing gets a nice momentum going," she replied as she pressed her palm against her tender wenus. Quiet. It's not what you think it is.

Ricky nodded. "Swing it out once and see if you can make it go around your stomach—like around the front—and then swing it back around to your back in one motion, and then keep it going back and forth like that. And keep your other arm out of the way. It might sting a little, but that's normal. And don't worry if you can't get it on the first try. Here, let me show you." Ricky quickly preformed the action with a weapon that was identical to the one in Sydney's hand, which he held on to as a *teaching tool*. The second pair in the perilous set. Giving Sydney more than one way to bash their big brother into oblivion right off the bat seemed like a bad idea at the time. "Okay, now you try."

Mildly baffled by how she would execute the seemingly complicated maneuver, the student took a moment to consider the motions and suddenly performed the action flawlessly.

"Nice!" Her sibling chuckled as he watched his inexperienced sister easily enfold the weapon around her waist over and over. "Now try it from the starting position and lob it over the top of your left shoulder and bounce it against your back again like this." He demonstrated the next maneuver for her. "Oh, and uh, keep your head still while it's moving. Yeah."

Watching his actions carefully, she placed the pendulous bludgeon under her arm before trying the technique in Ricky's most recent lesson. Her weapon gracefully danced over her shoulder before she followed through with the previous skill, bouncing it around her lower back and waist again effortlessly before allowing the weapon to dangle by her side. "That wasn't so bad."

"Dude! That was awesome! You're better than me when I started learning."

Sydney bowed. "Thank you, sensei. Can I try with both now?"

"Wait, you need to learn how to stop in a combat situation. After you attack, the nunchuck will still have tons of force, so to keep it from, like, smashing into your face or something, you gotta catch it in your armpit again."

"While it's *swinging*? Hope I don't hit my boobs by accident."

A distant voice sneered, "What exactly does she mean by *boobs*?"

"I fuckin' heard that you halfling..." Sydney shouted to Leunga as she swung the nunchaku inattentively, seizing it easily under her arm instinctively. "Oh! I caught it!"

"Nice job! You're pretty good. Like a natural or something."

"Thanks. Just like twirling around a softball bat."

"Now do it a thousand more times," Ricky teased.

Sydney snorted with laughter. "You're a good teacher. You should give lessons."

"Dude, I just did!" He smiled as he held out the second in the pair without a second thought, encouraging her to become the badass she was born to be. "Here, try it with both now. It's easy if you just try to mirror what your dominant hand is doing, but you gotta keep them from smacking into each other, or you'll lose your rhythm."

"Ooh, complex-icated."

As his sister took the nunchaku, he continued, "It might be hard at first, but just take it slow. Or if it's too hard, you can just go back to using one at a time."

Sydney made a tentative attempt at dual-wielding the weapons, surprisingly successfully, until she ran into a slight problem. As they often did, the unparted bangs draped above the girl's left eye lost their inhibition and flew across the bridge of her nose without warning, carefully blocking her ability to see anything.

Ricky's attention was drawn to the spinning danger in his sister's grip. He pointed at the duo of blurs to add, "And remember that those are made of really dense wood, so they're pretty strong, but if you hit something hard enough they might get cracked. So watch out for splinters."

As she swung the batons blindly, Sydney attempted to catch the twins under her armpits while her vision was obstructed. Repeatedly trying to whip the hair from her face, she struggled to multitask.

Without her knowledge, something strong whacked her brother's pointing finger with one of swift smack, right on the end of the nail. Ouch. Ricky screamed through his nose as he jumped up and down in pain.

"Okay, what's next?" his sister asked after trapping each of the nunchaku in their respective holsters beneath her arms and replacing her bangs back to their rightful place, diagonally dangling dangerously against her eyebrow, with a toss of her head.

Ricky bit his lip as he winced in agony. "I think you're ready..."

"Excellent. And just in time too, because I'm pretty sure we just passed the senseless bonding quota for today by a ton."

And Leunga agreed. "Yeah, so get out of the way and then give me the nunchucks. It's time...for Leungie's lesson."

Lost in the Woods

"Oh my god! For the millionth time, we are not *lost!*"

Leunga nodded to his sister, who had been leading their pack for the better part of a few hours. "Oh yeah, I know. You're totally right. We're just taking the really really really *long* way around to nowhere. Forgotten by time as we trudge aimlessly all the way across the world and back again without even noticing. Ricky-Dicky, how would you describe our dire circumstances? Would you describe them as...dire?"

Ricky tightened the fresh boxer's tape wrapped around his knuckles and wrists—his weapon of choice for battling evil: his own hands—as he pondered the query. "Hmm, um, I guess I would call us...replaced...or displaced maybe? Misplaced? One of those is probably right."

Leunga was impressed. "Nice ass-word cluster!" He turned around and held up an open palm facing his brother as they walked along the trail. Ricky attempted to high-five his brother a few times unsuccessfully before they each shrugged and gave up.

Sydney rolled her eyes. "Yeah, okay, but add the word *temporarily*, please."

Temporarily Displaced in the Woods

"I like that. It gives me hope," Leunga said, smiling.

"We still don't have any idea where we are though..."

Sydney whimpered, "Please don't say it..."

"Nice going, Syd. You lost us."

"Yeah, way to make us lose, loser."

"Damn it, you dumb bastards. We are not *lost*!"

"We're going in circles, I can feel it. Look! I recognize this leaf."

"We aren't going in circles," Sydney insisted and noticed a bit of proof in her favor along the future path, so she quickly jogged ahead a couple of yards and picked up the item from the ground. "See?" she claimed, holding up a small rock with a large black dot colored on it. "To make sure we get back to where we started, I leave little marked stones where we've been, just like this...one..."

"Oh, yeah. Here's that energy bar wrapper Lou secretly dropped when you were coloring stupid rocks with your marker."

"Oh! Ha-ha! So *that's* where I put it. Lemme just get that..." Litterbug Leunga bent down grudgingly and picked up what he thought was a masterfully lost piece of trash and shoved it into his pocket.

"Huh. Maybe this path is a big circle then?" a girl asked timidly in hopes that no one would draw attention to her obvious lapse in a sense of direction like I just did. Sorry, Sydney.

"So how do we get out of here?!" her younger sibling inquired with eyes shooting through the trees in search of escape.

Sydney scratched her head. "Well, we could go back the way we came, but I think we would end up here again..."

Ricky grabbed his brother by the arm and pulled him closer in order to whisper, "We're trapped!"

"Hey, it's kinda fun though, right?" Wanting to draw the attention away from her dazzling mistake, one teen tried to improve their outlook. "Think of how much exercise we're getting!"

The boys lowered their eyebrows as they looked to each other in disapproval over the wasted words of their sister's unconvincing justification of their predicament. "I'm taking point now." Leunga made the sound of a gun cocking and held up an invisible pistol. "You three follow me." The siblings rounded a nearby corner indicated by a very large tree, took ten paces, and then stopped at their leader's command. "Here we are."

Ricky folded his arms across his back, beneath the sling pack he was forced to carry once again. "Where is here?"

"Here is this."

"What is here?"

"We is here."

"Here is nice."

"You guys shut up," Sydney fumed while she readjusted her tightly coiled necklette. "Why'd we stop?"

"It's time for lunch, Ms. 'Placed.'" Nice.

"Nice."

"How do you know that?"

"My stomach does an amazing thing where it growls when it's empty."

"Ricky, what time is it..." she asked without asking.

Flicking his wrist up, the chrono mage replied without replying, "Eighty-eight eighty-eight?"

Leunga shook his head while he wrapped his hands around the back of his brain. "It can't be that late already."

Sydney moved closer to her little brother and sneaked a peek at his watch. "Uh-oh."

"What uh-oh?" Ricky frowned.

"It's dead."

"Ugh, are you serious?!" he cried and pulled his wristwatch away from the sister to hold the timepiece up to his face, squeezing the buttons on its sides to find some remaining life in the frozen display holding time in place for eternity. "Dude, it was working great yesterday morning...!" he said and then sighed to himself when he recalled the event that started a series of equally stupid events that could be held accountable for so many things, including this. "Before we went in that dumb spider cave and Lou got all yelly." The quest claims another victim. And it was a nice watch, too. "Awesome."

"I wasn't yelling. I was powering up. Apologize."

Sydney looked left to Leunga through her concealing bangs before flicking her head to remove most of the obstruction. "Now we have to rely on your disgusting phone for the right time. Great."

"What about bootyboy's phone?"

"I left it back at camp." Where it was ringing at that very moment. Caller unknown.

"Errr...why do we even need to know the time?" Leunga scowled at Sydney as he rubbed his rumbling stomach in anticipation. "It makes no sense!"

"Uh, duh! So we know when we should stop and eat," she mocked.

"Uh, duh! We should just eat when we get hungry," he mocked.

"Uh, duh! Then we'll run out of food too quickly," Sydney mocked as her older sibling and she simultaneously glared up at their brother. Much mockery.

Noticing their demonic eyes focused on him, Ricky furrowed his brow. "Why are you looking at me?"

"Said the teenage vacuum."

"All right, I'll get the old phoner out..." Leunga grunted as he dove into the large pocket by his right knee. He fiddled with the contents of the pouch for dozens of silent seconds before ultimately pulling out his flask. Jiggling the silver cask by his ear, he moaned in aggravation.

Ricky stared at Leunga blankly while his older brother took a not-so-discreet swig from the thin canteen. As his stomach began to snarl and twist with vacuity, he looked at his partner's languid nature and snapped, "The phone!"

Leunga jumped. "Oh, yeah...one sec."

"Just tell us the time so we can all shut up," Sydney calmly suggested as she continued to look through the trees while wondering how she could have so easily let the group become lost in the woods.

"*Temporarily displaced*! Forgetful trash thing."

"Thanks, Leunga."

...Anyway...he nodded courteously to his little sister as he traded the flask for the phone, holding the device dangerously close to his eyes. Leunga commenced a sequence of commands, pressing a series of buttons in a very particular order. Too many buttons. "Okay, here we go. Wait."

Ricky scowled at the amount of time it was taking to simply state the hour. He glared at Leunga with confusion as he shook his watch. "Dude! Come on, what time is it? Isn't the clock just right there on the desktop?"

"It is on mine..."

"I'll tell you guys in one sec; I just gotta close this awesome game I bought last night after Rick passed out. Juggle Monkey. Your character shouts commands at a wild ape until it learns how to juggle...and...okay. Hold on, I accidently started a new game. Okay, hold on. I just have to beat this game and then I'll tell you. One sec."

Sydney bounced in place, showing severe signs of impatience as minutes flew by. "Hurry!"

Ricky tapped his crusty temple with a duo of fingers while he wrapped his other arm around his ribs, holding his gi shut. He glared at Leunga and shook his head. "Man, this is madness..."

Leunga shot a glare at his brother and raised his brow. "*Madness...?* I oughta kick you square in the chest for tha—" Rapidly redirecting his attention elsewhere when someone suddenly stole the electronics from his hand while his attention was away, he was forced to cancel his original thought and turn to his younger sister to beseech, "Hey, don't kill my monkey..."

The phone played a somber sound effect. "It's dead."

"God, if you just waited nicely it would've only been like thirty minutes!"

"It's not letting me exit out of this dumbass game." Sydney squeezed the device angrily. "Son of a bitch, it started a new game. Stupid phone. One sec."

"Be careful with the stupid phone. I am very literally still paying for that thing."

His younger sister pounded on the touch pad and replied, "You should've waited for your birthday and got it for free like me."

"We can't all trick Pop into getting us whatever she wants in great addition to a goddamn car, goddamn it."

"There we go! Finally...okay, it's—whoa—way after two." Sydney glanced up from the screen in surprise. "We should've stopped almost thirty minutes ago, but I feel like we just barely ate..."

"Obviously that was many hours ago, according to the expensive new clock."

Ricky lit up eagerly. "Can we eat?!"

"We can eat." Leunga nodded.

Excited that the group was finally taking a much-needed break from their rigorous—and senseless—hike, the lone backpacker struggled with his satchel, trying to remove the beast, only to have the sack become hopelessly tangled in the creases of his loose martial arts attire.

A smug Sydney was seen to snicker as she sneakily slid her older brother's phone into her pocket with a thieving smirk. After her success, she dropped her hands into her back pockets and quietly watched her younger sibling fight for his life with his robe for minutes on end.

Leunga glanced around, completely studying each tree his sight came into contact with in a matter of seconds. His attentiveness succumbed to his mind's wanderlust, enticing him to lose focus on the task at hand. Squinting at treetops and hovering over underbrush, he listened to the sound of his breathing in tune with the breeze unnoticeably weaving through the pines. Under the effects of a tranquil atmosphere, he had the sudden realization that he and some teenagers were actually on a legendary quest surrounded by a forest in search of something that may not even be there. He inhaled cautiously and asked, "Am I crazy, or is us being out here looking for a fight the wrong thing to be doing ever?"

With the first piece of his assignment accomplished, Ricky quickly unzipped their grandfather's old backpack before him, using the tearing sound of the zipper to conceal his muttered answer. "Both."

Sydney swiftly warned her older brother, "Don't even think about starting that Ricky-bitching too, fartface. I'm not going to be the only one feeling like I have to drag us all to the end of this shit, so don't go anywhere near those words again. Yeah. Okay. I get it. If yesterday had never happened, this would be the stupidest thing ever, but after watching you whirling around those glowy swords and seeing that big fuckin' wolf with my own eyes, I don't really think it's wrong to want to stop some kind of evil wizard with violence. It's not *right*, but I get it. I can understand that we need to make sure it gets done. That's why it's us out here and not somebody else." The female furrowed her brow and shuddered at the odd sensation of sounding like Leunga and validating his spontaneous quest. "Shit..."

Leunga, empowered by his sister's shocking reminder of his aptitude and abilities in the world of his new existence, stood by her side and rested his elbow on her shoulder with his other hand on his hip—which remains to be an unnatural position given their vast difference in height. He being relatively short and she being relatively tall. I went over this already. The eldest spoke with newfound confidence, saying, "You're right! Now that we know what we're up against for true it's not so bad. These ugly bastards are kinda slow. Plus the swords make it so they can't even hurt us. Really takes away the suspense of danger if you think about it." Don't think about it.

Ricky watched Sydney agree with their brother and sighed at the sight while he held a hand inside the suspended rucksack in his clutches. As he glanced into the pack he added, "You know, before this *vacation*, my biggest problem this summer was avoiding my friends and Becky... But now I have to avoid getting killed too..."

"So wait, you *weren't* trying to avoid being killed *before* the trip?"

For no apparent reason—and without any apparent inflection—a young man with a pair of swords strapped to his back shouted, "Both." Just as he was feeling a steady sense of calm in his party's *displaced* environment, Leunga had a sudden fit of panic when he realized something was missing from his life. Plunging his mitts into every oversized pocket he could find, the pothead asked the world, "Where's my phone?!"

A young lady replied, "I do not know."

"Shit...did I drop it or something?" he questioned as his eyes flew around the dusty path they had trekked too many times before.

"Shut up."

Reaching a few fingers through the messy crop of crunchy locks beneath the well-positioned cap atop his head, Leunga scratched the concerns racing through his mind over the loss of his telephone. "Okay, well, if we see it on the way back around, someone remember to pick it up for me."

"I said shut up."

Ignoring the noise up until that point, Ricky rummaged through the sack as he took his siblings' orders. "What flavor do you guys want?"

Losing interest in his conundrum, Leunga looked to the trees with a thought of a different variety. "I will have a...green one, and the lady will have raisin."

"Ew!" Sydney objected. "Don't order for me, bastard breath... I hate the raisin. They use yellow grapes. It's gross..."

"You always loved the yellow ones when you were little! You ate them like this..." Her older partner proceeded to devour the imaginary raisins in the palms of his hands like a ravenous farm animal. Curious currant consumption. So unrefined.

Sydney could not recall an instance when she enjoyed yellow raisins, or ate them in such a way, but she had forgotten much of her childhood as the years went by. "How do you remember that? I can't even remember that..."

Leunga put a finger to his brain. "My mind is sharp. Like ice." Melted ice.

"Whatever. All that matters is that I don't like them *now*."

"Ooh, how picky for you."

"I'm not *picky*; I just have very high taste standards. Something *you* wouldn't know about. I don't just put anything in my mouth unless I can get something out of it—" Freezing her words where they were, Sydney's makeup-laden lids rolled shut and she gave an exasperated sigh at the awkwardness of her final statement in her present company, and the undoubtedly disgusting nature of Leunga's upcoming feedback. "Oh shit." Familiar with her older brother's history of sexually explicit verbiage regardless of company, Sydney knew what to expect from her misstep. Hoping to avoid any further referral to her possible allusion of oral carnality—no matter how secretively nonexistent her experience in the field of lust may be, despite the evidence to the contrary represented in her presented choice of alternative style—she quickly continued, "I mean, I don't *eat* anything unless I like the taste, or for its nutritious value. Food. Trying to stay skinny, you know? I knew today would suck monkeys..."

Seeing the possibilities for lewdness awaiting, Leunga smirked at her comments while he tried to find the most demeaning reply in his arsenal. He quickly turned to Ricky, who, at the time of his elder siblings' timely argument, was tapping his large metal watch in an attempt to resuscitate the

device while holding a protein bar in his teeth. Leunga shot a greedy glance at
Sydney, but noticed the obvious discomfort in her wandering expression; and
in a generous gift of brothery sisterish friendshipping, he consciously chose
not to comment on the crassness at hand and to spare her the embarrassment
of such a mistake. Plus, that was just too gross, even for him. She's his sister,
for crying out loud!

Thoroughly confused by his own behavior, the bladed boy scoffed
and gave a single nod to his little brother. "Yeah. Little thief probably didn't
even like the delicious taste of my extravagant *name-brand* whiskey either.
What a baby."

The youngest teen jutted his chin in agreement to the formless sound
of his eldest sibling's voice. "Uh-huh..."

Expecting a response more grotesque and uncomfortably vulgar in
her brothers' presence, Sydney's eyes went wide with unexpected shock
aimed at what was actually said as she laughed nervously. "Heh! I'm can't—I'm
not old enough to drink! What were we talking about...? I've never even had—
whiskey, did you say?" She shook her head and looked away. "Nope."

"Sure."

Sydney bit her upper lip, pondering how much information her
brother knew about *that* night...How could he know? No one else was home.
Oh great, now *I* want to know. She shook it off and mumbled something like,
"Just give me a peach."

Ricky reached into his magical bag and pulled out a ripe peach, one
of many different varieties of raw fruit to choose from in the pack. "Here you
go," he said quickly as he tossed the produce her way.

Catching the orb with one hand, she glared at it with confusion. "I
meant a peach protein bar, not an actual—never mind! This is way better."
Sydney sank her fangs into the juicy goodness, causing a reservoir of liquid to
dribble down her chin and splash against her shirt. She chewed the meal
slowly as she glanced down at the atrocity. "Aw, shit!"

"Language, young lady!" Leunga snapped off too much of his green protein bar between his teeth and spoke with a full mouth. "Use more language!"

Ricky ripped open his ration, remarking, "Hey, Syd, you got some crap on your tank top."

She growled angrily. "Fuck! Could this day suck any more?!"

"What the hell is that?" Leunga asked and chewed with vigor as he pointed a single pinky finger along the path before them.

"Was that there when we came around before?" someone slim wondered. "Looks like somebody's bike..." Suddenly filled with alarm at the high probability that another human being was close by—a person with eyes who might use those eyes to see his awful attire—Ricky nonchalantly hurled his lunch into the trees and dropped his hands behind his back, carefully concealing the wording on his tail behind his entwined fingers.

"Hey! Ideas from me. Firstly, we need horses or emus. This walking thing is bullshit. Also, let's find that thing's owner and ask her how the hell we get out of this damn maze—*or* we can hide the bike and run away! Or maybe...something like...hmmm..." His words trailed off, searching for their own direction.

As Leunga finished articulating his masterfully incomplete crime, a man's face appeared, peeking around a tree far down the path, only a few dozen feet from the abandoned transportation.

"Oh...never mind the second half. There's the guy," the cannabis kid commented, clearly crestfallen.

The man near the bicycle kept his face poking out from the safety of his tree as he glanced at the hikers far from his hideout. He watched the trio attentively until Leunga took one step toward him and he ducked behind the pine, reappearing a few seconds later slowly. Sydney squinted hard in an attempt to see the cyclist's face more clearly. As the man poked his head around the tree once more, she could tell that it wasn't the same attractive stranger as before—this man was much more hairy, and not a particularly handsome fellow. His brow was heavy, almost as if it were covering his eyes. His nose was average, but slightly discolored around the nostrils, perhaps by blood. His lips were thin, so much so that they were undetectable from her distance, but blackened all the same. And finally, his hair was incredibly spiky, much more than Ricky's fauxhawk. The man also seemed to have stylized his ample beard as well, because it too was as spiked as the rest of his mane. She strained to see him any clearer, but to no avail. "He kinda looks like he's hurt. Maybe he fell off his bike."

"Maybe an animal got to him. He's way-ass scared of us. But we are not animals?!"

Sydney turned to her bladed brother and grimaced. "What if one of the mage's *things* found him? It definitely knows that you have those swords by now. Maybe it's been sending out tons of giant monsters into the forest to search for us..."

"What a terrible thing to witness for someone who's not as awesome as us." Leunga took another step forward, causing the man to hide momentarily. "Huh! How the hell can we help him if he's gonna keep doing that?! And furthermuch, why help him at all?"

"Duh, because I just barely finished saying that it's probably *our* fault!"

Ricky pointed with a nudge of one shoulder of his occupied arms, palms pressing ham. "You could call out to him and see if he needs help. Or, you know, see if he can tell us the way out of this crudhole."

Sydney bit her thumbnail as she shoved her older brother in the back and whispered, "Ask him. In *English*."

"Me?! Why don't one of *you* ask him?!"

"You are the loudest person alive."

"Yeah, well, that must make you two the luckiest...because I'm here." Leunga carefully removed his cap and gently deposited it on one of Ricky's broad shoulders—either one, they are equally magnificent. He cleared his throat and formed a fantastic megaphone with his hands, drawing in a deep breath and shouting, "Ahoy! Excuse me mister, but are you better than okay there?!"

The man stared at them blankly with shadowy sockets for a moment before nodding slowly.

Leunga called back, "Oh! Good! Um. Hey! Do you know how to get out of this endless trail?! Me and my little peeps are kinda temporarily displaced right now. Can you help us the hell out?"

The man smiled politely with his clenched lips and nodded again.

"Radical!" The noise machine stopped shouting and turned to Sydney. "Ew, did I just say radical? Faux pas!" He continued to yell, "I mean...gnarly, dude! Most excellent and tubular and such. Hey, also, were you here when that huge noise hit yesterday?" Leunga snorted. "Seriously though, what was that? Am I right?!"

The man continued to smile motionlessly.

Leunga waited an entire moment for the supposed cyclist to respond before he took in a deep breath and shouted, "I patiently await your reply—aw, fuck it." He shook his head in disgust as he addressed his little peeps. "This guy is a dick...why do we keep running into quiet fuckers today?"

The coy little smile on the man's face began to grow wider at a slow pace. Growing and growing and growing, it became a large grin showcasing a beautiful set of perfectly white front teeth; however, it didn't stop growing. Very quickly, the corners of his mouth extended far beyond the possibility of any lips known to humanity. Reaching from one edge of his face to the other, his smile had literally stretched from ear to ear—if he in fact possessed any ears. With a grin as broad as a football on its side, the man gradually opened his mouth, revealing triple rows of fangs with no resemblance to his brilliant front stratum of teeth—several sets of chompers that were equally as broad as his grin. The face gnashed its tines together as its eyes opened to uncover large globes of orange light, and the rest of the creature slowly emerged from behind the hideaway.

Ricky sighed with relief as he removed his hands from his cheeks. "Oh good, I thought it was somebody hiking."

Friendly Sands That Smile Back

Unhidden by its tree, the fiend sat on the path, staring at the gawking group while blinking its bulging eyes filled with light like two electric bulbs and grinning its twisted mouth happily. Appearing on request, voltaic orange symbols coursed over its short, dark gold fur—like a fiery tiger without stripes— much in the same fashion as the yellow lights on the giant wolf from the previous day, but concentrated more on its deceivingly manlike face and the sides of its wiry feline proportions, with thick spirals of neon runes around the base of each of its few dozen immense, half-yard-long, light brown quills sparsely sprouting from all over the back of its torso, along with several larger quills protruding from the tip of its lengthy tail. Shifting its lightweight body forward, it stood, reaching a maximum height of roughly three-and-a-half feet on legs like that of a cheetah with overstretched paws bedecked in luminous claws completely created by its web of sunset markings. Atop each of its shoulders nestled a tightly folded clustering of thick quills unlit by its curse, held closely against its ribs for purposes unknown. All in all, the vision of an ancient actor hopelessly maintaining its false identity sat there on the path, one hundred yards or so from the triumvirate, persistently wearing the unattainable grin on its bearded visage as if to welcome them to the world of madness and monstrous mayhem they themselves made.

Sydney turned to her brothers to ask, "What the hell is this?"

"Definitely not the owner of a fine ci-bycle, I can tell you that," answered her smaller sibling. "Looks like a big spiky kitty-cat...with a fugly face." Leunga clicked his ring-shaped fingers together to reconstruct his hand-binoculars and zoomed in on the smiling monster blinking happily at their group. He nodded. "Yeah. A *really* ugly cat-type person, but this one is more cat than person, and I'm an expert on cat-type persons. My best character on Fantasy World is a catgirl...but she's a hot ass."

"Fuckin' dork. Does April know you're a freak?"

"She has one too. We make them kiss."

Ricky squinted at the animal, distraught by the continuance of yesterday's struggle against the impossible. He swallowed dryly as he noticed the many pointed spikes covering their prickly foe with a head of hair that greatly resembled a faintly brunet version of his own—but far more treacherous—and quickly came to the conclusion that its coarse facial mane was most likely constructed entirely of tiny quills as well; though, it was difficult to determine with certitude at his great, and welcome, distance from the beast. Ricky quickly wrapped his right hand over his left wrist to test the strength and durability of his combat support tape as he whimpered, "I dunno if this one is gonna be that easy, you guys. I mean, how are we gonna avoid all of its freaky giant pokers...?" Filled with a sudden wave of humiliation as he realized he was preparing himself to enter battle with a masked monster that would have only been a nightmare two days earlier, he held his tongue to keep himself from feeling any more stupider, but it was too late for that. And too late for me too...

"Don't worry about that!" Leunga reassured his younger brother. "Remember? That giant guy yesterday was super slow."

"That...doesn't answer my question."

Agreeing, his brother continued, "I bet you millions of dollars that this thing is the same way."

Sydney blindly groped for one of the weapons secured to her hip while she stared along the path warily, and remarked, "But this one's so small." Comparably, much smaller than the bestial Fenrir, it was like measuring a housecat against a normal-sized timber wolf. I assume those are animals—do not correct me if I'm wrong; I prefer not to know. "It might not be a big turd like the other one was. You never know."

While it may have paled in comparison to its lupine counterpart, this new demon was still relatively enormous, and although it was not quite as brawny as a true greater cat, anyone in their right mind would still label it a threat, especially after the creature crouched to the ground within an instant like a feline preparing to pounce, pulsing its slender leg muscles in alternating rounds.

Bracing for the inevitable onset of aggression, Ricky secured the pack across his back and altered himself into his standard defensive stance, holding his claw-formed hands high and keeping his knees bent and supple. The tight turquoise sweatpants stretched themselves constrictively over his thighs and buns, retaining their defining form as they too readied for the brawl. He threw a few words of worry to his brother while his eyes locked on the monster. "I think it's getting ready to come kill us. Shouldn't you, uh, be getting out the automatic katana or something?"

Leunga brushed away the threat and assured, "Nah, we got time. Look how far away it is."

In the blink of a wink, the smiling performer shot toward them along the path with incredible speed. Rapidly bridging the gap to its prey, it grinned as it huffed along the trail, covering a dozen yards in a matter of seconds. Each of the siblings' eyes widened in response to its unnatural haste as its faint image became clear. Sydney hurriedly threw her attention to her belt out of desperate need to uncloister her weapons, shouting, "Shit balls!"

MANTICORE. Legendary man-eating beast from the kingdoms of Persia. Known as a martyaxwar in the original Persian, the manticore is a devious demon that uses its triple rows of jagged teeth to swallow its prey whole, bones and all. Few travelers have survived an encounter with one of these creatures, but most of those that have managed to catch a glimpse describe the animal as having the carriage of a powerful lion with broad wings sprouting from the shoulders and a long tail tipped with enormous, hazardous thorns. Deceptive by their nature, manticores possess the face of a bearded

*human and use a call of beauty created by a roar with the quality of a brass
instrument. A nomad in need of direction may hear this lilting tone before
seeing the smiling face of a kind soul watching from afar and choose to greet
the friendly stranger, only to discover too late that it is a horrific villain intent
on feasting.*

Preoccupied with removing her nunchaku from their holsters
through her belt, Sydney panicked and neglected to keep a careful watch on
the beast barreling down on her group's location. Letting their instincts lead
the way, Ricky and Leunga darted off the path in opposite directions to take
cover from the rails of the luminous locomotive, leaving their dearly distracted
sister behind. Shooting at the trail in time to see the Manticore's gruesome
grin bounding at her from a few yards away, the girl's gawp moved up to meet
with the fiery glow of the beast's gaze just as she vacantly felt a pair of arms
wrap forcefully around her waist from behind.

Leunga locked his embrace around his sister and pulled her swiftly
off the path, taking refuge behind a tree as the nightmare ran by. It glanced at
them with a smile while it continued down the path, only to disappear into the
bosky backwoods and bushes beyond. Leunga and Sydney panted in
temporary relief as the disquieting chirping of the monstrosity faded. "*That*
was close."

"Thanks," the teen in tattered jeans exhaled in relief and agony,
having rediscovered her cruel collision's contact point from the previous day—
with the help of her older brother's increasingly constricting arms. "Damn it.
You can let go of me now..."

"Are you absolutely sure?!"

Sydney quietly scrambled to wrestle her way out of her older
brother's forceful clutch and eventually escaped. Holding a gentle touch
against her unquestionably bruised contusion, she sidled the tree by the boy
and joined him in listening to the atmosphere.

Leunga panicked when he realized they had forgotten something. "Oh shit! Where the fuck is Tricksy?!"

"Hey, you lanky bastard!" Sydney shouted uncomfortably to their absent companion. "We *had* a strategy! Remember?! *Stay together!*"

Silence followed, broken moments later by the sound of a brass section moving swiftly through the trees in a large circle around the two. Underbrush shifted out of sight of Leunga and Sydney as they attempted to pinpoint the location of the monstrosity, but the disturbance of the flora was inaccurate and indiscernible.

The shorter one whispered with deep intent, "Did you just hear a *trumpet?*"

"Did *you?*"

Peeking his face over the edge of their tree, Leunga coiled himself around its crust, tightly gripping his coniferous cover in search of marching bands that were nowhere to be seen. Following her tiny brother's lead, Sydney leaned out above him as a totem pole of vigilance and looked for signs of either their little brother or the other monster. After practically no time at all, Leunga gradually slid down the slick bark of the barricade and fell into the dirt without his occupied coinvestigator noticing. Landing on his elbows, he instantly sprang straight up and smacked the back of his head against his leaning tower of sister's teeth. Sydney's head flew back in shock while she cupped her hand over her traumatized lips. Leunga glanced to her and calmly added, "I don't see it. Let's go on the path."

Probably bleeding, she nodded silently.

The duo tiptoed into the open road. Clouds of dust pierced by beams of shadowshine hung low in the air at their sides while they slowly surveyed the ferns and trunks. They squinted into the endless void of monuments to nature, only to realize that nothing wanted to be found.

Suddenly, a giant needle fwhipped into the dirt by their feet. Leunga glanced around quickly, whirling in place a few times as he asked his sister in a dangerous whisper, "Did you hear that?!"

Her eyes traveled in a large circle through the base of the trees and she replied, "Maybe…"

As the pothead protector was preparing to demean his sibling's unacceptable response to his question, his attention was abruptly gripped by the pointy ears and jostled to life at the sight of an enormous foot-and-a-half pin poking the path several inches away from his foot. Thin and pointed like a fencing sword, the needle was far more flimsy and pliable than most maiming weapons. Mildly threatening. The fact that it was able to penetrate the beaten path is astounding. He pointed to the ground in haste and hollered, "A clue!" Wrapping his hand around the high end of the quill and ripping it from the dirt, he held it up like a sword to gasp, "*Mein Gott!* What do you suppose did *this*?! Someone tried to kill my shoes!" Whipping the switch back and forth, the stooge stood mesmerized by his own actions. "Ooh, this is cool. This thing is so long, but it's not as hard as I'd like."

Before anyone else had the chance, Sydney blurted out, "That's what *she* said," causing her to wince in embarrassment at her unexpectedly abrupt vulgarity. And she was concerned about her brother's possible lewdness. Such a change ten minutes makes.

Leunga removed the shaft from his sucking mouth and whacked the pointed tip against his tongue a few more times before asking, "Well, did she happen to say where it came from?" Suddenly, the quill in his clutches burst into a wisp of dark mist and splashed his face with cool, dry smoke. Frowning, he appeared disappointed. "That is just less impressive."

Sydney considered the angle at which the object protruded from the trail and used her basic physics class knowledge to calculate its trajectory, forcing her to look up. Her mostly uncovered eyes met with a broad smile looking down on her from halfway up a robust pine. The grinning gargoyle gripped its perch tightly, aiming its body toward the ground. The Manticore opened its enormously broad mouth, dripping with saliva, and asked in a hollow, grinding, pipe-organ-produced voice, "Lohst?"

Leunga's eyes went wide as his focus darted up the tree to the great pretender with its neon claws puncturing the bark. "Dude!" he said to his sister. "That thing talked!"

"See? It's not an animal. I told you they talk—hey!" Sydney became enraged as she realized what the fiend had done. "We are not fucking *lost*, you shit! We are temporarily displaced!"

The creature clacked its rows of teeth and laughed like iron. "Ye'll nae faind ehnehtheng ef yeh wolk en cearcles...foolesh lasseh."

Rolling his eyes, Leunga muttered, "Great, now it won't shut the fuck up."

One step over the line. Though the words were somewhat lost in the mire of a highland dialect—something which she could swear the other monstrosity was able to overcome—the tall girl's outlook shifted once more to the side of putting an end to the Summoner's malicious deeds, starting with this belligerent actor. All of her preconceived notions of animal hospitality aside, Sydney scowled angrily. "Bitchface!" she shouted. "Come down here so I can beat the crap out of you—oh, wha—wait, let me get ready first."

Leunga's gaze transferred from the beast on the tree to the tomboy athlete on the path as his sister noisily grappled with one of the two weapons trapped within her belt. Starting with the nunchaku on her right side—in her sibling's sight—she fidgeted with unhinging the duo of batons without an ounce of accomplishment of the task. Staring at her struggles with mild indifference as she changed her attempts to the opposite weapon on her left—not in her sibling's sight—Leunga looked up at her face and watched her annoyed expression flare while she hastily jostled the long black bludgeons snagged against her hips. Unable to contain his natural ability to annoy any longer, he blew a lung of air through his loose lips and made an impatient noise.

Sydney flicked her fluctuating bangs to the side and glared at her brother. "Could you not stare at me, please? Goddamn."

Staring with newfound determination to stare at her, he asked her a logical quandary. " *Why* do you have both if you can't even use *one*?"

"Shut up!" she replied curtly.

Leunga continued to stare as he imposed a follow-up in a contributory tone. "Do you want help? I'm never ever getting my hands anywhere near your pants or pieces, but you suck at this. I could've had those out and pummeled that ugly guy on the tree into a billion shards by now."

"Oh, yeah, you're a *pro*," Sydney mocked. "Just keep an eye on it." She motioned at the awaiting Manticore with a nod and replied, "This one is mine."

"Any day now." The slacker slid his fingers under his ravenous brown bangs and rubbed his forehead slowly with both hands, moaning. "Waiting. We are waiting for you, and this is the optimus of sucks. Was I to rely on your support at some point during this adventurous fight? I only bewilder because you take too long to arm up. Why didn't you just keep them shits in you back pockets or something?"

The girl growled at the revelation. "That is exactly something you should have said back at camp! Nut-ass!"

"But I just thought of it—oh, god!" Leunga slapped his hands against his left cheek and spoke carefully with his tongue locked between his molars. "I bit my canker sore!"

"Ugh, this sucks! They were so easy to slip in...Why the hell are they stuck?!"

Jamming his tongue against the inside of his face, Leunga tested and tasted the structure of his cheeky injury while he waited for Sydney to bring the pain to their bristly foe. A thought not occurring to him at that moment was why the monster had not taken advantage of their obvious unready status and allowed the pair a gratuitous formulation of their defenses to its inconvenience—but that is at the Manticore's discretion. Leunga slouched by the willowy young woman at his left and propped his hands around his hips. He began swaying from side to side, when Sydney made a startling announcement.

"Ha! I got one out...wait...*half* of it anyway..."

The second half of the nunchaku held steadfast with its grip on her metal-studded belt, compelling Sydney to pull forcefully at the liberated end with her inexperienced right hand. With one final jerk of the baton, she freed its sister from imprisonment. As the hearty club skyrocketed out of its holster, the swinging edge dragged powerfully over the broad side of Leunga's unprotected face. His head twisted around and he yowled while his sister brought the flailing baton to an abrupt stop over her shoulder like a baseba— *softball* bat. In an act of confidence, she locked her eyes on the monster in the tree and smirked. The teen swung the nunchuck forward and whirled it at her side blindly for a few moments, unknowingly hitting the open cudgel against her brother's elbow before she made the transition to catch the weapon under her combat neutral armpit, where she miscalculated and whacked herself in the breast from beneath. The Manticore had yet to move, and it was already winning.

In a mild daze, Leunga wobbled in place and held a hand to his temple. He shook his confusion and attempted to establish his sense of presence. "What is? What's goin' on...? What's all this then?"

The weapon dangled at Sydney's side as she wrapped her free arm over her chest. "Son of a bitch! I knew that would happen...!"

Leunga's eyes blinked out of sync. "A new what?"

"Yep," Sydney grunted, "that is painful."

The warrior shook his head slowly. "Naw, it's not so bad...I can still see." He waved his palm toward his face. "Out of *one* eye."

"Ugh, gonna have another bruise...this fuckin' stupid day..."

The Manticore watched the proceedings silently, soaking up information; after all, there was plenty of garbage that needed sponging.

Utilizing the time-honored healing technique of utter distraction, Sydney hopped on alternating feet back and forth from side to side and spoke calmly to herself. "Okay, just shake it off, girl. Just shake it off...you're fine."

Leunga followed her orders and jiggled his face. "Okay, shaking it all off."

The two eldest siblings alleviated their respective pains as much as possible given the short amount of time they were allotted before a flapping of cloth caused them to relocate their concentration back to the beast.

With a respectable span of at least a dozen feet, the Manticore spread its wings as it crouched against the tree. Connected quills thicker than the rest of its rapiers formed the structural base of its bat-like gliders while the broad patagium became alight with giant runes coating the back of each entire membrane protruding from its feline shoulders. The glow of its markings shined through the thinly stretched skin while the creature kept its massive wings unfurled to flap a gust of wind toward the gawking humans below in a plea for their attention. "Thess aes soo veereh ehntertieneng, baut Ah've bean waeteng setch eh loang taem fir thess. Wewhd yeh kaindleh combe weth meh? Ah wewhd trooleh ehppreaciette eht."

Leunga turned to his sister and pointed angrily at the monster. "What the hell kind of accent is that? Welshy or Zealander?"

"Doi! It's Scottish. The Summoner was from Scottish-land, so that makes it Scottish."

"Oh, yeah...so what did it just say?"

"I have no idea."

With a smile, the demon clawed its way around the tree trunk and launched, floating its way over the path while sounding its misleading roar. The Manticore flew from tree to tree, landing on one to glance back at the siblings before hopping to the next further down the trail.

"Hang on a tick. I think it wants us to follow it..."

Sydney scoffed, discreetly holding her new injury. "Fuck that! We gotta go catch Ricky before he runs home with the food."

With a hazy nod, Leunga took the lead as he and his sister turned around along the path and began walking away from the flying nuisance. Lagging behind a bit, his little sister studied the underbrush in search of their missing sibling—shouldn't be too hard to find; he's a skyscraper. The shaggy man in his early twenties drew in a breath for a shout to distinguish their younger brother's bearing when he was halted by outside forces.

The duo stopped quickly in shock as the Manticore landed with a thud in front of them abruptly, blocking their march. The swordsman's eyes flared with aggravation as he addressed the beast. "Please move."

The monster shook its head and cackled. The white centers of its orange eyes darted between the pair as if waiting for something to happen. Leunga was the first to react, hiking up his constantly plummeting pants with one hand hooked through a contemptibly empty belt loop and extending a complimentary middle finger at the abomination with one other hand. Sydney responded in kind, aiming both of her middle fingers at the Manticore as her brother raised his eyebrows with a kind smile for their obstacle and said, "Oh, I see. You want summa this, fuckface?!"

Unpredictably enticed by the offer, the demon's eyes brightened, and it trembled in anticipation. Gripping the overfilled, oversized pockets slipping down his scrawny thighs, Leunga lifted his tan shorts like a skirt and rushed forward to take a spontaneous kick at the cat's obnoxious grin but missed when it leapt back out of reach. Following the majestic punt, the pothead's untied boot continued onward in its momentum, easily slipping off his foot and arcing backward over his head silently, eventually landing with a thump against Sydney's bracelets behind him. Ceasing her double-insulting-gesture in a damaging slam, she made a horrified face that would've gone well with a scream and retracted her hands to her heart instinctively to guard against more agony, subsequently releasing the solitary weapon from her previously-occupied-middle-fingerless grip. As her nunchuck fell to the dirt, Sydney jumped back in surprise at the sudden strike from her brother and promptly twisted her ankle on an oddly placed stone with a large black dot on the top. Elevating her possible sprain, she hopped aside on her uninjured foot and howled, "Fuck! Today sucks!"

Leunga balanced on his sock-covered foot to lift his remaining shoe above the filthy ground, bouncing on one leg as he raised his fists up to his chest, keeping his thumbs and pinkies safely outstretched in preparation for the punches he would issue. Double shaka signs. Hang so much loose. The braggart boy was just about to break some noses, when he spied someone vaguely familiar along the trail ahead and paused.

Looking like a lone superhero standing with cape adrift as he watches over the injured city, Ricky appeared suddenly far down the path. His face was awash in anger while he stared at the Manticore from beneath his thick black eyebrows. Sinking into an attack pose, he yelled with enough force to draw in every combatant's attention. "*Hai!*"

The beast's bulging eyes widened as it glared over the folded wing on its shoulder to the hidden fighter who had traveled in an inappropriate direction; it threw a supplementary smile to the losers at its side and quickly sprinted into the trees again, sounding its horn and fading from sight within seconds.

Leunga hopped over to the misplaced footwear by his springing sister and slipped it on. "Chicken shit!" he accused and sighed at the disappearance of the devil. "Bloody hell."

Sydney gingerly set her wonky foot to the ground and used her brother's shoulder as an appropriately heighted crutch while she nodded in agreement with his statement. "What a tosser."

For Use in Self-Defense Only

Ricky dashed off the path, unknowingly leaving his inattentive sister in the beast's course. Smashing his way through ferns without concern for the plants' well-being, the guy glided over the dirt and rounded a wide-trunked pine to catch his pounding heart. He huffed heavily under the weight of his cumbersome burden of aiding his brother's quest, leaning into the tree with his broad shoulders, tensely keeping his back pressed against the gripping bark of his asylum. Pulsing muscles prepared for whatever may come next. Holding his breath, his wide eyes followed the blind sound of the monster thumping through the dirt behind his back before it disappeared down the path. The disquiet of his racing nerves was all that he had left in his unnerving new world.

A distressing stillness echoed over the bushes and firs jamming his vision. The muffled shock of his brother off in the distance said something similar to, "Oh shit! Where the fuck is Tricksy?!"

His sister then called out for him in the wrong direction. "Hey, you lanky bastard! We *had* a strategy! Remember?! *Stay together*!"

Ricky exhaled angrily under his breath and quietly muttered, "Shut up..."

Spending endless consecutive hours with his elder siblings was undoubtedly taking its toll. Generally growing weary of his recently high levels of tandem activity with Leunga and Sydney, the tallest of the trio was very near the point of almost being fed up with their company. Being grouped together with them was widely atypical in the history of their relationship, and it was especially rare for all three to be alone together at once for more than an hour at a time. Combine that with the fact that he didn't get enough sleep the previous night, and it's no surprise that he was sorely tested and tired of dealing with them at all.

But in a blink, survival became his prison—kept in captivity by fear and paranoia. Like the tree at his back, he had become motionless and still; only the flapping folds of his martial arts robe fluttered in the wind. Holding his breath out of fear that something other than himself may hear his trembling lungs, the statuesque Ricky rolled his vision over the forest before him in search of that which cannot be. He absorbed every tiny shift in his surroundings, becoming wild. The sudden confusing timbre of a trumpet in the distant trees at his back caused him to drop into a squatting position, landing with hands on the dirt.

Camouflage percentages in the negative thirties, he knew it was no use to try to hide out in the open wearing bright summer colors. As quietly as he could manage, he scurried away from the sound in a squatting crawl, taking refuge behind large ferns as he made his best attempt at following the previous trail blindly. His feral brown eyes scoured the pines while he slowly scampered from one hideout to the next, slinking through an overgrowth of underbrush. No sign of the monster was present, but he would not let any part of his guard down without first gaining a bearing on its location, if it even existed at all. The thought of letting his partners know of his current condition crossed his mind, but he was unable to allow himself to shout any form of reassuring reconnaissance. The fear gripped him tightly.

Alone at last.

Desperately seeking sanctuary from his fateless predicament, he found that wishing wouldn't solve the problem, but it helped. While he skulked from fern to fern in an attempt to elude the battle, moments adding up to minutes slithered by slowly while he strained to listen for any evidence that could lead to the whereabouts of his fellow alien individuals—be they human or, more likely, monsters. A large shrub with a concave opening presented him with the means to hide from his problems. Ricky crawled into the maw and knelt in the shadowy dirt, binding himself with gripping arms to contain his fear. Hiding like a stone, unnoticed and untouched under the greenery, he rocked back and forth on his knees and hopelessly waited for the all clear to rejoin his brother and sister on what should have logically been an average summer hike.

The blare of a horn echoed over the path once again as he tried not to picture his circumstances. He clenched his eyes tight. Ricky was electrified with shock, brought on by another auspicious reminder that the tenuous comfort of wilderness isolation he felt solely in the presence of his family could so easily be broken by the suggestion that they were never alone. A surge of thoughts suddenly bounced through his skull. He didn't need to be there. He never did. He didn't belong in the forest. This was not his fate. Such an uncontrollable string of events led him along so far before pulling him unsuspectingly into another predicament of his life like so many inopportune moments before, allowing the flow to take him where it may by whoever wanted control over him at the time, so that he could aim to please. Yet somewhere along the line, he forgot to keep track of his own desires, to give something to appease the neglected and forgotten boy always by his side.

He so clearly saw himself being two people at once for reasons he could never comprehend—two lives each expecting and wanting something different. Why did it have to be like this? Why couldn't he just force himself to be the assertive boy he wanted to be? Why couldn't he express his desires as they actually were and not as how they actually sounded to others, instead of trading his comfort for affability? If only he could go back to that day when he helped his sister in peril on the rooftop... Would he have been able to change anything? Had he not rushed out of the dojo and waited five minutes before walking home, would he be in their living room at that very moment instead of fearing for his life and potential humiliation in the woods?

But why stop there? Keep going. Go back before becoming friends with Hunter—back to a time when rolling tiny toy trucks through the dirt was all that really mattered—before the awkward expectations and selfish hedonism began engulfing his existence with the future. Adolescent leaders preparing to rule the world in the halls of a high school, all the while, fulfilling every flippant desire that crosses their mind without heed to the effect it may have on any other soul. Deeply buried flashes of his past fired through his mind without restraint, constantly bringing unrelated embarrassments back to life. Damaging events caused by the weakness of his boldness. The nature of his behavior, building an anchor in a cell of his own design. Like a sponge soaking in all of the pain and using it to fuel his character, assembling a power plant of angst.

Core critical. Meltdown. His eyes shot open in a fiery explosion of frustration and disappointment at his lack of will, burning with a deep-seated anger at his controlling siblings, with a growing torment over their oblivious dismissal of their dangerous circumstances and the sudden manifestation of the Summoner. In the ambivalence of fear and hate, the midteen's fight-or-flight reflex kicked in full charge. He felt his fighting spirit struggle against his natural instinct—that magic set of rules authored by all ancestors and forever burned into the genome of every living thing. His impulse dictated that he needed to run, and yet he didn't. Muscular education was fueling his dawning appetite for aggression. His will drove him to fight; after all, the quicker they weeded out the Summoner, the sooner he could go home and rid himself of one set of problems.

Erupting uncontrollably, Ricky frenziedly threw the backpack he was constantly required to haul deeper into the confines of his hideout for safekeeping. Maneuvering quickly out of his den, he stormed around the fern previously concealing his position and reentered the path. A sharp gust of wind struck him, pulling his open armor outward like a waving banner floating freely over the ocean as he angrily advanced on the feline in his slightly tight pants. Staring at the beast crouched before his hopping brother and sister through his furious brow, the boy stopped his march, ground his teeth, and snarled.

Ricky inhaled quickly and howled a halting, "*Ha!*" Eight years in the making. Pro karate. His hidden skills bloomed, revealing the buried seedlings of his combat development. Dropping his hips closer to the ground, he took on a wide crouch. With his left hand locked in the form of a slicing dagger, he thrust his arm forward with fingers held skyward while pulling his tight right fist back stomach-high. His target quickly turned nervously, making its long quills stand on end in surprise. After flashing an increasingly worried grin to the pugilist's elder siblings, it abruptly dashed off the trail and disappeared into the underbrush while sounding its horn of war.

The customary thrill of engagement was missing. This was not exhibition. This was survival. Ricky's disciplined disposition held back his desire to mercilessly bring his kung fu wrath upon everything that exploited his nature—which, of course, included his brother and sister—and to use his extensive training only at the appropriately intended moments. These moments. The lightly tanned skin over his arms and thighs became taut as his limbs filled with blood; his lean muscles tensed in the anticipation of the impending battle ahead. As he glanced through the wild growth surrounding the path for signs of the smiling monster, his knuckle crackled, clenching his fist tightly, containing it close to his ribs. The tightly coiled tape wrapped over his wrists expanded under the duress of his preparations, tightening their grip around his furious hands.

The hair along his toned arms and down the back of his head stood on end. He felt a presence in his hollow cage, something moving in a large sweep behind him out of sight, along with two more intruders approaching from the trail before his feet. Out of the corner of his eye, he witnessed his older sister and brother gradually making their way to his location, though he wished they wouldn't. The last thing he needed was for his family to interfere with what he knew needed to happen next.

With Sydney's fingers digging into his neck, Leunga greeted their younger brother pleasantly as the pair walked toward the young fighter. "Where the fuck were you?!"

Hopping at her older brother's side, the middle sibling spoke with eloquent poise and added, "You're so stupid, running off the path like that. Dipshit. You could've gotten *lost* out here..."

Ricky might've said something along the lines of, *We are lost*, or *I'm not a little kid anymore; this isn't some grocery store where you two can wander off and forget about me again*, but he was focused on something far more pressing. "Shh! I hear it now."

The muted sound of paws approached him from behind. He shot the disturbance a focused glance in time to see rows of glistening teeth ready to ram him with an attempted head-butt. The Manticore charged on eagerly, staring the pugilist in the eyes with a flattering smile and a mild shaking of its bobbing head in disagreement, a confusing expression for a sneak attack. Ricky locked eyes with the rushing rampage, his own dour brown stare set to a pinpoint as he braced for impact. Rapidly gaining ground, the monstrosity leaned forward and prepared to knock the young man away, leading him from the wrong direction of its desired path.

Feeling the flow of motion like a well-designed sonata, Ricky looked over his shoulder for accuracy and kept his crouching stance. With timing so perfect, he jabbed his right elbow back at the exact moment the Manticore closed in. Shotokan: age eight. The jagged force of his bone plunged into the monster's joyous face, stopping it entirely and lifting its feet several inches off the ground as its momentum dispersed completely. In utter shock at its halt, the Manticore's nose smashed against the fighter's strike, becoming a twisted concave mass in a brief shower of blood. The mist bathed Ricky's gi, peppering the rolled arm of his shining white armor with dark red speckles. Critical hit. Double damage.

Leunga and Sydney stopped along the trail in surprise and stared wide-eyed at their baby brother's brutality.

The Manticore landed in a daze. The vibrant orange rune running over its nose hovered in place where it once contacted the now destroyed structure; the symbol struggled to maintain its luminosity as it flickered wildly before bursting into tiny flecks of energy that slowly fell to the ground, disappearing before they got too far. As the marking exploded, a portion of the creature's face rapidly transformed; the broken remains of its nose's monstrous, lionlike bridge faded into a puff of smoke, leaving behind the dark brown snout of a rodent, elongated along its face to the point of indistinction.

"Whoa!" Sydney broke her awestruck silence at the discovery. "I think it's changing back..."

"Cools! I totally knew it could do that! Like a boss in a game where you gotta break off its butt and stuff. Bet if you bust it up a ton, you can turn it back into an animal."

"That'd be cool."

"Either that, or you'd end up killing it in the most agonizingly slow way possible."

"Yeah...probably be that one."

Ricky's rage burned ever brighter as he completely ignored his annoying counterparts. While the beast was stunned, the teen threw his right foot into its ribs with all of his might, snapping away several of its fragile quills with his size thirteen sneaker. Muay Thai: age fifteen. His impressive kick more than cracked the cat's ribs and may have even punctured its lungs, forcing it to slide on its paws before rolling to a heap in the dust. Symbols fluttered all over its broken body as it slowly attempted to stand on sinewy legs. Without remorse, Ricky dropped his hands to the ground and swept his foot through the Manticore's shins, causing it to plummet once again.

While his opponent wallowed in the filth, Ricky hastily gripped a handful of the spikes over its spine and bent them back to avoid sitting on them with his bootylicious seat as his spontaneous plan began to unfold. After clearing a path, he quickly sat between its shoulders and knelt against the ground, straddling its long, slender neck to keep it from moving. The pointed mane that had seemed so hazardous to the touch was no more dangerous than his own gelled head of golden hair. He entwined his fingers through its medium-length locks and quickly pulled back the creature's head to reveal its unguarded throat beneath, attempting to grant it a quick demise at the edge of his brother's blade—but something was wrong. He looked over to his sister's bewildered crutch and savagely growled at Leunga when he noticed that his sibling had yet to wield the swords. His voice was coarse with anger like a demon. "What are you waiting for?!"

Before he could be answered, Ricky felt the odd sensation of flight as his knees left the ground. The Manticore reared up suddenly with a burst of power, standing solely on its hind legs. The blond on its back struggled to hold on, but the force was too much; he shot off the feline's neck from nearly seven feet in the air on a headfirst course to the earth. Acting quickly, he threw his upward-facing palms over his head and preformed an improvised backflip, barely managing to land on all fours. He exhaled sharply with relief as he held the ground like a beast, his fingers trembling as they dug into the dirt awaiting his next move. Ricky looked at the Manticore as it set its front paws back on the path and glared over its back through a myriad of destroyed spikes at the young fighter.

The beasts stared into one another—each looking through the other's counterfeit guise at the dissimulator huddled before them. Ricky's nostrils flared as he waited and watched for the monster's next move. The Manticore shot him a look of disappointment as it crouched to the ground and prepared to circle its devastating foe, but the formidable fighter had another idea. As the feline hunched down, the berserker sprang from all fours into a lunging charge on two feet and threw his entire weight into the monster's side, tackling it and pinning back its long arms while he struggled to figure out his next move without the help of his uselessly captivated companions.

Trapped in the teen's grip, the Manticore laughed in metallic shades, fueling the flames in Ricky's anticipating fists. Craving an end to its derisive dismissal of its true danger, he set out to disarm its desire, and ability, to mock him further. Burning with an intense level of hostility almost exclusive to adolescence, Ricky grappled with the beast and rapidly took the Manticore in a tentative headlock, trapping its head against his kneeling leg. Locked in

Pankration with the horror, he slid one taped hand's protected palm inside the Manticore's mouth against its lower rows of jagged teeth, pushing outward as he pulled the rest of its horrified head back with his other hand gripping around its upper lip. The feline flailed in sudden panic as the creaking sound of its expanding jaws began to climax to a duet of loud snaps, completely and permanently unhinging its jaw. The monster's weak joints were no match for Ricky's unbridled fury.

"Jesus god!"

Leunga frowned unpleasantly at the sight. "Gross, Richard," he yelled. "That was gross of you."

Ricky grunted in annoyance. "I thought we were *supposed* to destroy these things before they hurt anyone..."

"Yeah, but this seems a little too...*gross.*"

"You made me do it!" Ricky sighed under his breath irritably. "You had a chance to end it without all of this. You should've had those stupid swords out when it all started!"

"Hey! I was supremely distracted! What are you talking about?!"

"Guys, shut up. Just end it quick, Ricky..."

Releasing his hold of the horror's head, Ricky shot up to run to its back and carelessly gripped its lengthy tail. He hauled the beast through the slobber-strewn grime and began dragging its surprisingly lightweight body in a circle around him by its barbed extremity. It's not as heavy as it looks. In a whirlwind of dust, he managed to swing if off the ground and whipped the limp creature against a tree, hoping to end its misery with one blow, but ended up breaking and bending more of its quills instead, subsequently pinning it to the bark with the shattered remains of its needles as it stayed mostly unfazed by its flight. Releasing the kangaroo-like tail of his foe, he started to back away, but not before the monster retaliated, thrashing its tail about and dragging the massive thorns on its barbed tip over the skin of his arm. Ricky roared in agony as he jumped back to a safer distance.

The Manticore left a trio of gashes along his forearm. While the beast was trapped by the clutches of its own spiked quills, Ricky held his arm in pain, careful not to touch the open fissures. Torn tissue gushed blood, running around his level forearm and trickling off his elbow. He stared at the slack-jawed monster struggling to break free from its entrapment with a ferocious rage evident in his furious brown eyes, ready to strike as much as necessary to destroy his enemy and protect the innocent—all of those people who, through no fault of their own, were oblivious to the trials Ricky and his siblings were faced with for the benefit of everyone. Just as his muscles tightened for their next attack, Sydney grabbed his injured wrist and pulled him out of his trance.

Leunga studied the lacerations carefully and assessed his brother's damage. "Dudeness! That freak got you good! This is bleeding wicked nice."

"You should pour water over it to clean it out a little. We don't want it to get infected."

"Yeah, bru." The bitty brother glanced suspiciously at his defender's empty back and then spoke rather loudly to himself. "Oh man, where's the bagsack?!"

The Manticore squirmed relentlessly under the livid watch of the pugilist as he sternly said, "I'm fine...this is nothing."

"Holy shysties, Sydney!" shouted a Leunga, smacking his sister's bracelet-veiled wrist. "Don't *touch* it!"

"I wasn't gonna!" she insisted and retracted her hand. "Not very much anyway..."

"I totally believe that, but we gotta be a little bit serious here! Infections happen to everyone when we're out in the wildernesses! This is what hospitals are invented for and stuff!" The geek of the gander glanced at the Manticore stuck to the side of the tree before returning his disgusted gaze to the torn flesh flooding blood on his brother's lean forearm. "Fuck damn!"

Feeling that her shorter relative was right, Sydney's expression soured as she addressed her taller sibling. "You'll be okay as soon as we get back to camp. I have some stuff in your duffel bag I got from Grandma's bathroom to stop the bleeding. If we can find our way back to camp..." She wasn't supposed to bring up her little navigational indiscretion. "You'll be all right."

Ricky's rage broke for a moment as he turned to his big sister. He had a sudden bout of concern for what items may be hidden in his luggage. "Left-side drawers?" he winced.

"Well, yeah, I think it was... It was the only place I could find them."

Unbeknownst to Ricky at the time, Sydney was actually referring to a cache of bandages and disinfectant she managed to relieve from their grandmother's possession without detection. Right side only. Limited by information gathered from his ignorant friends and through blurry conversations of the two female members of his immediate family courtesy of the thin walls of his room, the younger guy groaned disgustedly at his very vague, and uninformed, understanding of the hygienic nature of the unwanted intruders he could picture sealed away in the night blue bag. He rested his stance and felt the frustration of the overall situation pulse through his athletic frame. Blood poured like a leaky faucet from his wounds unknowingly and ran down his right wrist, coating the boxer's tape containing his hand with his red essence while the excess dripped off of his fingers into the dust—a small piece of him became part of the forest as a small piece of the forest became a part of him. At the sound of the beast's shriek, Ricky's temper flared once more.

Orange markings over the beaten body of the Manticore grew in luminosity to near-white light. The trumpet-like roar of the cat rapidly elevated to higher notes like a jazzy bossa nova as it ruthlessly tore its body from the clutches of its quills, leaving behind flimsy rapiers that turned to smoke in a matter of seconds. With its jaw dangling in place, it quickly looked up the imprisoning tree and pounced, deeply clawing its way along the bark up and up before the teenage brute had a chance to stop it. Disappearing from sight once again, it called out in a high-pitched squeal of a horn.

Ricky's eyes lasered in on the treetops, stunned by its rapid ascent. "Hey! Son of scum!" he shouted. "Where are you going?!" Quickly turning to his brother and sister now by his side, he panted nervously. "W—we gotta stop it before it hurts someone!"

"How?! It's in a tree! Besides, it's not gonna *bite* anyone anymore."

Rocking his head back and forth to the melody of the Manticore's terrible scream, Leunga added, "Still has claws and that tail. Why don't you go break those too? You beast."

Ricky was less than amused by his siblings' attitudes. He exhaled angrily. "We gotta go after it."

Leunga patted his brother on the back, dangerously close to his most-likely toned buttocks. Minor. "Don't worry, big guy, it'll be back. Nice."

"You think so?" Ricky asked while his focus darted through the flora, forgetting for the moment that the monsters were, for whatever reason, drawn to the swords still harnessed and sheathed against his sibling's spine.

"Yes. But we just gotta wait for it to come down." Leunga nodded gradually and suddenly gasped. "Oh right!" He pointed to an animal he noticed perched in a tree far down the path and informed his svelte sibling of something the youngest may have missed while he was hiding. "Also—forgot to mention—it can fly."

Ricky spun around and followed his brother's lazily pointing finger to a distant dot of fur and light hidden in the needles of a mighty pine. Hundreds of feet above the ground, the tree rustled violently as the tangerine terror leapt through the branches toward the siblings upon its apparent discovery. Falling on a controlled route to the ground below, its wings burst outward and immediately slowed its guided descent. Plotting a concealing course through the trees, it turned sharply and became hidden to the group once again. The faint sound of membranous wings vibrating in the wind while gliding around unseen haunted the trio as they each searched for the anomaly in different directions.

Suspiciously looking through the limbs above—one more cautiously than the other two—the hikers remained vigilant for the floating, broken actor and its dangerous demeanor. Being the first to notice something odd, Sydney pointed to the sky and blurted out, "Is that it up there?"

Leunga shaded his eyes with one hand lunged under his obnoxiously untamed bangs and squinted at the hovering lights. "Maybe...Either that, or it's another UFO."

Ricky quickly looked skyward, seeing the Manticore circling the branches high above their position before it immediately entered into a dive-bomb stance. With illuminated orange claws outstretched in front of its fall, it appeared to be reinforcing its notoriously weak joints to brace itself to land on, or near, its enemies with a tremendously powerful thump, keeping its forepaws aimed at the ground below. As quietly as it could, its wings retracted back like a hawk soaring to the floor to scoop up its prey, allowing the abomination to zoom toward the fellow trespassers in this sacred land.

The fearless fighter's focus narrowed to a point, once again becoming one with the creature's movements. Time seemed to slow, but his reactions were quickened. With honed, lightning-forged reflexes, Ricky powerfully thrust his stiff arms into the awaiting shoulders of the mesmerized gawkers at his left, accurately shoving each of his elder siblings off the path; both Leunga and Sydney stumbled at the unexpected force and toppled over, falling in unison into the embrace of a healthy hedge.

As the diving demon entered Ricky's proximity, he furiously, and accurately, gripped one of its thrusting forelegs with his left hand and jabbed his bloody right hand into its abdomen, using its incredible momentum against it and flipping the monster in midair. Judo: age eleven. The beast soared in the controlled grasp of the brawler and tumbled over; its back was slammed into the ground, knocking the wind from its lungs and creating a crater of tampered dirt. Without a moment's hesitation, Ricky's best fist plunged with all of his focus toward the Manticore's throat. Battling his autonomous restraint against actual contact—learned while on the mat in the safety of his dojo—his simple, yet tremendously sufficient, blunt weapon quickly creased the creature's unmarked fur mercifully, splashing the white hairs of its neck with dark red speckles dribbling from his shredded skin. The villain's weakened and elongated windpipe easily splintered under the force of the blow and collapsed beneath his knuckle in a deafening crunch, leaving it breathless in horror as its eyes very slowly faded away with the rest of its runes.

In an explosion of dense vapor the size of a delivery truck, their enemy was no more, and Ricky was consumed by the blackness, covering his world in an onyx blanket for the second time in as many days. He stood blindly in the cloud of mist, the last one standing, feeling his temper subside with the enveloping darkness and returning him to a more normal, if not comfortable, status. Reeling from such a fleeting taste of a bravery he craved, even if he didn't know it—courage in all forms—he leaned into the shadow and lifted his eyes to the sky. A constant trickle of sticky warmth flowed over his fingers and disappeared into the black. In his rage he had sacrificed something precious and taken something that he had no desire or right taking, but it had to be done. Unable to puncture the mist with his sight, Ricky closed his eyes, allowing the fog to hold him hostage and stain his mind with another haunting memory he would have to keep for the rest of his life.

In the gloom around him on all sides, he could feel something he couldn't describe. A presence that was not there, but wanted to be. In his ears he could clearly hear the sound of whispers, as if someone were standing at his side in the darkness, speaking in what he could only imagine was a language he had never heard before, nor ever would again. As the impenetrably dark fog slowly sank back into the ground, it revealed the cautious combatant breathing heavily; the echo of the tinny voice from the previous day returned to bounce mournfully across the trees over the loss of another enslaved sacrifice.

Leunga blew a massive heap of leaves from his mouth, granting the collection a brief flight before ultimately succumbing to gravity and covering his face with greenery. After cleansing most of the oral dilemma caused by the abrupt shove orchestrated by his combative baby brother, he sat up quickly and stared at Ricky but was far too late to witness any part of his grinning foe's brutal defeat. Leunga glanced around for the creature but noticed only a lifeless animal at the taller teen's feet. Nothing but a hapless porcupine runt bereft of breath.

Following her older brother's lead, Sydney sat up and spit out a mouthful of leaves like a blast of airy feathers before she began to collect her wits, having lost them to her crash landing. In a wave of disorientation she groaned, "What happened...?"

"Ricky won."

Ricky lost. He allowed anger to get the better of him, and it took more than it deserved. Feeling a persistent sense of dissatisfaction with his actions in the wake of losing his cool, he knew he could hide his feelings with ease for the sake of his brother and sister's potential badgering, even though he truly didn't want to, but that's what he'll do. Pretend—like so much else that happens in his life—that nothing really happened. Unwilling to view his victim in the light, Ricky held his gaze skyward, piercing the branches clawing high above with solemn eyes while he drifted away in the wake of adrenaline slowly taking its time to drain his ferocity. Trying to take his mind off of the anxious pain growing in his nerves, he turned away from the critter by his size-thirteens and walked down the path to a place he must have been before. "I'll be right back," he explained. "Gotta go get the backpack."

"Ding! Level up!" Leunga burst with a triumphant congratulation and smiled with a leaf stuck to his teeth while he sat with his sister in the gentle upholstery of their fern. He nodded his chin to their disappearing brother and shouted, "Bet you never thought you'd actually use any of that martial arts crap! I know *I* don't."

Sydney's face arched with worry while her heart did the same. Her larger little brother was too young to realize the gravity of his actions. Too young to see the line he crossed. Too young to understand...wasn't he? He *needed* to be for her sake. Despite the desire to be there for him in the event that everything wasn't right as rain in Ricky's reversed world, she felt the necessity to keep her concerns to herself; otherwise, she would run the risk of exposing her delicate demeanor to her siblings and lose her strong semblance. However, seeing the feral beasts her brothers had become over the course of a minute amount of days, Sydney was still consumed with concern that her humanity too would soon be lost in the woods...or hopefully just temporarily displaced. "Well, at least I'm not worried about *Ricky* anymore."

Leunga scowled with disgusted dissatisfaction. "You were *worried* about him?"

"This morning! That—I told you that *this* morning! Jesus! Don't you ever listen to the things I say?!"

"When?"

Knights of the Rock Table

Hours after the confrontation with the Manticore, the newborn afternoon was growing at a steady pace while Ricky and Leunga spent a little brotherly time together as a duo in the trees encompassing their camp at the behest of the eldest, discussing things of great importance, with the swordsman leading the conversational cavalry.

"Where were we? Oh yeah, high school. Best time of my life. I remember none of it. Except for April...she's so awesome," Leunga repeated. Desultorily drifting through the open pores of his susceptible mind, all issues were out in the open as he went tearing through unfinished topics like a goldfish slurping up flakes of food while simultaneously spitting them back out. Sure, we don't *need* to listen in, but I didn't have any plans right now anyway.

"Anyway," the stoner continued, "what's the deal with Sydno all of a sudden? Just when you start thinking she's cool—always acting like she doesn't care about shit, dressing all dark and wearing all that morbid metal crap—and then it's like, as soon I kill a monster, she shuts down. It was a monster! But then *you* beat the shit of that teeth freak the very next today, and she's fine with that. And actually, before you showed up, she was all in its ugly face trying to fight it. And here I thought she loved animals, which is another thing that doesn't make sense. Oh, and I couldn't say this in front of Sydkins, but you totally kicked that thing's ass! I mean, I don't like having to kill real things, and I don't think you do either, but what are we supposed to do? Come on, we're trying to save the world here."

"Right..."

"But, whoa. You know? Those monsters are seriously sending out some mixed signals, I say you what. Like how that wolf chased us down with that look of 'Hey, I'm totally gonna eat you, nom nom nom' on its giant-ass face, and then that smiling thing being all polite and shit telling us to follow it in some impossible-to-understand language, *but* then it attacked you for no reason! Also, I don't mean to nickpit, but maybe you need to calm the fuck down the next time we have to fight something from out of this dimension. You almost tore that guy's head out of its socket. I mean, yeah, he was incredibly annoying, but so am I. And speaking of Sydney, what kind of Gotholic girl joins a *softball* team?! What the fuck does it mean by *soft* ball anyway? I mean, *sports?* Really?! Is she *trying* to throw all her awesome punky darkness away to be some normal butthead or something?! She's turning into *you!* She should just stick to playing her electrigal guitar. Or join a band for once. She's almost good enough. Plus, she's like a hundred feet tall; why didn't she do basketball? She could just stand there and block every shot ever. Also plus, I think she has a hard-on for that douchebag jock from over the street, which I really don't get. How come we're so cool and she's not?"

"A question for the ages."

That was possibly the weirdest answer anyone could have given. Leunga nodded and fastened his pants, having finally finished using nature's restroom facilities. Giving a despondent sigh, he stated, "I don't know why I'm saying all of this. You'll probably tell her *everything* if she asks." He walked to the water's edge and stood over the burbling creek flowing from their camp's pond, rinsing his hands and sleeves in the flow haphazardly.

As the water pulsed against his fingers for moments on end, Leunga quietly performed a short play for the sole benefit of his own enjoyment—a prophecy of the events to come—speaking softly to himself in character voices he thought to be appropriate for each of his siblings: low for Sydney and high-pitched for Ricky.

"*Oh, hey guys. What were you talking about? I need to know all the time. I like punk rock sports.*"

"*Oh, um, hi Syd. We were just having a meaningful conversation about life, liberty, and how you don't make any damn sense.*"

"*What do you mean?! I'm perfect in every way! I need more tissues for my tiny bra!*"

"*Um, yeah, you know. Stuff about stuff and stuff.*"

With a satisfied grin, Leunga shook his hands wildly in the drying air and stood. He chuckled at his flawless representation of his brother and sister's predictable behavior and blindly turned to Ricky, wishing he could have performed for an audience. "Oh well. Come, my leggy blond squire! We make haste to our encampment. The hour is late. The blacksmith must have surely finished with my mare's shoes, or I'll have his head! Let us see what the old spit-hag has cooked. Probably more water 'cause that's all she knows..." The eldest's insult suddenly trailed off as he discovered the complete and utter absence of his leggy blond brother.

Leunga spun around clockwise, and then again counterclockwise. He wobbled in place as his squinting eyes combed the trees in search of a suspect: male, mid-to-late teens, above-average height, lean build packed with hidden muscles, blond hair, dark eyes, discernibly thick black eyebrows, last seen dressed as a kung fu mutant, goes by the alias *Ricky*.

"Where did he go...?" Leunga spoke through his teeth and took a very wide stance, bringing his point of view even closer to the ground. Rhythmically staring in one direction before cranking his head in another again and again, he saw no hint of his partner through the lines of pines—not even the slightest glimpse of a bootylicious tail, as horrible as that would be for me. I mean—um...ignore that.

Unable to hear much of anything except the slow trickle of the rushing spring nearby, the deserted quester cautiously rounded the tree designated as a toilet by the markings he left behind and plunged his wet hands into his pockets nonchalantly while his hidden worry began to grow. Suddenly realizing how much he craved that sought security of being around the people that he had an alternating relationship of protection and support with, Leunga felt the oddest chill run up his spine. He walked at a relaxed pace, but his paranoia began to kick in rapidly. He had not yet felt alone in the stifling thickness of the forest; it was an unexpectedly haunting feeling. Everything was against him. Even when he was wandering through the trees that legendary night of Fenrir's demise, he could always see the glow of the campfire and sense his brother's aching presence, but now there was nothing.

His mind hopped around maniacally. Leunga found himself yearning for the exclusive safety and comfort he felt only by his girlfriend's side, but moreover, he began to wonder why April was abruptly in his thoughts after all these days. A rush of panic took him quickly. Many more things began to beg for his attention, but it was up to him to ignore their importance and keep his current conundrum kicking; after all, the sooner he found a sibling to talk to, the sooner he could forget the stuff that actually mattered. So, looking back to hunt for potential followers, he jogged carefully over to a glorious beacon of salvation.

Rapidly removing his mount from its stable against some random nearby tree, the lone loser mounted the treasured treasure of the recently ditched and discovered mountain bike he chose to procure, previously left in the care of the Manticore not so long ago. With a newfound sense of comfort in his empty world, he stroked the fine metal handlebars shining in the light and popped a stationary wheelie. "Whoa, now! Easy girl!" It was a fantastic steed for a gallant champion, galloping together over meadows and rivers as the pair is chased by the wind. A horse is a horse. "Of course?" Of course.

Riding on the group's new, previously abandoned, and recently stolen, silver bicycle—an adult-sized ride designed specifically for those lucky few who have long legs—some might say adult-sized legs—Leunga kicked back blasts of soggy dirt as he searched for his kid brother, or any evidence to refute his solitariness, and awkwardly tiptoed along quickly on his tall roving seat. Pedals are for chumps. The weensy warrior wove around the same three trees over and over as he cautiously crushed most of the tinier bushes in his path while looking for Ricky, but the older brother's thoughts of search and rescue were overshadowed by his overabundant distance from the reassurance of their campsite, and he lost focus on his investigation all too soon, making his way back to camp in a hasty retreat to regain his sense of reliance.

The familiar wall of trunks and their exposed tangle of high roots approached at the end of his brief trail of trials. Passing through the conspicuously auspicious archway of low limbs reaching over his unpaved pathway, Leunga made his return trip without any fuss and began to wonder why he was so anxious in the first place—and why April remained in his mind even after successfully surviving his ordeal. With a relieved expression, the stoner sighed at the sight of Sydney and gradually led himself across the infertile blight of the clearing to rejoin his loser sister.

At the sound of a stolen bicycle tire galloping over the dirt, Sydney checked to make sure it was someone who had a right to just wander up to the camp like that. Glancing over her shoulder, she greeted her older brother pleasantly. "Hey, bitch."

"Hey, what's up," Leunga replied as he strenuously hopped off the tall bike and sent it careening toward the boulder wall. The vehicle wobbled as it rolled along without its operator until finally smashing into the rocks and toppling over, bringing it crashing to a safe stop. To hide his seemingly obvious shaken state over being abandoned for what felt like a couple of eternities in the trees, Leunga slid a scarred hand beneath the back of his mop and scratched his neck while he faced his little sister and nonchalantly asked, "Did Rickie come back yet?"

" *Who*?" she answered with puzzlement.

"Ricky."

Sydney kept her attention focused on something atop the bench by her side out of her brother's view. "What do you mean?"

"We were talking out there and then all of a sudden...*ninja*! He disappeared on me. I kinda looked for him, but I didn't find anything. So, like the greatest detective I am, I figured he just came back here. Where I did too."

His sister looked at him again, ignoring whatever it was she was studying on the bench by her side. Her bangs had fallen out of place once more that day and blocked his view of her eyes, but Leunga could tell she was just as confused as he was. She asked him calmly, "What the hell are you talking about? Ricky is right here."

Leunga was stunned when he suddenly noticed his brother sitting very visibly next to Sydney, especially because the brawling boy was camouflaged in no way. Ricky leaned his face around their middle sibling to wave to his older brother. The eldest of the bunch scowled and made a few confused gestures at the other boy. "Dude, why'd you leave me?! We were right in the middle of the good shit."

"Leave you? Uh, I was right here the whole time... Well, not right *here*, but you know, right around this general part of the camp," Ricky alleged, pointing to the ground to draw a circle in midair. "Ever since we finally found our way back from that trail of doom."

"Thanks to me and my awesome rocks," someone added under her breath.

"Duh!" Leunga threw his hands about. "Don't you remember?! We were just barely peeing like ten seconds ago when I said all of that stuff about the color orbit and Sydney..."

Sydney's inattentive attention snapped up.

Ricky glanced at his brother with concern and shook his head. "Dude, you asked if I wanted to go to the bathroom with you, and I said 'why?' and then you rode off on the bike, talking to yourself."

"Really? Then who was that guy agreeing with me?" A question for the ages.

"So." Sydney raised an eyebrow as she turned to her younger brother to ask, "What were you guys talking about?"

Ricky gave a confounded shrug. "I wasn't there!"

Leunga cleared his throat and answered, "I'll handle this one, Mickey. You just relax it. Ahem! Well, it goes like this, see? We were having such a meaningful conversation about life, liberty, and how you don't make any damn sense." My goodness, he ratted himself out. Fink.

"*Me* not make sense?!" said Sydney before she shoved Ricky in the arm.

"Yeah." Conveying all of the ignorant information he had, Leunga counted off his sister's attributes with his fingers. "Softsports, animals, you wanting to bone that freak across the street that you spy on, alternative musics, electronical guitar, your metal-studded shit... Rick, help me out here. What else did we say?"

"I wasn't there!"

Knowing full well she wasn't the only walking contradiction at hand, Sydney repressively rolled her eyes, instantly thinking of every little conflicting attribute she could point out at her two rude brothers' expense, but chose instead to ignore the whole thing, because confrontation was not something she sought at the moment. "Well, while you and Ricky were so kindly talking about me behind my back, Ricky and I found a trail map in his stuff. Grandma probably snuck it in when no one was looking." I noticed it right away. "Liar. No one asked *you*."

"Opp!" Leunga *said*? Without a moment's hesitation upon hearing the news, he whipped off his hat and tucked it under his armpit before bursting into a frenzy of spontaneous applause. Abrupt adulation. Caught up in the momentum of the moment, Ricky stood immediately and involuntarily joined his brother in the ovation of their group. Sydney watched the furious clapping of her brothers in awe. Not wanting to be left out, she hopped up from her seat and completed the trio's sign of approval. The three siblings clapped heartily for several prolonged minutes before they all ceased the activity in unison.

"With a cool map we get to go to every zone and dungeon and then mark off where we were with a big stamp of success! Now we can be just like all those paladins and rangers that came before us. Questing around on a dedicated journey while they scour trails and whatever the fuck else. We'll carry on their serious task. With swords, nunchaku, tightly wound fists of fury, bo staffs...bows and arrows...shields...double-sided axes...daggers...those really big scythes...claws that look like cat's paws...throwing stars...flails with really long chains...pointed sticks...and whatever other crap we can find. We'll take up arms and be the brave knights—dark protectors of the universe and almost everybody else."

"Wow...you're really stuck on that fantasy world samurai shit."

Leunga coughed. "Damn right! And now you are too." He walked around his younger siblings' backs and stopped at the end of their stony privacy barrier. "Whip that thing out," he demanded as he slapped his hand against the shortest of the half-dozen boulders shielding their benches. "Unleash that beast of yours all over this here rock, and try not to make a mess of it."

Fortunately for everyone in the camp, Ricky knew his brother meant the map. He stood with the chart in hand and lazily made his way to the end stone and unfurled his folded discovery on the table. With an elder sibling at each arm watching his every move in anticipation, the teen spread the massively oversized chart on the broad, flat boulder like a tablecloth and adjusted it accordingly. Taking a stand at their own solitary border of the clean sheet of paper, the knights gathered around the atlas, each of them studying the aspect they found most interesting at that moment.

Sydney stopped and slowly looked up to the distracted faces of her brothers. "Guys...? Where are we?"

"As far as I can tell, we might be in a forest."

Standing at the southern edge of the chart, with the most accurate point of view, Ricky placed a finger against the smallest pond on the map and stated, "I think we're right here, 'cause see?" He dragged his digit north along the trails to a large campground. "Here's that place we went to on Sunday, and then see?" He continued to trek the trails with one sliding finger. "We were like, walking this way, I think, and this lake kinda looks like the one right over there." As he pointed to their actual pond, Leunga and Sydney followed his directions and turned to observe the similarity. Ricky focused on the paper once more and said, "We are here."

"Yeah, see? The little trees on the map are probably trees."

Sydney grinned. "Dude!"—she rarely ever says that—"You know your shit!"

Justifiably jubilant at the new organizational structure his impulsive quest had taken, one dork was apparently pleased. With a mischievous grin, he glanced up at his brother's face and made a grand announcement for the benefit of the forest and its denizens. "I do solemnly hereby do swear to nominate Junior Richard to be our crew's map reader. Charting our course as we sail the green trees in search of the great evil unknown." Reaching up and placing his swelling hand on Ricky's shoulder, Leunga listed off the adventures his young brother would no doubt be sending them on in search of the Summoner as they came to his mind. "We'll crawl across snow-covered mountains, hop from stone to stone over lakes of lava in magma-filled caverns, walk the windswept sands of eternity, barter information from seedy townspeople in bustling bazaars and shady restaurants with nasty bathrooms, soar through the stars in a giant spaceship, search for treasures in the depths of the sea, swing from vines in dense jungles for no real reason, raid the halls of an enchanted castle, battle ancient dragons, save princesses and princes alike, and...uh...oh yeah, wander through this forest filled with faeries and bullshit." He seems to have borrowed dangerously romanticized fantasies from more than one genre. "If that's where you need to take us, we will go with confidence in your capability."

"Wait. What...?"

"Do you accept these terms, laddie?"

"Um, are we doing pirates now?"

The sweetly naïve child within Sydney's heart was overcome with sudden excitement at the aspect of any of the activities listed by her idealistic big brother. She shook the baby brother at her side by the shoulder roughly and added an enthusiastic growl to her voice when she announced, "He accepts!"

"We will call you Atlas." No they won't.

Without a full understanding of how or why he just agreed to take responsibility as the ship's navigator—or whatever it was Leunga was babbling about—Ricky replied with hesitant bewilderment, "Aye... Captain?"

"There! It's settled. And Syddley, you can be...the crow's nest...or helmswench. I really don't care."

She saluted. "Cannoneer!"

"I really don't care." Leunga placed his flask against his lips and scowled. "Why is the rum gone?"

His older siblings' sudden dependency on him left a boy with a feeling of pessimism. Ricky blew a gust of breath through his lips and shook his head. "Man, but I'd be no good at choosing where we go..."

Sydney scoffed and pointed between herself and her other brother back and forth. "And *we* would be any better?"

Leunga gave a tremendous nod, violently shooting his hat from atop his head onto the map as his liberated bangs bounced grittily against his face. He squeezed his lips together and replied to his sister, "Lest we forget—wait a minute, what is that supposed mean?"

Sydney made a mildly embarrassed face and averted his perplexed stare, sharing, "Well, it means I *might* have gotten us *temporarily displaced*." She shrugged. "And you're...you."

"No, I know that." Leunga furrowed his brow. "I mean what does *lest we forget* mean?"

The agitated gamine girl cocked her head to the side and sighed at the obtuse company she was currently forced to keep. "How can someone be so dumb? You're twenty-two. You should know stuff by now."

Leunga retaliated quickly. "No, I'm twenty-*three*, you idiot! How can someone be so dumb?! In ya ugly face!"

"In ya face, Syd," joined a disinterested Ricky.

"Oh wow! That is a humongous difference!" she stated with shocked sarcasm.

"Indeed it do." Leunga rolled his lips between his teeth and quickly raised his left hand in expectation of a high five from his little brother. Bewildered by the odd offer, Ricky clapped his hand vigorously against the pothead's palm in a thunderous gesture of accomplishment. As the youngest's attention went back to the unfolded paper at the core of their trio, Leunga's eyes screamed in horror as he scrunched his face and silently howled in pain, cradling his stinging hand against his stomach while he jumped in place, flushed with fantastic agony.

Her brothers' minor victory over her did not warrant that level of enthusiasm. Shaking her head, the unyielding shadow around Sydney's lids closed in deep darkness to complete her annoyed reaction. "Losers."

Returning to his concern about the map he suddenly wished they hadn't found, Ricky scratched various parts of his injured arm and neutral neck in an attempt to comprehend exactly what he was expected to do. His siblings and he stared at the large chart stretched across the top of the granite as he leaned the weight of his body against the countertop with his arms and sighed. "So what do you think you want me to do with all of this power?"

Sydney tapped a finger on the map, carefully avoiding the black hat sitting atop the display. "You'll be in charge of looking for places where a possible warlock-type mutant would try to hide, and then make us go there. And then we win."

The tall, pretty boy stared with widening nostrils growing in anxiety at his sister's pointing digit. His face contorted to express his worried enthusiasm as he chuckled in a nervous manner. Ricky was anxious, and not in the good way. "There's no deadline though, right? Like, we don't even know what to look for. What if it takes me forever to figure this thing out...?"

Ricky's slight smile faded as the villainously shadow-cast faces of his older brother and sister at each side of the chart slowly turned to glare up at him through their respective bangs.

"I don't care," Leunga grinned happily. Holding his throbbing palm delicately with his other hand, the older brother assured, "As long as we win at some point, we could stay out here until *August* and it wouldn't matter to us. Who's up with it?!"

"We're probably gonna run out of food in a couple days..."

"Whoa, shut up." Sydney quickly lost her stern demeanor and changed her focus to Leunga. "You really think it's gonna take that much *time*? I got stuff to do. This is my last summer, you know."

"It's *always* my last summer!" he exclaimed in response. Leunga could feel the morale of his siblings slipping wildly out of control, falling through his fingers like overcooked pasta burning his hands. "How is fighting legendary battles *not* the best way to spend your vacation?! Besides, you get to be out here with *me*, so why ever complain?"

"Yeah, but, I dunno... I kinda wanted to hang out with my *friend*. You know? Like a normal human being and not some battle-freak? She's not going to the school I am, so this could be... I dunno."

"Oh, bravo. Way to change the damn subject. Damn it! I can't remember a thing! Now what the hell are we talking about?" Leunga stared blankly over the pond while thoughts aimed at his sister's buddy bounced around uncontrollably in his head. Those two had been "best friends forever" since longer than anyone could remember—true BFFs—though...*those two* would never classify their relationship in such a bubbly term, but it seems pretty obvious to me—never really needing anyone but each other. Sydney and Addy—aka Adelaide Newcastle. A mysterious girl she was—dangerously clever but seemingly unmotivated, and, in many ways, mistreats the idea of acting feminine in almost every aspect of her individuality, with the obvious exception of her illustrious hair, which always seemed so elaborate, keeping ahead of the curve with fantasy style. Hey, wait. What were they talking about again?

Ricky was drawn to the eyes of his scary metal sister staring up at him through her hazardous hair, showing her serious severity. "Just find it, Atlas," she said. "I'm not wasting my whole vacation out here. Use those awesome spatial skills of yours to get us over to that secret lair." Sydney brushed the map, sending Leunga's hat to the dirt. "Then we can be done with the dumbshittery and go back home."

The younger teen swallowed dryly in agreement. "Epp. Yeah..."

While the image of Adelaide lingered hazily on the tip of his mind, Leunga jangled his flask by his ear, clanging its metal structure against the jagged edge of his temple uncontrollably. Calling himself back to the task at hand, he quickly sprang to attention at the reminder and frowned. "Bad news, kids. Looks like we're sober from here on out." Gasp.

Ricky ironed out the creases on his new responsibility and muttered an opinion under his breath. "And then nothing changed..."

"What?!" Sydney shouted, questioning her little brother's silent comment. Ricky recoiled in shock and stared at her for a moment before going back to his own business without answering.

Ignoring everything, Leunga raised his hands to the sky and pointed accusing fingers at the lone cumulus loitering over the central trees. "Tomorrow, Rickocity will be our guiding star in the cosmos, and all is right with the world. Fucking rum."

"Pirates..."

"Let's make it official." The knight with the swords sitting nearby held his scarred fist out over the map palm down and let it hover in place as he looked into the eyes of his younger siblings. "Hands in, everybody. You too, Ricky. We about to make a commitment up in here. A promise to ourselves to see this through to the end, no matter what. Or at least until we get bored. Right?!"

"Right!" Sydney smiled with wavering feelings of confused animal defense as she placed her persistently perspiring palm atop Leunga's floating fist, causing the short stoner to grimace in controlled disgust.

Ricky reluctantly clapped his hand over his sister's binding agreement and rolled his neck to the side. "Whatever, dude."

And thus, just as it happens on most any other camping trip in the woods far from the comforts we've come to expect, the knights were customarily conscripted into the brothery sisterish flock of fighters bound by duty to destroy the wicked of the world like so many that came before them, joining the ancient ranks of warriors ready to sacrifice it all and refuse to rest until the villains are vanquished and the innocents are saved. I give it another hour, tops.

Ending their unnecessary physical contact in a rush, the siblings stood by in solidarity while their minds began to wander once again.

"This is cool. Finally fuckin' feels like we have some goddamn direction on this bitch," Sydney stated swearingly. "Now I think we really might actually find that piece of shit bastardcan." She spoke to the boys in confidence, proposing, "I bet you nothing we find this booger-butt first thing tomorrow."

Ricky's squinting eyes shifted back and forth while he pondered her statement carefully, considering all of the evidence before he whispered to her. "I'm totally sure you're right about that, but why aren't there any pages left...?"

Leunga jumped in, his voice cracking with horrified shock. "What?! This is *it?! This* is the end?!"

The End?

You wish.